ACCLAIM NOVELS OF

SARAH LANGAN

"A MAJOR TALENT."
Tim Lebbon, author of *Dusk* and *Berserk*

THE KEEPER

"A beautiful, suspenseful novel . . . that sets out to do exactly what it should: scare the reader with a combination of well-crafted prose and page-turning velocity."
Baltimore Sun

"A smart, brand-new take on the haunted house story and it's a dilly—Crammed with startling images and framed by a sense of overwhelming dread. It's really hard to believe this is a first novel."
Jack Ketchum, author of *Offspring*

"[Langan] combines a witches' brew of toxic styles, mixing in bits of Stephen King, Lovecraft, Poe, and Peter Straub, then pours out a thoroughly nasty concoction all her own."
Madison County Herald

"Her book [has] a distinct and juicy flavor all its own. *The Keeper* begins what should be a very fruitful career."
New York Times bestselling author Peter Straub

THE MISSING

WINNER OF THE BRAM STOKER AWARD

By Sarah Langan

AUDREY'S DOOR
THE MISSING
THE KEEPER

SARAH LANGAN

AUDREY'S DOOR

HARPER

An Imprint of HarperCollinsPublishers

HARPER

An Imprint of HarperCollins*Publishers*
10 East 53rd Street
New York, New York 10022-5299

Copyright © 2009 by Sarah Langan
ISBN 978-0-06-162421-6

First Harper paperback printing: October 2009

HarperCollins ® and Harper ® are registered trademarks of Harper-Collins Publishers.

Printed in the United States of America

Visit Harper paperbacks on the World Wide Web at
www.harpercollins.com

10 9 8 7 6 5 4 3 2 1

For my parents, good eggs,
carrying on the good fight.

Acknowledgments

Some books are harder than others. I'm indebted to Joe Veltre for his encouragement and faith. I'm also grateful to my editors, Sarah Durand and Diana Gill, both of whom gave me the time to get it right. Finally, thanks to Arlaina Tibensky for the awesome line, and the people who've read this in its various stages: Who Wants Cake, Jon Evans, and Adrienne Miller. Thanks also to Diahann Sturge for the rocking design and Karen Davy in Managing Editorial. And, of course, first, last, and always, JT.

Then she goes pale, and her body shrivels up.
her glance is sideways and her teeth are black;
her nipples drip with poisonous green bile,
and venom from her dinner coats her tongue;
she only smiles at the sight of another's grief,
nor does she know, disturbed by wakeful cares,
the benefits of slumber; when she beholds
another's joy, she falls into decay,
and rips down only to be ripped apart,
herself the punishment for being her.

Ovid, on Envy, *Metamorphoses*
Translation by Charles Martin
W.H. Norton and Company, 2005

AUDREY'S DOOR

Preface

odern haunted-house stories build on a rich tradition. While writing *Audrey's Door*, I was particularly inspired by Shirley Jackson's *Haunting of Hill House*, Stephen King's *The Shining*, Ira Levin's *Rosemary's Baby*, Roland Topor's *The Tenant*, the films of Roman Polanski, and Edward Rob Ellis' *The Epic of New York City: A Narrative History*. I hope I did right by these guys, and by New York, the city that stole my heart.

Sarah Langan

September 18, 2008

Part I

The Seduction

Harlem Hills Triumph!

October 22, 1861

Delight! At dusk on October 20th, the doors to Manhattan's newest luxury apartment building, The Breviary, opened at last. Coal giant and primary financier Martin Hearst cut the ribbon to riotous applause. The teeming crowd's cheers resounded across both rivers, and were even heard by this office down in Times Square. Despite The Breviary's slanting Chaotic Naturalist architecture, independent engineers agree that the stately monolith is sound, and will stand for centuries to come.

The event raised a new standard in both architecture and society balls, which one can only hope Washington Square will answer with verve. After the ribbon cutting, guests reposed their mourning over this terrible war against brothers and waltzed inside the main lobby until dawn. In attendance were the future occupants of the building, its unkempt architect, Edgar Schermerhorn, two Union generals, three senators, and celebrities such as Claire Redgrave, Barry Sullivan, Fanny Price, and Hannibal Hamlin. Libations and decadent hors d'oeuvres floated on silver trays like river flowers, and the event was crowned by a sunrise marksman's contest on the building's roof. The worse for rum, not even Major General Winthrop hit a bull's-eye, though tragically, one of Hearst's Negroes took a bullet to the knee. The party broke at dawn. Guests watched the great building from the backs of their carriages. I do not think I was alone in waving it, and that perfect evening, farewell.

The building boasts every amenity imaginable, from water closets to gas-powered lights, and its future residents represent the finest families in America. What's more, its westward slant and unique design outwit its mundane brownstone cousins, heralding a style all New York's own. We deserve such a landmark—Manhattan is a Post Road way station between the wealthy South and Boston's aristocracy no more. We are the ascendant new America—hardworking, intelligent, and free.

From *The New York Herald*

1

The Tenant

Fate.

Audrey Lucas found the apartment through an online ad in *The Village Voice*. The real-estate section was updated on Tuesday afternoons, and she checked it as soon as three o'clock rolled around, just like she'd checked it last week, and the week before that, too. She'd seen twelve places this month, and not one of them had been fit for a dog. They'd had showers in their kitchens, paint peeling from walls, urine-stained carpets (pets or people?), and, once, the red chalk outline of a fat guy's body. She'd almost given up and started calling real-estate brokers in Queens when—bingo!—today's search brought up a match:

Morningside Heights Charmer. Landmark Building. Large, Pre-War 2br. City Views, EIK, $999. Priced to go!!! Call owner: (212) 747–4854. No Brokers, plz.

Her hand hovered over the phone's receiver. There had to be a catch. $999 was too good to be true. You couldn't share a fifth-floor walk-up for that price in this city. Still, she grinned: *Prewar, baby!* She dialed the number, and couldn't believe her luck when a man with an upper-crust British accent got on the line and told her the apartment was still available.

"An architect? What a lovely career. I dabbled in it myself once upon a time. Come straightaway, dear. I'll arrange a viewing," he said. His voice sounded old-timey, like a Harold Arlen song ("Let's Get Crazy; Let's Fall in Love!"), and she was charmed.

She prairie dogged up from her cubicle to avoid the sightline of her boss, Jill Sidenschwandt, and the rest of the Parkside Plaza team, then ducked out the back stairs to the street and was on her way. The #1 Train was flooded again, so she grabbed a taxi from West Broadway. On the passenger-seat television panel, Liz Smith reported the latest news on Donald Trump's toupee. Made from mink fur, apparently.

Twenty minutes after leaving SoHo, her cabbie let her out at 110th Street, where she wondered if she'd transcribed the wrong address: 510 was too good to be true. Its fifteen stories were sooty limestone brick, each with intricate latticework, curlicues, and gargoyled ledges upon which sky-rat pigeons, and even real birds, cooed. Like the Leaning Tower of Pisa, only less leaning, it slanted west toward the Hudson River. Its green copper roof converged neatly into a tidy spire that scratched a crooked hole through the September sky.

She squinted in disbelief. The building's details indicated a type of architecture that didn't exist anymore. Or at least, the textbooks said it didn't exist. Her grin spread slowly, like dawn, and lit up her entire face: but maybe the textbooks were wrong.

To the right of the main entrance, she found the cornerstone: THE BREVIARY, 1861. The name was familiar—

she'd read about it someplace. Her smile broke into a short laugh, and she pressed her fingers inside the crevices of its limestone skin, just to make sure this building was the real deal.

. . . And it was. *Holy cow.*

Chaotic Naturalism. She'd studied it in graduate school. Daydreamed about it, and in doodles, tried to make it work, not just in theory, but in application. But she'd never imagined she'd see the genuine item.

Back in the 1850s, a whole fleet of Chaotic Naturalist structures were erected, mostly in eastern Europe. Houses, libraries, city halls—from the lithographs she'd seen, they'd all been gorgeous. They'd also been unsound. Their foundations hadn't stood flush to the ground, so their support beams never settled right, and over time they'd collapsed. At least a hundred people, probably closer to an unreported 250, had died within their crumbling walls. Some instantly, as roofs had caved; others slowly, trapped in basements like miners, hoping their next breath would not be their last.

True to the Chaotic Naturalist philosophy, The Breviary's floors differed in height from one story to the next, and its walls didn't intersect at right angles but were either obtuse or acute. The gargoyles weren't evenly spaced but appeared at random intervals, like flowers on a vine. Inside buildings like this, dropped marbles rolled in all directions, and the furniture warped, so once a couch lived in a particular space for a few years, you couldn't move it, or it crumbled.

Supposedly, the last of these buildings had been condemned in 1929. And yet, here was The Breviary. Ten thousand tons of cement and steel, and not a single right angle. How on earth had it survived?

Once she got inside the building, her grin spread even wider. The lobby was grand as a ballroom. Cracked Italian mosaics along the floors depicted blackbirds in flight, and a low-hanging crystal chandelier emitted a sallow glow, like an archeologist's lantern unearthing a deep-sea relic. Dust specked the air, thick and itchy in her nose. The back of the room was elevated, as if it had once been a stage or pulpit, and behind it were randomly placed, art-deco-era stained-glass windows. This building was neglected; run-down; divine. She leaned into its entrance, cold butterflies cramming her chest, and thought, *I can see now, why there are wars, and people kill for* things.

At the doorman's post, she found a slender Hispanic man in blue coveralls whose name tag read EDGARDO. He looked about seventy. "You the lady who wants to see apartment?" he asked.

She nodded.

"I'm the super!" he announced, then hobbled with the help of a knobby cane toward the old-fashioned, iron-cage elevator without shaking her hand. She followed, thinking for a second that he had told her he was *super!*

They stood in silence while the car ascended. The metal dial slowly ticked the floors: one . . . two . . . three. She patted her thighs in three-second intervals, to hurry the thing along. If her boss found out she'd left the office, she'd be up some serious shit creek. At Vesuvius, they worked the first-years hardest. She was lucky most nights to get home before *The Daily Show*.

Edgardo smiled through brown, chewing-tobacco-stained teeth, so she smiled back. He smelled a little. Like garlic and tuna fish.

"I working here almost a year," he said. "I'm only one who takes out garbage and cleans. The rest all lazy. Don't even flush their own toilets. I fix everything!"

She nodded, hoping the toilet part was an exaggeration. "That's great." The cage wobbled as it ascended, like the cable attaching it to the top of the shaft was shredded to a single, thin wire.

"Yes. I fix roof and leaks. Exterminate insects—

roaches, red ants, everywhere! Everything run-down,
but I fix. I am super!" he said.

"Wow, that's fantastic," she told him. She didn't
intend the sarcasm; it just happened.

Chastened, Edgardo looked down at his penny loafers. He'd sliced the leather wider, to accommodate
shiny, matching quarters. There was something inher-
ently tragic about that to her, like watching a Martian
try to put on pants both legs at a time: they have no
idea.

"No, really," she said. "What you do is wonderful.
Places like The Breviary get torn down every day, and
the world gets worse because of it. People have no re-
spect for quality or history. They'd make houses out
of Styrofoam and throw them away every week if they
could."

The elevator creaked past the fifth floor, where she
spied dirty beige carpet that might once have been
white. "Yes! True! What I do is important!" Edgardo
announced, then used their newfound connection as an
opportunity to check her out. He started at her black
ballet flats, moved on to the legs of her loose wool trousers, and worked his way up.

When people first met Audrey Lucas, they were reminded of 1930s Hollywood glamour; lovely and un-
adorned, with a pointed chin, long, bumped nose, and
cheekbones sharp enough to cut rocks. She was pretty
but awkward. She kept her arms crossed in conversations to keep people from standing too close, and she
tended to shrink in crowds, making herself invisible,
because she'd learned from experience that the world
was cruel. She'd been working such long hours that the
skin under her eyes appeared smeared with charcoal,
and her pale cheeks had lost their rosy bloom. Still, the
few and brave who took the time to get to know her
unearthed their reward. She was smart, and funny, and
kind. When she trusted the people around her enough

to smile, the sight was lovely, and just a little heart-breaking.

If her life worked out okay, and she found happiness, the pinched angles of her body would soften. By her forties, she'd blossom into a stunning beauty. If her life worked out badly, those angles would calcify into stone, and she would become small, and bitter, and angry.

Edgardo's entire neck craned as his eyes grazed the v-neck of Audrey's loose blouse, her small breasts, hunched shoulders, and at last, her stark, green eyes. When he was done, his gaze settled on her bare, scarred-up fingers. Then he winked, to let her know he liked what he saw.

She frowned. She was thirty-five years old, with a good job and a decent head on her shoulders. Still, when she spotted strangers looking for that ring, she felt . . . exposed.

The elevator passed the seventh floor. The red hall-way carpet was littered with empty champagne flutes and confetti. A Monday night party? Edgardo smiled. She hid her hands in the pockets of her green, army-surplus peacoat, and imagined poking his eyes into pools of goo.

Edgardo shook his head, to let her know she'd gotten the wrong idea. "My daughter looks like you."

She raised an eyebrow, and he continued. "Really! She does! She's in Alaska. I visit her in the summer, but the winter"—he mimed being blown down by a gust of wind—"too cold!"

She shrugged. She'd never met a happy family, and wasn't quite sure she believed in them. They sounded as kosher as Scientology Aliens or leprechauns.

Edgardo waited for her response. She had none. After a few silent seconds, he flinched. The entire wrinkled right side of his face seized like a stroke patient's, then went smooth again. She realized right then, that he was lying. Maybe he didn't have a daughter, or else, they didn't get along. Maybe he was an ex-con, and had gone to Rikers Island for setting her on fire. Whatever the story, he was lying. She could sympathize. Sometimes you tell people what you think they want to hear, only you're not so good at figuring people out, so you never get it quite right.

He looked sad, flinching, inflation-shoed Edgardo. She decided to rescue him by letting him know that she was kind of a Martian, too. "Don't worry. My mom's in a mental institution in Nebraska. Bipolar disorder. I haven't seen her in years."

Edgardo crossed his arms, visibly uncomfortable. She knew she'd blabbed out of turn, and tried to fix it. "Not that I'm suggesting that your daughter belongs in a mental institution, of course."

Edgardo narrowed his eyes. They were blue, and either booze or hard work had threaded them with red spider veins. A second or two passed before he was certain she wasn't mocking him, and he chortled. "My Stephanie belong in Bellevue! Don't you worry."

They passed the ninth floor, which was stripped of carpet and light fixtures though it didn't appear to be under construction. The walls were broken in places, and the copper wiring torn out, as if this rich building had been looted for parts. Strange. Perhaps the co-op was late on its payments, and The Breviary was up for sale, but since nobody was buying real estate these days, they'd taken to pillaging their own infrastructure. From an apartment on the floor either below or above, "Dixieland" played. Its bouncing beat echoed through the shaft.

Edgardo continued. "Alaska is no good. My Stephanie won't write . . . I told a story. I never visited. She won't let me. These kids, they blame their Mamis for everything."

"Maybe some parents deserve to be blamed," she said. And again, once she spoke, she regretted.

Edgardo pursed his lips and looked genuinely pained by what she'd said. His eyes got watery. "So, what if we deserve it? Don't you think we had parents, too?"

She couldn't think of a sensible answer to his question, so they stood there, eyes averted, as the elevator creaked. After a while, he took a few steps away from her. She did the same, until, like boxers, they occupied separate corners.

Finally, excruciatingly, the elevator dial clicked fourteen. They stumbled out, blinking into the light, like caged animals dumbfounded by their freedom.

Once Edgardo keyed open 14B, she forgot the elevator's awkwardness, and the fact that she'd left work, and even the faulty foundation of this building, which might soon crumble. Everything changed. Everything was wonderful.

"Ha!" she cried. Edgardo caught her enthusiasm and smiled, too. She didn't wait for him to show her around; she galloped down the long, dark hall and into the den where it mushroomed. Then she ran its expanse like a kid. A stained-glass turret! Central Park views! Built-in bookcases! Original pocket doors! Fifteen-foot ceilings! This place was huge. If she wanted, she could get a friggin' pool delivered, connect a hose to the tub, and swim laps!

The apartment was run-down, but its bones were solid. Its western slant wasn't severe enough to warp furniture, and even its curved hall showed a kind of brilliance because it directed the eye toward the focal point of the apartment—the den.

On her way down the hall, she bit her lips and braced herself for the bad news. No way the rent here was $999. Add a zero. But then, something glistened. A crystal chandelier in the master bedroom cast foot-long rainbows against the walls. Red. Yellow. Blue. Green. Leaping Jesus, it was beautiful!

Her eyes got misty. Her heart pounded, like meeting the love of your life for the first time, and you *just know.* For as long as she could remember, she'd scratched. Everything she'd ever gotten was hard-won. But today, she'd arrived. That guy in the sky was showing some benevolence, and giving her something for nothing. About frickin' time.

She found Edgardo waiting by the turret in the den. He looked pensive, and she wondered if he was thinking about his daughter. She decided she liked Edgardo, which was unusual, because she never liked anyone unless she'd known them for years.

"This place is crazy. I love it. No catch? It's really $999 a month?"

Edgardo nodded.

"I'll write you a check. First, last, and deposit?" she asked in one breath, like if she didn't draw her pen fast enough, another homeless New Yorker would barge through the door with more money and better credit.

Edgardo frowned.

"I want the apartment," she repeated, then joined him at the window overlooking Central Park. A tiny red ant crawled across the glass, and he smooshed it with his thumb. Down below, ducks bobbed under the small waves of the Harlem Meer, and joggers sprinted along the reservoir. If she squinted, she could even see the Parkside Plaza renovation on 59th Street.

Edgardo tapped his cane. Once. Twice. Three times. Four. He was stalling. She was about to offer him a C-note bribe (it was all she could afford, unless she started turning tricks), when he finally spoke: "They want someone with your job. That's why you're here. Someone who can build things this time. Last one, fine voice, but no good with her hands."

She beamed. "I'm a real professional. It's very professional. A career. I'm not home during the day making noise or having part—"

He cut her off. "—But I like you, you see? You stupid, like my Stephanie."

"What did you call me?"

His eyes watered again. She decided maybe his tear ducts were broken. "They want it a secret. I could lose my job. But I should tell you."

Her stomach sank. Lead water mains. Asbestos-filled walls. Rats. She'd have to share the kitchen with fifty Chinamen. Well . . . still might be worth it.

"There was an accident," he said.

She cocked her head. An old lady fell out the window. A neighbor's malnourished pit bull developed an appetite for human babies. Whatever. For the last example of Chaotic Naturalism in the world, she could handle tag-team serial killers in tights.

"You heard about her. The woman and her babies. Happened in July. The bathtub?"

"I just finished school—architecture," she told him. Barely scraped by. Between Saraub and her final project, *using negative space to define boundaries in domestic environments*, she was still recovering. When she woke up in the mornings lately, she had a hard time getting out of bed, and not because she was depressed. She was exhausted.

"I haven't even seen a movie in three months . . . It's been hard. I broke up with my boyfriend. That's why I'm moving." She heard herself, and decided she ought to make some friends instead of burdening random building superintendents with her problems.

Edgardo's knobby walking cane *tap-tap-tapped* as he limped to the center of the den, where the floor buckled by about two inches. A piece of it had broken to reveal a rotted support beam. Something heavy and damp (an old-fashioned wet bar?) must have rested on it for years and years. "Well, you didn't miss *this* story," he said.

Edgardo, my friend, you overestimate me, she thought.

To get her attention, he banged his cane hard against the warp in the floor in four quick strikes: *Whock!-Whock! Whock!-Whock!* Then he cleared his throat. "The last tenant was fighting with her husband for the children. He lived in . . . New Jersey. A McMansion, you know? They go up overnight, as big as this whole building. Me? I'd rather live in a sewer. But the fights. Very ugly, the fights. The neighbors complained when he came."

Audrey nodded. "McMansions are designed by half-wits. You know, they waste twice as much energy as houses with plaster instead of drywall? The American family keeps getting smaller and its houses keep getting bigger . . . It's actually a very lonely way to live."

Edgardo waved his knobby cane at her. "Not the point! The point is she was wrong fit for The Breviary. That's why the rent is low. The board wants to be able to pick the right kind of tenant—no one like her ever again."

She nodded, but couldn't help but smile. Down the hall, the kitchen door was open. Sure, whatever he was about to tell her was a doozy, but you could fit a six-person table in there!

"The Mami, she drowned her babies in the bathtub. Then she slit her wrists and climbed in with them," Edgardo said.

"Oh, boy," she said.

He banged his cane on the rotten floor to get her attention, then showed her his clenched fist. "Four babies and Mami." He lifted his thumb. "One!" Then he lifted his index finger. "Two!" His middle finger. "Three!" His fourth finger, which she now noticed was adorned by a handsome copper ring. "Four!" Finally, his pinky, so that he was showing her his open palm. "And Mami makes five! All dead, right here."

Her heart sank a little, then rested in her stomach, and then—oops!—landed in her shoes. She *had* heard about this. The story had been on the cover of every newspaper for days: MOMMY KILLER, TRAGEDY STRIKES ON THE UPPER WEST SIDE, DISTRAUGHT HUSBAND BLAMES CITY FOR NOT ACTING ON ABUSE COMPLAINTS. She thought about that, and now she knew why the prewar bathroom tiles had been replaced with ugly white monstrosities and a half Jacuzzi from Home Depot: water damage. "No," she groaned.

"They repainted and tore up all the carpet. Didn't even resell the old—what was it—claw-foot tub. They had it destroyed," he offered, like he'd decided to soften the blow.

"How awful," she said.

He winced, so that his sun-damaged skin pruned along his eyes and mouth. "Yes. Bad. Worst part: her husband was on his way that morning. He was going to take them. Got the . . . the custody."

Audrey looked out the window. The sun shone bright, but strangely, this place didn't gather much sunlight. She sighed. So her luck wasn't in after all. Surprise, surprise.

Unexpectedly, Edgardo cupped her shoulder. He was shorter, so he had to reach. Maybe not tuna on his breath. Maybe sardines. "All people have dark side. A nice lady like you, best you never meet yours. You find a place where I live. In Queens. Is better for you. I rent this to a yuppie. They don't notice if it's haunted. Don't have gravitas to know. You . . ." He eyed her in a sympathetic way, and she understood that the way he'd winked at her in the elevator really had been paternal. "You'll notice."

She sighed. If she didn't find a place soon, she'd miss the October rentals and would have to pay another month to stay at the Golden Nugget Hotel through November. She'd be a fool to turn this place down. Still, those kids.

Queens, she decided. She'd find a short-term studio out there, get some rest, and after a few months, figure out her next step. This breakup with Saraub might be temporary, so why sign a yearlong lease? Yes, this place was amazing. She could spend her life studying it. But that didn't mean she ought to live in it. A terrible thing had happened here. Something so bad it was bound to have left a stain. She was about to tell Edgardo she'd decided to take his advice when he added: "Better you find a nice man. Girl like you should be married. Have someone to take care of you."

Her reaction was immediate, like flinching when someone jabs. "I'm taking it," she said.

He frowned and shook his head a few times, mumbling something under his breath: *Gringo?* Then he closed his eyes. "Okay. First floor, Apartment C. They'll interview you, and they have paperwork."

He didn't wait for her to follow when he clopped out of apartment 14B. As they rode down the elevator in their separate corners, she wanted to let Edgardo know that she appreciated his concern. Instead, the doors opened, and they parted, in silence.

2

Her Black Holes
(She Glimpsed Something Better
Before It Drifted Out to Sea)

On the morning of the move, Audrey packed fast. There wasn't much to take: a rolling suitcase full of clothes and a prickly cactus named Wolverine. She was leaving in an hour, and she didn't plan on coming back.

Life at the Golden Nugget was a downer. Prematurely aged hookers with bad hygiene (obviously) trolled the street corners, and the vendors who sold chick-pea samosas also sold crack. Their empty, blue-stoppered vials clogged the gutters like Harlem's answer to fall leaves. You get what you pay for, and this hotel was the cheapest place in Manhattan that didn't charge by the hour. She might have found her tenure here more disquieting if she hadn't spent most of it in bed, catching up on her sleep. Four weeks later, she was still exhausted.

She traced the letter "S" along the nightstand with

her finger and wondered: was she depressed? She shook
her head. No, her life had just moved too fast since she'd
moved to this city, and her body needed time to catch
up. She'd had a single weekend between graduation and
the new job. Looking back, she probably should have
taken some time to travel, or at least get a haircut. But
she'd been too excited. Vesuvius was one of the best
firms in the city. Besides, this was a recession; architects
weren't getting hired, they were getting fired. She'd been
lucky to get the offer at all. The *Daily News*' front page
last week had proclaimed the death of new construction, and the illustration below it had been a hairline-
fracture-cracked tombstone that read:

N.Y.C.
1524-2012
REST IN PEACE

In this economic environment, only a fool would take
vacation.

She noticed then that the red light on the hotel phone
was blinking: a message. Her stomach turned. Saraub.
Most of her stuff was still in boxes at his apartment, and
this morning he was supposed to oversee the movers on
his end while she waited at The Breviary. It was sporting of him to help. But that was Saraub: a pathologically good sport.

She lifted the receiver to her ear. It beeped like it was
alive. At first, he'd given her the space she'd asked for,
but as the month came to a close, he'd called more often,
and the pretexts had gotten increasingly lame: "Do you
want all your clothes, or just your fall stuff, so when
you come back to me, the move won't be so big?" and,
"Are you eating right? You know how you get when you
miss breakfast," or her favorite, "Do you know where
my Frank Miller comics are at? . . . You better not have
tossed them, because they're collector's items!"

He'd shown the patience of a saint until last night. She'd called to make sure he was set for the move, and after a little small talk he'd erupted. "You're really leaving me after everything we've been through? Can we talk about this? CAN WE PLEASE FUCKING TALK ABOUT THIS?" he'd yelled.

With the men in his family working abroad, Saraub had been raised by the shrew quartet—his mother and three aunts. They'd taught him early never to raise a voice or a hand against a woman. When he got mad as a teenager, his mother had cried and pretended to be frightened. Not surprisingly, until Audrey came along, Sheila Ramesh had won every argument. To this day, when he was pissed off, he drank neat double shots of Wild Turkey at Blondie's Bar, or waited until she wasn't home and punched something. It had only recently dawned on her that those eye-level round smudges on the white-painted walls in his study alcove were evidence of his fists.

So, when he'd raised his voice for the first time that she'd known him last night, she'd understood that something was brewing. One month after their breakup, they were about to have their first knock-down, drag-out. As soon as she figured that out, she'd hung up fast, like the phone was radioactive.

Now, the phone continued to beep in her ear. But she'd signed the lease at The Breviary. Even if she wanted, there was no turning back. So she hung up, then wiped her eyes, because they were wet.

Out the crud-covered window and a few stories down, horns bleated. The diesel fumes from trucks making their Manhattan produce deliveries darkened the air. Farther north, along the Marcus Garvey Housing Projects, families wearing their Sunday best headed off to church. They walked in groups of three and four. A pair of girls, twins she guessed, wore sailor dresses with matching straw bonnets.

Unbidden, she imagined her children with Saraub. Dark-skinned towheads with wise little eyes. She'd dress them in something obscenely adorable, and they'd complain it was child abuse. "Matching corduroy overalls?" she'd shoot back. "If that's your biggest problem, I win mother of the year."

As she watched, her grin faded. In her mind, the concrete sidewalk rose up like a boil until it burst. It swallowed the happy family, and like a wave, dragged them down underground. The trees and buildings, idle on a windless day, would make indifferent witnesses, and steel trucks would honk without cease, as if it had never happened at all. *Would the grown-ups go first,* she wondered, *or the kids?* Or did that matter, because eventually, this city swallowed everyone?

She closed her eyes, ran her thick, scarred fingers along the window. She'd been imagining holes a lot lately. Partly it was a real fear, partly it was the obsessive-compulsive disorder—she got ideas in her head, and couldn't evict them until they were ready to go. Over the years, she'd learned to control her disease, and took some pride in the fact that not even Saraub had ever guessed that her meticulousness was actually a pathology.

If she patted her left thigh and needed to even it out and pat the right, she did it so slyly that only someone looking for it would notice. Wrinkled knuckles reminded her of tiny baby rodents, so she never looked at people's hands, and when possible, kept her own in loosely curled fists. When she'd felt compelled to scrub the bathroom floor two times (or maybe three) while living with Saraub, she'd done it with the door closed and run the tub so he'd thought she was taking a bath. When she had bad thoughts, like imagining poking out Saraub's baby nieces' eyes with her fingers, or having gross sex with homeless smackheads, she'd learned that trying to expel them from her mind only gave them strength. Instead, she let them fade, like bubbles in a bath. Until now, all that had worked. She'd passed for normal, and, all in all, was probably only half as neurotic as your average New Yorker.

But these holes lately had proven stubborn. The more she ignored them, the stronger they got. She even dreamed about them: a yawning black mouth that gnawed her toes, then her feet and legs and arms, until she was a cripple. A flopping trunk, useless and terrified. And then the hole consumed her entirely, and she was nothing at all. Just a shadow—a dark stain left by the woman she'd once been. In her more paranoid moments, she got the idea that the images were portents of things to come.

The disease, and the fact that she never got treatment for it, had made her departure from Omaha all the more surprising. She still didn't know how she'd found the courage. It might have been Betty's hospitalization that had jolted her into action. She'd figured: now or never. Then again, maybe it wasn't Betty at all. Sometimes you get so tired of living in your own skin that you'll do anything to peel it off. Even the hardest thing: change.

From the day she'd arrived at the Port Authority Bus Terminal four years ago, New York had tried to spit her back out. She'd met with a thick-accented Corcoran Real Estate broker whose dyed black hair had matched her imitation Chanel Purse. (Chinel! The label had exclaimed, like it was excited to meet you.)

As soon as Audrey eked past the credit test, Chinel! took her to the East Village: "I've got some efficiencies on Avenue A. Ya'll LOVE it there!"

Chinel!'s three-inch heels had gone *crack!-crack!-crack!* like kids' cap toys, while beside her, Audrey had tried not to crane her neck and gawk at the finely crafted stone peaks of the old tenements on East 3rd Street. They saw three places, all of which Chinel! had promised cost less than $800 but magically turned out to be at least $2,100. A month!

"You can't get no cheappa than two grand," Chinel! had exclaimed with exasperation at apartment number four, like Audrey was insulting her hospitality. The place was a fifth-floor walk-up that smelled like mice.

"You don't understand. I can't afford this," Audrey had answered with tears in her eyes. Her whole life, she'd scraped. As a kid, she'd stolen Coffee Mate creamer out of motels, like "milk solids" was a food group. In college, she'd ladled slop at both cafeterias, just so she could afford the textbooks. To keep the grad-school application checks from bouncing, she'd skipped the sweet air for a month. Never once had anything come easy. Never once had a rich uncle died, so baby could wear a pair of new shoes.

"So take out anotha school loan! That's what all the kids do. Me, I live farther out. But you can't commute that fah. This is the best deal you'll get."

The tough, callused pads of Audrey's feet had rubbed against cheap linoleum because the soles of her special-occasion-only loafers had been worn to a thin layer of rubber. She hadn't changed her fancy corduroy jumper since the bus transfer in Pittsburgh, and as they'd entered each small, stuffy studio, she'd learned the hard way that the concentrated sweat dried to her underarms smelled a lot like piss.

Audrey sighed. She'd been in the city less than six hours, and already, she wanted to take the next bus back to Omaha. But by now her old job at IHOP was filled, and someone else had rented her tiny, black-painted studio apartment. She was alone, and home was gone.

Chinel! clapped her hands together like she thought they were going to make a deal, and Audrey had wondered: *Why did I think I could pull this off?*

She didn't know how to buy a Metrocard, or read

a subway map, or fix a blown fuse, or apply for a job other than at IHOP. She was weird Audrey Lucas, who hadn't learned to balm her lips in high school, so in the winter, they'd bled. Not to mention the maxi pads. It was too humiliating to even *think* about the maxi pads. She hadn't known about table manners, either. When she got to the new-student banquet at the University of Nebraska, she'd rolled her flat chicken cutlet like baloney and eaten it with her hands. Even the shit-booted farm kids had hooted their amusement. Weird Audrey Lucas: she raised herself, only she didn't do a very good job.

Chinel!'s cell phone had jingled to the tune of Prince's "When Doves Cry." She'd looked at its lit-up screen, then at Audrey, like she was trying to figure out which was worth her time. She grudgingly picked Audrey and dropped the phone back into her purse.

Maybe it was something in this New York air. Dirty, but dignified, like tarnished copper. Maybe it was Audrey's semiretarded busboy at IHOP who'd forgiven her two-hundred-dollar hash debt, and pressed five fatties into her palm for the road. "Shit on a stick: Columbia University! Forget about that stuff with your mom. You're going someplace. Write me sometime, even if I don't write back. I'm proud to know you, Audrey Lucas," Billy Epps had told her. She'd looked down at her black Reeboks before thanking him, because the kindness had been so unexpected.

If a nice guy like Billy Epps could think she was worth something, why was she letting tacky Chinel! get her down? Who was this woman to con her out of an education, a new life, just so she could make a quick buck on the signing fee?

Audrey made her decision. She wanted this new life so much she could fucking taste it. Sure, she might not be special or smart or tough enough. But not this way.

She wasn't going to let this fake-pursed phony be the bitch who took her down.

Chinel! beckoned toward the dingy, nonworking fireplace with shellacked red nails: "Look at this, sweetie. A real prewar detail."

Audrey didn't move, and Chinel! came back to retrieve her. Blood rushed to Audrey's face: hot and salty, like liquid fire. "I booked this appointment from Nebraska! You told me you had apartments in my range! You told me no problem!"

"Hun-ee," Chinel! clucked, then rolled her eyes. But when she looked at Audrey, whatever she saw there changed her mind. She smiled crookedly, a real smile, like suddenly the game was over—nothing personal— and they could part friends. "I had you pegged all wrong. I thought you was the daughter of a rich man when you said you was going to Columbia. Forget the East Village. It's Neva-Neva Land. Do ya-self a favor and go to stoodent housing up in Morningside Heights. They'll find you something cheapa."

Audrey didn't bother saying good-bye, or even shaking hands. She left Chinel! in the dirty walk-up. After a thirty-minute search up and down 14th Street (she refused to ask for directions because—Dammit!—she could do this!), she found the crosstown L. It was only after she held to the metal strap, and the subway roared through its noisy tunnel, that she smiled. She'd never guessed she had it in her to yell at another person. Better still, yelling felt pretty stinking good.

After that day, she kept fighting. And scratching. And working. And learning the little things, like why dental floss was good and the creepy old men on 113th and Amsterdam were bad. And then one morning, she looked in the mirror, and discovered that she'd lost her sad-sack slump. Her hair wasn't greasy anymore. And her smile happened to be kind of pretty. For the first time in her life, she looked happy. New York was where she belonged.

Even grad school worked in her favor. Turned out, she had real talent. If she'd been any good at reading people, she might have recognized the envy of her fellow students, and even a few of the teachers, whose snipes had not been intended to encourage but to undermine. But after growing up under Betty Lucas' thumb, the subtleties of academic pettiness flew right over her head. Nothing stopped her, or even slowed her down.

By the end of her first year, the department chair selected her to help design New York-Presbyterian's Pediatric Wing. Instead of shared bedrooms, she suggested small, alveoli-like rooms in clusters of three along the edges of the building, so the really sick kids still had their privacy, but they also got a view. Her design won the New York Emerging Voices Award in Architecture. That summer break, even though nobody else in her class landed so much as an interview for an unpaid internship, she had her pick of firms.

During her second year in school, with one aspect of her life in place, she decided to shoot for gold and shore up the other part, too. Her first effort was E-Harmony, but their standards against weird were too high, because after she filled out their hundred-item questionnaire, they told her she was unmatchable. Next she tried singleny.com, then smoked up with the last of Billy's hash before her dates because she'd needed the courage. She let the first guy kiss her even though she didn't like him, because a girl needs a first kiss. "Farmer's daughters are my favorite! You're as sweet as jelly!" he'd announced, and she hadn't corrected him by letting him know that the closest she'd gotten to a farm was when Betty had worked as a secretary at the John Deere in Hinton.

She let the next guy get to second base. She liked him a little better, but not much. He'd lived with his parents in the Trump Towers, and kept talking about how much money he would inherit when they died. From the broken veins across his nose and the half bottle of Bombay Gin he downed, she got the feeling that she'd hooked herself a boozer. "You're forty-two years old, right?" she'd asked, thinking such a question would shame him, but instead he'd answered, "I lied on the application. I'm forty-nine."

Compared to his predecessors, Saraub was Prince Charming. His name was pronounced Sore-rub but his friends called him Bobby, because, before political correctness, that was what kindergarten teachers at Manhattan private schools renamed all the Indian kids—they didn't like having to pronounce foreign words. Worse, she later learned, his real name was Saurabh, but the hospital got it wrong on the birth certificate.

From his short, no-nonsense e-mails she'd learned that he was a documentary filmmaker, he liked Frank Miller comic books, especially Batman, and he was teaching himself to play the harmonica. Badly. He'd never once written that she was *hot*, that he'd like to poke her, or that he wanted to fill a room with oodles of crisp hundred-dollar bills and swim naked through them with her. "Yours, Saraub," he always signed, and the first time she'd read that, she'd thought: *Okay, I'll take you*.

"Are you stoned?" Saraub had asked when she met him outside the Film Forum movie theatre, where they'd arranged to see Hitchcock's *Strangers on a Train*. Her pupils must have been dilated to the size of black aggie marbles. So far, he was the only guy who'd noticed.

"Yeah. I hardly ever smoke anymore. But I got nervous," she'd confessed.

He was about six-foot-six, and wide as a linebacker, but he stood kind of slumped, like he'd been putting people at ease about his girth for so long that he'd given himself bad posture. His online profile had framed only his face: clear skin and big, puppy-dog brown eyes. She hadn't noticed his twenty-inch neck. Probably, to get his blue pin-striped shirt to hang so nicely, he'd had it made special.

He bent down so that they were talking eye to eye. "Do I look that scary?"

She'd shrugged. This was her third date in a month, and already she was sick of the bullshit. "Yeah, you do look scary, but that's not why I'm high. I don't date normally, but ever since I moved to New York, I decided to try, you know? I don't come from much, but I'm trying."

He'd frowned. Maybe he'd expected the gleeful Audrey Lucas from the singleny.com profile, who ended all her sentences with exclamation points (looking forward to meeting you!!!) to be his soul mate, but the somber woman with crow's-feet waiting for him at Film Forum had dashed his hopes. He looked up at the sky, like he was just a little pissed off at God. It occurred to her that getting high before a date is kind of rude.

"Hey, I'm sorry. What can I do?" she asked.

Cars trundled down West Houston Street and toward the Holland Tunnel. "I'm trying, too," he said as a cab hit a pothole, so she wasn't sure she'd heard him right.

"What?"

He shook his head. "Forget it. I should go. I've got a lot of work to do."

Normally, she would have let him leave. Her tiny, four-walled dorm room whose bathroom she shared with three other girls needed vacuuming, and he was a fat Indian guy, so why chase him? She could call forty-nine-year-old contestant number two tonight instead. They'd go out and get sloshed, and in a way that would be easier because he wouldn't look at her the way Saraub was looking at her right now, like he was actually trying to *see* her.

He started to walk away, and it slipped out before she had the chance to censor herself: "Don't go. I like you."

Suddenly, she was red-faced and sober. Her heart beat in her ears (squish-squish!), and she looked around for a hole to crawl inside of and hide.

Saraub turned back and smiled like he was amused. He *saw* her. Her whole life, she'd been a phantom. She and Betty had moved around so often that she'd never had time to make friends, and when they finally did put down roots, it had been too late to learn how. Sometimes she got so lonely, she caught herself talking to the damn cactus. But, looking at Saraub, she glimpsed the promise of something better. His arms looked firm. Like if he wrapped them around her, he'd weigh her down and make her real. In her mind, she hugged him back. She pressed her fingers along his spine and let him know that around her, it was okay to stand tall.

"Come on," she pleaded, even though this was the first time she could remember ever chasing a man instead of running in the opposite direction. It felt scary. It felt alive. "It'll be my treat."

He narrowed his eyes like he was thinking hard on something. "The thing is," he said, "my family has somebody picked out. An arranged marriage. I thought . . . I'd see what else was out there. I've only ever dated Indian girls, but I'm getting married next month. Twenty-four days, actually."

"Oh," she said. She tried to swallow the lump in her throat, but it stayed there. She looked down at the sidewalk. His shoes were shiny loafers. Hers were ballet flats. The smell of popcorn was in the air. She wondered if she cleaned more often than necessary because she was lonely.

"I shouldn't complain. I'm no catch," he'd said, patting his ample gut. In his profile he'd called himself fit. Then again, she'd called herself an optimist. "The girl—she's not my type. She smiles all the time, but she never says anything. It's annoying."

"What's your type?" Audrey asked. She ached so

much at the thought of losing this stranger that she thought she might cry, so she bit her lip and looked at the man in the ticket booth, who was counting quarters one by one.

Saraub ran his hands along his suit, straightening the fabric. It was a Saturday. She didn't think he was going to work after this, which meant he'd worn it for her. "Complicated. My type is complicated. Would you mind seeing the movie, just as friends?"

She nodded. By the time the tennis star's wife got murdered in the reflection in Patricia Hitchcock's glasses, they were holding hands. By the third "just friends" date, he'd postponed the wedding.

She was afraid to tell him that she was a thirty-three-year-old virgin, so they didn't sleep together until their tenth date. To avoid the humiliation of such a confession, she'd considered breaking up with him. But she liked him too much, so instead she braved the adult section of Kim's Video on 112th and Broadway, and rented three pornos. *Dr. Cocksalot,* with his fingers made of penises, provoked the most giggles, though it had lacked the desired erotic effect. She studied it until she thought she could put on a decent show and make him believe she wasn't new to the world of love.

Her plan had one flaw. Sex is terrifying. As soon as he unzipped his jeans, and his little friend poked its way out of his blue silk briefs, she started crying. What was she supposed to do with that thing? Hold it? Compliment it? Give it a cute name? She'd never seen one before in real life!

Then she'd laughed, loud and braying, because this was absurd. After all the bad shit with Betty she'd faced with the kind of poker face that even a stoic would envy, she'd picked now to cry, when she was happy for the first time in her life, and a nice man finally wanted to touch her.

Saraub hiked his trousers. Shirtless and blushing so

hard his brown face turned red, he'd looked down at his stomach like it had done something wrong, hunched his shoulders, and tried to make himself small.

She stopped laughing, and leaped off his queen-sized bed. Melted Mallomar crumbs from one of his late-night snack sprees were stuck to her back like freckles. "It's not you. I—I love you," she'd blurted, so intent on keeping the immediate secret that she hemorrhaged the more important one. "But I'm. . . . I never dated, you know? I used to be kind of a shut-in. I was too scared. I never . . ."

He'd smiled then, a lazy, cat-that-ate-the-canary grin, and dropped his trousers again. "It's okay," he told her. "You don't have to say." She cried through the whole thing, but not because she was sad. She'd gone and done something stupid. After all the ways she'd let crazy Betty Lucas break her heart, she'd finally opened up and trusted somebody again.

"I'm glad it was me," he told her when they were done, and lying in each other's arms. "Because I really love you."

At those words, she'd felt something inside her crack apart. Her whole body got warm. Sometimes you can feel your walls as they break. "Me, too," she said.

Six months later, she and her cactus moved into Saraub's apartment on the Upper East Side. With his wedding officially canceled, his family, who lived twenty blocks away on Park Avenue, cut him off. No more ski trips. No more health insurance. All they had to live on was his freelance income and her tips from waiting tables on weekends at La Rosita. "I'm so sorry," she'd told him.

He'd rubbed the back of her neck in that way that made her purr. "I'm not. I'm relieved. I wish I'd done it sooner."

She tried to hide it for the first few months, but after a while, she couldn't help it; she rearranged his kitchen cabinets, moved the framed poster of dogs playing poker to the space behind the door so she wouldn't have to look at it, and scrubbed all the floors with a toothbrush. He was understanding because he had a few quirks of his own. He was a documentarian, which provided him the excuse of filming people with his camera phone when they weren't paying attention. At least once a week she caught him holding up his phone while she sipped her morning coffee. She shooed him with a wave of her hands like he was a fly: "Are you kidding? I haven't even brushed my hair!" But after a while she learned to ignore it. Some men buy flowers, others carry around footage of what their girlfriends look like at 6:30 A.M.

After their first year of domestic bliss, Saraub started talking about finding a bigger place. With his I ♥ NY tourism commercial editing gigs, and the job at Vesuvius, she was about to start, they could afford a house in Yonkers, maybe even start a family. She'd nodded and changed the subject, because she'd figured he wasn't serious. Besides, it wasn't *that* outlandish: she'd kept a cactus alive for five years; a baby couldn't be that much harder, could it? . . . Right? And the truth was, this happy family bullshit, with its white picket fence and healthy Campbell's-Soup-looking kids he kept dreaming about; it sounded pretty good.

One morning, he woke her up with a cup of coffee and the real-estate section of the *New York Times*, in which he'd circled about five house listings. "Let's take the train to Yonkers and have a look," he'd nudged. She'd rolled over and told him she had too much homework, which was true. She'd been working ninety hour weeks to get her thesis finished on time.

When the project was done and she'd been at the new job a few months, she couldn't put him off anymore. They went to Yonkers. Saw a classic Victorian overlooking the Hudson River. "It's run-down," he'd told her. "But the taxes are low, and I know you'll work wonders." As soon as the broker left to take a phone call, he got down on one knee.

"I've got a surprise," he told her as he reached into his pocket. A lock of black hair fell into his eyes, and she thought he was the most handsome and terrifying man in the world. The air got thin, and the walls felt closer. She pressed her hands against them to keep from getting crushed.

"I saved up the money for the deposit," he said. He was so proud that he'd done it without his family's help that she had to smile, and be proud of him, too. "It's our house if we want."

"Wow," she mumbled, while pushing hard against plaster and trying to remember to breathe.

He opened a velvet box. Something sparkled. "My grandmother's," he explained. "Do you like it?"

The ring was small and classy. Antique platinum. Perfect. She loved it. The house was perfect, too. She took a deep breath and held herself steady. Then again, it wasn't perfect at all. This was a man who burst into the bathroom while she was showering, just to announce he was leaving for work. This was a man who, no kidding, really did eat crackers in bed. His grandparents had survived famine, and as a result he thought that food equaled love. When she came home from school at night, he scampered out of the bedroom like a puppy dog: "How was your day? Did you have a good day? . . . I baked you this pie! Eat my delicious rhubarb pie!"

No matter how hard she tried, she couldn't get his shoes to line up nicely, or his furniture to shine quite right. She never wanted to admit it, but she knew why. It wasn't *her* furniture. It wasn't *her* apartment. The thing about other people is, they're not you.

"You make me a better man," Saraub said.

She took a breath. And another. And another. Imagined the house full of voices. A barking dog. Meddling in-laws with really good table manners, who corrected her when she used soup spoons to stir her tea. A kid or two. Indian kids! On holidays, she'd have to dress them in saris. The rest of the time, they'd want to know how to tie their shoes. They'd need burping, and bathing. They'd need mothering, and who was fooling whom, she could hardly take care of herself.

"What do you say?" Saraub asked.

She put out her left hand and told him the truth. "I really love you," she said.

He slipped on the ring, which fit as neatly as Cinderella's glass slipper.

When they got home that night, they made love. It was good, and slow, and for a little while, she thought maybe it would all work out, and they really would live happily ever after. But after he fell asleep, she was restless. She got up and rearranged all the dishes. Saucers in front, bowls in back. Then she took everything out, and relined the cabinets. Then she put the dishes back, and stopped eating.

Two days later they went out to Daniel Restaurant for a fancy French dinner to celebrate their engagement. They split a bottle of wine. On an empty stomach, the booze hit her fast. She turned into a blabbermouth. Everything she'd held in since they'd started dating gushed out. "I need a break," she said, "Not from you. From my life. I'm so tired, all I want to do is sleep. Don't you ever get sick of this city? It's so noisy. It never stops. I thought I'd move out for a while. Find a sublet or go to a hotel. Just to catch up on my sleep, you know?" The worst part was the shock that resolved into puckered hurt on his face, like she'd punched him, and he was trying to show he could take it like a man.

"Okay. I understand," he told her while smashing his wild okra into mush. Still drunk, unaware he was close to crying, she'd continued. "It's not that I don't love you, but you drive me crazy, you know?"

That was when he covered his face with his hands so she didn't see his tears. She felt so bad that she stopped talking. The rest of the dinner, she didn't look up from her plate because she was afraid that if she saw him crying, she'd start crying, too.

He slept on the couch that night. In the sober light of morning, she was ashamed. What a terrible way to break such news. Most of the time, she liked him just fine. More than anybody else, at least. She'd considered crawling onto the couch with him. When he woke up, she'd eat as many runny Velveeta omelets as he cooked, if that was what made him happy. "I'm neurotic and have limited interpersonal skills," she'd explain. "You know that. Next time, don't take me so seriously."

Then again, sleeping alone for the first time since they'd moved in together, she'd noticed a change. The bed was deliciously spacious, and the walls stayed where they belonged. Without Saraub, she could breathe.

So she moved to the Golden Nugget and told him it was temporary, when in fact, she was pretty sure it was permanent. She stopped wearing the ring on her finger, and now carried it in her pocket wherever she went, because she didn't trust the hotel staff not to break in and steal it. Probably, she should give it back to him. But she wasn't ready to, just yet.

And here she stood with a packed bag, checking out of a fleabag flophouse. Not so different from the Midwest no-tell motels her mother had dragged her through like a rag doll when she was a kid. Maybe this was how Betty had started her descent, too. A relationship that got too close. A move too many. And then the inevitable red ants of madness that had followed them from town to town, like they'd developed a taste for her scent.

Audrey took one last look at the room. She'd straightened, of course: folded white sheets, a Bible, and a sparkling ashtray. The blinking red message light on the phone and the letter "S" traced into the glass-topped nightstand with her finger were the only evidence that she'd lived here at all.

She imagined going back in time. Picking up her suitcase, and walking rearward out the door. Reversing the order of this thing she'd done, so that she'd never signed the lease for The Breviary, never done anything that couldn't be undone. She'd return home to Saraub and fall asleep alone in their futon, and when she woke, she'd be on a date at a fancy French restaurant, only this time, she'd take it all back. He'd talk about moving to Yonkers, and she'd tell him, "I hope we have enough kids for a football team!"

Yes, she decided. She would go back to him. It wasn't too late. If she stayed on this desolate road she was carving for herself, she knew what would happen. Her life would become an empty thing. Erased daily because she had no one to share it with. She'd become a phantom again, and this time her mother wasn't around to blame.

She picked up her bag.

Saraub, or The Breviary?

Saraub.

The idea of him caught in her chest and pressed out her breath like a weight. She imagined getting fat with a kid in her belly. She'd try to sit at her desk, and she wouldn't fit. They'd fire her, and she'd get stuck cleaning the Victorian and playing host to the bitch quartet while with every year, Saraub's center of gravity got lower, and his smile more fake, and the smudges on the walls became holes. Her breath got slow, and then was gone altogether. Before she found him, when the space in her stomach had been an empty thing called longing, she'd known the truth. Squandering love is the ugliest of sins. She wished she was a stronger person. She wished she could reach inside herself and fix this thing that was broken. But she couldn't.

In her mind, the asphalt outside opened again into a hungry black hole. It widened like a wave and crashed against all the families walking home from church. It crashed through the hotel window, too. The current pulled her back out and into its depths as it receded. It carried her to a small, dark place deep underground, where she became still as a shadow and she didn't need to breathe.

The Breviary, indeed.

3

All the Pretty Young Things in the Dark

I live here now. I'm moving in today," Audrey told the doorman at The Breviary. He was a skinny Haitian man wearing a faded gray uniform with silver buttons. It reminded her of a bellhop costume from the 1950s. She bit her lip and gave him a pleading look: she'd forgotten to call ahead and reserve the freight elevator, and it had only occurred to her now, looking at the sign that read, NO MOVING ON SUNDAYS! that she wasn't supposed to move in on a Sunday.

He nodded. "I know, Mizus Lucas. Fourteen B. They tell me. It's in the schedule."

She cocked her head. The owner? The co-op board who'd approved her application? "Did Edgardo tell you I was moving in?" she asked.

"Edgardo no work here no more," he said, then smiled at her and went back to reading Borges' *Labyrinths* in French.

"Where'd he go?" She was holding her cactus so its dirt didn't spill.

He shook his head, then returned to his book. Either they were divided by a language barrier, or else he was done talking and had decided to erect an imaginary language barrier. She moved on.

As she rode up the elevator, she noticed that the floors had all been cleaned, and the powdery hotel scent of Love My Carpet wafted through the iron bars. The only remaining evidence of a party on the seventh floor was the cigarette burns—perfectly round circles of black branded into a beige carpet. The ninth floor was still empty, but someone had hammered drywall over the plaster holes where the copper had been torn. The job looked hastily done, or else in keeping with the architecture: none of the boards were level.

She keyed herself into 14B and put down her suitcase. The ceilings were even higher than she'd remembered, and the fifty-foot hall was more cavernous. She pictured herself waking up at night and getting lost, so she took a deep breath and reminded herself that big was good.

Carrying her cactus, she walked down the hall and opened doors, one after the next. First, the small bedroom. A child's room, she guessed. Where the drowned ones had slept.

After signing the lease, she'd been foolish and had researched Clara DeLea. A divorced has-been opera diva. Worse than a has-been; an almost been. Big, beautiful, and full of temper, her drinking got the better of her and City Opera fired her. The low point in her life transformed her. She checked into rehab and became a new, more generous woman. A few months after her release, she met and married her lawyer husband at Betty Ford. They had four dewy-eyed kids aged ten, eight, five, and two. Their life was suburban perfection—a picket fence, good schools, nice neighbors, a short commute to the city. They grew apart.

The divorce got ugly. She accused him of cheating. He accused her of beating the children and giving the infant brain damage. At two years of age, Deirdre Caputo had still not spoken a single word. Her eyes, which had once focused on objects dangling in front of her (mobiles, human faces, her own fingers), became glazed. When the change in her behavior was proven in court, and her concussions linked to the dull handle of a metal spatula, Richard wound up with custody.

Clara and her kids had only lived in 14B for fifteen days before the tragedy, but in that short time, she'd managed to start drinking after more than a decade of sobriety. The *Daily News* posted one of the last family photos of the Caputo/DeLea family in its online archive. The father was absent, possibly because he'd snapped the picture. The kids, dressed in red-and-green finery, had stood next to the fake, white Christmas tree. Eldest Keith had cradled glassy-eyed baby Deirdre in his arms. The child's gaze had been eerily vacant, her pupils so dilated they'd appeared black. Beside them had been the second oldest, Olivia, with her hands fixed on toddler Kurt's shoulders. They'd formed their own family while, several feet behind them, Clara DeLea had lurked. She'd grown sloppy and obese, wearing black, horn-rimmed glasses and blue sweats.

Normally, Audrey might have wondered about Clara—whether the woman had suffered, was sick in the head, had some kind of reason for what she'd done. But looking at this miserable, lurking thing that had glowered behind those four innocents, all she'd seen was a monster.

Now, Audrey's eyes adjusted to the bright October light as it shone across the freshly glazed pine planks in the children's room. She didn't like to court these morbid thoughts, but unanswered questions tended to nag her into insomnia. So she imagined the room's many possible configurations. Then she nodded and pictured the one that fit best. The baby hadn't lived here, but in a crib with Clara in the master bedroom. In this room, there had been a bunk bed against the wall for the boys and a single bed by the window for the girl. Trunks for clothes, a shared closet, and an aisle of walking space between beds. She even thought she could guess the color. Jarring red, because the children would have argued between pink and blue, and Clara, by then, had gone mad.

She walked to the center of the room, then lowered her head in prayer because a tragedy this size demanded acknowledgment. "You poor kids. I'm so sorry," she said. The apartment did not answer her, and nothing creaked in the stagnant bedroom air, so she continued. "I'll change this place and make it warm, but I'll remember you." Her words didn't echo, even though the room was empty. Instead, they seemed to gather inside the walls, as if something there had received them. She bowed her head and left.

Across the hall was the renovated bath. The copper fixtures remained, but the antique yellow wall tiles had been ripped in places to make room for the new Jacuzzi, Home Depot vanity, and pressed-wood cabinets. She closed her eyes, and imagined a claw-foot tub. Deep enough to stack all five of them. After a few hours, the tops of their bodies would have turned pale, and their bottoms would have purpled with jellied blood.

Audrey blinked. When that didn't work, she held the cactus steady and tapped her ballet flats four times each (left-right-left-right: a slow-motion Fred Astaire). The sound was soft, and soothing. The hole in her mind from which the image had sprouted closed. She moved on.

The next room was the kitchen. Old built-in cupboards and oak floors. To her relief, the walls smelled like grain and decades of home cooking. The happy opposite of hunger. Finally, the master bedroom. She took a deep breath and opened the door. The chandelier threw rainbow shards of light along the walls. Small details like Guilloche molding and the handblown Mercury glass doorknob made her heart pitter-patter. She imagined green, Scarlett O'Hara velvet curtains, and knew exactly where she'd get the four-poster bed. That antique shop on Atlantic Avenue in Brooklyn that delivered. She laughed out loud, just thinking about it: she'd sleep until noon on Sunday mornings, and speak in the royal "We!"

She let out a deep breath she hadn't realized she'd been holding. She'd chosen right after all. This place was a dream come true. And, well, if it needed paint and a few wall sconces to brighten the mood and erase the bad history, she was up to the task.

At last, she marched to the end of the hall and pushed open the final door. The den. A rush of ancient dust, some remnants of the former tenants, sprayed her face. She swallowed fast, and it got inside of her. She felt it land in the pit of her stomach.

Murder! A man's voice whispered.

The hairs on the back of her neck pointed skyward. Instinct took over. She raced like something was chasing her and inspected every corner of the den. The turret, the rotted support beam, the double-doored closet. She looked high and low, felt the plaster with her fingers, ran her hands along wood and glass. Sniffed the stagnant, dusty air. Nothing spoke or leaped out from a hiding space. She was, quite clearly, alone.

Murder!—Had someone really said such a thing, or was she just nervous about this move? Perhaps this was one of her bad thoughts, like the black hole, that wasn't real? She hoped so. Good God, she didn't want to move *again!*

Just then, someone called to her from the front door: "Hey!"

She jumped. Down the fifty-foot hall leaned a skinny, potbellied young man wearing Janus Moving Company coveralls. WE GET YOU WHERE YOU WANT TO GO! The add in the phone book had read.

"Hey!" she said back, then walked fast in his direction, like the room behind her was on fire.

He pointed a clipboard at her. "Sign on the X," he told her, so she did. He walked away before she could tell him that actually, there'd been a mistake. She was moving to Queens instead. Wherever they could find a FOR RENT sign hanging out the window—that would be her new home.

She followed the mover out. There were four other apartments along the common hall: A, C, D, and E. As she glanced out from 14B, each of the other apartment doors slammed shut. It happened in a single, synchronistic motion. Blood rushed to Audrey's face, and she wondered: *Were my neighbors watching me?*

A few minutes later, all three movers returned. From their thick nasal accents, she guessed they hailed from the Bronx. In her mind she named the first one "Boss Guy," and the other two "Hot Guy" and "Improbably Gangly Plastic-Man Guy."

"Where do we put this?" Boss Guy asked, as the other two hauled the Steinway baby grand through the door. Rolled on its side over a dolly, it just fit.

"That's not mine," she said.

Boss Guy shook his head. "Naw. The guy at the other apartment told us it was a present."

Sweet Saraub. She smiled. His grandmother had given him the Steinway, but he'd never learned to play it. Back at his apartment, Audrey used to sit at its bench and bang out "Chopsticks" or half of "Heart and Soul" while he gave vocal accompaniment in a Monty Python old lady's voice, off-key and absurd:

Heart and soul, I fell in love with you
Heart and soul, the way a fool would do, madly
Because you held me tight!

"It's too much," she said under her breath, but the three movers heard her and glowered. They were skinny guys, and she was surprised any of them had the muscle to prop the jeans over their bony hips, let alone lift a baby grand.

"I don't wanna move this again, lady," Gangly Plastic Man said. He was sweating so much that the floor around him was damp. It was a warm October day, and this was, after all, the fourteenth floor.

Saraub. The man was a saint. She reached into her pocket and felt something sharp. The ring. Good. She'd never forgive herself if she lost it.

"Please! Where do we put this?" Boss Guy asked.

She startled. "Oh. Right. The den."

They followed her down the long hall, wheeling the piano on its side. When they got about halfway, the lone bulb dangling from the ceiling hissed, popped, and went out. All the doors were closed, and no light crept through their cracks. Everything got dark.

"Hold on!" she called, feeling her way toward the den with one hand, cradling her cactus with the other. Somebody, maybe Gangly Guy, yelped, like the piano had pinned him to a wall. She thought about those four kids, and Clara. What if their spirits had never left The Breviary?

In her mind, a hole opened up in the floor, and Clara's wet hands reached out. *Stop!* She scolded herself. *Stop it! Stop it! Stop it!* Then, to the movers, "You okay?"

"Fine! We're fine!" someone answered. But it was so dark in here. Was that one of the movers talking, or was there someone else in this apartment?

Breathing fast, she ran her hands along either wall as she walked. The hall ended. She slammed her forehead—*bonk!*—and reeled back. The den door creaked open. A rectangle of midday light shone through the turret and illuminated the hall just enough for her to see the movers' shapes. They blended together with the piano like a single, lumbering beast.

She found the light and flicked it. Everything got bright. The men blinked like moles. Their faces sagged in this less-forgiving light, and she realized they weren't as young as she'd thought.

"Where?" Boss Guy growled. They were sweating. They were pissed.

"Oh, right!" she said, after she caught her breath. She pointed to the buckle in the middle of the den. "Sorry about the light. You can wheel it right to this hole in the floor. I think somebody had a piano here before. Or *some*thing heavy, at least."

All three of them chose this moment to roll their eyes at her, like it was her fault that pianos are heavy. Then they wheeled it into the room.

After they made two more trips, Hot Guy finally spoke. "This place isn't right," he said. He wore a cigarette behind his ear and a pack of Pall Malls rolled into the short sleeve of his sweat-stained undershirt. "Do you know what I mean?"

"What's not right, the piano?" she asked. "Where else should I put it?"

He was a good-looking guy, and from the way he posed, cross-legged against the wall, she got the feeling that he was accustomed to the attentions of the fairer sex. "My cousin lived in a place like this," he said. "His dog used to bark all night long at the fireplace, like it saw something there. Then my cousin saw it, too. An old guy's face, watching him. All red-eyed and crazy-like. Turned out, some guy'd been murdered in the house, then buried under the fireplace with some extra bricks. His wife did it. Happened a hundred years before, and nobody who'd lived there after that had ever noticed anything wrong. Something about my cousin brought it out. Or, hey, maybe it was the dog that brought it out."

She decided he'd smoked a bowl before reporting to work. Who else but a stoner would say something so stupid to a woman about to spend her first night in a new apartment, all by herself?

"Did something bad happen here?" he asked.

A shelf dropped in her stomach. She thought about four children. Acknowledged the thing she'd been denying. She'd read that Clara DeLea hadn't emptied the tub from one child to the next. At those tender ages, they could not have understood what death meant. Had only learned what it looked like as their mother had plunged them underwater, and they'd witnessed its wild-eyed mask on their siblings' rigid faces.

Hot Guy pressed his ear against the plaster and listened. Then he ran his piano-string-greased hands up and down the walls, as if feeling for a vibration. She thought about tiny fists and pictured the monster, Clara DeLea, crawling across the apartment one night and sneaking up on her children while they slumbered. Her knees would have left an imprint on the old carpet. A slightly darker hue, where she'd pressed the nylon the wrong way. Or worse. Maybe, like a witch, she'd crawled along the walls, and her greasy, bloated body had left snail trails that hadn't been washed clean but instead painted white. They were coming through that paint now, psychic residue, in the form of this mover's dirty paws.

Audrey pointed. "You're making a mess!"

Startled, Hot Guy dropped his hands. His smears were everywhere. Nobody looked angry. Just uncomfortable. She tried to think of an explanation: *I'm feeling a little fragile . . . I just broke up with my boyfriend . . . Of course it's haunted. A woman slaughtered her four children here!*

Hot Guy looked like he was going to say something, but the boss interrupted him. "Look at what you did to the nice lady's wall, you mucker! Go get a rag."

When they were done, she handed them each a ten-dollar tip. "Don't listen to these numbskulls," Boss Guy said, pointing his thumbs at his accomplices. He waited until Audrey cracked a smile, then added, "You know the magic formula, don't you, sweetheart? If you want to be happy here, you will."

"Thanks. I'll make sure to tap my ruby slippers," she said, regretting her rudeness even as she spoke.

Boss Guy raised a puzzled eyebrow. "Uh, yeah," he said, and left without another word.

It didn't occur to her until after they were gone, that when she'd first arrived, she'd opened all the doors along the hall. But when the bulb went out, they'd all been closed.

So, who had closed them?

4

Going Gently Into That Good Night
(Iniquitous Darlings)

The first thing she did was situate the cactus. It went on the turret's ledge in the den, where at least some sunlight filtered. It was Saraub who'd named him. About a month after she moved to his place on York Avenue, he'd written "Wolverine" in neat, black pen on a swatch of masking tape, and stuck it to the side of the orange planter. "Little guy needs a name," he'd told her, like he'd been worried about the prickly member of their family for a while now and had finally done something about it.

With Wolverine securely placed, she painted the far walls in both bedrooms. She'd decided to go with Calvin Klein metallic white; cheerful, but not ridiculous. After that, she hung her drafts along the hall. Most were sketches of the mourning garden above the Parkside Plaza office building on 59th Street that she'd been working on since she'd started at Vesuvius. It was coming along more slowly than anyone had anticipated, which nobody at the office was happy about. Tomorrow morning was the next status report, and she wasn't looking forward to it. There was the distinct possibility that heads would roll, or at least shamble to the unemployment line.

After unpacking, she camped out on an air mattress in the den and flipped to the TBS Classic Television Marathon. Somebody was still paying the cable bill, which was handy, if unsettling. Clara had killed her family in July.

Out the turret window, couples and large groups scurried toward their destinations. A crowd spilled out of the Columbia hangout The Hungarian Pastry Shop, where grad students carved oh-so-deep aphorisms ("God is dead!"; "Let the river run, let all the dreamers take the nation!"; "I text: therefore I am"; "Rick Wormwood Will Light Your Fire!") into the pine tables. She was too high up to hear their laughter, but she could see their distant smiles. She looked at her watch: 7:30 on a crisp fall Sunday night. The kind of night so alive that you can almost hear the city's beating heart down in Times Square. Here she was, all moved in.

And it was very quiet.

Living with Saraub, she'd gotten used to low-level background chatter whenever she was home. He talked on the phone with Los Angeles a lot. Producers, agents, studio executives, secretaries, and crazy people, who tended to encompass all of the previous. For as long as she'd known him, he'd been trying to get financing for his documentary about the privatization of natural resources, *Maginot Lines*.

Last she'd heard, he was close. But that was Hollywood, he'd once explained. Even the shoeshine guy thinks he's close to a green light. He paid the rent by directing commercials freelance. I ♥ New York was his biggest account. He'd been doing it for years now, and the thrill had worn off, but they both agreed that it was significantly better than shoveling coal.

She repositioned Wolverine. This time his name tag faced east. A stained-glass bird caught her attention. Its red eyes were disproportionately small, beady. "You're weird," she told it. "No offense."

Her hands were spattered with paint, and she chewed on the cuticle of her left index finger. It tasted, well, metallic.

What was Saraub doing now? Had his mother set him up with another Indian dial-a-bride? Was he getting drunk every night alone? Or maybe his best friend Daniel, who never slept with the same woman twice because he didn't want her getting clingy, was taking him to strip clubs.

Did something bad happen here? The mover had asked . . . How had he known?

She wished she had a little hash. Make that a lot of hash. Old school, three fatties a night back in Nebraska hash. Instead, she turned up the volume on the television—where *Sex and the City*'s Carrie Bradshaw was explaining why sleeping with strangers is awesome, and sat Indian style on the inflated AeroBed, with her laptop balanced between her knees. Somebody close by had a wireless account (BettyBoop!), so she Googled "Remaining examples of Chaotic Naturalism."

On the television, Carrie wore a washcloth for a dress and wondered whether men liked freckles. Online, the first entry that popped was a reprinted Cambridge University psychology thesis in a critical journal called *Extrapolation*:

Diary of the Dead: Casualties of Chaotic Naturalism

She moaned. Oh, crud. Seriously? She wanted to shut the laptop, but now that she'd seen the link, there was no turning back. Its ominous title would fuel her nightmares unless she investigated. She clicked on it. The article was written in 1924, by a graduate student who'd trained under Carl Jung. She skimmed the introduction, which espoused the merits of alchemy, and started on page two:

—ravings of madmen.

Edgar Schermerhorn's religion, Chaotic Naturalism, waned more than a decade ago, and only a scant few of his buildings remain. Most people don't know that he was originally an architect, and did not found his cult until after reading Darwin's On The Origin of Species.

His theory was founded on the notion that the human mind had evolved into a pattern recognition machine: man perceives cause and effect, and from this, extrapolates reason. For example, plants grow from seeds. This fact is now obvious, but back in 1000 B.C., the idea that wheat could be harvested triggered the Neolithic Revolution and transformed civilization from nomadic to agrarian. Because of pattern recognition, society emerged. Humans transcended their biology and ceased to be animals.

But Schermerhorn believed that the human mind was overactive. It miscategorized, and forced patterns where they didn't exist. For example, natural observations assume that time is linear—Humpty Dumpty can't be uncracked, and returned to the wall—but such narrow perceptions don't account for Yeats' widening gyre, alchemy, particle-wave duality, or time travel.

In the stead of realism, Chaotic Naturalists' followers embraced chaos, which they reflected in their breeding practices (like good eugenicists, they abandoned or drowned imperfect newborns); the families they raised (most were bigamists, and it was not illegal for siblings to marry one another); and the buildings they designed (Schermerhorn had many disciples). In eastern Eu-

rope, they were hailed as visionaries, and even here in America, they achieved a brief celebrity. It wasn't until the 1880s that their membership dwindled as their buildings crumbled one by one, and popular religious leaders of the Second Great Awakening proclaimed that they deserved it, for having made an enemy of God.

There were twenty-six true Chaotic Naturalist edifices all told.

Schermerhorn honed his craft, then returned to America with what he thought was a perfect design. Like the modern Gaudis in Barcelona, they were modeled after nature, not Euclidian geometry. But unlike Gaudi, they borrowed from the snails' spiral, the winged bivalve, the honeysuckle vine, and then broke apart these natural patterns into a disjointed mishmash, as if to prove that not even God held providence over man.

The buildings' tenants were self-selected crews who tended toward emotional instability. With so many neurotic personalities housed under one roof, they fomented each other's afflictions, unleashing the anima and animus. It is Jung's contention that it was this release of unconscious desires, and not the architecture, that is responsible for the wealth of reported Chaotic Naturalist hauntings.

Jung has stated that the buildings functioned as repositories for their tenants' repressed desires, and over time, became closed universes unto themselves. Eventually, the tenants' suppressions became animate, not solely to the dreamer who'd dreamed them but to everyone in the building: the singular psychosis reached the critical mass of collective mania.

Mirroring the structures of the buildings that housed them, the tentants' thoughts fragmented, and they went mad. Their waking hours degenerated into Byronesque nightmares. Some took refuge in their opium pipes. Others ceased to go to work or care for their children, claiming that all efforts were futile, because the end of the

*world was at hand. In many cases, their journal entries
started out in pen, and finished in childish, nonsense
scrawl.*

*I would never contest the brilliant Mr. Jung's conclu-
sions, but in studying the history of Chaotic Naturalism, I've found cause to attach some qualifications to his
theories.*

*As we learned from the Freiberg philosophers, it is
anathema to his biology for man to embrace chaos. Even
if spirits exist (watching us, haunting us, inhabiting alternate universes that subvert time), granting them entrance through the spaces in our minds, or the structure
of our homes, and any other doors we might construct,
can only result in man's utter destruction.*

*Who is to say that the door, once opened, could ever
be closed? And in these alternate worlds, what capac-
ity might man inhabit? Witness? King? Or victim, host,
slave. Both author (Schermerhorn) and interpreter
(Jung) neglected one thing: because of pattern recognition, mankind has learned that kindness and fellowship
are in his best interest. Society evolves slowly, through
group effort and the education of its children. A world
without pattern recognition would be a cruel, inhuman
place. Forgive my sentimentality, but without consequences to our actions, there is no love. And without
love, man has no echo or memory. He can never be im-
mortal or transcend his own coil. He returns to the slop
with the swine.*

*Happily, few of Schermerhorn's buildings still stand.
Each pile of rubble tells the same wretched story. In
Dubrovnik, a woman refused to abandon her seaside,
Schermerhorn house with her family, despite the likeli-
hood that it would crumble. She insisted that the walls
spoke to her and that she had work yet to do. Her husband, recognizing that she'd lost her wits, removed all
the sharp objects from the house and stranded her there,
hoping that without food or the means to cook it, she'd*

*eventually surrender to the city where he'd moved with
the children. When he visited two days later, a plume of
black smoke frothed from the lopsided chimney. Inside,
he found the coal-fire stove burning blue flames, and her
head stuffed inside it. He was not at first able to determine how she'd written her epigraph across the side of
the house until he saw her right index finger, which was
broken and raw. In the absence of a knife or kindling,
she'd carved her last words with her own, still attached
index finger bone: "Gol deschis în sfâr°it." Translated
from Romanian: The void opens at last.*

*In Krakow, the Pigeon sisters Gwendolyn and
Cecily bludgeoned—*

Audrey stopped reading. Something squirmed in her
stomach. It felt like a worm. She scrolled past the rest of
the text and moved on to the lithographs and black-and-
white photos at the end. The first depicted a mansion
with its slate roof caved in. The spike of a four-poster
bed poked out from the rubble. The caption read: *"While
They Were Sleeping at The Orphanage,* Boston, 1887."
There were houses in Romania, Croatia, Poland, Boston,
and finally, the last photo: The Breviary.

Her mouth went dry, and her heart double-beat inside
her chest. Its limestone was white, and its gargoyles
sharply carved. 1900, she guessed, when the world had
still been new. The caption read:

> Schermerhorn's Iniquitous Darling. Its foun-
> dation is embedded in Harlem's subterranean
> granite mountain, so despite its slant and im-
> possible geometry, it is the only Chaotic Natu-
> ralist structure expected to stand.

She sat back. Oh, boy. She wasn't sure what "iniqui-
tous" meant, but she didn't like the sound. On the television, crazy Carrie Bradshaw decided that some men

like freckles, and some don't. But she wasn't going to bother with the men with freckles, because that would be self-destructive, wouldn't it? Except, she couldn't help but bother. Really, she was so depressed about it that she couldn't get out of bed. Why, oh why, didn't the man she kind-of-almost-loved, like freckles?

Audrey scrolled. In next the photo, a crew of blue bloods posed outside The Breviary, all dressed in three-piece suits and Gibson Girl swan-bill corsets. They smiled for the camera without a care in the world. New York's party elite. The caption read:

> Once the most lavish address in all Manhattan, by the turn of the century, a total of thirty people who'd lived within The Breviary's walls were committed to insane asylums. They fared better than the seven who were murdered, by their own hands or otherwise.

"Bees knees," Audrey moaned, then looked left, right, left, right. Okay, one more time: left-right! left-right! On the television, Carrie the idiot called her redheaded friend to commiserate about how they both had freckles, which clearly made them lepers.

Just then, the buzzer rang. She jumped. The buzzer rang again. Saraub?

She looked like crap! Her hair was a mess. The buzzer rang a third time. *Zzzzt-zzzzt!* It sounded like an outdoor bug killer. She smelled under her arms: musky. Good grief, had she even showered today?

Now he wasn't buzzing. He was knocking. Polite little taps. She jumped up. "Coming!" Then she looked through the peephole, and stopped shivering. "Oh," she mumbled.

A petite redhead in her early thirties grinned up at her, like she could see Audrey's blinking eye through the backward telescope.

Audrey swung the door wide. Immediately, awk-wardly, the woman stuck out her hand for a shake, and poked Audrey in the stomach. It didn't even slow her down. "Hi! I'm Jayne! I live across the hall!"

Audrey didn't know what to say. Except at cheap motels, where she'd known better than to answer the door, neighbors had never dropped by. Was this a joke? Was this woman a Jew for Jesus?

Jayne waited for Audrey to speak. Audrey waited for Jayne to grow wings and fly away. Her hair was the phony color of a fire engine, and she'd shaped it into a chin-length bob. Her mouth and teeth protruded, horse-like, from her face. She had three gold studs in one ear and two in the other. The skin surrounding them was swollen, like she hadn't worn jewelry in a long time and had recently popped open her skin with the sharp ends of her earring posts to get them to fit.

"I'll bet you had a long day," Jayne said. Her voice was sandy. She smelled like fertilizer and smoke—Winston cigarettes.

"I wanted to say hi. Also, I thought you might like these." Jayne thrust a pile of glossy papers in Audrey's direction.

Audrey accepted them with a tight-lipped grin. She was sure they had something to do with Hari Krish-nas, the evil Freemason conspiracy, or rescuing cats from cruel and unusual juggling. But no, she realized when she glanced down. Just take-out menus. Chinese, Indian, Greek, and Middle Eastern.

Jayne bopped her head up and down. "I figured . . . You know. You'd probably be tired. I heard it was some-body young moving here, and I thought, thank God. They're all, like a hundred years old, you know?"

"They are?"

Jayne puckered her lips and rolled her eyes to the ceil-ing, in what Audrey could only guess was an imitation of a dead person, halfway decayed. "Fossils! Bat-shit crazy, to boot. This one guy downstairs, Mr. Galton, only ever wears a plain, white mask. What is that? Fucking creepy." She leaned in close, and lowered her voice, "And 14D's a taxidermist. Evvie Waugh. Animals all over the walls. Basically, we live with Michael Myers and Norman Bates."

Audrey lowered her voice, too. "I thought . . . I haven't seen any of them, but they seem strange. I feel like they've been watching me."

Jayne nodded. "Totally. That's because they are watching you. They were born and raised in The Breve, and they've got nothing else to do but sit around and spy on the young people. I swear to God, sometimes I think they peek at me through the opposite end of my peephole. But they're harmless, and my place is dirt cheap. I moved in three months ago, and if I hadn't found it, I would have wound up with a twenty-year-old rich-girl-hipster roommate in Brooklyn. And not even near the park! Totally embarrassing. So, I'm never leaving. When I die, they can bury me under the floor."

Audrey chortled. A little at the delivery, a lot at the messenger. "Sorry," she said.

"Why? I'm very funny. I'm doing stand up at the Laugh Factory next week—my first real gig!" As she spoke, Jayne bounced against the doorframe with her hip like she was made of rubber. Back and forth. Back and forth. Audrey couldn't figure out if it was a nervous habit or a happy one. Maybe both.

"You should come to one of my shows. I've got like, three friends, but they're all married, so they don't count. I hate it when they make their kids call me Auntie Jayne, and what the hell do I care if they shit green or brown? Anyway, if you come, I'll comp you. That's what it's called: comping, for complimentary. But that's not my real job. The rest of the time I'm in sales at L'Oreal. Westchester office, so it's a backward commute. They laid off half the staff last month. Everybody was wandering out of their cubicles carrying cardboard boxes and crying. I hope I never cry when I get fired from a job I don't even like. I mean, what's the matter with them? You'd think they weren't going to get unemployment. Anyway, if you ever need makeup or whatever, just shout. I'll give you samples and shit. Oh, I hope you don't mind that I keep cursing. Do you mind? I've got a real potty mouth."

Audrey shook her head. "No, I don't mind."

"You're awesome!" Jayne declared. In her excitement, she hip-checked herself against the door hard enough to hurt, and her bounce-back wasn't nearly as resilient. She limped a little but kept smiling.

Audrey shook her head. Was this chick for real? Then again, nobody else had come knocking, so she decided to play along. "You're awesome, too!" she said, then chuckled, because she hadn't used the word "awesome" since . . . ever.

Jayne clasped her hand and squeezed, but didn't shake, like they were New Age hippies practicing touch therapy. Her skin was surprisingly cold. "Okay! It's so good to meet you! I'm on my way to a date. It's new, but I think I love him. Will you have dinner with me tomorrow? Let's have dinner! Anyway—oh!" She dropped Audrey's hand and ran back into her apartment across the way before saying more. Audrey fought with a sudden case of giggles. Just barely, she won.

When Jayne returned, she was holding a twelve-ounce minibottle of Moët & Chandon. "I've got, like, ten of these. L'Oréal Christmas parties—they hand them out like cards. Too bad they don't give bonuses. Welcome to the building!"

Before Audrey could say *thank you,* Jayne was heading down the hall in beat-up New Balance running shoes. She didn't jog. Instead she walked really fast, like those middle-aged ladies who circled the Central Park

Reservoir in the early mornings wearing nylon track suits. Determined as ducks, and just as graceless.

After Audrey closed the door, she opened the bubbly, sipping straight from the bottle to keep the suds from spilling. She was relieved to find that the "Betty Boop!" wireless connection had faded, and when she tried to refresh "Diary of the Dead: Casualties of Chaotic Naturalism," it was gone.

So she did her best to put the article out of her mind and watched as the *Night Court* theme song played. As she sipped Jayne's bubbly, she wondered when she'd last made a friend aside from her boyfriend, Saraub, or her drug dealer, Billy Epps. She reached back into her memory as far as she could and realized that the answer was never.

5

The Piano Has Been Drinking

ZZZZ!-ZZZZ!

After a big move and twelve ounces of fizz, Audrey dozed. The story line from *Night Court* entered her dream. A smarmy lawyer with short, slicked-back black hair hunkered over her piano. He wore an old-fashioned notch-collared shirt and three-piece suit, and when he winked, he reminded her of all the charmers Betty had dated on the road. She'd always been surprised when they got tired of her bullshit, and walked.

"Have you ever built a door, darling?" he asked. His eyes were dilated like he was high, and in her dream, she smiled, because "darling" was a pretty word.

ZZZZ!-ZZZZ!

"Shouldn't be hard for a bright girl like you," he said, then turned back to the Steinway and began to bang out "Heart and Soul":

—*I beg to be adored, Heart and Soul!*

His voice was low-pitched and strangely plural like that of a locust.

"I tumbled overboard . . ." His face hollowed as he played, and she saw now that his chin was dark with stubble, and the circles under his eyes were deep.

I fell in love with you madly! he sang, then he leaped up from the piano bench and ran at her with open arms. His voice got louder as he charged:

"BECAUSE YOU HELD ME TIGHT!"

She woke with a start. A man, in the room with her! A man, coming after her! But then, the television played a courtroom scene. A laugh track crescendoed with John Laroquette humping the blond defense attorney, the bailiff, the judge, then the camera. Equal-opportunity hump.

She rubbed her eyes. A dream. But the man in her dream had been different from the one on television, hadn't he?

ZZZZ!-ZZZZ!

She spun in all directions and peered down the hall toward the front door. What the hell was that? A plague of locusts? Was this her tiny studio in Omaha? Saraub's place on the Upper East Side? Oh, right, The Breviary.

ZZZZ!-ZZZZ!

She staggered out from the den and down the long, dark hall. Felt her way with her hands. What was making that noise? Still groggy from sleep and champagne, her thinking was murky.

ZZZZ!-ZZZZ!

She jumped, then sighed, and said aloud, "shit-all." The intercom. She'd ordered Tandori Chicken from one of Jayne's menus a half hour ago, before falling asleep. She pressed the TALK button and got staticky feedback in reply. "Hello?" she asked.

The she pressed LISTEN, and heard the Haitian guy

with the 1950s uniform: "blah-hiss-blah-guy-blah-up?

Her stomach growled. "Send him up!" she said.

The bell rang a few minutes later. She swung the door wide without looking through the peephole. Saraub blinked at her. She blinked back.

"Hey!" she said. A rush of warmth filled her cheeks: *You know, I just had the craziest dream,* she nearly told him.

He leaned into the door. His breath was bad: whiskey and dog biscuits. He was a big guy; that meant *a lot* of whiskey and dog biscuits. "Want my piano back," he slurred.

"What?" she asked.

He balled his fists into the pockets of his wax rain jacket. "You took my Frank Millers, too, didn't you? I fucking knew you'd be petty like that!"

She'd been about to step aside and let him in. *Let me show you Wolverine's new home!* She'd planned to say, and then, by implication: *Let's both live here! Better yet, Oops, my bad! This place freaks me out. Let's both live someplace else!*

"Are you tight?" she asked.

"I want my piano . . . and my *Batman.* Just because you don't like something doesn't mean I can't have it. You were always doing that—taking my stuff and moving it when I wasn't around. Bruce Wayne is awesome. You have no idea!"

She looked at her bare feet. This was true. She'd thrown away the "Bless This Home" welcome mat he'd carried back from CVS Pharmacy (*Come on! Those things are breeding grounds for bacteria!*), and she'd hidden his favorite cutoff sweatshirt, because its red color had faded to pink. When he'd worn it, he'd looked gayer than a Lucky Cheng's drag queen. But how do you tell the man you love something like that? Kinder just to hide the evidence. Well, maybe not kinder. Maybe just easier.

"I don't have your comic books. They're in the crate

under the futon. Sober up, you turkey," she said, then closed the door on him. He kicked it back open. The wood shivered as he shoved past her and headed down the hall.

Countless times growing up, men had busted down the front door, looking for rent money or a fight with Betty. She hadn't liked it then, and she didn't like it now. Something squirmed in her stomach (the dust she'd swallowed?). It felt like a worm, writhing in bile. She chased him deeper into the apartment and shoved him from behind. He lurched. She pushed again. Hard. He stumbled but kept walking. She'd never been so angry in her whole life. She didn't know she had that kind of anger inside of her. She wanted to throttle him, just a little, with her hands or a knife, or the water in the tub. "Get out! Don't you ever do that! Not ever!"

He opened doors along the way. Room after room. Not a stick of furniture in sight. Just the new bedroom curtains blowing in the breeze, and metallic white paint. Their emptiness shamed her. Like the apartment was her life, and he was peeking inside it and finding nothing.

"What are you going to do?" she asked as he stumbled into the den.

Saraub kicked the air mattress aside. It slid across the wood and into the turret. The vibrations unbalanced Wolverine, who fell. "Hey!" Audrey cried. "Watch it!"

He was too drunk to notice. "I'm taking my piano," he said, but he stepped too wide, and stumbled into the Steinway's closed lid to keep from falling.

Audrey raced across the room and righted Wolverine. He'd lost some potting soil, but was otherwise unharmed. She held on to him for just a second longer than necessary, then placed him on the floor, so he didn't fall again. "You're the one who had them move it. How do you think you're going to get it out? Are you going to carry a piano on your back?"

Saraub wedged his shoulder against the baby grand. Its wood was polished and black, and its ivories shone. She came to the other side of the behemoth. *Thank you. This piano is probably the nicest thing anyone's ever done for me, and I'm grateful*, she wanted to say. *So stop being such a jerk!*

Then something happened. She felt like she was on a ship. Everything was moving. Even her feet. The piano began to slide. Its legs groaned in protest. The floor groaned, too, as a layer of its varnish peeled back, and the wood began to splinter. Saraub was pushing the piano!

She shoved back, in the opposite direction. "You'll break its legs!" she shouted.

He kept going. Shoulder against its bulk, legs spread, knees bent, she pushed back with all her might. This was crazy. This was petty, like those families at the trailer parks back in Hinton and Sioux City and Yuma, who couldn't be bothered to loan each other a cup of milk or a few extra bucks. They were cheap with each other. She'd always figured that rich people knew better, or could at least afford to pretend they did.

"Stop it!" she shouted. "Just stop it!" He didn't move. She heard him groan, but didn't look up. Didn't want to give him the advantage. She loved this piano. She loved him, too. Had she been wrong in that?

The piano slid away from her and pulled open the hole in the rotten wood floor. She pushed harder. She was winning!

"Fuck!" he shouted.

"Wha—?" She looked up, worried he'd hurt himself, but no. He'd simply let go. Already he was out of the den, staggering down the long hall. He lurched from one side to the other, steadying himself with his hands, like he'd downed a whole bottle in an hour, and the liquor was hitting him harder with every second that passed. He wasn't just drunk; he was blotto.

She took a few fast breaths to keep from crying, then chased him. Her bare feet slapped against cold, hard wood, but didn't echo. All the doors were open, like the empty rooms were watching.

He was waiting at the end of the hall.

"I didn't take your comics, and if you—huh-huh"—she panted—"if you want the piano so bad, you can have it."

He shook his head but didn't leave. She waited for his apology. It didn't come. She tried to make it easier for him. "You looked gay in that shirt. That's why I hid it. I didn't like people thinking you were gay. It embarrassed me." Then she heard herself, and winced. This was her idea of an olive branch?

He'd drunk so much that his eyes were dilated and black. It reminded her of the man in the three-piece suit from her dream. A chill ran from the tip of her neck to the small of her back. "Not my pro'lem," he slurred.

"What?"

"Tapping yourself—" He imitated her, bending down low enough that they were eye to eye, and slapping his thighs. The sound was a muffled whip:

"One leg—" *Whack!*

"The'other leg—" *Whack!*

"One leg—" *Whack!*

"The'other—" *Whack!*

He stood tall again, holding the wall for balance, and kept talking. "—Moving stuff when I wasn't looking, like a spook . . ." He glared at her, his jaw set firm and furious, and she knew that whatever was coming next was going to be bad. She squinted, like not looking directly at him might soften the blow.

"You don't have any friends. Nobody likes you. You never leave the house except for work. It's like you're a ghost. Like you don't even exist." Hundred-proof spittle flew as he shouted. The blood drained from her face and pooled at her feet, making her dizzy. She squeezed her hands into fists. Blinked once. Twice. Three times. Felt the tears as they cooled her cheeks.

Though she'd never seen it, she'd always assumed that, deep down, he had a cruel side, just like Betty. But she'd also always hoped she was wrong. His eyes were so dilated they looked black, and he squeezed his hands into fists. It occurred to her that he was about to hit her. Show the true self he'd been hiding from her all this time. A violent man who would one day trade his study walls for her soft flesh, or their children's bird-like bones. What was worse, she wanted him to do it, so she'd never have to speak to him, or feel bad about leaving him, again. She turned her cheek, to give him a better shot.

His fists tightened briefly, then dropped open at his sides. But his rage remained, a palpable thing.

"I hate this," she said.

"Yeah? Well, I hate you."

He turned fast and didn't wait for the elevator. Instead, he jogged down the fire exit stairs. She heard the echo of his steps. Quick *tap-tap-taps* followed by a loud tumble (*thump! thump!*). Then he got up again and went slower.

Audrey shut and locked the door, then threw herself down on the air mattress. An old episode of *Law and Order* played. A doctor conducting an autopsy removed a sheeted body's spleen, heart, and liver, then dropped them into a metal bowl. The corpse looked cold without those things. Vacant.

Saraub. Every time he'd told her he loved her, or pretended, when they were sitting on the couch playing Honeymoon Bridge, that he was happy; every offhand glance she'd spied, in which he'd coveted her rear, or else just watched her move, like he was so proud of his girl; every surreptitiously snapped photo; every time he'd run his two fingers down her spine, and traced every bone: all lies. Because his love had been conditional. All along, with his camera and cold eyes, he'd been watching her, and in her mannerisms, and cleaning, and shyness that people so often mistook for coldness, judging her *not good enough*.

As she lay there, she cried for the first time since she'd left him. Before this instant, she'd never really believed that their breakup was real.

Too tired to pull her air mattress into the bedroom, she fell asleep in the den, with the sound of the television to keep her company. A few hours later, she jolted awake to find the man in the three-piece suit watching her from the piano bench.

His beard had thickened with black whiskers, and his long teeth now came to sharp points, wolflike. He tapped his knuckles against the bottom frame, and said, "Satinwood, yes? They don't make anything like they used to, do they darling? Build the door, Audrey. We love you madly."

Part II

The Walking Wounded
(The Dead Have Always Outnumbered The Living)

Auld Lang Syne in the New Breviary

Martin Hearst, Jr., Society Reporter
and Harvard University historian

January 2, 1894

Last night's annual New Year's Eve Gala at The Breviary was the social event of the decade. More ambitious than the Flavian Amphitheatre, more architecturally significant than the Sistine Chapel, The Breviary was the perfect venue in which to host the coming out party for the most elite and important generation the world has ever known.

The gala's attending cast shone more luminous than the café society perched in balcony seats at the Paris Opera. These included the fifteen original investors in the building, whose names grace the streets of half of Greenwich Village (Reade, Astor, Worth, Bennington, and of course, my father, Martin Hearst). But out with the old, in with the next generation! This was the hour for The Breviary's children to shine, and indeed, we donned our finest. Stars from the stage, both Paris and London, cheerfully handed off their engraved invitations and mixed with senators, oil and steel moguls, and diplomats. But they were the side attractions: it was we luminaries of The Breve that everyone wanted to know. Russian caviar, French champagne, roast pig drenched in genuine Canadian maple syrup; never was a party so lavish or so fine!

Our women sparkled in diamond earbobs, and we gents donned towering stovepipe hats and velvet coats. The air could have crackled with our confidence. *Behold your inheritance,* the reverberating walls full of giggles and raucous chatter announced, *finally, a building fit for American Kings.*

I know you'll indulge me, as this column has won three People's Choice awards from the Know-Nothing party, so here is my aside: I have never felt so loved or happy as I did last night.

At exactly eight o'clock New Year's Eve, the guests assembled. Fox pelts adorned the spiked iron gates from a small hunt early that morning, and gas lamps burned the winter darkness into submission. A string quartet conducted by Arms Bueford of Carnegie Hall played Dvorak's Quartet 12 in F Major. Champagne bottles popped and glugged, glasses passed, the music crescendoed, ceased, and my father, with an imperious wave at the crowd, handed his scepter down to me, his eldest son. Upon a fusillade of applause, I signaled for the party to begin.

The first waltz was reserved for The Breviary's first generation. The second dance, for us. After freely given and wrested kisses (these foreign prudes!), a light second meal of foie gras and fresh venison was served at midnight, followed by more dancing, and a tour of each 5,000-square-foot floor. Later in the evening, we determined that Mr. Pingree of the Boston Pingrees was the best shot, as we'd set loose pheasants off the roof for the annual hunt. God knows, in that dark, where, or upon whom, those bullets and birds rained.

I chatted with every kind of celebrity, but in the end, felt most comfortable with my own kind. We are destined for greatness. Even the building tells us so, as it rocks us to sleep as lovingly as a wet nurse. Naturally, despite some of our parents' objections, we've all converted to Chaotic Naturalism.

The party broke after dawn. I did not sleep but instead watched the sun rise with my sisters and brothers. It was then that our realization, hithertofore unacknowledged, was spoken. We'd started the evening as children and had ended it as men. Soon we would run our parents' companies and change the fate of the world. With great powers come great responsibilities, and the crown, at last, weighed heavy.

After some sleep, we gathered again, and found that our collective resolve had remained. Our parents travailed a bloody civil war, the relentless English who impressed our ships, and the foolish French, who insisted upon aiding our wayward brothers. They untethered themselves from the mundane and soared free. It is my hope and earnest promise that my own generation, standing on the shoulders of giants, will soar even higher.

And so, rest assured, dear readers. This is our resolution. We speak for you, too: the elite; the crème de la crème; the divine. My generation will blacken the skies with burnt coal and oil. We will drill holes with a vengeance, until this nation swims in gold. In mines and servants' quarters, there will be jobs for all those willing to work, even the Irish, Negroes, and Italians. The stock markets will forever soar while the British sterling sinks. We promise this as a fulfillment of our birthright and as the execution of our destinies.

I close, with a sincere parting wish, my friends, old and new: Peace on Earth, Good Will Toward Men.

From The *New York Herald*

Debauchery in Central Park

January 5, 1894

The bodies of two women were discovered early this morning at the northern end of Central Park. They are assumed to be the Parisian actresses reported missing from the December 31st New Year's Eve Gala at The Breviary building on 110th

Street. Families were unable to identify their bodies, but matched their gowns (blue and ivory, respectively) to what they'd worn that evening. Because of the high-profile nature of the case, the names of all parties are being withheld. The young women's bodies were disturbed and their gowns torn in such fashion as to imply acts untoward.

From The *New York Times*

6

She's Thirsty Because Her Neck Never Stopped Bleeding

The air mattress deflated. Her shoulder and bony hip jabbed the hard, wooden floor. Around her, the walls of 14B creaked, and the stained-glass birds peered out from the glass, captured in midflight.

Her dreams moved like sludge through her consciousness. Heavy and relentless. Always, the man in the three-piece suit was with her. Always, he was watching.

She was standing outside the Film Forum in Manhattan where the marquee read: STRANGERS ON A TRAIN. She loved that movie! But wait, no. The letters rearranged, slip-sliding into a knot, then pulling apart again to spell something different:

Audrey Lucas: This is Your Life.

An usher waved her into the lobby. He was dressed like a 1950s bellhop: tassels on his shoulders; a thick, wool coat. She got closer, and saw that he was Saraub. He smiled blankly, without recognition. "This way, ma'am."

"But I haven't paid for my ticket," she told him.

"That's fine," he answered "You're the star of the show."

She walked down the fifty-foot hall, and into the theatre. Lights flickered against the screen. Credits rolled familiar names: Betty Lucas, Saraub Ramesh, Billy Epps, Jill Sidenschwandt, Collier Steadman . . . To get a closer look, she climbed onto the stage and stood against the screen. Then, suddenly, she was in the movie.

The room where she found herself was empty and white. Her mother Betty stood next to her. Their skin was joined at their hips and chests like Siamese twins. Down below an audience filed into the theatre and took their seats. They munched buttered popcorn with greasy fingers, and slurped red wine from paper cups.

"Good to see you, Lamb. I've been waiting a long time," Betty said, and the audience began to laugh.

The man in the three-piece suit was in the movie, too. He lurked in the far corner and shushed the audience with a single, furious rasp.

Audrey tried to leave the stage, but something caught her. She looked to her left and saw that she and Betty shared a single heart: *lub-dup*; *lub-dup*. A soothing, symmetrical sound. Ventricle to ventricle. Left side, then right. Left side, then right. She struggled to pull away, but the tissue binding them held firm. "This works better," Betty announced, then pulled a knife out from her pocket and began to saw. The left twin cut, and the right twin bled.

Down below, the audience cheered. *Hooray!*

Fade to black. Another dream. Another. Another. Relentless. She found herself in an empty room, pulling a black thread from her toenail, only to pull her toenail away, too. And then, compelled to continue, to make everything neat and even, she kept pulling, until the lower trunk of her body unraveled into a perfectly wound coil of cotton.

"Is this what you came here to see?" she asked the man in the suit, the dandy with wolf's teeth. She could hear his rasping breath as he watched from the edge of the screen, and another dream began.

The dreams played all night. Fucked-up Audrey Lucas: Greatest Hits. The audience cheered, and jeered, and laughed, and cried. Their fingers and lips smacked with grease.

The worst dream was this: going back in time, to the double-wide in Hinton with the hole in the kitchen floor. She'd forgotten all about the place until she found herself standing inside it. Then it all came back: the white, diamond-shaped adhesive paper meant to look like linoleum; the pine cabinets so filthy with grime they'd been soft; the Murphy bed she'd shared with Betty; that musty scent of dead field mice, whose source she'd never been able to detect but which had permeated all her clothes, so that at school, the townie kids had held their noses.

"Please, no. I don't like it here," she whispered in the old kitchen. Her sleeping body spoke the words, too. They circled 14B, and woke the stained-glass birds.

In the closet behind the old-fashioned string mop, she found the man in the three-piece suit. His skin had thinned, and through it she saw the eggshell ridges of his bones. It occurred to her that he might not be a man at all. He might be The Beviary: ever-changing and relentless.

"Did you bring me here?" she asked him. "I don't like remembering. I'm not that girl anymore. That girl is dead, and I hate her." He turned his back and faced the corner of the closet, like a little boy who's been bad. With his fingers, he began to scrape the wall: *Scritch-scratch!*

From the darkness, the audience laughed. The sound was canned, and without humor. Their black eyes glistened in the dark.

"Fine. Be that way," she told him as she shut the plywood closet door and mated the hook to its eye latch, locking him inside. "This isn't for you, so you're not allowed to watch."

Then she sat down at the kitchen table. Out the window, was a dirt road that stretched for miles, and along the cul-de-sac were more RVs and autumn trees red as fire. Hinton, 1992. She'd been sixteen years old when she lived here, and Betty cut up the floor. It had hit her worse than most other things Betty'd done, though in retrospect, it shouldn't have.

The first time Betty's red ants arrived, they'd been living in a white clapboard house in Wilmette. Betty had been a beauty back then. Miss Cornhusker, 1980. Blond hair, deep dimples, and the kind of curvy saunter that strangers had followed with their eyes. Roman Lucas would have cut off his hands for her if she'd asked. Given enough time and boredom, Audrey had no doubt she *would* have asked.

Still, they'd been happy. Two bedrooms, a study full of Betty's medical illustrations, a darkroom for Roman's pictures. Audrey had slept in a dressing closet off the main bedroom where the deep pile carpet had warmed her toes. After they fell asleep, she'd sometimes crawled into their room and slept on the floor, pretending she was their dog.

And then one night, Betty painted every wall and ceiling of their two-bedroom house rust red. Audrey had been five years old, and in her imagination, she'd pictured it like a possession, in which the ants that had infested their untended lawn began to swarm. They'd crawled though the cracks in the back door, then marched like a living red carpet into Betty's studio. Thrashing and swiping, she'd tried to fight them off, but they'd stolen inside her ears and nose and mouth, then chewed their way underneath her skin. Infected, she'd painted life as she saw it. Her canvases, the bed, the walls, the ceiling, the whole house, squirming with red.

The next time it happened, Audrey was six. Betty took off without a note or even a phone call. She'd left the oven baking, so the lamb got burned to char. The smoke ruined the new corduroy couch and killed their pet parakeets, Harold and Maude. Their curled feet had pointed up. A week later, a short, skinny man with a half-eaten Slim Jim sticking out of his shirt pocket dropped Betty off at the curb, then peeled away in a clunking blue Hyundai. By then the red-ant manias had burned out and turned their characteristic black. Betty was so tired she'd had to crawl to the front door, where Roman had found her and carried her to bed.

Creeping, creeping. Things got worse in the in-between. The unused tea service tarnished. Arguments supplanted back rubs and scotch. Dinner became soggy, microwaved Stouffer's pizzas and Hungry Man pies. Harold and Maude's cage stayed empty and hanging, months-old bird shit stuck to the bars.

Nine months later, it happened again. Betty left for two days, and when she came back, she broke into Roman's darkroom and exposed all his negatives to the light. "Your camera eyes stole my soul!" she'd screamed so loud that even with the pillow pressed against her ear, Audrey had heard. Roman left that night with bags he'd already packed, like he'd been waiting for the excuse to go. He peeked into Audrey's bedroom only once. "Are you coming?" he'd asked, even though neither of them had ever spoken of the problem out loud. She'd squeezed the pillow to her stomach and felt the air against her wet cheeks. He'd mistaken her silence for an answer. After he left, he never wrote or called or sent a dime.

They got evicted a couple of months later. "I'm sorry you got stuck with me," Audrey said, as they'd stuffed the white Pontiac with so much crap—the sewing machine, Betty's illustrations, garbage bags full of clothes, the empty cage, its wires still caked with shit—that its chassis grazed blacktop.

From her back pocket, Betty had produced Audrey's second-grade class picture. A scrawny kid with a lopsided grin to match the lopsided hair that she'd shorn, all by herself, because scissors were cool. "Funny girl, even when you're at school, I keep you with me," Betty told her. "I see your face in my mind.

"You do?"

Betty had nodded. "I'm not like other people. There's something missing, and I'm full of holes, but never when it comes to you. You're the only person I've ever loved. We're the same that way. You'll see, you'll break hearts you never wanted." Betty had smiled when she said this, like she was happy, but it was a pretend kind of smile. Audrey got the feeling that if she could fix the broken thing inside her, she would.

"You won't leave me?" Audrey had asked.

Betty hugged Audrey tight. She'd smelled like Winston cigarettes and Baby Soft perfume, and Audrey had wanted so much right then, to climb inside her mother, and eat her red ants, and fill the empty space with better things, so they could both be whole. "Let's make a deal, Lamb of mine. We throw our lots in together. Nobody else counts. Just us. I'll never leave you, and you'll never leave me."

Weeping with relief, Audrey had put her mouth around Betty's sharp shoulder and sucked on it. "Deal, Momma," she'd mumbled. "It's us, forever."

Low points of life with Betty: the time she locked them both inside the Yuma Motor Inn because she was convinced the cleaning staff was trying to poison them. Burning her boyfriend's clothes in his own oven, dancing a circle around the smoke, then running across his backyard in their pajamas like maniacs, so they didn't get caught. Trying to convince that state trooper with the gun that nine-year-old Audrey really was of legal driving age, because Betty's burnt-out red ants had made her too depressed to get behind the wheel, and they'd needed to blow town, since they'd owed three grand in back rent. Waking up to find that Betty had shorn the hair from both their heads, so they'd looked like Sigourney Weaver in *Aliens. So they don't recognize us, lamb. We're wanted!*

High points with Betty: see previous. Crazy is often fun.

For a while, tramping was a thrill. Betty knew how to sing into a pretend microphone with perfect pitch, talk a waiter into a free meal, tramp it at the Lakeshore so they spent every morning swimming in warm waves, every night in a kind stranger's guesthouse. She taught Audrey early how to read and draw, so even though she wasn't often enrolled in school, the staff at the local libraries always knew her name. They were renegades, who knew the secret most people would never learn: the trappings of life are just that: traps. They moved because it was carnival season, and Audrey had never won a teddy bear, or a storm was passing, and if they rushed with their windows rolled down, they could chase the lightning; or Betty'd had a fight with a boss or a boyfriend, or the debt collectors were knocking, or because her red ants had come and trashed all the things they'd worked to build, so that they had to start over again.

Packing and unpacking. Twice a year. Three times. Four. After a while, the drifting frayed Audrey's nerves. She got the idea that with every ditched motel or trailer, she left a tiny part of herself behind and became more like a ghost. Was it so strange that she began scrubbing bathroom tiles, patting her own thighs, and running her fingers along hard objects, just to reassure herself that she was real?

At twelve, Audrey started sleepwalking. Every time they moved to a new place, she pissed the corners of the room like a dog marking its territory, then marched right back to bed, like she'd un–potty trained. When Betty would tell her about it the next morning, Audrey would always wonder if it was true, or a story her mother had invented to shift the blame from herself.

At thirteen, she developed a rash across her entire body, itchy and throbbing, as if in sympathy with Betty's red ants. She spent fourteen high or drunk. Sneaked out and traded sips with the neighbors, who thought a boozy kid was cute, or found another street urchin, and together they scored what they could from panhandling. She cut her wrists, but chickened out once the water in the tub turned pink. If Betty noticed the scabs that became scars that Audrey had to this day, she'd never mentioned it.

At fourteen, Audrey gave up hurting herself for attention because she knew she wouldn't get any. At fifteen, she passed the tenth-grade equivalency, and enrolled in high school, then kept up classes, or at least the school-work, wherever they moved. By then, she'd wised up, and had finally started to wonder if indeed, they were alike at all, or if Betty'd only told her a story that last day in Wilmette, so someone would follow her from town to town, and clean up her messes. She'd started to plot her escape.

Briefly, she got out. Through perfect math ACT scores and a lot of begging, she landed a work-study scholarship to the University of Nebraska. That fall, before her freshman year, she sneaked out with a packed bag, just like Roman, and was free. But three years later, Betty knocked on her dorm door carrying a stale box of Russell Stover cherry-filled chocolates. In that short time, without Audrey to come home to, the woman had contracted a full-blown case of hepatitis C, and grown old. Her blond hair had gone wiry, old-lady gray, and she'd pinned it from her eyes with pink barrettes, like she'd mistaken herself for a little girl.

Caring for her after that had been inevitable. Giving up on graduate school in architecture had been inevitable, too. So she got that job at IHOP, rented that little tomb-sized studio, painted its walls black, then set Betty up on disability in the outpatient community residence down the road. Betty'd lost steam by then and finally agreed to take her lithium, which had coincided nicely with Audrey's newfound hash habit. They spent ten years in Omaha before Betty had to be committed. During that time, Audrey had watched the days go by, grateful that at least, now that she was the one paying the bills, they weren't running anymore.

And here she was, dreaming of Hinton, Iowa—1992. Long before college and Omaha. Long after the slits in her wrists had healed into narrow white lines. Smack in the middle, when things had been bleakest. The man in the three-piece suit *scritch-scratched* against the closet she'd locked him in. The theatre seats below were dark, but she could see the audience's glassy black eyes. The hole in the kitchen floor was broken faux linoleum and plywood, whose edges could have been teeth. Yes, she remembered this. It all came back.

As she watched, the show began. Starring characters reprised their roles like a movie on repeat that had always happened, would always happen, forever and ever.

Suddenly, Betty Lucas was kneeling in front of the hole. Blond still, and surprisingly young. She grunted as she pressed the knife against the tile and broke open more plywood. The hole widened. She cut her fingers as she worked, but the blood didn't slow her down.

Audrey watched from the fold-out chair at the kitchen table. Hand cupped over her mouth, knees pulled under her butt, chin tucked close to her chest, she tried her best to make herself small.

Outside, an early frost. A cold walk home from school. The girl, sixteen years old, opened the double-wide screen door. The hole over the crotch of her tan, Salvation Army coveralls was closed by a row of safely pins, and her hair was so greasy it looked wet.

"What are you doing, Momma?" the girl asked.

Audrey cringed. The girl was dirty, wretched, ignorant. What would the admissions director at Columbia, or the head of human resources at Vesuvius say, if they knew that Audrey Lucas came from this?

Betty looked up from the floor and bared her cigarette-stained teeth. "Who are you?"

"Momma? It's me," the girl said. Her voice cracked. She wiped her eyes, then took a breath to stifle the sobs. The cuts in the floor were sloppy, irregular angles that made the white tile stickers jagged, and Audrey felt a sudden fury, that Betty Lucas had allowed her daughter to dress in rags while she'd always made sure to buy her own clothes new.

Betty shoved the knife into another chunk of floor. It sounded like slashing a tire, the way the air whooshes as it rushes out. "See what you made me do?" she asked. Her manic words came fast: "Seewhatyoumademedo!!!!"

"There are doctors. There's medicine you can take," the girl said. Only, she was so frightened, defeated, that she whispered, and Betty didn't hear.

When she'd dug deep enough, Betty dropped the knife and tore open the subfloor with her hands. The dirt underneath came out in blood-mud fistfuls. She threw it against the girl's legs, where it splatted. "Iseeyouwatching-meYoucan'thaveher!" she shouted into the hole.

"Momma, stop it!" the girl cried.

"You hear them?" Betty asked. "They climb through holes, Lamb. That's how they get inside us. We've got to kill them. You'd do murder for me, wouldn't you?"

Scritch-scratch! The man scraped the door, and in the dark down below, the audience murmured.

The girl patted her thighs. Once. Twice. Grown Audrey, watching from the table, did the same: *pat! pat!*

Suddenly, Betty jerked to her feet. She teetered for a moment, like the unbalance in her mind had also unbalanced her body. Then she charged. Fast as lightning, she spun the girl into a half nelson, and wedged the knife against her throat. "Who are you really?" she asked. "And what have you done with my daughter?"

The girl didn't struggle. Instead, she mirrored grown Audrey and tried to make herself small.

This had happened before. It had already happened. And yet tears came to Audrey's eyes. Why didn't the girl run? Why didn't she scream? Didn't she want to live?

Betty drew a light line along the girl's neck with the knife. Blood beaded against her pale skin like tiny red pearls. The girl bit her lip, squeezed her hands into fists, closed her eyes as if counting backward, but never once budged, or even whimpered.

Audrey flinched. She knew what would happen next. She remembered. Betty would see the blood, and regret. She'd let Audrey go, and a little while after that, she'd run out the door, and ashamed, stayed AWOL, living in bars and with strange men for six weeks. The cut would heal in less than a day, and the on-duty cop who showed up on a noise complaint would look her up and down, then snicker, and tell her that with a mother like Betty, she ought to wear turtlenecks.

But none of that was so terrible. People survived worse. No, the terrible part was the lesson Hinton taught her that she'd forgotten until now. Always, before Hinton, Betty's red ants had raged outward, at boyfriends and bosses and imaginary conspiracies. But this time, they'd attacked Audrey, and she'd finally understood that the pact they'd made long ago had been a lie. There was no one Betty loved, not even her daughter, and that second-grade photo of her favorite little girl had met the bottom of a garbage can long ago.

Betty's grip on the knife loosened. The girl's chest heaved. Blood gathered along the neck of the T-shirt under her coveralls. The effect was a macabre red-and-white carnation.

Poor girl, Audrey thought. Time slowed. Audrey unfolded her legs and arms and sat straight in her chair. Sat larger. She wanted to be a good influence. Wanted the girl to glimpse the possibility of a better future.

The girl peered at her from the corner of her eyes, and Audrey thought they saw each other. Had somehow reached out across the void that divided past and present.

The girl nodded very slightly, as if to say, *Yes, I see you. I know you, too.* Something inside Audrey cracked open. A wall she hadn't guessed existed. She remembered being that girl. The pain, the shame, the bravery of every tiny revolt against Betty, that had been so hard to commit. Those revolts had laid the groundwork for all the other battles she would fight in her adult life, and win. She realized now that she'd left one good thing behind in Omaha, and she could still claim it, if she wanted: herself.

"Help me," the girl mouthed. Audrey's resolve returned. She leaped from the folding kitchen chair, and charged. "Get out of this! You don't need her. . . . RUN!" she shouted at the girl.

The girl (little Audrey!) hesitated. Betty did not hear. Only held the knife, and her daughter, too tight. Behind the closet door, the man *scritch-scratched* against the plywood.

"GO!" Audrey shouted as she ran, as if to tackle Betty. The girl heard. Her lips turned up. Only slightly. Only if you were looking. She smiled, then jerked away from her mother in one fast motion. The knife cut deeper. Blood streamed as she spun, but the wound didn't slow her down. She raced out the screen door and down the dirt road without looking back.

Audrey watched her go. Dirty, inconsequential girl. Wretch destined for a career in early motherhood and crystal meth. Audrey was so overjoyed by her escape that she shook with relief. "Good girl. Smart girl. I love you," she said, because even if Betty and Saraub were inconstant, at least she would always have herself. And this girl she'd been, it turned out, was worth something, after all.

In the audience, the crowd oohed and aahed. The lights got brighter, and she could see their faces. There were about fifty of them, and they were all old, in their seventies at least, but their skin was pulled preternaturally smooth and tight. "You see!" Audrey cried out at them. "Don't screw with me. I'll fight. I'll win!"

She expected to wake up, or to enter another dream, but instead the lights got dark again. *Scritch-scratch.* That sound remained. Only it carried more of a hollow echo, like the man was close to breaking free from the closet. The kitchen brightened like a stage set. So did the hole in the floor, and Betty's wild blue eyes. In front of and behind her, letters briefly lit up the stage:

Audrey lucAs: thiS is Your Life!

Audrey felt a breeze. She looked down, and saw that she was now wearing those same coveralls as the girl, only the safety pins had come undone. No panties. Her nakedness, exposed. She covered herself with her hands. A thick tuft of dark woman hair.

Betty turned and looked straight at her. Saw her. The feeling was like a stab in the chest. Audrey's blood pooled at her feet. "Who are you?" Betty asked.

Scritch-scratch! Audrey could hear the wood shavings as they fell from the plywood closet. The man had almost dug his way out.

"This is a dream," Audrey said. "You're my subconscious. You're not even Betty. I'm not your daughter. It's just me, talking to me, because I'm upset about Saraub."

"Really?" Betty asked as she cleaned the girl's blood from the knife with her hands, then licked her fingers, so that the corners of her lips got bloody. Betty nodded at the screen door. "Little girl won't get far. Only a few years. Twenty on the outside. Wounds like that bleed slow, but they're fatal."

"She'll make it," Audrey said.

Betty shook her head. "No, she's damaged goods. Now come with me. Come see the floor."

(*Scritch-scratch!*)

The audience got very quiet, and Audrey understood that something bad was coming. She and Betty stood on either side of the broken faux linoleum. Audrey's coveralls flapped. "We're the same, Lamb," Betty said, as they both peered down. The hole was deep, and at its bottom lay a mirror. The two women's black-eyed images were indistinguishable, because both were riddled with squirming red ants.

Scritch-scratch. The sound was very close. The man in the three-piece suit was almost out.

"Please wake me up, I don't like this game anymore," Audrey begged. Flap-flap, went her pants. So exposed. The red ants wound between mother's and daughter's reflections, then mounted the sides of the hole and climbed out.

Betty grinned. Her silken hair and dewy skin channeled an old Hollywood movie, where the people were charming, and nothing bad ever happened.

Scritch-scratch!

In a quick, jerking movement, Betty reached across

the void. She squeezed the hole in Audrey's coveralls. So shameful. So exposed. "You come from me. I own you," Betty said.

The hole pulsed wider, its jagged sticker linoleum like teeth, and the ants a red tide bubbling up from its depths. "It wants to live inside us, Lamb. It smells our weakness. It climbs through our holes. Don't you hear it?"

Scritch-scratch.

The hole got bigger. So did Betty's frozen grin. "Get out while you can, Lamb," she said as she squeezed. Only her fingers were red with blood, and now, so was Audrey's crotch.

"No. It's not after me, only you," Audrey tried to say, but her words got garbled. Her throat hurt. Bad. Something wet. She felt her neck with her fingers. Red.

Still bleeding, she broke down and began to cry. In her dream, and in real life, too. The sound carried through 14B's air shafts, and halls, and even the elevator. Through the vibrations in the walls, it roused sleeping and vigilant tenants alike. A weeping, desperate sound that made their hearts flutter in carnal delight. Down below, in the theatre, the black-eyed audience grinned.

Scritch-scratch! The sound was close. A tiny hole in the closet door near the eyehook appeared, and a long, pale finger reached through it. The latch came undone.

The ants swarmed Audrey's ankles. Pins and needles on fire. "I'm thirsty. Someone cut my throat," she gasped as she cried.

Betty loosened her hold on Audrey's crotch. A red, broken thing. "Better run, Lamb. It's a bad place, where you live."

Audrey traced the curving, open wound on her throat. "It never healed," she said. I'm still bleeding."

"Better run, Lamb."

Audrey backed away from the hole. Betty stayed.

The man burst from the closet. Betty lurched as the red army riddled her skin from the inside out. She didn't scream, though the sound was high-pitched and hysterical. Even as the insects bit, and her face swelled unrecognizably like a dry thing left too long in water, Betty Lucas laughed. The audience laughed, too.

Audrey turned to run. The man in the three-piece suit caught her by the shoulders.

"You're stuck to something, my dear," he told her. "A tumor. Let me get that for you," he said. Then he raised his finger, which he'd whittled to a sharp bone point, and sliced her throat open.

She jerked in her sleep, and stopped breathing. Everything got quiet, except the television in 14B, which turned on and off and on again, like the fluttering eyes of a large animal. Across the screen the late-night movie read:

Audrey lucAs: ThiS is Your Life!

7

Home Keeps Changing

"Great to finally talk to you, too, Bob!" Saraub Ramesh enthused into the mouthpiece of his cell phone. Reception was terrible, but at least he sounded less nervous than he felt, due mostly to a serious hangover. Thread-sized sparks of lightning flickered across his eyeballs, like he could see his own blood circulating there. He'd been dry-heaving half the night, and only remembered fragments of what had happened before that: a pole dancer, somebody sucking on his ear and making it sticky. God, he really hoped that meant she'd been gnawing on a mouthful of taffy. After that, there'd been a piano, and an apartment building with slanted floors and cockeyed windows. He remembered Audrey looking out from a crooked doorway, seeming small and alone, like the first time he'd met her in front of the Film Forum.

She'd been pacing beneath the marquee that day,

and he'd noticed that she looked both prettier and older than the online photo she'd posted. High, chiseled cheekbones, and heavy circles under her eyes from either drugs or an obsessive personality. After he got to know her, he'd learned: both.

He'd loitered near the side of the building before approaching, because it was his nature to watch. She'd worn flats and wool trousers instead of belly jeans and sparkling eye glitter, which had made him wonder if she was the last woman in New York who dressed like a grown-up. She'd held her arms crossed around her chest and taken deep breaths, as if reminding herself to remain calm.

From the second he'd clicked on her profile, he'd understood that there was a story in her, the girl from the Midwest who'd started her life fresh after thirty years. Left her family and friends behind, to worship the glittering man-eater called Manhattan. From her hunched shoulders and the pinched guardedness of her expression, he'd understood that she was a wounded person. But still standing. Still carrying on. He'd never lived much, except through the eyes of a camera, and he admired people who had.

Seeing her there, he'd known that if he started talking to her, he'd never stop. Good-bye to Tonia, who'd never read a book for pleasure, and expected him to start working for the family business as soon as they got hitched, and build her a mansion in Jersey. Good-bye to his family, too, and the life they'd planned for him. But he also knew that if he walked away, she'd wait under the *Strangers on a Train* sign for at least an hour before going home. And it was cold out there.

He'd never imagined, two and a half years later, that she'd be the one to leave. He'd always seen himself as the weaker link.

Now, head throbbing, Saraub switched the phone

from one ear to the other. Its ringing had woken him this morning—make that, afternoon. And good thing. It was the CEO of Sunshine Studios.

Reception was bad. The connection was all static. But then he walked to the window, and Bob Stern's voice returned. "Before we juice this thing up, I wanted to get you on the horn," Bob said. Saraub could only make out half the words: "wan et you on e orn."

"That sounds about right," Saraub answered. A white dot floated over his left eye, like maybe he was having a Wild-Turkey-induced aneurism. He considered this briefly, then decided there wasn't much he could do about it either way, so no point worrying.

"Just want to get a handle on where you see this going," Bob said. He had a staccato way of talking, like he was stabbing his words with a pitchfork.

"I've got one or two interviews left, then I'll start my final cut. My hope is for a small art house release. Ideally, after good word of mouth, it would grow from there. Anything you want to know, shoot. I'm happy to go over details," Saraub answered. Then winced, because he might not make it through this call: Wild Turkey's anti-Thanksgiving was gurgling its way through his stomach.

"How much you spend so far?" Bob asked, only it sounded like: "Ow uch end so far?" When Sunshine declared bankruptcy, a multinational called Servitus bought it in a fire sale and appointed Bob Stern its new CEO. He was an investment-banking executive who'd never produced a picture, but Servitus had made the gamble that he'd steer the studio back into the black. He'd been clearing off his predecessor's desk last week when he found the proposal and reel for *Maginot Lines,* then called Saraub's agent and asked if anyone had made an offer yet.

"I spent about $150,000," Saraub said. "Since I had my own equipment, I mostly only had labor expenses, and I didn't pay myself. I've got an assistant on salary, and I cover all our travel, but that's it." He opened the window, hoping to get better reception. "I can send you an itemization."

"Naw," Bob said. "You can worry about all that when you pitch it for my people. Your prospectus—or do they call them pitches here?—is pretty thorough. Cheap, too. Cheap is Jehovah, Allah, and Christ, all rolled into one. I just wanted to tell ya, I saw the rough cut, and I came. Man, love. I'm in love!" Bob gushed.

Saraub's stomach gurgled. He'd heard about half Bob's speech, and really hoped he'd correctly interpreted the rest. For three years, he'd been trying to get studio backing, but even his good leads had always turned sour. By now, most of his film-school friends had given up and gotten jobs in software development. But so far, he'd never let the turkeys get him down. One rejection, ten, one hundred. He smiled and said thank you so he didn't burn bridges, ate an extra bag of chips, punched a wall, then kept going. He'd resolved to wait every last one of them out until he got the answer he wanted.

"I'm so glad to hear it, Bob," Saraub said. "But seriously, anything you want clarity on, let me know."

"No, no. That's all fine. Sore—How do you call that—Sore-rub?" Bob asked.

"Yeah. Sore-rub. Thanks. No one ever gets that," he said as he tripped over the metal IKEA lamp on the floor, then covered the receiver to muffle the grunt. Audrey had been gone five weeks, and already the place was a sty. The carpet was littered with take-out containers, spilled soy sauce, and, inexplicably, pennies. The thing about food in early fall is, it attracts flies. They landed on his face at night as he drifted to sleep, and every time that happened he'd think: *It really wasn't so bad when she moved my shit.*

"It all sounds square. My worry here is experience," Bob said. "You say you want to edit it all yourself, and we can cover the suite. But you've never worked on a feature before. No bullshit, kid. Can you deliver?"

"I edit commercials every day. It'll be cheaper just to let me see the thing to completion. I've got it all figured out," Saraub said. In fact, he'd never edited a feature-length, and he'd never selected accompanying musical scores, either. But *Maginot Lines* was his baby, and what Bob didn't know wouldn't hurt him. "It shouldn't take more than six months in postproduction, and the legwork is almost done."

A phone rang in the background from Bob's end. Papers rustled. Saraub pictured a high-floored but depressingly sterile office in Studio City, and ten frenzied assistants with earphones attached to their heads, praying the new boss didn't give them the axe. "Obviously, if progress stalls, we retain the right to bring in our own people," Bob said.

Saraub frowned. Out the window, he could see holes all down the block, where luxury condominiums had lost investors midway through construction. Behind boarded planks, they were open sores of dirt. So this call was about ownership, and Sunshine planned to acquire controlling rights. But three years, no takers, and his bank account nearly drained, he was in no position to dicker. "Yea—yes. I hear that's standard."

"All right, then. This has been enlightening. I'll need a list of all your interviews and their info for legal if we sign a deal, and I'll get back to your agent in a few days."

"Thanks, Bob. I apprec—" Saraub started, but by then, the phone was already dead.

He sat down at the kitchen table and, despite the throbbing in his head, grinned. For as long as he could remember, he'd wanted to make a feature. Every weekend the last three years, he'd conducted interviews. Every morning, he'd gotten up early and cut film or placed calls. Even Audrey had gotten into the act, sending out questionnaires from her office and using Vesuvius stamp machines to save on postage. Opposite their futon was the time line she'd made on poster board, itemizing his subjects. Each branch represented an interview, the date it was conducted, and its overall significance to the film. It was preternaturally neat, with perfectly straight lines like she'd used a giant typewriter. "So you remember what it is you're doing," she'd said with a smirk when she finished it, which had been kind of funny, and given his lack of organization, kind of true.

At first, the movie was supposed to be about the trend of multinational corporations, often subsidized by the World Bank, to privatize third-world natural resources like water, forest reserves, fossil fuels, and even air. But the more he learned, the more he'd realized that the story wasn't abroad, but local. Privatization was happening in America, too, but because of this deep recession, people cared more about jobs and food than breathable air. No one wanted to blow the whistle on corporations that doubled the price of tap water, because at least they were cutting a profit and providing their employees with health care.

As it happened, Sunshine Studios' parent company, Servitus, had invested heavily in New York water rights, as well as Appalachian coal, Arctic oil, and the verdant timberlands of the South. They were based in both Atlanta and Beijing, and so far, they'd drained the upstate Hudson Valley and were selling their spoils to Europe in the form of bottled water. Riverbanks and natural springs had dried up, and a few of the houses surrounding them had collapsed. Small farms couldn't afford to irrigate because in its scarcity, the price of water had become too high.

When this recession ended, people would lift their heads to discover that America didn't belong to America anymore. By then, it wouldn't be worth much, anyway. West Virginia and Pennsylvania were already flooded from all the coal mining and the Alaskan pipeline had almost run dry. If you looked at this country from space, you'd see that it was filling with holes.

He knew it was cheesy. His married cousins, who'd been smart and joined the family rug business, now lived grown-up lives, complete with wives, kids, suburban McMansions, and Cuban cigars. They had things that, after toiling thirty-five more years in film, he'd probably still never be able to afford. But days like this, he saw through all that bullshit and remembered what mattered. He was trying to make the world a better place, and that made life worth living.

There was only one person who'd understand how he felt. His enthusiasm got the better of him, and he flipped open his phone and dialed Audrey's number.

As soon as it connected and began to ring, his stomach gurgled. An image that he'd blotted out returned. He remembered yelling, and a piano. Oh, crap, he'd gone to her place last night, drunk as Caligula! Had he . . . what the hell, had he told her he *hated* her? Oh, no. This was really bad. The floating white lightning returned to his vision, only bigger. It kind of looked like a hovering alien spaceship.

He'd said worse things, too. He tried to remember them, then tried even harder not to remember them. In his mind's eye, she was looking at him through a crooked, half-open door. Its length had dwarfed her, making her appear fragile and childlike. So very un-Audrey. He'd been so blotto that for a moment, he'd genuinely been worried that the ceiling of that place had been about to collapse. He was worried about her now, too. Something about that apartment building had been *wrong*. Or had he only imagined those humming walls?

Her cell phone clicked directly into voice mail: "I'm not here right now . . ." His pulse raced, and his stomach jake-braked. He owed her an apology. Big-time . . .

But until those movers showed up yesterday, it hadn't

hit him that she really was leaving. She'd had so few boxes that he'd felt compelled to send along some dishes, a couple of blankets, and the piano. Girls are different from men. They need nests. He'd thought about the money he'd poured into *Lines,* so that all he'd been able to afford was a broken-down wreck in Yonkers. It had only occurred to him then, that while he wanted kids, unless she worked full-time or he gave up freelance, they'd never be able to afford the health insurance, let alone the diapers. And then he'd thought about all those rich Wall Street scions in her office, who probably presented their wives with diamond-crusted nannies every Christmas, and he'd started to wonder if she'd hadn't left because she'd needed more space at all but because she'd been looking to trade up.

So, the drinking. And more drinking. And inevitably, the late-night antibooty call.

Audrey's message beeped. Saraub hung up. Yeah, he'd tell her he was sorry. But not right now, when his head was about to explode, and any moment, the toilet might beckon.

Who else to ring? The sun outside was bright. A perfect fall Monday. Great weather for a hot dog in Carl Schurz Park. He dialed Daniel's number. After the movers, he and Daniel had gone out for steak at Hooters yesterday afternoon, and then to Dick and Jane's Cabaret on 71st Street. Six strippers slathered in Crisco had swung from poles. The girl on his lap had assured him that she liked tall Indian men, which, even after four whiskies, had seemed like a convenient coincidence. After six whiskies, he'd taken her to the backroom and paid her three hundred bucks to strip to her birthday suit, then get on his lap again, and dance.

"Oh, big man," she'd said, while feeling his turgid crotch. The whole thing had been pretty humiliating, mostly because he'd wanted to tell her to stop but hadn't wanted to be rude. So instead, when she'd asked for three hundred more to suck him off, he'd given her fifty, and said, "I'd really rather you got dressed," then walked out. He waited at the bar another hour for Daniel, who apparently liked getting sucked off by twenty-four-year-old mothers who commute from Queens and dream of one day becoming Vegas show-girls, just like that movie.

Daniel's voice mail beeped. Saraub didn't leave a mes-sage with him, either. He'd been going out with Daniel a lot lately, and it was starting to hurt his liver. More importantly, his wallet had gotten a lot thinner. So he dialed the only other person he knew would be happy for him.

"Hello?" Sheila asked. She had a slight British accent, because that was where she'd gone to prep school.

"Mom?"

"Saraub!" she cried. "How are you?" He kept in con-tact with his cousins and siblings, but hadn't talked to Sheila in almost a year. He'd brought Audrey to meet her only once, and that meeting had gone badly. Sheila had referred to her as "that farm girl" all night and sug-gested that their dinner was unnecessary because the relationship was clearly a fling, before he settled down with a nice girl like Tonia. Despite all that, he'd hoped that over time his best girl and mother would learn to get along, but when Audrey got home that night, she'd locked herself in the bathroom and run the water until dawn so he didn't hear her crying. He'd realized that it was finally time to put his foot down.

"How are you?" Sheila now asked. He had to admit, it was nice to finally hear her voice. Also, and this thought did not illustrate his finest hour, he could always use that trust fund. He'd been burning through his cash lately. Hardly a single meal cooked at home. Turns out, eating alone is depressing.

"I'm good, Mom," he said. His head wasn't though.

It felt like a splinter had lodged in his cranium, and was slowly working its way out.

"Oh, Saraub, I miss you! Your uncle will be so happy. We're celebrating Ganesha tonight. Just in time. Will you come?"

"We celebrate that? Wasn't it last month?"

"It's a new thing. For good luck with the business. Would you come?"

He pictured their cook efficiently dropping pappadam in hot oil, cooking rotis special, just for him, and he grinned. Homecoming. He'd missed that apartment. For one, it was so big he could stretch out on the rug in front of the television. For another, it was on the thirty-sixth floor. So high up that the air was actually clean, and his stuffed nose always miraculously cleared. "I've got news, Mom."

There was a long silence on the other end of the line, and he realized that she thought he was about to announce his engagement to Audrey. She probably had no idea that it had already happened, and unhappened. "I'm not sure I want to hear . . ." she said.

"*Maginot Lines,* Mom. I might get a green light. Like, fifty percent chance they'll finish the funding and distribute it in theatres. A real, feature-length movie. Can you believe it?" He was so excited he hopped up from his chair. Crumbs came with him. He really was a slob. No joke. For a neat freak, Audrey had put up with a lot.

"And now, which one is that?" she asked.

He reddened. "The movie about natural resources. I've been working on it for three years, Mom."

"The hippy thing—your young-life crisis."

He made a fist and squeezed. "Right."

"Well, that's wonderful! But don't be too hard on Servitus. We've got half our stock invested. They paid for your college. And that beautiful wing at the Met, too."

"I know," he said, though it seemed like crappy timing to bring it up, just now.

"Only company that's up this year. Thank God! Anyway, this is wonderful news, dear. We can celebrate tonight. I'm so happy you called. I was just thinking about you because I don't have any recent pictures for the refrigerator. What do you want to eat? I'm about to give Innocencia the list. I thought puran polis—you like them, yes?"

He nodded, still wiping the crumbs from his backside. It occurred to him that he'd been down lately because normally he washed his clothes after wearing them. Working at home this last month had come at a bad time. He needed to be around people. "Dinner sounds great. What can I bring?"

"Wonderful! I'll set an extra place. So much to catch up on. Did you know your two cousins took over the business? It's still Ramesh and Ramesh, of course."

He smiled. Better news than he'd hoped. It meant his mother and aunts had sold their shares, and likely, each eldest son, except for Saraub, was now a partner. Which also meant that he was out of the rug business for good.

"Great news. I'll bring red wine. How's that?" Saraub asked. He walked as he talked, feeling energetic for the first time since Audrey left. Feeling good. He started picking up clothes off the floor. Maybe the worst of it was over. Maybe that first two weeks after she left, when he hadn't shaved or brushed his hair, were in the past. Hell, maybe he was even ready to start dating again.

"Yes. How about a nice Bordeaux? Two bottles. Oh, and Whiskers is good, but he'll be happy to see you. No one ever scratches his ears."

Saraub by now had piled his clothes into a heap on the kitchen table and was deciding whether to carry them to the Laundromat two blocks north, or burn them. "Okay. Two Bordeaux!" He was surprised by how well all this had gone. It was as if they'd never fought. And why had they fought? Over Audrey? It all seemed so ridiculous now. He'd built Sheila up in his mind as unreasonable, but maybe it was Audrey's influence that had done the damage.

"Six o'clock for cocktails. Seven for dinner. But come earlier if you want."

"Great!"

"Oh, and one more thing, darling. I'm only setting one extra plate."

Saraub's pulse throbbed in his temples. "How's that?"

"Only you."

He took a breath. Thought about telling her he wanted to come home for a night, and have a meal cooked, and be loved, and safe, and treated like he was special. He thought about telling her Audrey was gone, and he was the most down he'd ever been in his life. "You know that won't work, Mom," he said instead.

There was a long silence. He counted to ten. The silence continued. Always a game with her. Always about winning, because she was so sure she was right. His father, when he'd been around, had softened her. After he died, she turned into a frightened, clinging person, and even for his younger sisters, home stopped being home.

"I should go," he said. "I just wanted to tell you my good news."

"Don't," she said. "Come for dinner. I miss you. And we should talk about your trust fund, too. I've added to it, but I haven't put it in your name. Tax reasons."

He winced, and remembered now, why they'd stopped talking. It hadn't just been about Audrey. "I miss you too, Mom. Take care of yourself, and call me if you need me." He didn't say good-bye; he just hung up.

When he got off, his head was pounding. The apartment was veiled in a layer of filth. He shoved the clothes from the table, so they landed in a heap on the floor. In the kitchen, he mixed a large, crusty bowl with flour, milk, and eggs, and fried it in butter so that it resembled a huge pancake. It tasted like the stuff inside a horse's feedbag, but some syrup did the trick, and soaked up the acid in his stomach. When he was done, he looked around the home he'd made with Audrey, with its empty space where a piano had been, and punched another hole through the wall.

8

Everything Old Is New Again (Rats!)

onday morning, Audrey woke with a start. Her alarm clock read 3:18. She jumped up from the air mattress. Her throat! The man! The swarming ants!

Heart pitter-pattering, she rubbed her eyes and spun around the room like a windup toy. Her body was wet. Was it blood? Was she dead? No, it was sweat. Her black cotton trousers were soaked through. She felt uneasy, ashamed. A dream?

And then her cheeks turned crimson. Something was really wrong. Her thighs itched, and were too hot. She inspected the coat she'd slept under, and the wet mattress, and her crotch. Her breath came fast. She didn't want to believe it. She hadn't done this since Hinton.

But the smell. The heat. Oh, God.

The piano bench was askew, so she righted it—exactly hip distance from the keys. Her ballet flats were scattered, so she placed them next to each other, then on top of each other, then next to each other, then willed herself to drop them. The muscles of her face contracted into quiet sorrow. Saraub. The nightmares, and now, good grief, she'd pissed the bed!

She took a breath. Then another. One! Two! Three! Four!

(And Mami makes Five!)

She swiped the air mattress with a wet rag, peeled off her pants, and headed for the shower. Her wrist ached. Something sore and tight. She looked at it, then sighed with disappointment: she'd been so out of sorts last night that she'd fallen asleep wearing her watch. Its knob had worn a welt into the bone there. She unclasped the steel band and freed her inflamed skin, then glanced at the time. 10:05 A.M.

What!

She scrambled to the turret. Chiaroscuro shadows rushed as she ran so that the stained-glass birds looked like they'd been freed and were crashing against the walls. It was so dark in here—how could the sun have risen already? But when she got to the window, she saw that her watch was correct. It was midmorning. She'd slept twelve hours for the first time since . . . her hash-smoking days back out west. Down below, college kids rushed toward Columbia University, and throngs of Manhattanites disappeared into the sooty mouth of the 110th Street subway.

The alarm clock, she realized, was dark. Why had she thought it read 3:18 A.M.? She picked it up and found the problem. Its wire had been severed. Not cleanly sliced, but ragged, so that pieces of copper hung loose like Shredded Wheat.

A rat? A lot of rats? She *hated* rats!

She started for the bathroom—a quick shower. Saw that even after an entire night's sleep, the bags under her green eyes had deepened. She ran the tub, since the shower didn't seem to be working. Brown water glugged. A red ant crawled out from the drain, and she smashed it. She really hated ants. Always had. Then she remembered the thing she'd forgotten: she had an eleven o'clock status meeting. Big day. Huge, career-making day. And she was *really* late.

She raced. Found the only business attire that wasn't wrinkled—a black skirt, white polyester blouse, and clashing turquoise pumps, then reached for her jacket inside the double-doored den closet.

She would have missed it if she hadn't bumped into it. The sound was pretty, like the light footsteps of small children (One! Two! Three! Four!). Boxes scattered. They didn't bounce against the hardwood floor, or roll. Instead, they skated.

The empty cardboard boxes from her move. About twenty of them. They'd been recorrugated into new shapes; doubled-up triangles, squares, and rectangles, and were taped together end to end with clear packaging tape. Leaning against the far closet wall, they formed a solid, six-foot-by-four-foot rectangle. At the center edge of the rectangle was a circular cutout. A hole for a handle . . . This thing was a door!

She ran her hands along the side of the structure. Sparks of electricity ignited in her fingertips like touching dry ice. The materials were shoddy, but the construction professional. The various shapes fit perfectly, like a jigsaw puzzle, and each one buttressed the next. They'd all been turned inside out, so their writing (PALMOLIVE, SERVITUS, PFIZER, HAMMERHEAD, UNITED CHINESE EMIRATES) didn't show.

She remembered a snippet of her dream. The man in the closet, and her mother's accusation: *It's a bad place, where you live.* . . . and something else, too. Something about Hinton that she couldn't quite remember: a mirror layered with ants, down a muddy hole.

Who had built this door? Edgardo, playing a mean prank because he'd gotten fired? One of the neighbors? Saraub? Clara? The man from her dream?

She sighed. But her sharp box cutter lay on the piano, its blade open. Her arms hurt, and so did her back. Even her legs ached. But it's hard for your watch to dig a welt into your wrist when you're sleeping soundly. A truth she preferred not to admit was now too obvious to deny: a professional had done this thing. *She* had built this thing.

She took a deep breath and turned away from the closet. Its evidence was too unsettling. Sleepwalking. Strange dreams, sleeping in front of a television instead of in a proper bed. Moving into a haunted and crumbling apartment like a modern-day Miss Haversham. These decisions were pathologically stupid. No doubt about it: she was turning into her mother.

Audrey's lower lip got quivery. But no. She wasn't like Betty! Why couldn't she ever give herself credit? She'd gotten herself to New York. A scholarship to Columbia University, for Christ's sake! Everybody knows those programs aren't easy. It's like being a doctor! She paid rent once a month, and on time. When Saraub got cut off, she'd been the one to draw up a budget so they'd been able to afford orange juice and winter coats. She'd been the one to keep him from taking an office job, so he could push forward on *Maginot Lines,* too. So yeah, she'd peed her pants last night. But that didn't make her crazy.

As for the boxes and alarm-clock wire, she'd just been sleepwalking. Growing up, she used to sleepwalk all the time. Pretty reasonable, given the circumstances. Whose subconscious wouldn't run from Betty?

She sighed and put her hand to her throat. Sore. She knew what she had to do next. An unpleasant but unavoidable necessity. She needed to find a shrink. Fast.

Because Saraub wasn't around anymore, and there was nobody left to catch her if she fell.

Then she looked at her watch, which she'd put on the other wrist: 10:30. "Cripes on a cross!" she shouted. How the heck had she just wasted an entire half hour? She opened the door and fled.

While waiting for the elevator, a tubercular-skinny old woman with a yellow, spray-on tan peeked out from 14C, the apartment next door.

"Hi, darling," she said.

Audrey startled. It took her a second before she realized to whom the old lady was speaking.

"Hi!" Audrey said. The arrowed, ivory button pointing down was carved, not stamped, and time had worn a finger-shaped groove into its center. She pressed it again.

"A lot of unpacking, sweetie?" the woman called. Her face shone, pasty and slick with what looked like cold cream. Something about her was off. It took Audrey a beat before she figured it out: plastic surgery. The woman's pale, paper-thin skin was without wrinkles, though she had to be at least eighty-five. Her cheekbones were preternaturally high, and her chin was too sharp, as if its bone had been sawed to a point. The effect wasn't pretty, but insectile—a praying mantis. Even her eyes were wrong. They were too wide for her narrow face, and as Audrey looked more closely, too perfect in their roundness, like a doll's. Man-made holes like slits in fabric. Audrey couldn't help it. She gasped. The woman looked inhuman.

"I said, a lot of unpacking?" the woman repeated, slower this time, like maybe Audrey was simple.

"Uh-huh," Audrey answered. She tried not to look at the woman, then couldn't help looking, and imagining the surgery. Skin sliced open, pulled tight, stapled closed. Bone and flesh separated like strangers.

The woman opened the door wider. Audrey blinked, then blinked longer, but both times, she saw the same thing. The woman wore an aged and yellowed dressing gown. Nineteen-twenties vintage silk—something Jean Harlow might have strutted through an old gangster movie. It fit her like the clear plastic casing butchers squeeze over sausages. Her saggy arm flesh disgorged from its short sleeves, then hung all the way down to her wrinkled elbows. Oh, Audrey hated wrinkled elbows worse than knuckles. They were like giant gerbil babies!

"You building something in there?" the woman asked. Audrey saw now, that her eyes were clouded with cataracts. Partly this was reassuring. Maybe half-blind, she didn't realize she'd gone overboard on the surgery.

"What do you mean?" Audrey asked. A few floors down, the elevator hummed.

The woman smiled. "All that hammering about last night."

Literal hammering? Audrey wanted to ask, *Because I don't remember that so well.* Instead she said, "Sorry if I kept you up."

"Oh, don't you worry, sweetie. Everybody here builds. We all try our hand, but I know you'll be the best," she said. Then, with one useless eye, she winked.

The elevator pinged, and 14 lit up. Audrey got inside and pressed "L" just as the woman planted her bare feet on the hallway carpet. All that money spent on a wrinkle-free face and a liposuction-skinny body, but her toenails were yellow with fungus. "Don't be a stranger!" she called.

Audrey nodded, too shocked to speak. The metal cage closed, separating her from 14C's strange beast. "Leaping Jesus!" she muttered, as the car plunged.

9

The Business of Grief

shooting spree in Times Square closed off Broadway, extending gridlock all the way into Harlem, so she took her chances and headed for the subway. On her ride, the #1 train slammed to a stop at Columbus Circle. Audrey clung to the metal strap in the ceiling with both hands while a middle-aged Dutch tourist in an "I ♥ NY" T-shirt and Mickey Mouse backpack stumbled down the aisle with his arms outstretched, like he was racing toward his long-lost true love, lederhosen-clad Minnie.

Before impact, he squeezed his deli coffee cup. Its lid saucered into the air. As he plunged into her chest, he crushed the cup between them. She swung from the strap while he held her shoulders for balance. The good news: The coffee was lukewarm and didn't burn. The bad news: where to begin? Her shirt was sopping wet, and by the time she got to the office, it was 11:10.

As soon as she walked through the door, Bethy Astor

popped out from behind her narrow reception podium like a restaurant hostess, and announced in a loud whisper, "You're in so much trouble. Jill shit a brick. She shit two bricks. It's shit-brick-splatter all over the walls." The sun shone bright through the windows, so Bethy's auburn hair looked like it was on fire. Devil Bethy. Slightly less annoying than regular Bethy.

"That bad?" Audrey asked. Her shirt from the coffee spill on the subway was wet and cold. Sticky, too. Figured Mr. Mickey Mouse was a three tablespoons of sugar kind of guy.

Bethy leaped across her desk so that half her body dangled. She was a friendly, nervous girl just out of college who couldn't transfer callers without disconnecting them. Like most of the people who worked here, she wore thousand-dollar suits and her blood was blue. Also like most people here, she'd gotten her job through connections. "Sooo bad," Bethy exclaimed with both hands on her heart, like it might break if she didn't hold it together.

Audrey sighed. Something squirmed in her gut like acid indigestion, only more, well, squirmy. What kind of a cutesy name is Bethy, anyway?

"And the thing is, I like you, Audrey!" Bethy said, like she was auditioning to perform Audrey's eulogy at the annual Luck Strike Smokehouse company retreat. "If they boot you, I'm gonna put Ex-Lax in that bitch's coffee."

Audrey took a deep breath. "Well, for that it might be worth it."

Jill Sidenschwandt was Audrey's supervisor, and one of only nine other women in the eighty-person office. Jill had entered the business back when architecture had still been a boys' club, so even though she'd given Vesuvius thirty years of hard work, she'd never made partner. She was bitter about that. Or maybe she was just generally bitter, Audrey couldn't tell.

Since Jill's fourth kid got diagnosed with leukemia, she'd stopped working the same long hours as the rest of the 59th Street team. Instead, she'd been delegating, and leaving Audrey in charge. But Audrey was bad at delegating, and besides, she didn't have the job title to back her up. As a result, some parts of the project were in great shape, others, a mess. And Jill hadn't been paying enough attention to know the messes from the successes.

The meeting was a status report on the 59th Street, Parkside Plaza Project. Six months ago, a Ukrainian man with two hundred pounds of urea nitrate strapped to his back got past security. The metal detectors hadn't sounded, and, remarkably, the guards hadn't questioned the note he'd written on the sign-in sheet: "End Servitus Tyranny." On the elevator, the terrorist had unstrapped the bomb from his waist and held it in his hands. A Good Samaritan had strong-armed him to the roof. During the struggle, the bomb detonated. Twenty midmorning smokers were killed up there, and another eighty-four died on the top floor when the ceiling fell. If not for the Samaritan, mortalities would have been in the thousands. It took the FBI almost two months to identify his remains: Richardo Monge, an illegal immigrant from Costa Rica who operated the street-level bagel cart. He'd been in the middle of a coffee delivery when he'd seen the bomb and saved the building.

Allied Incorporated American Banking (AIAB), which held a one-hundred-year lease on the 59th Street property, had picked Vesuvius to rebuild the gutted floors and erect a rooftop memorial for those who'd died. Jill was team leader because, before her son got sick, she'd asked for more responsibility. If her team design saw completion, the firm's founders had promised to finally make her a partner.

Silk blouse sopping wet, Audrey raced to her workstation cubicle, where Jill stood with crossed arms.

"You're late. We're all waiting," she said. Her skin looked pale blue, like her blood had been replaced with black and blue ink, and if you touched her, she'd bruise.

"I'm so sorry," Audrey panted.

Jill was tall and slender, but big-boned. Her uniform was loose-fitting pantsuits and fussy silk blouses that tied into bows at the neck, like an ERA poster from 1972. "I just finished going over floors forty-seven through fifty in the boardroom, but not the roof. That's up to you."

"What?" Audrey panted. As project manager, it was Jill's job to give presentations.

"I decided you should do it," she said. Her voice cracked, but only if you were listening for it. Audrey knew then what had happened. Jill hadn't bothered looking at the plans over the weekend. Instead, she'd come in early and expected Audrey to brief her. When Audrey hadn't shown, she'd panicked and decided that somebody had to take the fall, and it wasn't going to be the lady with the chemo bills.

"Hurry up!" Jill said, her arms still crossed.

Audrey took three long breaths to collect herself. This was bad. She wasn't prepared. She squeezed her hands into fists and let go. Tried to think of a bright side, could come up with only one: she no longer smelled like pee. It was something, at least. "Okay," she said, and started toward the conference room.

"Oh, no you don't," Jill answered. "You can't go in there looking like that." She pointed her chin at Audrey's chest.

Audrey followed Jill's gaze. The blood rushed to her face, hot and uncomfortable. She was reminded of her dream, and the coveralls. Her mother's red-stained hands, and the girl she used to be, because the wet, spilled coffee had rendered her blouse see-through. Her sexy Victoria's Secret nylon bra, which had been a handy, albeit impractical choice this morning, wasn't thick enough to contain the damage. Through the wet was the very obvious outline of nipples.

Jill frowned in disgust.

Audrey looked down at the pink hills of her skin. It wasn't cute. It wasn't sexy. It was white trash, and she wondered, not for the first time, whether she belonged in this nice, clean office among civilized people. She folded her arms across her chest, and remembered depressed teenage days of unbrushed hair and soiled clothes that she'd worn, again and again. What was happening to her? Alone again after all this time, was she falling apart?

"Here," Jill said, taking off her blue cashmere suit jacket that reeked of rubbing alcohol and vitamins, and plopping it over Audrey's shoulders.

Audrey pulled it tight around her chest, pressing the brass buttons through their holes. In that second and that second only, she loved Jill Sidenschwandt. "Thank you," she said.

Jill lifted Audrey's chin in her cold hands. Her bloodshot eyes were wet, either from exhaustion or weeping. "Pull yourself together and stop making me feel sorry for you. I'm not getting fired over this. Do you understand? You can do this. I believe in you. I wouldn't ask if I didn't."

Audrey nodded. "Thanks. Yes. I'll be fine. Don't worry."

Jill held on for a second longer than necessary, and Audrey couldn't tell if the gesture was friendly or hostile. "I'm sorry if you've got troubles," she said. Her tone was dismissive, like because Audrey didn't have a family to care for, she wasn't entitled to bad days. Her kid wasn't dying, and she had no real responsibilities or attachments, so what was the problem?

Audrey looked at her ballet flats. The thing that had recently invaded her stomach writhed in acid bile.

What the hell did Jill know about her personal troubles? Unlike every other fat cat around here, she'd never shown up to work crying, or fought on the phone with a lousy husband who couldn't remember to buy the milk. She'd never whined about idiot kids who didn't study hard enough, or forced people to look at professional photos of her terrier poodles (whoodles!). Crazy, yes. But Jill was out of line: she'd never bitched about it.

"You don't need to worry about my troubles or my performance. I've never given you cause in either department," she said, then picked the plans up off her desk, pushed through double oak doors, and stormed the Vesuvius boardroom.

About twenty men in suits were waiting at the long conference table. Its window gave a cityscape view of downtown Manhattan. In the distance were construction holes, the circle line, and Lady Liberty.

Jill took her seat with the rest of the nine-member Parkside Plaza team. On the opposite, windowed side of the long, Japanese teak table were Vesuvius' founding brothers, Randolph and Mortimer Pozzolana. Flanking the Pozzolanas were the hierarchy of nondesigners, from accounting, to vice president of operations, to manager of public relations. Basically, this room represented everybody who was anybody at Vesuvius. She'd kept them waiting, and they did not look happy. Audrey gulped. For the fiftieth time this year she thought: *I really ought to own a suit. I also ought to start wearing lipstick.*

"I'm so sorry I'm late," she said.

"Audrey's doctor's appointment ran longer than she expected," Jill chimed in.

Audrey nodded. "Right."

Scritch-scratch! Scritch-scratch!

She headed for the empty seat near Jill, but Randolph Pozzolana, the friendlier, younger partner who referred to his twenty-eight-year-old wife as "my-old-lady-number-three" shook his head. "Other side. Use the podium." His voice was matter-of-fact, but polite, like a British Navy captain who's aware that the boat is sinking, but sees no reason to shed good manners. She realized then that he knew. Everybody knew that something was up, and *somebody* was going down. Jill had sold her out.

She walked the long gallows. When she got to the podium, she surveyed the rest of the team, but none offered an encouraging smile. She had the least real-work experience at Vesuvius, but Jill had made her second-in-command. Because of that, Audrey Lucas was nobody's favorite new girl. She stood at the front of the room. Swallowed, hard. The air expanded inside her chest like a reverse burp and left her breathless. This was her first job outside a greasy spoon. Other than telling truckers and Omaha art-school crankheads to keep their mitts to themselves, she'd never given a speech or even raised her voice before. She was fairly sure she'd be bad at it.

Scritch-scratch! Scritch-scratch!

Was someone cleaning the windows outside?

The faces peering at her looked alien, as if she were viewing them from upside down. She took a breath. At least she wasn't sleepwalking in The Breviary right now, or fighting with Saraub. In its way, this office was a relief. She tried to remember that.

The faces kept watching, so she squeezed her hands into fists and closed her eyes. Pretended the room was empty of people and perfectly symmetrical. Opened her eyes again, but tried to keep the image there, of black nothing. She could still see, but the trick calmed her enough to continue.

"Sorry to hold you up. I love this project!" she said. She tried to sound excited, but the effect was more used-Hyundai salesman: unctuous and just the wrong side of smart. Mortimer frowned. So did Jill. David Galea, who brought Cokes to her cubicle when she worked through lunch, looked down at his notepad like he was embarrassed for her.

She unrolled the plans. Lots of lines on oversized white paper.

Scriiiittccch!

What was that? The sound was dull and had give, like shell dragged against concrete: it rattled, leaving pieces of itself behind.

"Hydroponics are environmentally friendly, and the running water buffers plane and traffic noise pollution. The design of the future." She continued, talking to a room she'd decided to pretend was empty.

"These plans were made by Manny in design, and he did a great job, but I should remind you all that they're rough," she announced as she handed out the five-by-seven replicas of the latest design, ten to each side. The hands that took the papers were disembodied. Unrelated. Papers rustled as they were passed, like phantoms.

SCRITCH!-SCRAAAAATTCCCH!

Who the heck was making that sound?

"I don't like the colors—orange is for hazard signs, not plants, and those grid lines will be gone when we present this to the client." Her voice trembled as she spoke.

Someone at the far end of the long table wrapped his fingernails against the wood—she couldn't see whom. She unrolled the master plans with her hands. The details were marked with light ink and hard to distinguish from the blue paper and small graph boxes. She didn't remember what they represented. That sound, so distracting:

SCRITCH!-SCRATCH! SCRITCH-SCRATCH!

She turned to the corner behind her. Because of the mind game she was playing, everything seemed dark. Something twitched. She closed her eyes. When she opened them, it was bright again. Her imagination? The OCD?

At the far end of the table, Mortimer wrapped his slender knuckles against the teak table. He wore red Santa Claus suspenders under his blue wool jacket, and they made him seem deranged. *What seventy year-old man wears suspenders?* "Go on," he said. "We don't have all day."

She continued, trying not to look in the corner. Not to look anywhere. "What the client liked about Jill's proposal was its unique style, but . . ." the words left her. She focused on her hands, whose wrinkled knuckles looked like newborn gerbils. Jill's boxy, Brooks Brothers jacket was too big. Its sleeves met her fingers, and it smelled like a hospital, which of course reminded her of Betty.

Scriiiiittccch! Scraaaaaaaaaaaaaatttccch!

She couldn't help it. The sound was too big to ignore. She jerked her head toward the corner behind her, and *saw*. The man from her dream. He stood with his back to her, and he appeared as a shadow, only darker; the reverse outline of a sunspot when you blink.

She broke out in a quick sweat. Can OCD make you hallucinate? Can you get flashbacks from hash? She looked away, hoping he would disappear. No one else was reacting, which she knew meant he could not really be there . . . right?

"Practical considerations . . ." she said. Sweat dampened her temples. She tried to remember those considerations, but her mind drew a blank. Her team was boring holes through her skin with their eyes. Little lasers of humiliation. A few looked nervous, like her discomfort was contagious, but most were openly hostile. Limping chickens in coops are always the first to get pecked to death. Nobody likes the weakling of the pack.

Scritch!-Scratch!

She couldn't help it. She looked back into the corner.

The man's shape had gotten more distinct. Pieces of the plaster wall fell to the floor as he worked: *scritch!-scratch!* To dig, he was using his index finger, which he'd worn to the bone.

Another tap from across the room, and then, "Ms. Loomis? Lucas? Is something wrong?"

SCRITCH! SCRATCH!
SCRITCH! SCRATCH!

She covered her ears with her hands. The scratching got faster. His bone wore as he worked and left a chalky residue.

SCRITCH! SCRATCH!
SCRITCH! SCRATCH!
SCRITCH! SCRATCH!

There was a hole in the plaster now. She remembered the article she'd read, about the doors of chaos that civilized men had no business opening. The thing in her stomach slopped. The hole the man had made was black and deep. If she looked hard enough, she thought she could see something on the other side of it, peering back at her.

Above the hole, he began to scribble with his chalk bone. His body bent and jerked as he wrote, and he worked inhumanly fast, like time moved differently for him than for everyone else in the room. *SCRITCH! SCRATCH! SCRITCH! SCRATCH! SCRITCH! SCRATCH!*

His hair had gone gray, and his sharp teeth fell out one by one. Not a dandy, anymore. His three-piece suit was worn to threads. When he was done, he stepped aside to let her see his message. In blood and bone above the black hole, he'd written:

Build the Door

. As she read, the hole underneath the letters expanded like a breath, and the void inside it widened. And then, oh, no. Out from the hole, a swarm of red ants crawled.

"Stop it!" she cried.

The entire room jolted. She turned back to the board-room table, where shocked faces peered back at her. She faced the man in the corner again, but he was gone. So was the hole.

Ragged breathing, she closed her eyes. Opened them. Nothing there. Not even a crack in the plaster. A bead of sweat rolled over her brow and into her eye. The salt burned.

Scritch! Scritch!

This time, the sound was Mortimer, scratching his manicured fingernails against the wooden table. She realized he'd been doing that for a while now. The blood rushed to her face. She looked in the corner again. Nothing there. Could she really have imagined such a thing?

"Are you ill, Miss Loomis?" Randolph asked.

Audrey blinked. The room was bright. A sunny fall day. Twenty rich people with good jobs sat at a long teak table, politely observing Audrey Lucas have her first psychotic break.

Mortimer glared, like he wished his eyes would burn holes through her skull so she'd keel over, and he could kick her dead body. Jill was up and heading in her direction. There were tears in her eyes, and Audrey wasn't sure whether they contained self-pity or sympathy. Randolph pushed out his chair as if to stand, excuse her from the podium, then insist Jill continue. Do the honorable thing and put her out of her misery. She'd be fired if that happened. Maybe not immediately, but eventually, because screwing up a major meeting wasn't something anybody was going to forget. She couldn't let that happen. Not without a fight.

"I should explain. I had light surgery over the week-end. Nothing serious, just a polyp, but the doctor gave me Vicodin. I think I might be allergic because—I'm dizzy, and a little confused. But I'll stop wasting your time and get going now. Okay?" The lie came out in such a nervous rush it sounded natural.

Nobody moved any closer, and she seized the opportunity to continue. "Now . . . Where was I?" she asked while unrolling the plans. The lines on the page were a jumble. She fixed her eyes on them and shut everything else out. The shuffling papers. The eyes, watching. The sound of her own rapid pulse. The thing in the corner. Was it invisible, and still watching her even now?

She counted backward quickly from ten. Imagined the shapes of the numbers as she thought them. Moved her gaze from left to right, small to large, and willed herself to *see*. After a few seconds, the plans coalesced. Right angles and arcs, beautiful straight lines. They intersected, and spoke.

"It's a maze," she said. Mortimer narrowed his eyes. Randolph shrugged. The middle men shuffled their feet. She realized they thought she'd said *amazed*.

She looked at each person in the room, one by one, so that they knew she was back in control. She started with her team. Realized that they hadn't been hostile before, just concerned. If this went badly, Audrey wasn't the only architect facing an unemployment line. Then she nodded at Jill to reassure her. The underarms of her frilly blouse were wet with sweat. Then the department heads. Finally, Randolph, then Mortimer. Dead in the eyes. She'd be damned, after all she'd done to get here, if this was the way she was going out.

"A garden maze in the clouds." She let this sentence hang for a while, because she liked the sound of it, and she suddenly realized that she was proud. These long, late hours, she'd extended Jill's idea into something new, and good. She'd been so busy working and looking for a place to live that she hadn't noticed it until now.

She cleared her throat. "Tragedies happen. But life

goes on. Buildings go on, too. They have to, or else they're shrines to the dead."

A few people shifted uncomfortably, and the Pozzolanas returned her gaze with something cold. She'd hit a nerve. Since the recession, architecture firms, unable to build, had gotten into the business of grief. Angelfaced memorials were popping up like weeds all over the country, and Vesuvius was responsible for a lot of them. It had become a commonplace Sunday afternoon hobby for people to visit the memorials of people they'd never met and leave flowers. And not just soldiers who'd died in war, either. Plane crashes, car accidents, stray bullet shootings. They were all marked with stone angels, slabs of marble, or plaques posted to trees. The grief industry was burying the country in white baby's breath flowers, and the scent was sickly sweet.

"New York is about the future and living your dreams. Nobody left Omaha because they liked it. Or Sioux City. Or Des Moines. Or Portland. Pick a Portland. Any Portland. You can have 'em. I'll take Manhattan."

A few people chortled. She smiled, because she knew they'd decided to give her another shot. "So! We designed an outdoor roof garden. Like flowers, it'll be an offering to those who died, but it'll exist for the living, too."

She looked down at her hands, which she'd squeezed into fists so she didn't have to see her knuckles. She straightened them now, so her audience didn't mistake the habit for hostility. The thing about her work was, she loved it. She was never more comfortable, or happier, as when she was designing, or seeing her plans come to fruition. What could be more satisfying than changing the architecture of the world, and maybe even making it a better place to live?

"We've done something new here, and I think you'll be pleased. Instead of low-lying plants or grass, we chose six-foot-tall hedges. We'll assemble them into a winding maze, not so different from cubicles, with fixed places for benches and picnic tables. At the center of the maze we'll place a mourning wall, where the names of the victims will be carved in marble." She lifted her copy of the plans, and pointed with her pen. "You can see these will be areas for reflection, but here and also here"—she pointed while holding up the plan—"we'll place sculptures and picnic tables. Finally, we'll dedicate the mourning wall to 'The Good Samaritan,' and the inspiration he has been to all of us. And now, for the really good news: we've made preliminary inquiries, and so long as AIAB green lights the fee, Joseph Frick is on board to carve the wall. He's the same guy who built those steps in New Orleans after the second levees broke."

A few people sat back in their chairs. Randolph smiled. Her team smiled. Jill smiled. She exhaled with relief so pleasantly contagious that Mortimer finally stopped glaring.

She went for gold, delineating the structure of the roof and the floors below, for the next half hour. When she was done, the room stayed quiet. Her cheeks burned like a fire lived in there. She'd screwed up, yes. She was nuts, maybe. But at least she'd come through when it counted.

The seconds passed. Jill's eyelids fluttered, and Audrey realized she'd fallen asleep. Randolph scribbled something into his paper datebook—the last man on earth to own one. Mortimer tented his fingers.

"I like it," Randolph finally said.

"But no statues? No reflection pool? Is a wall enough?" Mortimer asked.

Audrey answered fast, so no middlemen cronies had the chance to chime in and blow the deal. "It's enough. You make people feel guilty with big memorials. Besides, if it's too big, AIAB will have to take it down one day because their staff will want something pretty. But by then they'll have to fight the city and the families, because once they have a memorial in place, any changes they make will look like a betrayal of the dead. With this structure, you're honestly remembering them, and moving on, too."

Mortimer nodded. "I'm sick of these bullshit memorials, too. I didn't get into this business to design cemeteries. When this recession is over, we're a skyscraper-only operation. Still, I don't like marble for the wall. Too mausoleum. I want something that blends. The maze is good, but it's uptight. Like you, Sidenschwandt," he said to Jill, whose eyes popped open. Next he turned to Audrey, but like his brother, got her name wrong: "And probably you, too, Loomis. Show me something better by next week." Then he rapped his knuckles against the table, and said, "From the way this meeting started, I thought I had a lemon on my hands. Nice surprise."

Then, shockingly, Mortimer smiled. "Next time, less pills, sweetheart. Send me the plans in an e-mail so I can run it through engineering. I'll set up a client meeting for the end of the month. I've got to run." He was standing fast and turned back once to add. "One more thing."

"Yes?" Audrey asked.

"This whole room was waiting for you. By my watch, almost five minutes. Everybody here."

Audrey looked to Jill. Jill looked to her hands.

He lowered his voice. "That can never happen again."

Audrey nodded. "Yes, sir."

Then he and Randolph, who gave her a surreptitious thumbs-up, were out the door. The rest, including the 59th Street team, followed slowly, like herded sheep. What surprised her—a couple of them patted her on the back. Dave Galea even whispered, "Fuck yeah! Lunch is on me."

She and Jill were the last to leave the room. "Did you really have a polyp?" Jill asked.

Audrey shook her head. "No. I don't know what's wrong with me. But I had to say something."

Jill looked at her for a beat longer than necessary. "Well, take better care of yourself. I can't afford to give you time off."

"Oh." Audrey's shirt had dried. She took off the jacket and tried to hand it back, but Jill wouldn't accept it. "Keep it. You'll need it." Then she lowered her voice so that no one outside could hear. "You helped me out on that. Decent job. Thank you."

Audrey beamed. "Yeah. Rough start, but I think they liked it. I wish you'd give me some notice next time, though."

Jill flipped her cell phone open and began to text a message. "The nurse is sick today, and nobody's watching my son."

Audrey frowned. "Sorry." They stood at the wide boardroom window overlooking downtown Manhattan. Sun-soaked tourists crowded Battery Park to ride the Circle Line, then snap photos of former monuments turned holes.

"Technically, as my second-in-command, it's your job to develop presentations. I don't have to give you notice." Jill didn't look at her when she said this, and a bolt of genuine rage thundered through Audrey's chest. The worm inside her began to gnaw. She thrust the jacket in Jill's direction until she had no choice but to take it back.

"Smells like sick people," she said, and left the room.

10

You Like Me? You Really Like Me!

David swung by her cubicle ten minutes later, with the other members of the team in tow. "I was thinking Balucci's, so we could sneak in a couple of beers," he said. He was wearing a crisp blue suit and pressed trousers. He could have made the cover of *GQ*.

"Lots of beer," Craig chimed in. He was a junior designer, but he acted like an intern. His dad worked for AIAB, though, and had referred a lot of business to Vesuvius.

"What?" she asked. What did David expect her to say, that it was okay to drink on the job? Meanwhile, she had to get these plans done and didn't have the time to swallow a bagel?

"So Balucci's is okay with you?" David asked.

She got a little hot under the collar. "Actually," she said. "I could use some help on this."

David frowned. "You don't want to go to lunch?"

Now she was more confused than ever. Rather than getting herself into deeper trouble, she decided to say nothing at all.

"Lucas," Mark said. "It's our treat. For the presentation. If you hadn't done it, one of us would have been in the hot seat."

"Really?" she asked. They'd never asked her to lunch before. Usually, they just sneaked out one by one. She never imagined they all met up at the same place. "You guys always eat together?"

Simon nodded. "Some of us aren't machines." Simon wanted her job, and had made no secret about sending out his résumé when Jill stopped delegating to him and hired Audrey. There was a note she didn't like in his voice, envy or contempt or both. She decided to ignore it.

The rest of the team, Jim, Louis, and Henry, Craig, Mark, and even Collier Steadman, the head of Human Resources, were smiling . . . Was the watercooler spiked with liquid nitrous or something? "Come on!" David cheered.

They spent sixty decadent minutes at the restaurant. As the only woman at the table, she felt like a star. They pulled her chair out and poured a Bud for her. What could be more fun? "How do you not get caught, going out every day like this?" she asked.

Jim, whose family owned an entire apartment building in SoHo, finished chewing his food, and answered, "We just go. If you ask the bitch, she'll always say no. So don't ask."

"Won't I get fired?"

Collier from Human Resources, who was drinking his vodka-tini with his pinkies outstretched, moaned theatrically. Once, while she'd been filling out 401(k) beneficiary paperwork in his office, he'd broken down in tears because one of his poodles was sick. Bewildered, Audrey had patted him on the back, *I'm sure he'll be fine*, she'd promised. *These vets work miracles.* He'd grabbed her hard and hugged her as he'd wept. Crazy, but who was she to judge? She talked to a cactus.

"Audrey, darling—" Collier scolded like the grand, barrel-chested queen that he was. "You're so delightfully green. It's a law: full-time work requires a sixty-minute break. Also, Jim, Jill Sidenschwandt is not a bitch. Her child is dying, and she's watching it happen. You, however, are a ridiculous person."

Audrey smiled. Collier saluted her with his martini.

"Bi-itch," Jim repeated.

"I second. Motion carries," Mark said.

It occurred to her that men could be catty, too.

Collier sighed. "Repeat. Dying son." He'd sipped a third of his vodka-tini, and looked dizzy.

"No, I'd call her a bitch," David said. "I took this job to learn something. It was a demotion from graphic design. She promised to train me." Audrey frowned. She'd always assumed he was idle because he was lazy. She'd never guessed he might not know how to do the job. No wonder he was always leaning over her shoulder when he bought her those lunchtime Cokes, asking basic questions like, "Which of those dots represents the plumbing?"

"I have nothing to do. It's like I'm fucking dying inside," Mark said.

"Kafka over there," Louis scolded, then took a gulp of his Taj Mahal. He showed up late every morning and left early, but nobody cared, because he never did anything.

"You guys want work?" Audrey asked. "I figured you'd get pissed if I asked, because I'm new."

"I'd get pissed. Count me out," Craig said, then ordered a third neat gin. The trick, he'd told her when they'd sat down, was ordering something that didn't smell.

Simon dropped his fork and knife so they made a

clamor against the aluminum plate. All eyes turned to him. He squinted at Audrey, and she could see that he was trying to contain no small measure of fury. "You're obviously some kind of genius," he spit. "But if you'd screwed up today, don't kid yourself, they'd have fired you. And a few of us would have packed our desks up, too. On paper, you realize, I'm the second-in-command. Not that the bitch cares. I don't know what she says to you in that office. None of us even know half the time whether the plans are the same from week to week. We need something to show for our paychecks, Lucas. We've got families. Christmas around the corner." He glared. Nobody interrupted him. The idea that they wanted direction had never occurred to her, mostly because she'd never really believed she was in charge. Also, they were grown men: couldn't they have rolled up their sleeves before this and simply found work that needed to be done?

"I'm sorry," she said. "Of course. I didn't think. I've been preoccupied. I'll put something together for each of you as soon as we get back."

"You'd better," Simon said, and she realized that celebration wasn't their only reason for taking her to lunch.

Collier began to clap, which broke the tension. "And that, ladies and gentleman, is our lesson for the day in passive aggression. Simon has lots of grumpy little demons to work out. And here's my contribution in aggressive aggression: if you keep using the B word to characterize Ms. Sidenschwandt, I'm going to write you up for disciplinary action."

David hoisted his beer. So did Collier. Then Jim, Craig, Louis, Henry, and Mark. Finally, jealous Simon. "To Audrey. For a job well done, and more work for the rest of us," David said.

She looked around the circular table. For the most part, they were a smiling, convivial group. Was it possible, after all these months, that she'd been at fault, too, and ought to have tried harder to get to know them? Further, what would that sixteen-year-old in torn coveralls have said if she'd seen this dream job snapshot of her own future? She'd have giggled with her hands cupped over her mouth, then given up the ghost of subtlety and jumped for joy.

She elected not to acknowledge that none of them seemed particularly equipped for the work, that only half had requested it, and that they'd probably resent her when they realized how much needed to get done. She decided to save those worries for later, and instead, clinked her half-drunk glass against Collier's, then David's, then Simon's—one person to the next, and saw this happy moment through a certain sixteen-year-old's eyes.

11

This Petty Pace from Day to Day

The rest of the afternoon was a slog. She delegated the entire lower engineering and plumbing plans to Simon, David, Mark, and Craig, and to her shock they were grateful to have something to do. After that, she sat at her cube, refining the roof-garden plans for the brainstorming session Jill had scheduled for the next morning (they needed to position return drains in a way that kept mold to a minimum), and thought about what had happened during the night. She'd sleepwalked, obviously. It could happen to anyone, given enough stress. Still, those cut wires. That lunatic cardboard door. And the man in the three-piece suit with the bone finger today, at the meeting. She hadn't guessed she was capable of imagining something so bizarre.

She looked down at her paper, and saw that over the mourning wall, she'd drawn a rectangle with a handle. A door.

"That's it," she mumbled aloud, as the plans rolled

together, and she visited her health-care plan online. Three local shrinks looked best. She made appointments with each of them. The earliest she could schedule was Wednesday afternoon.

"Sleepwalking? Delusions? . . . Siamese twins. Like Chang and Eng?" the last woman asked.

"Who? No. Like De Palma. *Sisters*. But forget that part," Audrey whispered. "I'm under some stress, obviously."

"Is there a possibility you'll hurt yourself?" Her accent was Staten Island: Ya gonna hoit yaself?

"I don't know. Is that a thing people know?"

"Yeah. Ya'd know," the woman said.

"Then I doubt it," Audrey told her. "But I do have OCD. The kind that can't be medicated." She whispered this part and made sure no one nearby was listening. It was four o'clock, and everyone was playing with the new espresso machine in the kitchen. It infused chocolate, apparently. Jealous Simon, pleased with the role she'd given him as manager of all nonroof floors, asked her to join them, but she'd decided to make this call instead. "When I got diagnosed, they told me I didn't need pills or therapy. It's psychological only. Not physical," she said to the shrink.

"Who told ya that?" the woman asked.

Audrey prairie dogged over the cube wall, but she didn't see anyone nearby. "My nurse practitioner in training at the University of Nebraska . . . about fifteen years ago. She told me I could fix it myself—I'm just a nervous person," she whispered. Even as she said it, she knew her mistake. A diagnosis that serious, you get a second opinion. From a real doctor, and not the kid with the clipboard.

"Sweetie, I don't know what kinda Kool-Aid they fed you, but all obsessive-compulsive disorders are physical."

Audrey blushed. "Really? What about the kind where

you're so nervous that you change your own neurons and give yourself the disease because you had a traumatic childhood?"

"That's the nuttiest thing I've heard in . . . twenty minutes. There's no extraspecial self-created disorder. It's not your fault if you got blue eyes, is it? OCD is OCD. If you've got records, bring them. See you Wednesday, honee."

"Okay," Audrey said. She must have sounded shaken because the woman softened.

"Hey. It's life. Ya learn, right? You can't start off a genius, or there's no point."

"They pay you to be an optimist. That's your job," Audrey said, then squinted. Sweet Jesus, she was socially inappropriate.

"Sure," the lady said. "Between the malpractice insurance and Blue Cross, I'm a billionaire. Take care, and go to the hospital if you have an emergency. Bellevue's the best, if you live near there. If they're full, try NYU at 34th and First."

"Thanks."

Audrey hung up, then looked at the black phone. Her desk walls were adorned with a David Hockney calendar for creative inspiration, two Parkside Plaza sketches, a photo of her and Saraub at the Long Beach Boardwalk in February, and the framed *New York Times* twelve-line article about her New York Emerging Voices Award in Architecture. Their sizes varied, but she'd assembled them so that their corners aligned, and the spaces between them were equidistant. Her pens were arrayed in a jar by color and thickness of tip. Her desk reeked of bleach because at least once a day, she swiped it with Clorox. In her lap, she noticed that her hands were not evenly placed. She separated them now, so that each hand held an equal amount of each corresponding thigh, and her thighs were equidistant apart, too.

"Crap," she moaned. For how many years had she been like this? Triple-checking that the toaster was unplugged, worrying that the floor would open, lingering in bed some mornings, because she was afraid the day would bring something that she couldn't tame by rearranging it into right angles? Of course this was physical. How could she have gone so long without getting a second opinion?

As if willing it to do so, the black phone rang. She picked it up, a welcome escape. "Hello?"

Saraub's voice. "Aud—" She hung up. The phone rang again. She took it off the hook. Her cell phone chirped. She pulled out its battery, too unnerved to spend the time turning it off. It didn't matter what he had to say; apology or condemnation, the sound of his voice would start her bawling.

She put down her drafting pencil and did something she'd sworn she'd never do at any job, ever. Not even when the high-school kids at IHOP smeared her face with Reddi-Whip, or when she'd organized all the Jell-Os at the college dining hall by color, and the fry cook had told her, "You're pretty weird. Like somebody broke you, and you keep trying to put yourself back together, only you do it wrong. You know?"

She ran into the Vesuvius bathroom and cried in a stall. When she got out she saw Jill at the mirror. Her eyes were also red and swollen. They nodded at each other, then Audrey headed out. Before she got to the door, Jill called her back. "Audrey?"

"Yeah?"

"Are you okay?" she asked, wiping her hands on her trousers, because the women's room never had towels.

Audrey shook her head. "No."

"Me, neither," Jill said.

"Well, that's some consolation," Audrey answered.

Jill's somberness cracked, and she gave Audrey a lopsided grin. "Cute," she said, then peeled open her purse and applied a coat of jarring, bright red lipstick, as if to let Audrey know she was excused.

Audrey lingered, thinking about what Collier had said over lunch. "I'm sorry your son is sick," she said, then headed out.

Before she got to the door, Jill stopped her. "Audrey?" she asked.

"Yes?"

"Thank you." She seemed genuinely touched, like it was the first time anyone at the office had offered their sympathy. Audrey nodded, and started out. As she opened the door, Jill called, "Take care of yourself. Whatever it is that's troubling you . . ." She paused for a second, and Audrey understood that the sentiment bore a specific, human-sized weight: "It will pass. Good or bad, nothing lasts."

For once, Audrey thought before she acted, and chose not to speak but instead to nod.

When she got back to her desk, she rolled open the plans and began calculating distances between hedges and the building's internal plumbing. She worked until her shaking stopped, and her worries left. After a while, she got lost in it, as only someone with OCD can do.

An hour passed. And then another. Pretty soon, she looked up at the clock, and saw that it was eight o'clock. Most of the lights in the office were out, the cleaning staff was vacuuming near her feet, and upon the blueprints, she'd drawn nearly a hundred doors.

12

Girls' Night Out (Everybody Screws Up, Sometimes)

As Audrey keyed her way back into 14B at The Breviary, Jayne came thumping out of 14E on a pair of wooden crutches. On one foot she wore a strappy, three-inch black stiletto. On the other she wore a green wool knee-high sock. Beneath the sock, an Ace bandage peeked. She pointed the socked foot at Audrey's trim waist, like she was challenging her to a karate foot duel. "Lady!" she cried.

Audrey was in no mood. She'd had enough crazy for one day. Besides, this was nutty. Jayne must have been listening for the sound of Audrey's jingling keys all evening.

Jayne wiggled her toes inside her socked foot. "Lady!" she repeated nervously, like this wasn't the first time she'd stalked a new friend, and if she got ignored right now, or insulted, that wouldn't be new, either.

Audrey put her out of her misery. "Tramp!"

At 14C, the same old woman who'd worn the vintage dressing gown this morning opened her door and stuck out her nose. Not her face, but her small, sharp nose, and a spill of glossy white hair. On the other side of 14B, at 14A, another door opened a crack—just enough for Audrey to see the tip of a gender-indeterminate, old, and sun-damaged forehead. The moment was surreal. Just as quickly, both doors closed.

Jayne dropped her socked foot gently to the floor. "I fell," she announced. "Now it's sprained. My knee. I'm a gimp. I'm still appearing at the Laugh Factory Saturday night. Wild horses couldn't drag me. This shit happens all the time, but you've got to keep going, you know? You can't ever give up . . . can you?" Jayne looked up at Audrey with tears in her green eyes and Audrey thought: *This woman is a raw nerve of emotions. More aptly put, this woman is plain raw, like skin rubbed so tender it's bleeding.*

"No. You can't ever give up, Jayne. I'm so sorry. What happened?"

Jayne wiped the water from eyes by running her thumbs just under the skin of her lower lashes so she didn't smudge her makeup, which looked like it might have been applied with a spatula. For the first time in a long while, Audrey was tempted to touch another person. So she did. She put her hand on Jayne's bony shoulder, then wasn't quite sure what to do with it.

Smiling brightly, but with a quivering voice, Jayne said, "Cab hit me on my way to work. I didn't sleep well—I've been having nightmares for a while now. So, anyway, I wasn't looking when I crossed the street. Like an idiot. I'm so stupid!" She shook her head in disgust, still wearing that uncomfortably bright smile. "I rolled over the hood, like a stunt man or something. I'm all scraped up, but nothing serious except a bruised knee-cap," she said, then her voice got higher pitched, like at any second it would crack. "Wouldn't you know it? I have a big break on the eve of my big break?"

"That's awful," Rachael said. To her surprise, tears pooled in her own eyes, too. What a crappy thing to happen to such a sweet, fragile girl. "Did they catch the driver?"

"No. Some towel-head Indian guy. They should deport them all back to Iran. Bomb that whole desert into a sheet of glass."

Audrey frowned. "India, or Iran?"

Jayne nodded. "That's right, I forgot. Indians are from India. Whoever's hoarding those nukes. That's who hit me . . . The thing is, I'm so funny, Addie—do you mind if I call you that?"

"I guess not." Audrey dropped her hand from Jayne's shoulder. *Bad idea, this touching thing.*

"Good. I like Addie better. Audrey's so uptight, and you're so cool."

Audrey smiled. She'd been called a lot of things in her life. Cool was a welcome newcomer.

Jayne kept talking. "You wouldn't believe how funny I am. Really, you wouldn't. This won't slow me down. I'll make it part of the routine. They'll piss their pants."

"Of course they will," Audrey said.

Jayne grinned so sweetly that Audrey grinned, too. "I KNEW you were awesome. Are we still having dinner? I'm starved."

The idea was tempting. But she was tired, and not sure she could hold herself erect while Jayne blabbermouthed her way through an entire meal. "Sure," she finally said, deciding she'd prefer the company.

She opened the door to apartment 14B, then remembered the thing she'd built inside the open closet door and stopped short.

"What's wrong?" Jayne asked.

She let out a breath. Impossible to explain. Still, it

was far away, down the long hall and in the den. Maybe she could hide it before Jayne saw. Maybe Jayne was so batty she wouldn't even notice it.

"Is it boys?" Jayne asked.

Audrey was about to shake her head, then realized that yes, in a way, it was boys. "Yeah . . ."

"Are you okay?"

Audrey looked at the brass lettering that read 14B. The movers had left a black skid mark, which she wiped clean with the heel of her palm. "No. I don't think I am. I've got obsessive-compulsive disorder, and it makes me do things. I never got treated for it, but I guess I should have. There are other problems, too." This was a perfect stranger. She couldn't believe she'd confessed such a thing. For cripe's sake, she'd never even been able to say it to Saraub. But maybe that was why she was saying it now. Because she *should* have told him.

"Does OCD make you sleep around?" Jayne asked.

Audrey laughed in a quick burst, then sobered when she realized Jayne was serious. She walked into the apartment, and Jayne followed at her heels like an eager puppy, so she broke into a jog, and widened the distance between them. Jayne couldn't keep up.

"Sorry. Was that stupid? I was thinking maybe it compelled you to go home with strangers. That's a compulsion, right?" Jayne called down the long hall.

Audrey jogged. The doors to the empty rooms were open. Their white paint shone. "No. It's just funny, because I was a virgin until two and a half years ago," she called, so worried about hiding the door, that she was more honest with Jayne than she'd intended.

Behind her, the sound Jayne's crutches made was a light *clip-clop!* followed by the slipping sound of her sock as she dragged it along the floor. "Oh. Not me. I lost my virginity when I was twelve." Jayne twittered.

"Really?" Audrey asked, though she wasn't paying

attention. She was in the den now, looking at the door. It was smooth and strong, and charged in a way that spread pins and needles through her fingertips. The cardboard fibers were soft as sparse feathers. She'd planned to tear it apart and let the boxes tumble into a pile once the tape was gone, but now that seemed like a waste. All it needed was a handle and frame.

Clip-clop-Slip!

Jayne. The sound got closer, and Audrey shoved the closet closed just as Jayne limped through the hall and inside the den. She was talking, and Audrey realized she'd been talking for a while now.

"—are so mean. I have an act about it: 'Men you dated who never called: pretend they died.' Not so clever, but you have to admit it's true. I've got, like, fifty dead boyfriends."

Jayne's crutches shrieked against the hardwood. It was strange having her here. Like her organs—her stomach and lungs and heart and even her brain, weren't inside anymore. They were on display, her body an open autopsy. She wasn't used to guests. She wanted to be alone.

I want to finish the door, she thought.

"Stuffy," Jayne said, and headed with her crutches toward the turret. She tried to pry it open, but it wouldn't budge. Audrey watched, infuriated. What was this woman doing, touching *her stuff*?

The wormlike thing she'd swallowed when she first walked into this den unfurled, as if stretching awake. This thing, she knew it was her imagination. A fleeting obsession that in a day or week or month would disappear, only to be replaced by something just as outlandish. Such was the nature of her disease. Still, it *felt* real.

With a final shove, Jayne pushed open the turret window. Stained-glass blackbirds with red eyes lifted and doubled on themselves. A crisp fall breeze rushed the room. Fresh air replaced stagnant dust. The change was good. The thing in her stomach went still.

"There!" Jayne exclaimed. "So, can we eat here? I've been cooped up all day."

"But I don't have any furniture," Audrey said.

"Got any food?"

Audrey shook her head. "I got lint. That's about it. Maybe this was a bad idea."

Jayne balanced on her crutches, then clicked open her cell phone. "No way! It's a great idea! Chinese. Speed dial. It comes fastest. What do you want?"

Audrey sighed, and surrendered. "General Tsao's Chicken?"

Jayne placed the order, and added steamed string beans with garlic for herself. "I'm on a diet, so I can only eat every fourth meal. You would not believe how hungry I am right now!" she mouthed while waiting for the guy on the other line to provide a dollar tally.

After she clicked the phone closed, Jayne surveyed the mattress and coat-turned–sleeping blanket, and the ten-year-old box television and piano bench on which it was perched. "You need stuff," she said. "We should go shopping before my act at Laugh Factory this weekend. It's kind of *Zombie Apocalypse Meets the Olsen Twins* in here, you know?"

Audrey pulled two folding chairs that she'd found in the kitchen closet and arranged them in front of the turret. "You think it's creepy?"

Jayne eased herself into the chair and perched her injured foot up on the ledge. "Totally! You should wash the walls with bleach to clear the bad psychic residue. Fuckin' A, you should set a Raid bomb off in this place. That lady was like a roach, anyway."

"You knew her?" Audrey asked.

Jayne nodded. Her foundation and blue eye shadow were cartoonishly thick, like a Mary Kay lady from

1986. Up close, Audrey could see chicken pox scars under her makeup, as if her cheeks and forehead had been scored by a putty knife.

"What was she like?"

Jayne sighed. "She was supposed to have this great voice. All the papers wrote about it, like since she had a talent that never got expressed because she turned into a murderer, it was tragic that she died. Like it's less tragic when normal murderers die. My sister is a nuclear physicist. She invented those bacteria that eat oil spills in the Arctic. She's got double my IQ. I've got a below-average IQ, but I'll bet you guessed that. Anyway, nuclear physicist. You'd think that was a made-up job, wouldn't you?"

Audrey shrugged. "Maybe she lied. She's really a fry cook at Sizzler."

Jayne beamed. "Exactly! You're funny, too. I could tell the second we met, that you were funny and cool."

"It's true. Most popular girl in Hinton, Iowa," Audrey said. She meant this to be a joke, but Jayne didn't laugh.

"Obviously. I'd kill for those cheekbones. You don't even dye your hair, do you? Natural brunette."

Audrey winced. It took her a few seconds before she was sure Jayne wasn't teasing. Then she laughed. "Thanks, Jayne."

"Like a model! Anyway, for all that buildup, I never heard her sing. Just the kid. The girl. Clara's daughter—"

The sound of the monster's name dried the saliva from Audrey's mouth.

"—The kid used to knock on the walls in the halls singing 'Hard knock life.' She was Annie in the school play. You know: 'It's the hard knock life, for us! Steada kisses, We! Get! Kicks! When you're in an or! phan! age!'" Jayne sang-spoke the words Henry Higgins-style. Her high-pitched voice was surprisingly dulcet.

"—Cute thing. Really cute. If she was older, I'd have

given her a free minibottle of champagne, but not the mom. She could drink Tidy Bowl toilet water for all I care. And then one day . . ." Jayne's voice cracked. "And then I came home, and the hallway was wet, because the emergency workers' boots were soaked in all that water."

Audrey squeezed her hands into fists and looked out the window. The blackbirds, doubled on top of each other in the open window, looked like they'd been captured inside the glass. Those poor fucking kids.

"Did you have any idea?" Audrey asked.

Jayne pushed down her green sock and unwound the Ace bandage beneath it. Then she pressed her fingers against the wet wound, which was blotted with iodine and green wool sock threads. She pulled the wet threads, strand by strand, from the clot. Squeamish, Audrey averted her eyes.

"I've been through a lot, you know? So I should have guessed. But who imagines something like that? It's unthinkable." She pulled another thread, and looked at it as if fascinated. Then dropped it to her lap, and pulled another. The clot broke open and began to ooze.

"Is that why the rent is so cheap?" Audrey asked.

Jayne shrugged. "I moved in the same time she did. Before we came, it was only owners. We're the first renters they've ever had. They might not know any better . . . Since she died, I get nightmares."

Audrey was looking out the window. She could see the dark top floors of the Parkside Plaza. A lot of people had died when the bomb went off. When you considered all the tragedies that happened, it made the whole world seem haunted. "Do you ever see a man wearing a three-piece—" she started to ask, but Jayne interrupted her.

"I know what we need! Would you mind going to my place and getting some wine? I've got a bottle of red on the kitchen counter. Same layout as 14B, except not so *Romero Meets Cronenberg: Smackdown!*"

Audrey started from her chair. She decided that she liked having Jayne around. It was better than being alone. By a mile. "I'd be happy to. Do you mind my going in there without you?"

"Pffft!" Jayne said. "Hell, no!"

"Don't I need your keys?"

Jayne shook her head. "I never lock it. What are they going to do? Steal my plastic Mardi Gras beads? The people in this building own Picassos, the salty dogs. Old money and bad surgery. You can dress a hag in Dior, but you can't make her a Cover Girl."

"Totally! The lady next door is a mutant."

"Oh, yeah. Mrs. Parker in 14C. The writer. Well, critic, I think. She only calls herself a writer. She drinks, that's why those funny clothes. They all drink. Too much inheritance and not enough small dogs to spend it on. So, wine?"

"Okay! Wine!" Audrey giggled, and started down the hall. As she walked, she closed the bedroom and kitchen doors. Open things, she'd never liked them. Like something half-done, or an invitation to the unknown.

Jayne's apartment was brighter, but not by much. It faced north and gave a view of Columbia University's Miller Library. The air was just as oppressive, though, and the place reeked of cigarette smoke, too. The master-bedroom door was open, and she saw that the white sheets and satin, hot pink comforter were unmade. A foam mattress sealed in what looked like a rubber sheet peeked out from under the pink . . . Was Jayne a bed wetter, too?

In the spare bedroom were stacks of magazines arranged into piles (*Entertainment Weekly, Vanity Fair, Variety, Star, OK!, People*). There wasn't any furniture save a pink Pier I satellite chair—small and cumbersome, as if made for a little girl rather than a grown woman. In the kitchen were more ashtrays, all full. She'd smoked the butts down to the filter, not a speck left of white. A beach shell full of Winstons lay half-submerged in gray, ashy water at the bottom of the kitchen sink. Apparently, Jayne didn't have many guests, either.

The wine and a couple of clean glasses were on the counter, along with a thin line of red ants that crawled up through a crack in the backsplash. She smooshed them with her fingers, then picked up what she needed, and surveyed the apartment. Except for Saraub and Betty, she'd never been inside someone's apartment by herself. It was nice to be trusted this way. Then she remembered that right now Jayne was alone in 14B, maybe peeking in closets (the door!), so she hurried along, and searched for a bottle opener. She found it clipped to the old GE refrigerator by the *Sex and the City* magnetic poetry (*Cock-a-Doodle-Dooo! 30 is the new twenty! Mine is bigger than yours!*).

Also on the GE were about ten photos of redheads ranging in age from infant to octogenarian. Related, clearly. Blue eyes and fair skin. A huge family of cousins aunts, uncles, parents, and siblings. There was also a single, recurring brunette in every photo. She stood back from the others and did not smile. Audrey pulled the "Cock-a-doodle" magnet, and lifted an overexposed Technicolor that looked like it had been snapped in the 1980s. Jayne. The brunette's small features looked mouselike rather than delicate, and she squinted at the camera, a duck among swans. "Jayne, sweet Jayne," Audrey clucked, then replaced the photo. No wonder she dyed her hair red.

Before she left, Audrey quickly sponged the counters clean of ants, crumbs, dried coffee, and ashes. She'd never been good at explaining it, especially not to her freshman college roommate, who'd kicked her out after a month, but straightening things for the people she cared about was her way of protecting them. When everything was in its proper place, there wasn't room for bad stuff to creep through.

She reached 14B with the bottle just as the intercom buzzed, and Chinese food arrived. Jayne was sitting quietly when she returned. She seemed calmer than when they'd met in the hall a half hour ago. Maybe making friends was hard for her, too.

They dug in. Her General Tsao's was mostly beef grease and MSG, but it did the job and plugged the hole in her grumbling stomach. She finished half the container without looking up.

To her left, Jayne puckered her nose at the green beans but didn't eat them, then slugged the wine. "Can I have some of yours?" she asked.

"Trade," Audrey said, and they exchanged cartons.

"Want to watch TV?" Audrey asked after a while. She felt like she was on a date. What do two women do together when they're alone? She shouldn't have paid for dinner. Now Jayne had probably gotten the wrong impression, and decided they were going to become lady lesbians.

"Not unless you do. I watched it all day. Luke and Laura are fossilized now. *General Hospital* with mummies. I used to sneak the soaps when I was a kid because that kind of thing wasn't allowed where I come from—I'm Mormon. Now I'm thinking of suing ABC for making me stupid. Either that, or Bumble Bee tuna fish. My mom ate it when she was pregnant with me, and I think the mercury gave me brain damage."

"Oh." Audrey had never seen a soap opera, except the Spanish ones at the Laundromat on Amsterdam

Avenue. Lots of close-ups of lone tears streaming down maudlin cheeks. Out the window, the Parkside Plaza was the only building in the 59th Street row whose top lights were dark. The scaffolding only went to the forty-fifth floor, and not all the debris had been cleared. For months after the bombing, people had found human bones strewn all over the block.

" . . . I had to give a presentation today," Audrey said.

Jayne beamed. Her pockmarks were more evident near her smile, where the blood drained and her skin went taut. "You did? What happened?"

"I kind of freaked out at first. I saw something . . . But then it was okay. Everybody liked it. Even my horrible boss, who was supposed to be the one to give it."

Jayne clicked her glass against Audrey's. "Hooray, Audrey! Boo, hiss, bad boss!"

Audrey lifted her glass and took a sip. "Thanks," she said. She suddenly felt warm, and happy. She'd been very lonely this last month, and because of that she'd acted more squirrelly than usual. Funny, but she only realized that now, after lunch with the boys, and now dinner with Jayne, when she wasn't lonely anymore. "The thing I saw . . . Did you say you were having trouble sleep—"

Jayne cut her off. "You know what my problem is? I'm needy. I'll call, like five times in a day. It's crazy. I can't help myself. I know how it looks to a guy. I'm this hyperlunatic with wrinkles and a bad job, but I can't help it."

"Oh, you're all right," Audrey said.

"I'm skinny at least. That's important. Not as skinny as you, but skinny."

Audrey looked at herself. Jayne was right. If she wanted, she could pull her skirt down over her butt without unzipping it. The result wasn't flattering. In the mirror at work today, her face had seemed gaunt and her eyes sunken unrecognizably deep: she'd looked old. "Have you gone on any dates lately?" Audrey asked. Something told her the answer was yes, and that they'd been a train wreck.

Jayne bit the sides of her cheeks and rolled both eyes. "A few losers. There's this one guy I like. He's kind of a senior if you know what I mean. That's not so terrible is it? Do you think it's terrible?"

Audrey shrugged. "Depends. Does he wear Depends?"

Jayne clapped her hands together in delight at the very thought of him. "Probably. He's so old! But he's good to me. I'm being superstitious this time and not talking about him until I'm sure . . . Wait! What's your man problem? Don't you have one, too?" Jayne asked. She slurped as she drank, even though the wine was in a glass. Not an easy task.

Audrey thought about the fight last night, and her time at the Golden Nugget, and the years she'd known Saraub before that. She summed them up. "I'm a jerk," she said. "But he's no saint."

"Commitment?" Jayne asked.

"How did you know?"

Jayne nodded. "Because in a breakup, somebody's always the jerk, and somebody else is always needy. I'd rather be on your side than mine."

"Naw. It sounds like the better side, but it's not."

"Yeah, but I'm like the walking wounded over here. My bruises have bruises," Jayne quipped. The joke fell flat because it was so clearly true.

"Yeah, but people like you will wind up with somebody, because you're open. You're out there taking risks," Audrey said. Then she looked down at her coffee-stained shirt. Her hands were poised over her lap, the exact distance apart. Perfectly even. Next to her, Jayne was slumped in her chair, limbs akimbo, her teeth stained red with wine. It dawned on her that while Jayne would probably break free of this strange, lonely, single-woman existence in New York, she would not, because she was on the wrong side of the fight. She was the jerk.

She reached into her pockets for consolation and was alarmed to find nothing there. The ring! She took it everywhere. Not once since he'd given it to her had she let it out of her sight. So where was it? Still in yesterday's pants? She tried to sit still, but the compulsion overcame her. She hurried to the double closet, exposed the half-built door, then bent down and pulled yesterday's trousers free from the towel she'd wrapped them in. A sharp thing inside their damp, ammonia pockets cut her knuckle. She grabbed it hard, and tucked it inside her skirt pocket like a secret. When she returned to Jayne, she was crying. Little sniffles and hitches in this cavernous, terrifying apartment. "I screwed up," she said.

Jayne scooted in her chair (*Screetch! Screetch! Jiggle!*), then leaned over and rubbed Audrey's back with the heel of her hand. The gesture was comforting enough to allow her to release and cry harder.

"I screw up, like, twice a day. My dad says I'm a bigger disappointment than his dog, which is dead, by the way. A dead pit bull named Pudge, and I'm the disappointment."

Audrey laughed a little, while still crying.

"Everybody screws up unless they're boring," Jayne said.

"Have you ever screwed up, and it was because you loved them so much?" Audrey asked.

Jayne leaned to the other side of her chair, reached down, and took a quick slug of wine. Then she returned. "No man wants to get to know me that well unless he's related. I never get that far."

"Oh. Sorry."

"That's okay. I'm not jealous," Jayne said. "Everybody's different. I gave up jealous a long time ago because I'm not good at anything except comedy."

"That's not true," Audrey said.

Jayne shrugged. "I sound like a Sad Sally, don't I? Who cares. How did you screw up?"

Audrey sniffled. "He proposed, and I said yes. But then I got scared, because I have this problem, we both have problems, so I said no, and I moved out," she explained.

"The OCD?"

Audrey heaved her breath one last time, then brought herself under control. "I guess. I'm coming unhinged lately. This apartment—I might really be crazy."

"That's too bad," Jayne said. Then she leaned to her side, refilled both glasses, and handed one to Audrey. The act was natural, and Audrey wondered if it came from growing up surrounded by family.

"I hope you don't mind that we just met, and I'm telling you my problems," she said.

Jayne shrugged. "I'm in the market for more friends. Eight brothers and sisters, and I'm the only one still single. Oh, hey! I know what'll cheer you up! A game!" Jayne leaned back and scratched her knee. It was a real raspberry of hurt: her fingers came away glistening red.

Without thinking about it, Audrey folded a take-out napkin to its clean side, and handed it to her. "Stop picking at yourself," she said.

Jayne nodded, like she'd heard the line a thousand times before, and it no longer registered. She dabbed the napkin against the broken clot. "What's the most embarrassing thing that ever happened to you?" she asked.

Audrey shook her head. "Thinking about something like that does not make me feel better Jayne, just so you know."

"It will. It always works. Trust me. Normally I'd

throw out some stock bullshit for a laugh, but I'll give you something real. I'll give you my tenth most embarrassing thing." She leaned back, and giggled. The sound was pure delight.

"Tenth? You count?"

Her reply was serious. "It's very important, the stuff you find shameful. Funny should come close to hurting, or it's just slapstick. I've studied funny." The lights of the city reflected in her green eyes and she stretched out the silence to make sure she had Audrey's full attention. Showmanship. It made Audrey curious about her act.

"Okay," Jayne finally said. "This happened a lifetime ago. I'd just run away to New York, and I was going crazy because it was so free, and different from Salt Lake. My hair was purple, if you can picture that. Superpunk. I was waiting tables at the old Howard Johnson on Broadway, and living in that girls' dormitory on the Upper West Side. I used to walk the city and watch people when I had time off. I'd look at them and think, they don't know, but one day I'll be famous."

"Anyway, I was a real baby face, so I had to use a fake ID to get into the comedy clubs. The laminated kind you used to buy in Times Square that said, 'OFFICIAL IDENTIFICATION CARD'—you probably don't remember them, but they were about as real as three-dollar bills. Anyway, this one night I went to Caroline's Comedy Club, and met this guy who'd been on *Letterman*. Twice! It was like talking to a famous person. So I went home with him."

Audrey sat up, shocked. "How old were you?"

Jayne smiled like a sphinx. "Fifteen."

Audrey paled. She had a hard time imagining being in this city at such a tender age. The metaphor it brought to mind was: lamb for slaughter.

Jayne continued. "Anyway, the guy took me to this rent-controlled palace on the Upper West Side. He'd grown up in New York, so he inherited it. That's how those people get trapped. Same with the folks who live in The Breviary. They inherit, and then they never have to work real jobs, so they forget how. They don't even have any kids. They're the last of their lines. We ought to get in good with them. We could inherit the whole building! Anyway, he gave me a few drinks—screwdrivers, maybe? After that, he showed me how to blow coke up his ass, and then he did it for me. Best high of my life."

Audrey shook her head back and forth. "That's really gross."

Jayne nodded. "Especially when you're allergic, because your colon spazzes. I pooped his bed. Then I was so embarrassed I ran out. Never even gave him my number. Maybe he's my soul mate, but I had to leave because I pooped the bed. Fancy slate gray sheets, I'll never forget."

The seconds passed. Audrey didn't know what to say. Was she supposed to console Jayne? Was this some kind of test? What a terrible story! Worse, it was rehearsed. She'd told it before! Finally, Audrey couldn't help it. Laughter burst, then roared from her chest. "No . . . no way," she said between breaths.

"Way," Jayne said, laughing, too.

"Couldn't you have made it to the toilet?" tears came to the corners of her eyes.

"No," Jayne said. Now she was laughing really hard. "Huuh. Huuuh. I thought I was all sexy, and then . . ." Her face got splotchy, apple red. "It fell right out! Too late to do anything but run."

"Oh shit!" Audrey cried.

"Exactly!" Jayne screamed.

Audrey was laughing so hard that her stomach hurt. "I'm embarrassed for you right now, just thinking about that," Audrey said. "You just made me vicariously embarrassed."

"Yeah. I'm embarrassed, too. Good thing it wasn't

my nose or it could have been a lot worse. I don't know if I was allergic to the coke or something it was cut with, but I bled for a while. Everybody tells you that can't happen the first time. But it did happen to someone. It happened to me."

Audrey flinched. This part wasn't so funny. "Oh . . . That sucks."

"So did his dry-cleaning bill."

"He deserved it. You were too young. I hope he got E. coli poisoning and wound up in a hospital."

Jayne snickered. "Fifteen isn't that young."

Audrey shook her head. "No Jayne, it's too young. You were a girl."

Jayne inspected her wounded knee, basking in Audrey's concern. Then she clapped her hands together. "What's your most embarrassing thing?"

Audrey shook her head to both sides, fast. Once, twice, three times, four. "I think I repressed it. I can't remember."

Jayne kicked up her good foot. "Come on! Don't be a sissy. You've got one."

Audrey sighed. Her smile faltered.

"Come on!" Jayne whined.

Audrey looked out the window. The collateral damage to the lit-up buildings on either side of the Parkside Plaza had been repaired after the explosion, but if you looked closely, you could see the difference between the old concrete seams and the new ones. She felt her neck. Smooth, unblemished skin. No one would ever guess she'd once been cut. "Okay. I've got something, but I'm not good at stories, like you. It's not a story. And it's not funny, either."

Jayne's smiled stretched ear to ear at the compliment. "Of course not! I'm a professional. Tell me!"

Audrey's voice echoed in the apartment, and she had the feeling that something in the walls was listening.

"I was thinking about how young you were, and I remembered, I was pretty young, once, too. You ever go hungry?"

"All the time," Jayne answered.

Audrey sipped her wine. Absurdly sweet stuff. The sugar alone would induce a hangover. "Yeah. It's worse when it's not by choice. It's not like how they say, you know? You don't get fuzzy when you're starving."

"Really?" Jayne asked.

"First it's fuzzy, but then things clarify. Everything distills. You ache. Your fingernails hurt. You want calories so bad that even the air tastes like sugar. But it feels good, too. It feels like flying."

"Like you're high?" Jayne asked.

"Better, I think. Little instants of better when you're not trapped in your body like everybody else. You're free from it, and numb. Things you'd normally be sad about don't matter. The rest of the time, it hurts. Like there's this hole in you, that keeps growing . . . My mom left once, for six weeks. And I was starving like that. It was the worst feeling of my life."

"Wow," Jayne said.

Audrey had forgotten about most of this, but now, it all came back. Like a scab reopened, the pain was surprisingly fresh. She felt her throat as she spoke. "My mom is bipolar." It still hurt to say this, even after all these years.

"I'm sorry," Jayne said.

"Me, too." Once again, she'd surprised herself. Her voice sounded bitter. Unkind.

"Anyway, the disease worked in cycles. I came home one day and found her tearing up the kitchen floor with a chef knife she'd stolen from a neighbor. A serious German number, sharp enough to cut through bone. She kept saying she was digging—she thought something bad was down there. In the hole. I remember being so upset, but mad, too. I liked that double-wide, and we got kicked out for what she'd done. And I kept thinking, you know? Maybe it would have been better if she'd turned that knife on herself instead.

"She cut me with that knife. On purpose. Not deep or anything. It was more just upsetting. It was the first time she'd ever done anything like that, and she never did it again, either. But afterward, I hated sleeping in the same room with her. I couldn't trust her anymore."

She hadn't thought about this in a long time, and she knew there was more to the story than she remembered. Something about the hole in the floor, and her mother's ants. Something about her dream.

"It must have scared her when she saw the blood on my neck, because she ran off. Six weeks. That was the longest she was ever gone. I kept expecting her to come back, but she never did. Those asshole neighbors at that park didn't share. I was so skinny my knees didn't touch, and they never even offered their leftovers because they didn't like my mom. She'd done stupid stuff like spray-paint their cars and steal their newspapers, and she slept with a few husbands. They wouldn't forgive her for it. Really, they wouldn't forgive her for being crazy. They were scared it might be contagious. Like one of those sick houses during the Black Plague in Europe. They nailed human skulls to their doors, so people knew not to come knocking. Everyplace we ever lived felt marked like that. Like a sick house."

She leaned back, suddenly ashamed that she'd started this story. It was a real downer. Not remotely funny. "I stopped going to school—I'd enrolled that semester, passed into my junior year even though I'd missed tenth grade. I started working full-time instead. I told myself it was the freedom, but looking back, I think I was just ashamed. She'd abandoned me. Most kids, their parents care enough to teach them things, and show up."

"So what happened?" Jayne asked.

"She came·back. I still don't know why I took her back after all the things she'd done. I'd moved by then, and the new place was pretty bad, but we didn't stay long. We found another town. Except for when I ran away to college at U of N and she couldn't find me, I took care of her for twelve more years after that . . . I should have left," Audrey said, shocked by the words as she spoke them, and by her tears, too. She'd thought she'd outgrown self-pity. "I should have let her die. I'd have been better off."

Jayne didn't say anything. Audrey wiped her eyes. She thought about taking it back, but she didn't. That dream last night, that sad girl. It was time to stop hating her. "So, that's my embarrassing story. I got abandoned. A lot. Sorry it's not funny."

"That's okay," Jayne said. She didn't seem shocked, like Audrey always expected people to be when she told them about how she'd grown up. But everybody's got troubles. Even rich people in cashmere suits. Maybe they had OCD, or a kid with cancer, or couldn't find love. Or they were the black sheep of their families for no good reason. It's such hubris to think your problems are bigger than the person's sitting next to you, just because they have the fortitude not to complain.

Audrey sat back. The night had gotten late. It was past eleven. She felt heavy, and tired. But good, too. She liked Jayne. "On the plus side, my growth got stunted, so I didn't have to deal with having a period until college. Actually, I have no idea if I can have children."

"That's not funny! That's sad. I'm so sad for you!" Jayne exclaimed.

"Are you trying to tell me that the coke thing is happy?" Audrey asked with a raised eyebrow. "Because it sounds pretty bad, country mouse."

A beat of silence passed. Then two. Jayne laughed

first, and was quickly followed by Audrey. "It's the hard-knock life," Audrey said, and Jayne banged the floor with her crutch, and chimed in: "For! Us!"

And then, together. "It's the hard-knock life!" They laughed hard and long. Tears filled Audrey's eyes, and she wasn't sure whether she was sad, or happy, but the release felt wonderful.

"We are *so* fucked up," Jayne declared, and they laughed harder.

13

Humans Raised as Cows!

By glass two-point-five, they were loaded. The wine was so cheap that Audrey's headache had already started. Her dried-out tongue was stuck to the roof of her mouth, so she took another sip to set it free. On the television, Leno was reading nutty-but-true newspaper headlines— "Humans Raised As Cows Graze the Countryside!"—when the buzzer rang.

Audrey hoisted herself up on wobbly legs. The stained-glass crows looked like they were following her. Their red eyes shone especially bright. "Demon birds," she mumbled.

Jayne waved her hand. "It's Clara. She wants to raid your fridge. Chick was an orca. Like the woolly mammoth, I mean."

"Whale." Audrey simultaneously pressed talk and listen on the intercom. She could vaguely detect the doorman's French-Haitian accent, but it was mostly just static: *blah blah blah Mizz Lucas?* She had no idea what he wanted, but it could wait until tomorrow.

"Okay, good!" she said into the speaker, then staggered back to her chair and clawed a handful of string beans into her mouth. They were overcooked, and liquefied on her tongue. They were hot, too, and like everything hot and soupy, hurt the gums under her temporary crown. "Vegetables are bullshit!" she announced.

Jay's guest was sweating through an act about terrorists with funny accents using canned city smog as a weapon. US 405 in Los Angeles had gotten another bomb threat this afternoon. No one was hurt, but the traffic jam caused two asthma-induced deaths.

Audrey glanced at the pull-down map of Los Angeles behind the man and admired the clean perpendicular roads that counterbalanced its jagged coast and highways. That got her thinking about changing the topiary on 59th Street to something less symmetrical because unless they've got OCD, too many right angles make people nervous.

The comedian sprayed his bottle of Aqua Net, over which he'd pasted a smog label illustrated by a black death skull and crossbones. Not a laugh in the whole house. A fury rose inside her, and she wanted to reach inside the television and slap him.

"Amateur," Jayne grumbled. Then she cupped her hands around her mouth like a megaphone. "Too soon!" she heckled.

"What is this, Beirut?" Audrey asked. "I don't wanna live in Beirut."

"Like the band? That song 'No More Words'?" Jayne asked.

"No, that's Berlin."

"I don't wanna live in Berlin," Jayne said.

"Well, who asked you?"

They were laughing when the doorbell rang, and Jayne

hopped up in her lone high heel, leaving her crutches on the floor. "It's Jay Leno!" she announced. "He needs me to save his ass."

"You know, a boot would be better for your knee," Audrey said.

"Better than Leno? I do *not* think so," Jayne said as she hopped down the hall.

Still seated, Audrey scooted in her chair until she turned 180 degrees. "Are you answering my door?" she asked. "It's very rude."

Jayne's face was pressed against the peephole. "It's a guy. He's really big. Like he could lift a car."

Audrey's ears got hot. "Brown skin? Short black hair?"

"Yup."

Audrey got up and walked down the hall. Jayne stepped aside. She didn't look through the peephole. She was afraid he'd able to see her eye.

"Audrey, you in there? I need to talk to you." This time, he didn't slur.

She turned and started in the other direction. Jayne hopped after her. "Are you going to open it?"

Audrey stopped and leaned against a wall in the hall. *Clack-clack!*

He banged the knocker, and they both jumped. Then he used his fists: *Bam! Bam!* "Please. Let me in. It's important." The sound of his voice resonated in her chest. She wished she could be like the normal people of the world who, in her place, would probably not want to pee their pants right now or smoke so much hash they saw stars.

"Audrey!" he called again. She got the feeling he could see her through the wood. Right into the hall, and her eyes, all the way to the curved sockets of her skull. Into her thoughts. She touched her throat, and thought, *I'm wounded, and you know it. So why do you keep knocking?*

She pressed her cheek against cool plaster. Jayne

leaned against the opposing wall and wrapped her arms around her waist like a lonely hug.

"Does he hit you?" Jayne whispered with the phlegmy rasp of a habitual smoker. In the gray light, her eyes shone bright and wet. Audrey understood then, why Jayne called men five times a day. She needed reassurance. She expected the worst from them because the worst was all she'd ever known.

Oh, Jayne, you poor thing, she thought. She considered taking the girl's hand in her own, but it wasn't her way to touch other people, so instead she matched Jayne's honesty with her own. "He's never hit me, but I worry. He holds it in. I'm afraid he'll burst. He used to hit the walls when I wasn't home . . . There's this place in his study nook with holes in the drywall from his fists"

Jayne nodded like, of course, she'd expected this. Weren't all women afraid of getting hit? On the other side of the door, Saraub slammed the brass knocker into wood three times: *Clack!-Clack!-Clack!*

Audrey looked down the drab hall and the doors that opened upon cavernous rooms. She remembered what Jayne had helped her forget: murder had happened here. New grout and Home Depot tiles didn't change the truth: this was a bad place.

"How long have you been together?" Jayne asked. Her cheeks were boozily flushed, and runny eyeliner had congealed into black gook in the corners of her eyes. She acted late twenties, but looking at her in the harsh hall light, Audrey realized with some shock that she had to be at least forty.

Audrey looked down at her turquoise pumps and tried to forget the lines cut into Jayne's cheeks like scored glass. Tried to see Jayne the way she wanted and deserved to be seen: fresh and young and fearless. "We've been together two and a half years . . ." she said.

Jayne answered in a whisper. "That's a long time. I don't know for sure, but I think he'd have done it by now."

"Probably," Audrey said. "But it's still not a good sign."

"If you love him, you should answer it." Jayne fixed her eyes on Audrey, like she was willing her to be brave, because maybe she didn't think she'd ever find love, but she wanted it for her friends.

"*Bam!*" Saraub knocked again, but she could tell that he was getting tired, and the knocks were becoming less frequent. Soon, he'd give up and go home. And pretty soon after that, he'd move on and find someone else. It can happen like that, even when it's the real thing: love dies all the time.

"I *should* answer it, shouldn't I?"

Jayne's dimples deepened. "Well, duh! He's a total hottie."

Audrey took a breath and headed for the door. She realized then, that if Jayne hadn't been with her, she would never have answered the intercom. She would have stayed in this vast, miserable apartment, lit only by the light of the television, as she'd rearranged the furniture, or God help her, worked on that door, and the night had passed into day. And another day. And another. Until this mistake of an apartment became her prison. Thank God for Jayne.

As she pulled the latch on the door, Saraub banged once more: *Bam!*

Then, suddenly, an old woman shrieked, "No subletting! I'm calling the police!"

This was followed by another raspy, feminine shout: "She's not home. Leave her alone!"

And then a baritone: "What's this, young man? You don't live here!"

Audrey swung the door wide and wondered for a moment if she'd accidentally moved into an old-age home. About ten residents were standing in the hall. Unlike at Betty's loony bin, none had shoulder dandruff, or drooled. Instead, their hair plugs, wigs, and sprayed-over bald spots were coiffed into Claudette Colbert curls and dapper pomade comb-overs. A few clutched gimlet glasses filled with brown liquid and cherries—Manhattans? They wore cocktail dresses or dapper suits that had faded over the years, but were fine nonetheless. Their skin was pulled taut, so she could see the ridges of their skulls and blue veins. More surgery. Some of it was good, some of it, horrific. It was close to midnight on a Monday night, and these fossils had been having a cocktail party.

One of the old men was even wearing a white porcelain mask with holes for his eyes and nose, but no space for his mouth. She thought he might be recovering from a recent, drastic procedure. Galton—Jayne had mentioned him.

The old lady from 14C next door—Mrs. Parker—had traded her dressing gown for a sequined black cocktail dress that revealed dimpled chicken legs. Bad. Worse, her orange lipstick feathered along the skin of her upper lip. "No subletters!" she shrilled.

"I don't like strangers. They give me terrible dreams," Galton mumbled through his mask.

A tall man wearing a bow-tie tuxedo bellowed, "Siamese twins belong in Siam!" He banged what looked like Edgardo's knobby cane . . . In a fit of senility, had he stolen from his own super?

"Shaaddup, Evvie Waugh, before I throw a drink at you!" Mrs. Parker shrieked back at him.

The guy closest to Audrey's apartment crouched, so that his center of gravity was level, then raised his Parkinson's-shaking dukes at Saraub like he was going to throw a punch. His face got so red that she thought it might burst: "You leave the little lady alone!"

Audrey's eyes met Saraub's, and they exchanged a single, half-formed thought: *what the hell?*

Saraub lifted his hands above his head, open palms facing out. Sweat rolled down his thick, black brows, and he wiped it away with his raised shoulders. His wax jacket lay in a crinkled pile in front of her feet, where he must have dropped it.

Parkinson's didn't budge. Audrey feared that the stress would give him a coronary seizure.

"I'm sorry," she announced to the cocktail party. "It's fine. Please, it's a personal matter. I hope we didn't disturb you."

Instead of backing away, the shaking old man inched closer, like he'd decided she was a battered wife defending her abusive man.

Evvie Waugh (14D?) lifted the knobby cane like a baseball bat, and got ready to swing. The sight was both terrible and ludicrous.

Saraub panted, and his eyes bugged. He hated getting in trouble, even imaginary trouble. "Really, folks. It's fine," she called out.

Jayne peeped her head from behind Audrey's shoulder and waved at them. "It's fine!" she agreed with bouncing, irrepressible delight. "We were having a girls' night!"

Audrey put her hand on Saraub's back and he lowered his arms. "This is my boyfriend"—she winced at the misuse of the word, but now wasn't the time for fine distinctions—"I'm very, very sorry. We don't usually fight . . . This won't be a regular midnight show," she said. "You can all go back to. . . . your party."

"Boyfriend! Edgardo said she was single. I wasn't expecting it. I don't like surprises. Party's over! My whole night is ruined!" Mrs. Parker screeched, then stomped back into 14C.

Evvie lowered the knobby cane. He, Galton, and a

handful of others followed Mrs. Parker back to 14C, where Audrey imagined they'd been having a Bengay orgy. They smelled like it. Thank God for soundproof, plaster walls.

"Just as long as you're okay," Parkinson's announced to Audrey without ever looking at Saraub.

"Marty Hearst, she's fine," Jayne told the shaking man. Then she waved her hand at him like it was a broom, sweeping him away: "Skedaddle!"

Sheepishly, Marty Hearst dropped his dukes and retreated with the others. Drinks in hands, the rest of them meandered toward the apartment near the fire stairs.

"Good night, everybody," Audrey called, then picked up Saraub's wax jacket from the floor where he'd dropped it and entered 14B. Hopping at her heels, Jayne followed. Saraub brought up the rear and shut and locked the door behind him.

"Bananas!" Audrey announced.

14

We Pick Our Own Families

They walked down the fifty-foot hall. Though they'd never met, Saraub took Jayne's upper arm and helped her as she limped.

"Jayne," Audrey heard her say, and he answered, "Saraub Ramesh. Pleased to meet you. Do you live in the building?" He sounded flustered, but polite.

When they got to the den, he helped Jayne into the fold-out chair, seeming immediately to understand that she required kid gloves. Jayne grinned, delighted by the attention.

"That was, indeed, bananas," he said to Audrey.

She smiled. "Yes, but could you have taken Marty?"

He shook his head, like she was incorrigible. "Funny girl." Then he picked up the mostly empty bottle of wine and pointed it at her. "Liquid dinner?" His eyes followed her shape from turquoise pumps to coffee-stained blouse, and the slack belt that cinched nothing, in between. "Looks like too many liquid dinners."

She shrugged. "The breakfast of champions." She was out of breath as she spoke. Surprisingly nervous. Surprisingly happy. What if he'd come here to apologize? What if she left with him right now and never had to breathe the depressing air of this apartment ever ever EVER again?

"You should know that my phone got stolen by a band of roving dwarfs. I hope you didn't call and get hung up on by one of them," she added.

"Oh, I just thought that was you, being a bi—" he didn't finish, and looked down.

"Bird?" she asked.

He shrugged. "Something like that." Their eyes met. She willed herself not to look away.

Jayne grinned ear to ear like a kid, and Audrey felt a swell of affection for her, and Saraub, and even for herself. They were all pretty okay people. *You make me happy*, she wanted to tell him, and Jayne, too.

Saraub sighed, as if just then remembering something. "I came here for a reason. Can we talk alone?" he asked.

Audrey nodded. "Yeah, but Jayne's my friend. It's fine."

A car alarm resounded, beeping and thrumping like a siren getting closer, then farther away. He closed the turret window. Doubled birds became single. The room got darker, and the air thickened. She hated this apartment, she really did. She hated everything it represented, too.

"It's bad news. You should sit down." His grin had gone from tense to rictus. She noticed that he was wearing a suit instead of his usual corduroys. A job interview? Had *Maginot Lines* finally gotten backing?

"I tried to get you at work, and here, too. I stopped by a few hours ago, but you weren't home yet."

"What?" she asked, still without sitting. She tried to

sound natural, but her voice had a frog in it. Was he leaving town?

Saraub squatted, so that they were eye to eye. "The hospital's emergency contact was the landline at our apartment," he said. "I didn't give them your cell-phone number. Maybe I should have, but I wanted it to come from me."

Something clicked. It took her a second, her mind raced forward, then back. At first it was a possibility, then she knew without a doubt. There was only one thing it could be.

"There was an emergency at the Nebraska State Psychiatric Hospital?" she asked.

Saraub nodded.

She got breathless. In her mind, the birds flapped their wings inside the stained glass but couldn't break free, and the rotted floor under the piano opened along broken, uneven lines. Something intelligent, but not sane crept out. She looked down at the wood, and thought about how high up she was—the fourteenth floor. What hubris to believe that men could erect buildings in the clouds and trust that they didn't collapse into ashes. What hubris to believe that she'd escaped the Midwest, when all along, it had only been biding its time, waiting to snap her back. Clever Betty.

Her knees buckled, but Saraub clamped his hand around her upper arm and held her steady. Crippled Jayne reached up from her seat, and held her other arm with an ice-cold claw.

She knew what had happened. Betty had gone AWOL, just like in Omaha, and Hinton, and Sioux City. "Have they looked in the bars nearby? That's usually the first place. I'll need them to come up with a list. Or maybe you guys could help."

Saraub pushed her down into a chair, and then knelt in front of her. His skin had gotten sallow since she left. Drinking? Eating every meal out? The man was good at taking care of other people but terrible at taking care of himself. She regretted that it hadn't occurred to her to worry about him until now.

"Audrey," he said.

She nodded, to let him know that yes, she was ready for this. She was prepared.

"Your mother tried to kill herself. She's in a coma."

15

Children's Hour

It didn't hit her. She didn't believe it. "You're sure? Betty Lucas?"

Saraub nodded. "Positive. Betty Lucas. Nebraska State Psychiatric Hospital. An overdose. She'd been hoarding her pills, they think."

"A suicide," Audrey heard herself say. Her tongue was dry and flopping in her mouth. "She cycled again."

Saraub let out a breath. "That's the word they used, too . . . They said you needed to get out there right away if you want to see her before . . ."

She nodded and touched her throat, which was dry. "Did they tell you what pills, or when?"

He shrugged. Only one bulb in the ceiling was working, so the room was pretty dark. The television still played, but someone had turned down the volume. His shiny face and the water in his eyes reflected the miserly light. "I don't remember what pills. But I checked the airports—there's a flight out of JFK tomorrow morning through the Twin Cities, to Omaha."

"Lithium? Depakote?"

He nodded. "That's right. Lithium, I think."

She let out a breath. Bad sign. Most people don't wake up from lithium comas, and even if they do, the brain damage ruins them.

"They said . . . she's dying. So if you want to see her, you'll have to leave first thing."

"Dying," she said. In her mind she rearranged. She placed dishes atop one another, stacked papers and topiaries and engraved mourning walls. (How many dead over the years, the centuries? They piled and piled, the ghosts of this world. There weren't enough living to mourn them.)

"Yeah. That's what they said."

In her mind, she repeated all the things he'd told her, and heard him. Her mother and best friend had tried to kill herself.

It was then that her thoughts kaleidoscoped into discrete segments of shock, pretty and fragile as stained glass. She looked around the room, and like a compound-eyed insect, saw each shard clearly:

There was the green Parkside Plaza, whose design was too cold. For the first time, she understood why she'd never liked the feel of grass between her toes, or dogs, or countertop clutter; she was frightened of them because they were unpredictable, like her mother.

There was yellow Jayne, who'd played cheerful for so long now to mask her sorrow that even she could not distinguish the woman from the act.

There was blue Saraub, holding her hand. Like her mother had predicted so many years ago, she'd broken the heart of a man she hadn't wanted.

There was the black Breviary, which she knew right then, without doubt, was haunted.

The center of the kaleidoscope was red, and in it she saw weeping Betty Lucas. An abandoned wretch in a backless hospital gown, no family save the daughter who never called.

The kaleidoscope narrowed until there was only Betty, and for a moment everything around her went red, too. The air, the floors, Saraub's shirt, Jayne's gauze bandage. All like blood.

Saraub knelt at her chair. "It's okay," he said, with his lips so close to her ear that she could feel their warmth. The sound of his voice echoed at first, then went dead, like something in the walls was stealing his words as they reverberated. She knew in that moment that Edgardo and the movers had been right. She was too emotional. Her heartbreak, first from Saraub, and now this, had roused something terrible.

Her grief made all these things clear, and fleeting. They existed as a distraction, flitting about the memories of Betty that were too painful to bear.

Her eyes watered, and to steel herself from a crying jag, she thought about the broken promise Betty had made to her, so many years ago. That lost photo. Thought about the lines on her wrists, unacknowledged. Those bullshit coveralls with holes in all the wrong places.

Her eyes dried, and in the place of tears, a slithering thing radiated from her stomach to the edges of her skin. It unfurled as it grew like a vine. Black spores of rot in berry clusters hung from its branches. It filled first her chest, then her limbs, and the space between her ears, and then her eyes, so that she lost the knowledge of color, and finally, her mouth, so that even her appetites were gone. The spores of fury were dry and bitter. They shriveled her insides, smaller and smaller.

"A nurse found her early this morning," Saraub said. "I called all day . . . I came to your apartment before, too. But you weren't home yet."

She thought of Betty in a bed, all by herself. One moment an angel, the next, a villain. And the thing is, do you blame the sickness, or its host?

The spores thickened. The mold overtook her until she was dry and bitter, too. There were others trapped here with her. Four children and a woman. They opened their eyes, cornflower blue that coalesced, like running ink, into black. Their mouths opened, too.

Build the door a voice whispered. The man in the three-piece suit. Did they hear him, too?

She turned a cold eye on her visitors. Drunk, ugly Jayne, who reeked of cigarettes and stupid decisions. Saraub, a doormat. He'd told her she was a ghost, and she wondered at the irony, if she slit his throat right now and trapped him here forever.

Would you like that, Breviary? She wondered as she watched them. *Shall I cut them for you?*

In her mind she covered them with mold. It grew over and inside them, through their mouths and ears and noses, until all was black. Until the vine wore their skin, and used them dry, and they became dust. Everything, like dust. The whole world a barren place.

"Do you need a glass of water?" she heard Saraub ask from far away, as if beneath a bathtub full of water.

"I have cheese. I could cut the freezer burn off," Jayne volunteered. "Do you want some cheese? Or half a pita pocket?"

Audrey shook her head. She grinned at her stupid friend. A mean grin. Saraub stroked her neck with too-warm fingers.

"It's cheddar or American, I can't tell the difference," Jayne said, then reached down under her bandage and began to scratch.

Audrey looked at the woman. "No, thanks," she said. The mean grin left her face. Jayne was crying. Saraub's eyes were wet, too. Here she was, numb and furious, and here were her friends, crying for her. The vine got smaller.

"Or tea. I could make a cup of tea . . . What can I do?" Jayne pleaded, still scratching. Her sore broke open and began to bleed.

"Stop picking," Audrey said. "You'll hurt yourself."

"Oh, right. Sorry," Jayne said.

"Don't be sorry. It's just, stop hurting yourself," Audrey told her.

Jayne's face crumbled as she closed up the gauze. She squinted to keep from crying. Audrey reached over and squeezed her shoulder. "Hey. It's okay. Thank you. You're helping. Really."

Jayne nodded, wet-eyed, and smiled heartbreakingly. The vine curled itself small again, a worm that lay in wait. Audrey turned to Saraub, and though she didn't yet feel the sentiment, she knew that soon, she would. "You were right. It's better it came from you."

Saraub leaned in, and said probably the only thing she wanted to hear. "I love you."

She scooted off the chair, and onto the floor, where she buried her wet nose in his chest. He put one arm around her back, the other around her bottom, so that he held her whole body. There, finally, she cried. Soft sobs. "I hate her. But I love her, too."

"You don't need to explain," Saraub answered.

"I know what you mean," Jayne said. "It hurts more because you wish it could have been different. And now it might not ever be."

Audrey nodded. "She was bad, but when I look back, I wasn't so great either. I blamed her for everything. Even when I was thirty years old. She was practically a vegetable, living in a group home, and I wanted her to tell me I was pretty. I wanted her to cook me dinner and make up for all those years she'd screwed up. I blamed her for everything. I held it over her head that I was a waitress, because she needed me in town to help her, and there weren't any jobs in architecture in Omaha. But the thing is, there were jobs. If I hadn't been high all the time, I could have applied for one. I just . . . it was easier to hate her than do something about it."

Jayne nodded. "Isn't it funny? When you have to raise yourself, you never really grow up."

"I guess we can grow up now, if we want. Can't we?" Audrey asked.

Jayne shrugged. "Good luck with that."

Audrey smiled.

Saraub cleared his throat, and she could tell he was uncomfortable. He'd never been big on discussing feelings, or, for that matter, criticizing loved ones. "Is there anyone I should call?" he asked.

She wasn't sure she liked the question. Did it mean he wanted to leave? "Well . . ." she said.

"Are you seeing someone?" Saraub asked.

"Like a shrink?" she asked.

He tried to hide his amusement when he answered by looking down. "No, like a dude."

"Of course not."

Suddenly, Jayne jumped up. "I'm going to leave you guys alone, but I'll be next door if you need me." She winked, not at all subtlely, at Audrey.

"Okay," Audrey said. Then she added, because she knew Jayne would be pleased to hear it. "I had . . . it was fun, Jayne. I had a nice time with you."

Jayne's entire face brightened. She lingered before hopping away on her crutches. "Me, too. So, I know this is bad timing and all, but if you're in town, you should come to my act. It'll cheer you up. Also, I'll need the moral support. And then I'll give you support back, too. That's what friends do. I'll buy new cheese and cook for you."

Holding her crutches for her, Saraub came to Jayne's side and took her arm.

"It's a deal," Audrey said as she rose, and walked with them.

"I'm sorry about your mom, Addie. It hurts my stomach to think you're sad . . . but don't forget about my act. She grinned widely at Saraub, then back at Audrey. Both of you!" Jayne said as she waved good-bye.

They waved back at her, new acquaintances tried by fire into friends.

If they had known the circumstances under which they'd see Jayne again, they might not have let her go.

16

Howard Hughes Flew Planes Too, You Know

They closed the door upon seeing Jayne safely enter 14E, then walked back down the long hall and sat in the folding chairs at the turret. She moved her ballet flat so that it brushed against the sole of his leather loafer. The hair above his ear hadn't been trimmed in a while, and loose strands descended from the razor line in a jagged arc that she wanted to touch. His skin was damp and jaundiced. Probably, he was hungover. "You look bad," she said. "You're not taking care of yourself."

He didn't move his eyes from the window. "It's a draw. You, too."

She sighed. "Still want your piano?"

"No. Are you in shock?"

She shrugged. "Yeah. I think so. But I'm also just dry. I don't have a lot of feelings left when it comes to Betty."

"Did she take that much work?"

The television was still playing, and the light in the den flickered. She was reminded again of something from her dream. "Yeah. She was a good person in a lot of ways, but it was too much for me." She touched her throat. "I think it broke me a little, you know?"

He shook his head. "I don't know why you always see yourself as a weakling. You're one of the bravest people I know."

"If you saw what I used to be, you wouldn't say that," she said. "Dirty. Lice. I could have put on a better show, but I was so depressed I didn't bother."

He was looking out the window while he talked. The city lights were cold and pretty. "That's hard for me to imagine."

"Yeah. I try not to think about it."

He nodded. "I need to tell you something."

She didn't like the expression on his face: apprehensive. "Okay . . ." she said.

He continued, still looking out the window. "The timing is bad, but I don't know if you're going to shut me out again—maybe this is the last time we'll talk."

She shook her head: no, she'd never do that again. Things had changed since she'd left him, or maybe she'd changed. From now on, she planned to let him in anytime he came knocking.

"I'm glad it happened, that you left," he said. "It never could have worked between us."

She looked down. Blinked once. Twice. Three times.

"Not the way things stand, at least. I know I'm not perfect, or even close. But you've got a problem, Audrey. The cleaning. The rearranging. When you've got a deadline, you get so nervous you can't sleep, and then you stop eating, too. The more comfortable you were living with me, the worse it got. You need a doctor. I love you, and I hate watching you hurt yourself," he said, calmly and without histrionics. It made her feel, for a moment, that the problem was not hers alone, but theirs.

He sighed with relief, and she knew that saying this hadn't been easy for him. She was reminded of Betty. Probably, she'd confronted her mother with a speech nearly identical to this, once upon a time: *I love you. For me. For yourself. Get help.* But Betty had always ignored her. Or worse, thrown something.

She thought about all that for a while, then answered, "You're a turkey. My mom's in a coma; this is totally the wrong time. And I didn't take your stupid comics."

He looked down at his feet. "Oh, yeah. I found them under the futon."

"Also, not that it's your business, but I made appointments with three shrinks this week. Three!" She held up three fingers and pointed them at him, as proof.

"Really?" He blinked in surprise.

"Yeah, really. I have obsessive-compulsive disorder, and I need to work on it."

"That's great, Audrey."

"And you're a real jerk for bringing it up," she said.

He raised his eyes up to the ceiling, and didn't answer. "Do you have anything to eat?"

"No. This place scares me. In another month I'm going to start peeing in milk bottles like Howard Hughes, just so I don't have to go into the bathroom. The lady who lived here before me drowned all four of her kids. We'll have to go to a restaurant."

Saraub's eyes wide as aggie marbles. "Not the Mommy Killer Murders?" That was what the *New York Post* had called them.

"Yeah. Them. There are temperature variations in every room, and they've got nothing to do with drafts and vents. Sound and light carry differently, too. I can't figure it out, but it's not a structural problem," she said. "I think it's an effect of the architecture. You've probably never heard of it, but this is Chaotic Naturalism. The last of its kind. Also, and this does not at all prove your stupid point, but I've started hallucinating. I've been dreaming about this guy in a three-piece suit who wants me to build a door. It's not good."

He stood, obliterating her view of the Parkside Plaza, and looked around the den. Took it in for a long time, then asked, "Why would you live in a place like this?"

She shrugged. "You're the one who said I need a doctor."

He touched a plaster wall, then put his ear to it. "You shouldn't stay here. There's something wrong. I felt it last night, too. Sorry about that, by the way."

She nodded. "That was mean, what you said."

He leaned on the turret seat, next to Wolverine. Gave the little guy a pet, prick side down. "Yes. It was. But you can be mean, too."

She noticed the neatly tailored suit he'd worn to call on her tonight. Almost three years later, the gesture still charmed. She got up and leaned next to him. "I don't want to fight."

"Good. Let's get out of here. Let's eat."

"Amir's Falafel. Open all night. Or Tom's Diner."

"I'll treat."

"Thanks, 'cause I'm broke . . . Would you come to Nebraska with me?"

He took a labored breath, like he hadn't exercised, or even left his apartment, in six weeks. She realized that she really was worried about him. In her absence, who was cleaning the sheets?

"I know I shouldn't ask," she said.

"No. You shouldn't."

She waited. The seconds passed.

"I'll come. There's an American Airlines red-eye. To-morrow morning at six," he said.

She was so relieved that she burst into tears, then averted her eyes and flapped her hands in front of her face, so he didn't feel obligated to comfort her.

"Thanks," she said. "Also, I'm glad you told me that stuff. You never tell me when you're mad, so it's good. I'll fix it if I can. I want to fix it."

"Audrey," he answered, his voice gruff. Then he took her in his arms, and she let loose, and cried harder.

"I don't want to make any promises. But I hope you know I love you. You're the most important person in the world to me."

"I know. Start making some promises," he whispered as he held her, and she squeezed tighter.

She packed in less than ten minutes. As they left 14B, they found a L'Oréal business card taped to the door, over which Jayne had written, "So sorry, Addie. Call me if you need anything: (917) 274–6639. She'd drawn a blue daisy in the corner, shaded in with a light-handed Bic. The flower was open, its layered petals sharp points like gardening spades.

At Tom's Diner, they ate American cheese and broccoli omelets while on the overhead speakers, soft rock Beatles "Penny Lane" played. When she tried to filch a fry from his plate, he forked her wrist. "I've killed men for less," he grunted.

"Fair enough, heart attack," she answered.

Before they caught the bus, she worried that she'd left something plugged in or turned on at 14B. A toaster, maybe. Or the hair dryer. Or worse, the alarm clock, whose frayed wire might cause an electrical fire. "I'm going to go back up for a sec," she told him.

He was unfazed. When they'd lived together, she'd had to run home for no good reason at least twice a week. Never once had anything caught fire. "Need me to come?"

"No. I'll leave my bags with you. I'll just be a second."

The lobby was empty, and the Haitian doorman was sleeping at his post with an open issue of *Playboy* draped over his face. She took the elevator up and opened 14B. She unplugged the severed alarm clock wire, then searched all the other outlets and lights, not once, but twice, and in her mind made a note, so that she'd be able to visualize it while she was gone, and not worry: *The toaster is unplugged. The oven is off. You checked,* she would tell herself.

As she was leaving, she took one last look at the den, then turned out the overhead light. In the dark, her mind played a trick on her. A heavyset woman sat at the piano bench while tiny red ants crept across her fingers. She was so still she could have been a doll, but softly she sang that tune from *Annie*:

> *"Send a flood*
> *Send the flu*
> *Anything that You can do*
> *To little girls."*

The tune was lovely. The woman's voice smooth and deep as a river. Something wet dripped to the rotted wooden floor. The woman looked up. She wore black glasses and a blue sweatsuit. It was Clara DeLea. Only, her skin hung slack from her face like a mask, and her eyes were black. *"Build the door, Audrey Lucas. Your mother's waiting."*

Audrey ran down the fifty-foot hall, and out the door, and down the emergency stairs, all the way to Tom's Diner, without stopping.

Part III

You Can't Go Home Again

A Letter to the Editor

December 31, 1926

It has come to my attention that in small factions of the civilized world, Chaotic Naturalism continues to flourish. I would argue that said religion is worse than Satanism. At least Satanism is laughable. It's possible that Chaotic Naturalism is real. Where, after all, did our base instincts go when we rose from the slime and became thinking, social creatures? As a physicist, I'm inclined to believe that all energy is preserved. These instincts persist. Chaotic Naturalism seeks their reunion with the human body, and the consequential demise of the human soul. I'm obliged to your article; it opened this old man's peepers. The Breviary's architecture is stunning, but these idiot flappers conducting séances in its old church play with fire. Sometimes I think I should have been born fifty years ago, when people weren't so stupid.

Sincerely,

M. M. DeVoe, Arthur Avenue, Bronx

From the *Christian Science Monitor*

Another Dodo Tries to Fly

December 29, 1937

This city has been raining socialites for eight years. The most recent fall took place at the once-regal Breviary apartment building last night at 5 P.M., soon after the stock market closed. Martin Hearst IV discharged his hunting rifle from the roof, then followed the path of its bullets down the westward side of the building. His body struck and killed a young man, Eta Murphy, who was selling apples from a cart. Hearst is survived by his wife Sarah and son, Martin V. This marks the 211th high-profile banker suicide in the city, and the 28th that took place in The Breviary. Out of deference to his mourners, The Breviary's annual New Year's Eve Gala is canceled.

From the *New York Tribune*

17

I've Always Lived With You

As she slept, the thing in her stomach unfurled.
Behind her was the dilapidated Victorian in Yonkers. Faded picket fence with missing planks like broken teeth. Ahead of her, a yard plush with wild sea grass that slipped between her toes. For once, she didn't mind the mess. Little voices shouted: "Higher!" "More!" "You guys, wait for me!"

Under the big oak, Saraub pushed a tire swing. Maybe too high, but the dark-haired boy hooted happily, so she let them have their fun. And then a small hand reached up and clasped her fingers. A little girl in green corduroy overalls with a bowl haircut. She had Saraub's brown eyes and Betty's high cheekbones.

The driveway was marked with chalk. Numbered single upon double boxes. Hopscotch! She'd only ever seen this on television, but the rules looked simple enough. Audrey leaped inside a box, and coaxed the girl to do the same. One foot! Two foot! Three foot! Four! They hopped back and forth, laughing, while in the distance the boy shouted, "Higher, Daddy, higher. I want to fly!"

Her family unborn. How she loved them.

But dark storm clouds swallowed the puffy white cumulus. The sky opened, and black rain poured. The sticky little fingers holding her hand disappeared. The chalk washed away, and the empty tire swing creaked. Sadness carved a whole in her stomach: Saraub was gone, too.

A gaunt woman with wiry white hair and pink plastic barrettes watched her from the window. Betty. Audrey's blood went cold as it pumped.

It's a bad place where you live, Lamb, she'd said, and now Audrey thought: *But I live with you, Mom. I've always lived with you.*

The woman receded from the window, and into darkness. Black rain fell. Something pricked her bare toes. Sharp pins and needles. The ground swelled with black water. Red ants seeking higher ground thrashed. They crawled up her legs in uneven clumps that looked like weeping scabs. She swiped, but not fast enough. Tiny mouths pinched. They chewed her insides until she was hollow and bleeding like a full-term miscarriage.

Once inside, they met with the thing in her stomach and expanded. They took her over, mind and body. Her eyes went black. Against her will, she walked through the Victorian's cardboard-box front door. At the end of a long, dark hall was a den: 14B. They were waiting for her there. Clara and her rosy-cheeked children, the man in the three-piece suit, Mrs. Parker and her tight dress, Marty Hearst and his shaking dukes, Evvie Waugh and his stolen cane, masked Mr. Galton. The rest of the tenants, too. All except Jayne. They parted like a splitting sea to reveal another door. It was built on a slant, and instead of cardboard, its frame was made of satinwood.

She walked toward it like a bride meeting her groom, while on all sides, the tenants clapped.

Her family, unborn. How she hated them.

The door opened. Shining black eyes peered back at her, just as 14B's ceiling buckled, and everything came crashing down.

Bam!

She jolted in her seat as the plane touched down into Eppley Airfield Tuesday evening. Rubbed her eyes. The dream fled from her, and she remembered only black rain, and a door.

One row over, Saraub peeked out at her, and waved. "We're here!" he said.

She patted her thighs with corresponding hands at exactly the same time. Once, twice, three times, four. That wasn't enough, so she went for five times, six times, lucky seven. "Yup," she said. "We're here."

18

Sweet Air

As soon as they got their bags, they rented a
white Camry and started the short drive from
Omaha to Betty's hospital in Lincoln. Since it
was after five, visiting hours had ended at the hospital,
so they didn't rush. They took the long way through
downtown, then west along Cornhusker Road.

After a few miles, they passed her old apartment
building. She didn't recognize it by sight, only by street
address. Its white paint had chipped, and its tin cornices
had rusted. The three-level boardinghouses that used to
surround it had been converted into stucco efficiencies.
Fold-out chairs with slashed leather seats and a broken
red barbecue lay rusting in its front yard.

She slowed as she passed. Funny, she'd missed this
place a lot when she first moved to New York. She'd
imagined its black walls, and the days that had passed
there without expectation. Now, she remembered hash
exhaustion, the constant phone calls, always from

the same person—Betty—and the loneliness of wind against a drafty house on a dark night. She'd grown so comfortable with those things that she'd mistaken this dump for happiness. Next to her, Saraub dozed. She didn't wake him up to point the place out as they passed, or even look back.

The US 480 sign (which read "U 80") directed her left, but habit guided her hand, and she turned right. The street looked like an empty strip mall: Appleby's, Outback Steakhouse, Sizzler, IHOP. Between them were large tracts of land that couldn't be traversed by foot, only car. Since she'd left, most of the dime stores and folksy diners serving cold cheese sandwiches had folded.

Audrey pulled into one of the lots, then took a fast, nervous breath like she'd swallowed something cold.

"Hey— Where are we?" Saraub yawned.

She peered through the tall glass windows that ran the length of the restaurant. Waitresses in blue uniforms and black shoes scurried to and from the heat-lamp counter in the kitchen while out-of-shape truckers ate breakfast for dinner. In the back was that blasted convection oven that had burned her hands into claws. She remembered the smell of the place—grease, boysenberry-flavored syrup, coffee. She'd been afraid of germs back then and had used a rag instead of her hands to lift dirty dishes. Tips she'd placed in her apron pocket, then washed her hands once or three times, but never twice. Unless Billy Epps took her out back and smoked her up. Then she relaxed. Of course, getting high had been part of the reason she'd burned herself.

"Is this your old job?" Saraub asked.

She nodded. They looked for a while. She didn't turn off the ignition, even though her stomach growled, and buttermilk pancakes sounded pretty good. Instead, she pointed her chin at the white-and-blue-painted IHOP sign. "It doesn't spin anymore. I wonder why."

"Looks like its seen better days."

"It has." Audrey looked down at her fingers. The right hand was scarred worse than the left, but both were oversized for her body, like oven mitts. The first and only time Saraub had brought her home to his family, Sheila Ramesh had run her thumb and index finger along Audrey's scabs while they shook. *You're a working girl?* she'd asked, and at first Audrey had thought she meant hooker.

"Let's go in. You can show everybody you're a big shot now," Saraub said. His hand was on the door.

Audrey peered into the restaurant. Her old manager looked back at them through one of the cracked windows, like she was trapped inside a giant web. She wore exactly the same beehive Miss Breck hairdo she'd sported fifteen years ago. The same old ladies were waiting tables, too. Even the same hostess stood at the podium—she'd started the job as a high-school kid, and nobody'd died yet, so she hadn't gotten her promotion.

And then, oh, no. No way. Two cars over, Billy Epps leaned against his rust-bucket VW van, smoking a blunt. His hair was gone now, and his chest had gotten concave. Hard living. How old was he? Forty? And still a busboy. When she left, he'd only just started the switch from hash to crystal meth. Looked like he'd been smoking his product, because most of his teeth were gone.

I'm proud to know you, Audrey Lucas, he'd told her on her last day of work. If only he'd known how often, during those first scary days in New York, she'd replayed that sentiment in her mind, and found courage. Sweet Billy.

"I can't go in there," she said. "It's the same people I used to work with. I'd feel uncomfortable, having them wait on us."

Saraub's brows knit in confusion. "That's their job. They don't care."

She shook her head. Saraub had never been a waiter, only waited on. It was moments like this that reminded her of the difference. "Trust me, they'll care. I don't belong there anymore." She pulled out of the lot and back onto the road.

A few turns later, they were at the highway. The sky above was open and blue. In her mind she folded the grassland scenery on top of itself, to give it boundaries. "Think you can hold out for dinner until Lincoln?"

He nodded, wincing as he turned his neck back and forth, like he'd gotten a crick. "Let me," she said, then reached out and rubbed it with her thumb and index fingers. "Least I can do for your troubles."

He smiled in a way that meant nookie. "I've got all kinds of aches."

"We'll see," she said.

"I'll hold you to that. . . . Would you change anything about this place?"

"What?"

"About growing up, I mean. Do you wish you'd gone to school in Chicago after college, or had a dad?"

She let go of his neck. "I try not to think about it. There's nothing I can do, you know?"

"Yeah. That makes sense. . . . I miss my dad."

"Why don't you ever talk about him?"

He shrugged. "He's dead. What's there to say?" Then he changed the subject. "I didn't expect Nebraska would be like this. There's something about it that's sad. Like it's too raw. Exposed, you know?"

"I'm sorry I never got to meet him. You'll have to tell me about him sometime . . ." She left him some time to answer, and when he didn't, she continued. "Nebraska is God's Country. That's what my mom called it, at least."

Just then, a sixteen-wheeler full of chickens packed as tight as jigsaw pieces passed them on the right. He lifted her hand and placed it on his neck. "Needy!" she said as she rubbed. "Since you asked, I thought of one thing I'd change: I wish I'd tried harder to make friends. I'd have been happier if I hadn't been so lonely," she said.

"Did you get teased?" Saraub asked.

She veered onto US 80 West toward Lincoln and Betty's hospital. "Teased?"

"Yeah. Who picked on you?"

She shook her head. "We moved too often. I didn't have a bully. It was more—I was invisible. I didn't stay in any one school more than a few months. Sometimes girls wrote stuff on the bathroom walls, but nobody ever said anything to my face. I think they knew better. I was too weak to defend myself, and they just weren't that mean. You've seen the scars on my wrists. They were a lot thicker then. I couldn't cover them up with a little face makeup like I do now. Trying to kill yourself is a lot bigger than being a misfit, you know? They were decent people. They left me alone. My whole life, until I met you, I was invisible. Sometimes I'd be walking down 42nd Street after seeing a movie by myself in one of those big stadium seat theatres, and someone in the crowd would accidentally shove me and keep walking, and I'd have this moment, you know? Where I'd wonder if they saw me. If I was even alive."

"I see you," he said.

"I know," she said. "That's why you're scary."

He shrugged. "Thanks. I thought it was because I'm Indian. You know, I didn't fit in, either."

"No?" she asked. Signs pointed for the open plains of Ashland. Another city where she and Betty had lived for a few months, hoping for a fresh start, and instead finding the same old mess. "But you were a lineman on the Choate football team. Who fits in better than that?"

He adjusted his seat belt so that the harness wasn't against his neck, and she dropped her hand, because it was tired. "I don't know. The *white kid* at Choate?" He said "white kid" with a bitterness that surprised her. She'd never known him to hold a grudge. Mr. Laid Back People Pleaser. Once, he ate undercooked chicken at his second cousin's restaurant in Queens, just because he hadn't wanted to complain. He wound up in the hospital the next day with a bad case of salmonella.

"It didn't help that I was a day commuter, and my parents wouldn't let me date." He let out an audible breath. "Some of them, you know . . ."

"What? I don't know. People are like aliens to me. I can never guess what they'll do."

Saraub smiled wide enough that she could see the tiny space between his incisors, but once he started talking, the smile turned stiff. "Well, you know me and cameras. I was always filming things, kind of a Peeping Tom."

"And then?"

"So I took a camera into the locker room after a game. I was interviewing everybody. You know, stupid stuff: how does it feel to be division champs? I thought everybody liked it—I'd make copies so we could all remember the season. And then, I don't know. I went to my locker the next day, and somebody had spray-painted 'fag.'"

She squeezed the wheel. "Who? Who did that?"

"These puffy red letters, like subway graffiti. Andrew Lafferty."

"Andrew Lafferty is a stupid asshole and I hate him and I'm going to find him and punch him in the face."

"That helps, Audrey. You fixed that real good."

"Right now I'm scanning his brain until it explodes. You'll see it on the news tonight."

Saraub nodded. "Take out my cameraman for me while you're at it. He's been drinking again."

"Oh, good, we're being mean. I hope Jill Sidenschwandt gets explosive diarrhea. Truly. So what happened after that?"

"Well, Andrew thought I'd been coming on to him. I, I guess I did like him. I wanted to be his friend. Mr.

Captain America. When I was interviewing him, I didn't punch him in the shoulder, you know? Instead"—he winced with shame—"I slapped his ass."

"So?" Audrey asked.

"So, men don't slap each other's asses in locker rooms."

"I thought that was a thing. You were all into that."

He shook his head. "I thought so, too, because the Giants did it on *Monday Night Football*. But no. So Andrew didn't say anything when I did it, but I guess he didn't like it. After the graffiti, the rumors started. Everybody thought I was a fag. By the next season the team wouldn't change in front of me. Maybe they really believed it, maybe it was just an excuse, because I was this Indian kid with a weird name, and I smelled like curry."

Throughout, his voice was level. Matter-of-fact. She marveled at how good he was at keeping his feelings tight as piano strings. "It's embarrassing, when you have to explain to your coach that the reason the team makes you put your jock on in a corner is because they think you're perving on them."

Audrey shook her head. "You have such a good personality. You could get along with Hitler. I always figured you'd fit in anywhere," she told him.

His smile was an empty grimace. She was surprised by it. "Thanks. It was just that year. Mostly, I did fine. But to be honest, I never tried very hard, either. I liked my movies and football, and until you came along, that was about it."

"Well fuck 'em. Fuck every one of them." The anger in her voice came as a surprise to herself. "Why would you want to fit in with people like that?"

He shook his head. "We're just different. Both of us. We want stuff most people don't care about. With the stuff we make, we want to change the world. We want to live forever. It's a funny kind of vanity, and I can't figure out if it makes us better, or worse."

"Whatever. That's no excuse. I hope all those losers who teased you have tragic hair now. Middle parts and dandruff. I'd be gratified by that knowledge."

"No hair. Cue balls," he said while combing his fingers through his own receding hairline. It was about a half inch higher than when she'd met him. It occurred to her that their backgrounds were different, but in one basic way, they were similar. They didn't like themselves. Or more aptly put, they were never content with what they were but were always striving for something better. Which seemed pretty dumb, given the boys on the 59th Street team, who probably built shrines to their balls in their attics but couldn't figure out how to unscrew a lightbulb without instructions.

"Do you regret being Indian?" she asked.

He looked up her, surprised. "Sometimes," he said. "Not just my skin. The way I look, generally," he said, with his hands on his belly. It wasn't nearly as big as he imagined.

"But I love you how you are," she told him, then reached her hand across the seat and pulled the wool fabric of his trousers between her fingers. His voice was hoarse. "Thanks."

She veered off the highway at Lincoln but kept her hand in his lap. He picked it up and squeezed. The moment felt too good to ruin with words, so she didn't.

This was the first time they'd driven in a car together, and it felt more real than anything they'd ever done. Like the two of them had sloughed their city shells, and the skin underneath, unaccustomed to exposure, was soft and easily bruised.

Ten miles down, the road narrowed. Farmland stretched in every direction. There weren't any cars anymore. Only the sound of wheels on cement.

"What's that smell?" Saraub asked.

She smiled, because it had been a long time since she'd smelled air this sweet. "Corn. The combines do the threshing right there in the fields. Farmers, they'd get squirrelly in summer if a couple of weeks went by without rain. Whole towns would be on edge. You could practically hear them collectively grinding their teeth at night like crickets. They prayed for rain, then when it came, they prayed for it to stop. That's why my mom called it God's Country."

"God's Country. I like that."

They were still holding hands. Warmth threaded through her stomach, and in this quiet car, on this dark road, on the way to visit her sick mother, she felt safe. She wondered if she'd lived for so long without happiness, that now that it had found her, she couldn't recognize it. "Why do you punch walls?"

He let go of her hand, then pressed his nose against the passenger window, so she couldn't see him. "What do you mean?"

"The walls in your study. You punched them. I saw the marks. There were holes." It seemed important to her now to know. Maybe she'd driven him to it, with her endless bleaching and straightening. Maybe she'd driven Betty to her red ants, too.

"I guess I get mad," he said, still showing her the back of his head.

"At me?" She was close to crying all over again. Surprising how hard this question had been to ask.

He nodded. "Yeah." The tears came fast to her cheeks. He didn't notice them. "But not just you. A lot of things . . . I've always done that. Punched things when I'm alone. So no one knows when I'm mad. Did it scare you?"

She waited a while, until she knew her voice wouldn't break. "Yeah," she said. "I don't think I realized it until now, but it did." By the glare of the windshield's reflection, she could almost see the skittish kid with greasy hair that she used to be. They weren't so different as she liked to pretend. They'd each kept their fear, a gnawing thing.

"Is that why you left?" Saraub asked.

She shook her head, and the tears returned. "It's not you—"

"—It's me." He finished for her, then laughed a bitter, humorless laugh that let her know a part of him, at least for now, had changed for the worse because of what she'd done.

"I'm sorry," she whispered.

"Yeah."

Three miles later, at the intersection of Main Street and the Nebraska State Psychiatric Hospital, was a Super 8. She thought she'd stayed in it before, but she couldn't remember for sure. These motels all looked the same. She waited in the car while he checked in. Together, they drove to their room. Silently, they unpacked their clothes into separate dressers, ate vending machine Snickers bars instead of dinner, talked on their cell phones with work from separate sides of the room, and fell asleep in separate beds.

19

Your Black Wings Are Showing

ebraska State Psychiatric was a hulking, im-
personal monolith the size of four Manhattan
blocks. A sterile, industrial-park-style Walter
Gropius box construction, its tripod of wards stretched
out from the main administration area. The wards were
long halls with block rooms on each side. Common areas
at ward vertices consisted of two couches, two coffee
tables, and mounted televisions that the patients could
not reach and which the orderlies tuned to comforting
old programs that didn't require much thought—*Andy
Griffith* and *Bewitched*. Though she'd been lucky to
place Betty here (it was one of the few inpatient hospitals that accepted disability), Audrey hated it, and she
didn't like coming back.

First thing Wednesday morning, Audrey and Saraub
were sitting in general administration executive office
A3. The fluorescent lights inside the cheap gypsum

drop ceiling emitted a sallow, nauseating glow. On the other side of the desk, Dr. Burckhardt wrote something in Betty's chart. He was about six feet tall, and though he was still young, his thick head of hair had gone completely white. She'd met Burckhardt when she'd signed Betty's commitment papers, and had pegged him as a blandly pleasant man with too much on his plate to help anyone in particular. Her impression of him had not changed. Since being shown into his office, they'd been waiting at least five minutes.

She counted the words on his Creighton University Medical School diploma (106), then looked up just as Dr. Burckhardt closed his chart. "Well, then," he said.

Audrey waited, and reminded herself not to get so nervous that she blurted.

"Betty Lucas, you're her daughter, Audrey. We've met, yes?" His voice was monotone and without affect. Her new name for him was Captain Bland.

She nodded. "When I had her committed. But were you her doctor? I thought it was some guy from Texas."

Burckhardt doodled with his pen while he spoke. Up-and-down lines that intersected, but no curves, which tended to mean no imagination. "She was never my patient. I'm an administrator. State agencies like this have high turnover. Your mother has had several doctors."

She nodded, and neither of them acknowledged that if she'd called once in a while, she'd be more up to speed on her mother's care.

He looked at his pen, then his doodles, then put the pen down. "Your mother overdosed," he said.

"Yes," she said.

He continued. Blandly matter-of-fact. "A combination of lithium, Valium, and Depakote. One of our orderlies discovered her late Sunday night. She lost her ability to breathe without intubation Monday morning"—he looked in his chart—"5:18 A.M."

Something about that time sounded familiar, but she couldn't place it.

"She's on life support," Burckhardt said.

"How likely is it she'll come out of the coma?" Saraub asked.

"She won't. After you see her and say your farewells, I'd like your permission to terminate," Burckhardt answered.

She cleared her throat. "I read up on this online last night. When people come out of comas, it doesn't usually take more than a month. So I think we should wait, just to make sure." She squeezed her knuckles tight, unaware that she was showing both men her fists.

Burckhardt picked up his pen again. A Silver Cross with smooth, blue ink. He touched it to the paper, but didn't draw. "That's a very large expense. You have to consider the chances, and I'm telling you, they're slim to none. Her quality of life won't be the same, either." His voice was low but still without emotion. Possibly rehearsed. Maybe people at this place overdosed all the time.

"So there's a chance?" she asked.

Saraub covered her closed fists with his palm. She shook him off. Maybe Betty would wake up. Maybe they'd made a mistake, and it wasn't even Betty in the fucking coma, so why the hell were they having this conversation at all? What did this asshole doctor know about Betty Lucas? She'd survived fire, bad boyfriends, drunk weekends, hepatitis C from a dirty tattoo-parlor needle, a husband who left, parents who didn't care, a daughter who abandoned her. Surely, like a phoenix, she would survive this.

Burckhardt put down the chart and looked directly at Audrey. "Ms. Lucas, there is a slim chance she'll wake up. One in a thousand. There is absolutely no chance she'll regain brain function. Would you like to see her CAT scan?"

"I don't understand. It just happened two days ago. It's a coma. People wake up all the time. I read about it."

Burckhardt rubbed his temples with his thumbs. She wanted to grab the wooden chair she was sitting on and smash it over his head.

"I'll show it to you," he said, then reached behind him and flicked the built-in light against the wall, illuminating the CAT scan film on top of it. It looked like an X-ray, only with more resolution, and it showed the outline of a double-layered sphere—the brain. Two long ovals overlapped inside the sphere like black butterfly wings. He pointed at them. "As you can see, there was a lot of internal bleeding, then swelling. All of these neurons are dead."

Audrey closed her eyes, but the light had burned a temporary impression into her retina. In the dark she saw the outline of wings, and thought, nonsensically: *she tried to fly away, but her wings were heavy iron, and trapped her here.*

"No," she said. Her voice was pleading.

Burckhardt didn't understand. He was looking at the film and not at her. "Yes. There was a brain hemorrhage. You can see it clearly. Her entire frontal lobe. She'll be a zombie. No language. No inhibition. No basic reasoning. She won't know you. She won't—"

Saraub let go of her hand and sat up. "Turn it off," he barked.

Burckhardt turned away from the screen. "What?"

"—She doesn't want to see it!"

Both men looked to her, and waited for her to speak for herself. She thought about that, then sat forward in the chair and put her head between her knees. Counted back from ten.

Burckhardt flicked the light and pulled down the film.

His voice finally showed an emotion: contrition: "Now you know."

"Give me a sec," Audrey answered. She closed her eyes and willed back the tears. Reminded herself that her mother needed attending. There was work to be done. Still, in her mind, she saw those heavy wings. Below her, the chair wobbled, like the floor underneath it would soon open, and red ants would pour forth. She wished she was back at The Breviary, where everything was dark, and still. She wished she was building a door.

She patted her thighs. Once, twice. Blinked away the X-ray light. Cleared her throat. Took a breath. Okay. Good. Enough? It would have to be.

"Where is she?" she asked.

Flustered, Burckhardt took a second to answer, and Audrey knew she'd judged him harshly. He was the chief of psychiatry here and had to oversee more than two hundred patients. If he was any good at what he did, he saved his compassion for them.

Still, her new name for him was Fuckhead.

"Room 27, Ward B1 of the ICU. You should be prepared. She doesn't look the same, physically, as when she checked in."

Audrey stood. Saraub followed. Burckhardt handed her his card. "My number's in there, if you have questions." Then he handed Saraub a short stack of papers with two yellow signature stick-its attached to the last page. With a lowered voice, he added, "And if you reconsider. For Miss Lucas to read over and sign. In my judgment, she should be taken off life support."

Audrey averted her gaze. They started out the door. She thought Burckhardt might remember himself, and offer his sympathies, but he didn't.

20

The Hull

The desk at Ward B1 was unattended. Audrey buzzed the bell, but no one came. She wanted to see her mother and couldn't wait. She kept walking. The sound of the respirators preceded her. Like a vacuum turning on and off. It reminded her of iron wings, struggling to flap.

There were two beds jammed close together in the small room, and a body lay in each of them. During their Omaha years, the medicine had made Betty slow and round, so Audrey headed for the large woman lying in the near bed. But this woman's lips were thick, and her hair was dyed brown. Audrey cupped her mouth with her hand: a mistake? Betty, alive?

She headed for the other bed, where she found a skinny woman aged far beyond Betty's fifty-eight years. Folds of skin pooled in the crook of her neck like rippling water. Her jaw hung slack. Someone had recently given her a quick, jagged haircut (before, or after the coma?) so that her Brillo-like silver bangs were crooked and high up on her forehead.

Audrey leaned in closer. Thin lips, wrinkles where once, there had been dimples. On her shoulder, a faded Playboy Bunny tattoo, and along her forearms, needles secured with gauze-colored tape. A breathing machine pumped, slow and predictable. Audrey swallowed, patted her thighs.

"Momma," she said.

She took Betty's hand. It weighed heavy. The sockets of her eyes were hollowed out and skeletal.

Betty Lucas, a madwoman, who'd spray-painted trailers, set her own shit on fire in front of a bar to piss off the patrons, and yes, once tossed all of Audrey's belongings into the street because she'd been so ungrateful as to complain that she had nothing to wear.

But it hadn't been all bad, had it? No. She never let herself admit this—it was too painful, but it hadn't been all bad. It was no coincidence that, growing up, not a single stranger had ever laid a hand on Audrey. Like a heat-seeking missile, every place they'd lived until Hinton, Betty had befriended the most large-hearted neighbor. In her absence, that neighbor had kept Audrey safe from harm. At night, they'd almost always shared a bed. Betty's arms had always banished the nightmares, even if she did squeeze too tight. Betty had taught her to draw and read, too. Two skills that had proven very handy.

And here was the other thing. The big thing that she had pushed so squarely to the back of her mind that she'd forgotten it. She'd been lonely at the University of Nebraska. Two separate roommates had kicked her out. At night she'd sat inside her small studio and listened to the kids playing their games in the halls. Sometimes, she'd come out, pretending to need to take a shower, hoping they'd invite her to watch television or take a swing at beer pong. Instead, they got quiet and waited until she was gone. Weird Audrey Lucas, who reported them to RAs for talking after quiet hours and wore flip-flops and panties in the shower. Her wrists were scarred like damaged goods. Before Betty came back into her life, she'd been on the verge of dropping out. Without that Russell Stover cherry candy appearance her senior year, she would have done it.

She sat down in the fold-out chair and watched her mother. An hour passed, then two. Saraub got coffee, then came back, then got lunch, then came back. Nurses shuffled in and out, shouting baby talk to the slumbering women, as if to show they cared, they really did: "Time for your penicillin, sweeties!"

The day passed and visiting hours ended. She kissed Betty's cheek and rested her head in the crook of her bony shoulder. Betty Lucas, hometown beauty. Talented artist. Saucy heartbreaker. Mother. Psychotic.

And now she knew the answer to the question she'd been asking for the better part of three decades. It wasn't her mother she hated. It was the disease. That fucking disease had cheated them both.

21

Where Do They Go
When The Light Leaves Their Eyes?

Betty's old room was in Ward C4. After Audrey collected herself, they headed there. The scenery was familiar, only more depressing. Apparently, recessions hit hospitals, too. Over the last four years, the white walls had turned dingy gray. Instead of clean Lysol, the entire wing smelled like cream of corn.

While Betty got adjusted to hospital life, Audrey had visited once a week. They used to watch television in the community room, which had been tuned to soothing programs like *Golden Girls* and *Seinfeld*. "Why can't they just shut up about their stupid problems?" Betty would ask while dipping an IHOP buttermilk biscuit into packaged margarine. "I want to watch cowboy movies, Lamb."

Saraub flipped through the document Burckhardt had given him as they walked. "I read this over. It's fine, but it says you won't sue them for wrongdoing. The thing is—how did she get all those pills? And by the way, what kind of doctor uses the word 'zombie'?"

The corridor was long. At least a thousand feet. They were halfway down, and the only window was at the far end. It was quiet in Ward C. Nobody was screaming they were Marie Antoinette, or fleeing from their rooms because big black spiders were chasing them. She peeped inside the doors that were open and saw something even more disturbing: patients sitting quietly. Perfect-posture erect, gazing at nothing. Wearing open-backed hospital gowns, street clothes, jeans, and frumpy dresses. It didn't matter how they looked, they each acted the same way. They stared at the gray walls ahead of them with dead eyes. Biding their time until the inevitable big black.

"It was a suicide," Audrey whispered. "I'm not going to sue. She wasn't old enough for Medicare. Most places wouldn't have taken her at all."

The administrator in blue scrubs propped open the door to C4–38 for them, then hurried off to answer a ringing phone.

Audrey stopped short in the doorway. She could smell her mother. Winston cigarettes and cheap, baby-powder-scented pink perfume. There were two beds. A heavyset woman wearing Betty's orange-and-black geometric muumuu sat farthest from the door. Her hair was a wild white tumble.

"Oh!' Audrey cried. "Momma?"

The woman turned, and Audrey saw she'd been mistaken. This was not Betty. Her skin was too pale and her face too long. Thick dandruff crumbs dusted her shoulders. "Who are you?" Audrey asked.

The woman took some time to answer. Coarse white whiskers poked out from her chin, and her eyes were doped-up vacant. It was possible she wasn't even stoned on meds. A whole generation of these older patients had been lobotomized, and a lot of them wound up in institutions for the rest of their lives. Back in the forties, doctors across the country had shoved ice picks into the corners of their patients' eye sockets, then scraped wing-shaped pockets into both temporal lobes, leaving them incontinent, childlike, and occasionally, soulless. Brain abortions, all the rage. Even Rose Marie Kennedy got one.

The woman turned to her. Audrey noticed the white scars in the corners of her eyes and shivered. Yeah, lobotomy. "We lived here together, in this beautiful place," she said with a dreamy smile.

"My mother? That's her dress." Audrey pointed.

"There's television here, and black walls where nothing scary ever happens, and that sweet air you like so much. You can stay here forever, Lamb. All you have to do is build it. She's waiting. We all are."

Audrey swallowed once, twice, three times. She patted her left leg with her left hand, her right leg with her right hand. Looked at the adjacent empty bed, upon which a pile of Betty's shapeless muumuus were neatly folded. Next to that was a bric-a-brac of odd items in a box. Effects.

"What did you just say?" Audrey asked. The woman smiled, but didn't answer.

Audrey fought an impulse to shake her. She felt something warm, and jumped. It was Saraub's hand on the small of her back.

"Siamese twins belong in Siam," the old woman said.

"What?" Audrey asked, remembering vaguely her dream.

The woman grinned wider. Something in her expression was *knowing*, and not so empty, after all. Her pupils were dilated and dark. They reminded her of the man in the three-piece suit. Of The Breviary.

Audrey turned away. Wiped her eyes. This was no time for hysteria. "Don't talk to me, old woman," she muttered.

"Come on," Saraub said, and steered her to the empty bed. It was stripped down to the mattress. She took a breath and lifted the stack of papers from the box. On top was her birth certificate. Audrey Rachel Lucas, it said, which was funny, because she'd never guessed that she had a middle name.

There was a photo album, too. Audrey's throat made a sound. A laugh or a cry, or something in between. The first page of the album displayed a clipping from the *Columbia University Record* (how had she tracked it down?) describing her New York Emerging Voices Award in Architecture. The next page, a double-sided list of city names in Betty's hand, with numbers beside them:

1. ⊗Yuma: 7
2. *Sedona: 8
3. ⊗Des Moines: 8
4. *Torrington: 8
5. *Scottsbluff: 9
6. *Cheyenne: 9
7. ⊗Fort Collins: 9
8. ⊗Oberlin: 9
9. *Plainville: 10
10. *Trenton: 10
11. *Maco: 10
12. *Ladysmith: 10
13. ⊗Winnona: 10
14. ⊗Epworth: 11
15. ⊗Cascade: 11
16. ⊗Belle Place: 11
17. ⊗Muscatine: 11
18. ⊗Leavenworth: 11
19. ⊗Lockney: 11
20. ⊗Carlsbad: 11
21. ⊗Mescarolo: 12
22. ⊗Las Cruces: 12

23. ⊗Duncan: 12
24. ⊗Clifton: 12
25. ⊗Maricopa: 12
26. *Yuma: 12
27. *Sedona: 12
28. ⊗Solana Beach: 13
29. ⊗San Clemente: 13
30. ⊗Blythe: 13
31. ⊗Prescott: 13
32. ⊗Winslow: 13
33. *Grand Junction: 14
34. *Aspen: 14
35. *Lincoln: 15
36. *Sioux City: 15
37. *Spenser: 15
38. *Mason City: 15
39. *Rochester: 15
40. ⊗Hinton: 16
41. ⊗Cedar Rapids: 16
42. ⊗Hannibal: 16
43. ⊗Ashland: 17
44. ⊗Marshaltown: 17
45. ⊗Fort Dodge: 17
46. ?18–20?
47. *Omaha: 21–31

It named every place they'd lived for more than a week.
It took her a while to figure out the numbers, but eventually, she understood. They represented the age Audrey
had been while they'd lived there. The ones with stars
denoted the happy occasions, and the ones with frowns,
the miserable ones. Funny that Betty had noticed that
some had been sad and some happy. She hadn't guessed
her mother could distinguish the difference.

On the next page of the album, she found something
she hadn't seen in a very long time. Her second-grade

class picture. Sloppy bangs she'd cut herself, and a blue dress that Betty had sewn. The glossy corners of the photo were worn to paper, as if Betty had carried it in her wallet every day for the last twenty-seven years.

So Betty hadn't forgotten that promise they'd made in Wilmette, to cast their lots in together. All this time, these years she'd been alone in this shithole, she'd been thinking of her daughter.

Audrey started to flip another page in the album, but knew that whatever she saw next might start her crying all over again. She snapped it shut and put it back into the box with the rest of the clothes and papers, then looked around the empty room. "Trade," Saraub said, and handed her Dr. Burckhardt's papers, then made as if to carry the box and clothes out the door.

"Just a sec," she told him, because she knew this room would haunt her. It would burn into her memory like that butterfly had burned her eyes. She wanted to make sure she saw every detail, so her guilt didn't fill its unseen crevices with images even uglier than the truth.

She started with the mattress. It had been flipped recently, so she turned it over again and found urine stains. Then she ran her fingers inside the places where the fabric had ripped, but found no roach droppings nor red pinprick evidence of bedbugs.

Next to the door was the closet. She dragged a chair over to it and ran her finger along the plywood, looking for hollowed-out hiding places. Found one on the sweater ledge. Obvious if you're looking for it, which meant nobody had cared enough to look. Her hand came back with a fistful of 5mg Valium, which she pocketed.

"Shit," Saraub said.

"Yeah. But I could have guessed. Betty hid things for rainy days. I want to make sure there's not a note. If it was a suicide, she'd hide it and expect me to find it, because she wouldn't want anyone else to read it. I'm not getting high enough to see this ledge. Give me a boost?"

Saraub bent down, and offered his joined hands. She took off her black flats and stepped into his palms. With a grunt he lifted her up above the ledge inside the closet. She ran her fingers along the dusty edges in search of a note. Nothing. He put her down. She walked the perimeter of the room, peeked under both beds. The old woman sat, hands clasped and smiling, like she was waiting for her big close-up. Audrey climbed up on the desk chair, and unscrewed the glass light fixture in the ceiling. Pills fell like rain. They hit the floor and bounced, then rolled in all directions.

Pills from heaven! she thought.

"Why so many places?" Saraub asked as the two of them got down on their knees and played 52 pickup with Valium and lithium; neither wanted Betty's roommate playing monkey-see monkey-do and following Betty's lead after they were gone.

"It's what prisoners do. They hoard, because it's the only way they can have any control . . . Actually, that's why people with OCD rearrange, too. To control the unknown."

He peeled off his wool jacket and tied it around his waist. It had been a while since he'd had the money for a custom suit, and she saw that its lining was full of moth holes. "That's a terrible way to live," he said.

"Can't have everything," she said, then handed Saraub some of the pills she'd swiped from under the bed, so they both had a handful. "Now we can be drug dealers."

She was about to leave but spotted one last hiding place. The desk screwed into the wall—she pulled out the middle drawer and flipped it over. A sealed white envelope was taped between wooden slats. On it Betty had drawn a young woman with a half grin. Prettier than Audrey, with a warmer, more symmetrical face, but then, about certain things Betty had always been kind. Beneath it she'd written in neat cursive:

Audrey Rachel Lucas

Audrey's face burned. Her breath came fast. Just then, the old woman leaped up from the bed. She was surprisingly agile. In one fluid motion, she and Audrey were nose to nose. "That's mine!" she shouted. "I'll cut your throat!" Reams of spit flung from her mouth. "Go away! This is my house now!"

Audrey made a fist. Saraub almost charged. Then they remembered; this was an old woman.

Her socks were brown support hose. Betty's muumuu fit her like a loose Hefty Bag. "Mine," she snarled. Drool hung from her chin, and dandruff drifted in the air like snow. *She's got no soul*, Audrey thought. *That's why she's acting so strangely. Ever since the surgery, there's a hole where her soul used to be, and through the vacuum its absence left, something slithered.*

"Give it to me!" the woman shouted.

"No, it's mine!" Audrey answered, then balled her free hand into a fist. They faced off, noses inches apart. The woman's breath was animal crackers, and she was the first to flinch. The animation faded from her scarred-up eyes. She retreated and sat back down again, then smiled blankly, as if her outburst had never happened.

Audrey pressed the paper to her chest to smooth it, then put it in her pocket with the pills.

"Let's get out of here," Saraub said.

She nodded. "Ooooh, yeah." They walked out, and as they did, the woman called: "I know who you are! You're the one who builds, but you do it all wrong. You're no good to anybody!"

Audrey bit her lip and squeezed the note tight.

When the doors to the elevator shut, she pressed her openmouthed face into Saraub's thick arm, making a round, wet mark on his shirt, and cried dry tears.

In the parking lot, they sat in the car but didn't drive. The sprawling hospital spread out like a mirage, as far as she could see. Birth and death, and nothing that resembled living, in between.

22

Icarus' Wings Burned Black

She spent all of Thursday and Friday at Betty's bedside while Saraub worked in the lobby, or at the motel. Friday night, they ate BLTs at Shorty's Diner. In her mind like low-level noise pollution, heavy wings flapped.

Their waitress was a big-hipped high-school girl with rosy cheeks who spent her downtime giving them the stink eye from the lunch counter across the room. They looked different from everybody else. They weren't wearing jeans, for one. For another, Saraub was Indian. Strike three, she'd returned her baloney sandwich and asked for the butter to be scraped from the bread. Upon its return, she'd checked for spit, then worried it might be snot, then decided to be safe, since her temporary crown was bothering her anyway, and not eat it at all.

The table where they sat was greasy, and a wire poking out from the vinyl booth had scratched her thigh. She blotted now with a napkin and fought the strange temptation to taste the salty redness.

"When are you going to take her off life support?" Saraub asked.

She looked out the window, where the sky out there was too big, and found herself homesick for The Breviary, whose sheltering walls would never permit such a question. "I'm not."

"But you heard what Burckhardt said. She's not waking up."

She thought about that photo. And the list of the places they'd lived. And the promise she'd made to Betty, that she'd broken. Too soon. She could not have this conversation right now. Maybe not ever.

"You worry about your own family. I'm not abandoning her because of some doctor. She's my mother, and I promised never to leave her."

Saraub opened his mouth as if to speak, then swallowed a french fry instead. Then the rest of the fries, all in a few bites. "Bob Stern from Sunshine called my agent," he said when he was done.

"Yeah?"

"It's a go. Contracts went out last night. I start in D.C. with Senator McCaffrey, then back to New York to interview that former Servitus CEO. After that, the editing starts. Probably in Los Angeles, where they've got cheap suites."

"Oh!" she clapped her hands together in delight. "That's wonderful!"

He nodded. "Call came last night. I might have to leave tomorrow morning, but my agent's trying now to see if he can push it back a week."

She was so happy she beamed. "Well, don't screw it up on my account. The movie's more important."

"Is it?"

"Of course. This is your dream. Aren't you thrilled? I

think I might pee my pants I'm so happy for you. Why aren't you happy?"

He leaned forward, and she saw what he was going to ask before he asked it. Leave it to Saraub to make lemons out of lemonade: "Why won't you be my wife?"

She looked down. Then reached into her pocket, and felt the hard ring. Her face turned red, and even as she did it, she knew she should keep her big mouth shut. But it had been on her mind all week. She'd been hiding it from him every morning, moving it from one pocket to the next. And why had she brought it, anyway? Had she really thought one of the rich crones at The Breviary was going to pick a lock? "You should take this back," she blurted.

He wouldn't touch it, so she put it down between them on the plastic table, while the teenaged girl at the counter gawked. "I can't do this right now," she told him.

He picked it up and turned it, so that the diamond faced up. "You should grow up."

"Don't. Let's do this nice." She was crying as she said it, so she shielded her eyes with her hand like a downward salute, to keep him from seeing.

"My dad died two months before we met," he said. "You know that, right? Or maybe you don't. You're so caught up in your own bullshit, maybe you never even put those two things together. Why do you think I was looking for a woman online? Because I'd become the man of the family, and my aunts and uncles and mother planned this life for me that I didn't want. So I found my own life. I found you. You're what I want. The whole package, OCD and all."

"I don't know what to say," she said.

"Try."

She shook her head. "You have to understand. I can't think straight. I'm not myself right now. . . . Ever since

The Breviary, I think I had some kind of break. There's this door I've been—"

He jerked up from the table and threw down a twenty-dollar bill, then leaned over her, furious. "After all we've been through, you pull this. You're a real chickenshit," he said. His mouth was close enough to her ear that she could feel his breath. Then he stalked out of the restaurant, while the stink-eyed waitress gawked.

He was waiting in the white Camry when she got there, which probably hadn't been his chosen method of dramatic exit. They drove back to the hotel. For a moment she thought he planned to call a taxi from the lobby, but he accompanied her to room seven.

She didn't dare turn on a light, or listen to voice mail, or watch television. Instead, she sat on her bed, and he sat in his. Five feet apart. Silence. The room was so dark that she could see the shine of his eyes.

"I'm sorry about all this," she whispered.

He sniffled. Crying or congested? She couldn't see to tell. "No. I shouldn't have brought it up. You've got things on your mind."

She could hear the frustration in his voice. The urge was strong, but she fought it and closed her eyes. Tried to sleep. Imagined folding the distance between their beds until it disappeared. The sound of his sniffling was terrible. It ached inside her like thawing frostbite.

She got up and felt her way toward him. The frostbite burned. She climbed into his narrow bed. She was crying again. Chest hiccuping with sobs. A nameless pain, upon which the past and future were both heaped. She was the old Audrey, full of hurt and dreams, and the new one, scarred and bitter.

She took his warm hand. Congestion, not tears, after all. He pulled away, but she held his fingers firm and pressed them inside her nightshirt. After a while, he faced her. She closed her eyes, and felt his breath as he brushed the hair from her neck with his lips.

This moment was new and frightening every time. Like a magic trick you have to trust will work, over and over again. The doubts. Why bother? She wasn't in the mood. Too tired. Too sad. She wasn't much good at touching, anyway.

She hesitated, and he waited, done now with coaxing her affection. The duvet was prickly green polyester. Dirty, she guessed. She peeled it from the bed and let it drop. Then pulled off her shirt and trousers, too. He did the same. They were both naked on the sheets. He hid himself, sucking in his belly, and she ran her fingers along it, then kissed his skin until he sighed, and let go.

"What do you like?" he always used to ask. She'd never known how to answer that. Instead, she'd pretended, even though it had shamed her to look at him, and with her smile, lie. She'd never come, not even by her own hand. And every time they'd made love, the lie had gotten bigger, and she'd dreaded it more. But the lie was better than the truth: she was dead inside. A ruined person who would never be normal. Would never feel pleasure, or accept love. There is only so much from which any person can ever heal.

Now, he kissed her, and ran his hands along the curves of her body. The parts she liked, and the parts that shamed her with their imperfection: lumpy thighs, pointy breasts, hips so narrow they belonged on a boy. He touched them, and she closed her eyes, and let him. Always, at this moment, she'd have pretended her delight, then distracted him away from her. This time, she stayed quiet. With nothing to lose, she decided to be honest.

She expected nothing. Silence. The night would be ruined, and he would know the extent of her betrayal. He'd leave in the morning, as he should. It had not been fair to ask him to come to Nebraska.

His hands worked slowly, and then fast. She lay back, and as he touched her, an unexpected thing happened.

An unfamiliar release. Her first instinct was to roll away. Run into the bathroom and hide. But she stayed.

He was different than before. Less tentative. She wondered if, in her absence, he'd practiced with someone new. Something happened. A shiver inside her that grew. Unexpected and terrifying. "Stop," she wanted to tell him, but she didn't because she liked it.

Soon, they were both breathing fast. The shiver built up like a bubble that suddenly burst. She stifled herself, confused and panting, thinking it was over, but there was more. The bubble burst again. And again. She cried out, then laughed, then screamed.

Afterward, they lay like spoons, still never speaking a word. She'd missed the feeling of his skin, and his warmth, and the weight of him in the bed. They stayed like that for a long time. "Ummm," she said, as if to tell him, *wonderful*.

She thought he'd fallen asleep, but then he whispered, his voice low and resigned, like something inside him had broken. "I can't go through this with you anymore. It's too hard."

Her smile went slack. His words were familiar. She remembered that once, she'd said them, too. Only, not to him, but to Betty. "I understand."

He squeezed her tight. And then, he let her go.

She woke the next morning to discover that he was gone. He did not leave behind the ring, a stray Snickers wrapper, or even a note.

23

Madhouses Always Have Broken Teeth

Saturday. Another day at Betty's side. This time, alone. She listened for the sound of black wings flapping, unable to fly. Then wondered: are all people born with holes, or just God's mistakes?

She opened the letter. It was written on unlined paper and short:

> *Lamb,*
>
> *I'm sorry. I got tired. Remember Hinton and the ants, even if you don't want to.*
>
> > *I Love you now and always,*
> > *Betty*

She tore it up, along with the good doctor's papers. They littered the floor like sloughed skin.

When she returned to the empty Super 8, she was too depressed to order dinner and instead took two Valium and a lithium, and crashed. Something squirmed in her stomach, and she dreamed of doors and crushed houses and black rain, only this time, they were soothing.

In the middle of the night, she sat up fast, and thought she saw the man from The Breviary in the corner of the room. A dark shadow without a body. "Come home, Audrey," he said.

She didn't bother seeing Burckhardt again. Didn't sign any papers. Sunday morning, she ordered her ticket home. She cried during the long drive back from Lincoln to Omaha. Roads she'd traveled, so many times before.

Above was the wide-open Nebraska sky that sheltered sane people with families and children and car pools. Content people who knew how to calm the gnawing monsters inside them. As she drove, she understood that she didn't belong here, and neither had Betty. They were too damaged. They'd never belonged here, in the country of God.

She returned the Camry early and beat the approaching hurricane back to New York by a few scant hours. She arrived back in John F. Kennedy Airport late Sunday night, a week to the day since she'd moved into The Breviary.

It was still dark when she collected her suitcase from the baggage carousel, then stood inside the plastic taxi-stand enclosure, while all around, rain pitter-pattered. She hesitated as she told her driver where to take her. Even as she said the words, she knew they were a mistake.

"One hundred tenth and Broadway. The Breviary."

Part IV

The Spaces in Between (Holes)

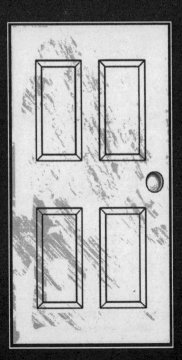

Weekly Police Blotter

November 8, 1992

On Wednesday, November 3, at 5:30 P.M., Officer Raymond Passman was called to a mobile home parked at 621 Station Street on a noise violation. The home is currently occupied by Betty Lucas (39) and her daughter Audrey (16). Through the window, Officer Passman believed he saw blood on the kitchen floor, and forced his entry when the young woman at home would not allow him access. Alleged blood was determined to be the crushed remnants of a red-ant infestation. As this was the third complaint, a $250 fine was issued for noise.

From the *Hinton Weekly*

"Edgardo! You-hoo, Smelly Pants! When ya gonna get rid a all these ants?"

Crazy Mrs. Parker from 14C,
hollering down the elevator shaft.
August 3, 2012

24

Audrey Makes Five!

The man in the three-piece suit played "Heart and Soul" at the piano while the children ran in circles. Keith, Olivia, Kurt, Deirdre. Audrey was there, watching. Wishing that just once in her life, she could join in on the fun. They played Ring Around the Rosy, hide-and-seek, hopscotch—all the games she'd never learned growing up. "One! Two! Three! Four!" they shouted while leaping from cardboard box to box.

Everyone was at the party. Loretta Parker from 14C. Galton in his mask. Marty Hearst, red-eyed and weeping like a pussy. Evvie Waugh from 14D. He swung a rebar instead of Edgardo's cane. Its head was clotted with hair and gristle. The rest of the tenants were there, too. Dapper and self-made, clasping cocktails in crystal glasses. Even their skin was their own creation.

The man in the three-piece suit scratched the ivories. This time, his skin had sloughed to reveal a faded beige skull, like he'd been dead for a very long time. "One!

Two! Three! Four!" he shouted. Clara's children ran in time, leaping from box to box, and Audrey sucked in her courage and joined them. What fun!

After a few stanzas, the piano began to play on its own, and the man curled his bony hands into a fist. "One!" he shouted, and extended his pinky bone. "Two!" his index finger. "Three!" his middle finger. "Four!" his ring finger. Finally, he opened his palm at her. "And Audrey makes five!"

The tenants in faded vintage finery clapped: right fingers against left heels of left hands like dainty sophisticates at the Metropolitan Opera. "And Audrey makes five!" they cried.

She smiled at the sound of her name (famous!), and broke away from the rest of the red-throated children, whose pajamas were so wet. Then she stacked the boxes together over the hole in the rotten wood floor and assembled them into the shape of a door. "Tah-dah!" she announced with her arms outstretched. "Look, you guys! I *made* that!"

The children stopped playing when they saw what she'd done. Motionless feet over swaying torsos, wet puddles at their toes. Doleful little blue peepers gazing floorward while they shivered. Little brats. They ought not to complain. At least the water hadn't scalded them. Like any devoted mother, Clara had tested it on her wrists.

. . . Funny. How did she know that? And if this was a dream, why did her arms ache so bad?

The children wept with sniveling little faces. Dimpled fingers and cheeks, she could tell just by looking that they'd never missed a meal. Store-bought comic-book-character pajamas. The eldest was Iron Man. The girl, Pepper Pots. Audrey's envy squirmed in her stomach like a worm. It got bigger as it writhed.

The children jogged in a circle around her and the door. Their hands were joined like a spinning wheel.

They spun once, twice, three times, four as they sang with pretty voices: *It's the hard-knock life!*

As they raced, the room changed, and time raced backward, too. Red velvet furniture, not hers (Clara's?), rushed to the center of the den. Empty ice-cream cartons, wine bottles, and dirty diapers littered the now-carpeted floor. Flies buzzed. It got hot. High summer. July. The fourteenth floor; closed windows and no air-conditioning.

The children kept circling, and as they ran, their bodies grew gaunt and their clothing soiled. The velvet furniture crumbled and became a smashed pile in the center of the room that rose toward the ceiling and covered Audrey's cardboard construction. The pile took shape, and became a door made from cherry oak and walnut, jigsaw puzzles, pulped self-help books, and toys. Shoddily made and lacking a frame, it rattled as if about to topple.

The children stopped circling. The door began to hum. And then, from down the long, dark hall, a woman's deep voice cried, "Keith! Olivia! Kurt! Deirdre! Don't hide from Momma!" Her voice carried, strong and resonant. It belonged on a stage.

The children shrilled as they ran: high-pitched screams and barks and moans. The red on their throats clarified into handprints. Thumbs up front: the better to squeeze you with, my dears.

Did something bad happen here?

"Keith! Olivia! Kurt! Deirdre!" the monster sang while the tenants clapped their polite, half-assed claps.

Audrey crouched toward the turret and tried to make herself small.

The boys, holding Deirdre, fled from the den and down the hall while the little girl stood still. She was thinner than Audrey had thought, and not blond, after all, but a green-eyed brunette. Her throat was bleeding. She leaned toward Audrey as if to whisper a secret, but shouted instead: "Watch out. You're it!"

Then she tore from the room and was gone. They were all gone. She couldn't see them, but she could hear them. Her stomach slopped. The thing inside it gnawed. The man in the three-piece suit played the same C flat-E sharp combo, again and again. Jangling and discordant. Off-key, the tenants sang: "You're it! You're it! You're it!"

The shoddy door creaked open. The opening made a vacuum. Pieces of the door, velvet furniture and children's toys, collapsed upon themselves. The vacuum sucked the light, too, and stole its own reflection from her eyes. When she looked directly at it, all she saw was black.

The children shrieked. The tenants cheered: "YOU'RE IT! YOU'RE IT! YOU'RE IT!" C flat-E sharp, C flat-E sharp.

The worm got big inside her and shrank her organs small. She hated the sound of these people. She hated the sight of them. She hated the door. She hated her life.

She charged down the hall with her hands outstretched. But her body had grown bulky, and these runts were quick. They weaved just out of reach. She checked the bedrooms; empty. Then swiped under the kitchen table and sink. The walls went red as she lurched. The ceiling, too. Blood or ants or simply paint, she couldn't tell which.

Running. Panting. So hot in here. High summer. The extra bulk she carried made it hard to breathe.

"Olly-olly Oxen free. It's safe to come out. Don't hide from me!" she cried. Her voice was a sweet soprano.

The children screamed. The sound didn't echo. But maybe they weren't screaming. Maybe they were laughing. Finally, she spotted them as they darted: Keith, then Olivia holding the glassy-eyed baby, last Kurt. She followed. Out of breath. Down the hall. It got longer. It got darker.

"Keith! Olivia! Kurt! Deirdre!" she cried, her voice

more charming than an incantation. She belonged on a stage, beguiling presidents. She belonged on the other side of the door, where her adoring fans waited. If only these little bastards had never been born.

One by one, the children dove underwater. Keith. Kurt. Unmoving bodies. Olivia, holding baby Deirdre, was the last to leap. Audrey clawed the sole of her foot and pulled her back by the ankle. Braced her like a slippery fish, then squeezed her bloody throat. Thumbs in front, fingers in back. A terrible snap.

Clinking their cocktails, the tenants cheered her on in the doorway: "Kill your love. It's the only way to open the door!"

The work was hard and thankless. The girl fought back. "She can't breathe!" Loretta declared with glee. The man in the three-piece suit played "Heart and Soul," off-key and dissonant, while Evvie Waugh beat his knobby cane in time.

She watched as little Ol-lovely's eyes bulged, then kept watching, to make sure the girl wasn't just playing dead. When she was done, she looked at her hands, which were wet with blood, then at the mirror over the sink. Clara DeLea grinned back at her, and limp in her arms was a small brunette in tan coveralls, her throat bleeding now, as if it had never stopped. Young Audrey Lucas, dead.

25

The Worm Turns

Another Monday morning at The Breve. Rise and shine!

She slid off the deflated air mattress. The dream departed fast. Acute panic remained. Had she hurt someone? Would she hurt someone?

Her body ached. Her knees, her hips, her shoulders, even the sockets of her eyes hurt. She stretched her hands along the floor. They sank into something wet—the tub! But then, no, it was only the rotten hole in the floor. . . . Had it grown? It looked about three inches wider in diameter, and its broken wood was jagged now, like teeth.

Zzzzt! Zzzzt!

As she sat up, a laser of searing pain sliced her temporal lobes in two. The separate parts throbbed out of sync like the ventricles of a heart. "Oh," she cried out, and squeezed her skull as if holding it together. "Oh, jeez."

She was in 14B, The Breviary, instead of Nebraska. Tears came to her eyes. What was happening? How had she gotten here? Hadn't she planned to leave The Breviary, and move back with Saraub? Weren't there papers left to sign back in Lincoln? Betty. The coma. Had she really left her there without pulling the plug?

"Crap," she moaned.

Zzzzt! Zzzzt!

And the room, oh God. At first she didn't know why the floor was covered in sparse carpet that rippled near the heating ducts like a field of butterflies. But a split second later, she understood. All the clothes from her suitcase. All her other clothes, too. She'd hoarded them for years. Her army peacoat from Saraub, her never-worn but much-loved, skimpy polka-dot bikini, her thrift-store slacks and blouses, grad-school overalls, I ♥ NY T-shirt. Every one of them signified an event she'd survived; another move, another episode with Betty, finals week at UN, the blue paisley blouse she'd worn to the Film Forum that first night she'd met Saraub. All gone now. Everything she owned but the clothes on her back, gone.

The fabric of her former clothing lay in pieces on the floor. They hadn't just been torn, but shredded small as flower petals. Red, pink, green, gray, black, blue: a motley rainbow. As she walked toward the turret, the breeze her body made carried them with her.

Zzzzt! Zzzzt!

She realized now, that the sound was coming from her pants. A bug? A bone finger, scratching? Was she still sleeping? She reached fast into her back pocket. Her phone, set to vibrate. "Oh Goddamn it!" she whispered, then flipped it open.

"Hello?" the woman on the other line asked.

"Yeah," she said. Her voice was raw, like she'd been screaming all night.

There was a pause for a second or two. Then, "Audrey?"

"Yeah." She looked around the room. A mess in here. She felt her crotch, to make sure she hadn't pissed her pants. Wished she hadn't felt it, because her hand came back wet. Seriously? Again?

What was the last thing she remembered? The taxi driver, who'd smelled like patchouli and Jheri Curl. And then, the brass letters that read 14B. She'd stood in front of them, not wanting to open the door, but having no place left to go. The door had been unlocked. Open, even. And inside . . . a shiver ran down her spine. The man in the suit had been waiting for her. He'd played piano. "Heart and Soul." Had she been awake, or sleeping?

"Audrey?" the woman on the other line asked. It sounded like Jill. "Are you okay?"

"No," she said. "I'm all fucked up. But you figured that, right? It's pretty obvious." Out the turret, the storm had arrived. The wind gusted the rain sideways. She realized she didn't know whether it was morning, or afternoon. The blackbirds trapped in stained glass watched her. She punched one of them with her fist, but the glass didn't break.

On the other end of the line, Jill didn't speak. She started to close the phone, then heard, "Yeah. Well, kiddo, who isn't fucked up?"

She sighed. "I've been sleepwalking. Hasn't happened since I lived with my crazy mom. I woke up just now, and the place is a mess. I trashed my own apartment."

Another pause. Because nobody ever knew what the hell to say to her when she came out with this shit.

"Are you hurt?" Jill asked. Audrey could hear the frustration in her voice. Imagined her sitting at her desk with a pile of work, looking for somebody to dump it on.

"No," she said. "I'm in one piece."

Another pause. And then: "Do you need a therapist? I

can give you a few names. My second son has emotional problems. Lack of emotions, really. He sees someone good."

Audrey shook her head into the phone. Rich Manhattanites, they loved their shrinks. "I think I'll start with sweeping up the mess."

"Are you alone?"

"What do you care?" She'd clearly forgotten she was talking to her boss.

"Nice, Lucas. That attitude's gonna get you far. I'm asking because I need your input, but if you want, I can come over and help you clean while we talk about it. Also, as a fellow human, I'm concerned about you."

Audrey frowned, then pulled the phone away and inspected it, like maybe it was defective. Jill Sidenschwandt, showing heart? She put the phone back to her ear. " . . . No. But thank you. I'll clean it myself. But that's. Well, it's thoughtful."

"A rain check, then," Jill said.

This time, Audrey looked around the walls of The Breviary and wondered if they were playing a mean prank and speaking to her through the phone. "That sounds nice . . ."

Another pause, and then, the moment they'd both been waiting for, that let Audrey know this was her boss and not her concerned buddy. "I know the storm outside is bad, but do you feel up to coming in to the office?"

Audrey's face crumpled. She didn't breathe, because she knew it would sound ragged, and she'd start crying. They'd stare at her in the office. They'd know she'd lost her marbles, just like Betty. Or worse, maybe they'd pretend not to see her, because over this last month, she'd become a walking sick house, with a skull nailed to her chest.

"Audrey?"

She reached into her pocket for reassurance. The ring. But instead, out came three Valium and a lithium.

She dry-swallowed them as she talked. The bigger one didn't go down, so she chewed it into bitter little pieces that dissolved on her tongue. "I was sleepwalking last night," she repeated, as if to prove it to herself. Only, she remembered little bits, didn't she? The fabric shears that she'd used to cut the clothes. And the music. And the boxes. She'd worked on the door again, too, hadn't she? And when she'd finished, she'd put it back in the closet like a secret from herself, because something about it was very bad. Something to do with killing what you love.

Her face went pale as the blood drained, and the thing in her stomach began to slither. She punched it to keep it still and covered the phone, so Jill didn't hear the sound as she gagged. Had she been sleeping last night, or possessed?

"I can take you out for lunch if that works better," Jill said. In her mind, Audrey folded the room upon itself. Made it a box that got smaller and smaller. Put herself inside it, where she was safe from the world. Where the world was safe from her, too.

"Audrey? You're on the East Side, right? I'll meet you halfway. How about Smith and Wollensky? The company's treat, obviously."

She pictured a knife through Jill Sidenschwandt's head. Ear to ear. Perfectly symmetrical. If she did it right, the point would line up with her eyeteeth and temporal lobes. She'd keep talking for a few minutes before she bled to death. The brain has no sensation. No pain. It would be interesting to see which faculties she lost and which remained the same. "I'm not hungry."

"Okay, the office? I hate to do this, but you were gone all last week. I saw the work you gave to Simon and David. They're not as quick as you. Besides . . . It might be good for you to get out. You don't sound yourself."

Audrey grinned the way the children in her dream had grinned: bitterly. Sure. She'd come down and lend a hand. She'd cut off this bitch's head. "I'll be right there," she said, and snapped the phone shut.

Her shower was quick. She didn't see her own reflection in the mirror, only black. At times the water was pink. Pretty color, she had to admit. Especially the way the red diluted in ribbons. She'd cut up her clothes, but in the master bedroom's built-in bureau, she found a blue sweat suit, extra large. She remembered it from the *New York Post* photo she'd seen of the DeLea family. The monster in black glasses had worn it. She pulled it on and cinched the drawstring waist very tight. The soft lining felt like a hug.

At the back of the drawer were a pair of glasses. Her head still throbbed like someone had shoved an ice pick through both temples. She put on the oversized black glasses, Jackie Kennedy, only prescription. The headache immediately abated. "Thank you, Breve," she whispered. The worm writhed as if in acknowledgment, and she headed out the door.

Outside of 14B, she found a present wrapped in shiny silver paper. She tore it open. Pulled out a ceramic lamp with a Hawaiian hula-girl base. Her skirt and shade were decorated with drawings of banana bunches. The note read:

> Dear Addy,
>
> Bananas, for bananas ladies, like us! Feel better.
>
> > Your friend,
> > Jayne

Gratitude penetrated her haze. She smiled. Sweet, meek Jayne and her dyed red hair. May she inherit the earth. Then she turned it over, and thought about the note. In her mind, she heard the children from her dream, laughing.

Did Jayne think she was crazy, too?

Through the glasses, everything seemed a shade darker. The squirming thing fed on her insides with sharp teeth. Gnawing, gnawing.

She dropped the hula girl. Black hair and lithe body. A bikini top, like the one she'd lost to the floor of 14B. The lamp thudded as it landed on the red shag carpet. In her mind, it wasn't carpet but red ants. They swarmed, sweet and insane.

She looked at the hula girl's flesh-colored skin and imagined it was Jayne. Idiot Jayne, who thought an orca was a dinosaur. Beirut, a band. Indians from Iran. Blithely happy Jayne, whose job at L'Oréal was probably forty-year-old copy girl. Of course she could stay up late getting drunk, dating grandpas, and hanging out in coke bars; nobody gave a shit whether she showed up at all. Infuriating Jayne, who didn't know she ought to be miserable.

The hall was quiet. Not a sound. The overhead light blinked and buzzed like a locust. She looked at the brass letters behind her: 14B.

She knew it was wrong, but the compulsion was strong. Fragile grass skirt. Little fingernails painted red. Idiot dimpled smile, just like those monstrous children. In her mind, the red-carpeted hallway glittered like an artery, coursing with blood.

She looked down at the lamp and saw herself do it. Played the image over and over again until it became inevitable, like a thing already done. Finally, she stomped on the ceramic girl with both feet.

Muffled by the carpet, the sound was delicate, like eggshells cracking, or Jayne's bones. *One! Two! Three! Four! And Audrey makes five!* She did it again and again. Imagined Jayne's face beneath her feet, cut up and marred by ceramic shards.

Dumb Jayne, who would accidentally stumble into the better life that Audrey had been scratching for with both hands. A year from now she'd be running down the aisle with the old guy while redheaded bridesmaids in tacky pink taffeta threw rice. Strolling into never-never land, where fucking bluebirds chirped. And Audrey would remain trapped here in 14B, watching television in the dark.

As she stomped, she remembered a tub. Keith! Olivia! Kurt! Deirdre! But that wasn't the right order, was it? No, first had gone Keith, then Kurt, last Olivia, who, in her terror, had squeezed the baby too tight, so that by the time it got to the water, it was already still.

. . . How did she know that? No matter; the truth is the point. Olivia. Clara. Jayne. Betty. Jill. These needy bitches always squeezed too tight.

She smashed again. Again. Again. Until the wires separated, and hula girl's face became flecks of flesh-colored sand.

The sound didn't carry, soft as a secret. You'd never know what was happening unless you were out here, watching. During her time with Saraub, she'd missed her secrets. At least now that it was over with him, she could stop pretending that she was happy, or even that she'd ever loved him. That love was anything more than a lie people needed to believe, to keep from slitting their own throats. The world was idiots and dope fiends, and if you weren't one, you'd better be the other.

The lamp sliced the soles of her shoes, but she kept going. Ground her feet so that they bled. Didn't bother pulling out the shards from her wounds. The pain was evidence of her devotion. A gift to The Breviary.

When she was done, she looked down at the mess. A red, dusty paste with wires running through it, and a broken lampshade. She imagined Jayne coming home and finding it, and for a moment, her senses returned. "Oh," she moaned in quick remorse, and bent down to lift the shards, but quickly reconsidered.

Twittish Jayne and her dependence on the kindness of

strangers. Someone ought to teach her to stop knocking. "Fuck you, Jayne," she shouted down the hall, then punched the elevator button. Feet bleeding, she slammed the iron gate and headed down.

If she had glimpsed along the hall, or stopped panting long enough to hear the tenants' emphysemic wheezing, she might have reconsidered her course of action. Checked herself into a mental hospital, or called the police. Perhaps even joined Saraub in Washington. But she did not look, or see the cold eyes behind shut doors all down the fourteenth floor, that watched through the man-made slits of their skin.

After the elevator descended, the tenants opened their doors and began to clap.

26

Some People Burn Their Own Wings

Monday morning, at the same time that Audrey's phone buzzed in her pocket, Saraub Ramesh looked out the window of an American Airlines 767. His camera assistant Tom Wilson squeezed into the seat next to him, packed tight as compressed styrofoam. They were parked on a Dulles runway, headed back to JFK. The Eastern Seaboard was about to get hit with Hurricane Erebus, reportedly the worst storm of the season. Right now, raindrops smacked against his small, round window, and the skies above were black. Takeoff had been delayed thirty minutes so far, and they were waiting for an announcement from the captain about whether they'd be lifting off at all.

This hitch in the weather wasn't surprising. Since Bob Stern had countersigned the contracts to acquire *Maginot Lines,* nothing had gone right. Not the movie, or his subjects, or his cameraman, or even Audrey Lucas, the first and only woman to whom he'd offered his heart.

The ring scratched inside his right trouser pocket. He wasn't sure where else to put it, and it wasn't beneath Wilson to steal it. So in his pocket it stayed. When Audrey had dropped it on the table of that greasy spoon in Lincoln, he'd been surprised by how small it was. Lighter than he'd remembered, too. He'd wondered whether she'd have parted with it so easily if the stone had been bigger than half a carat, and the band had been platinum instead of sterling silver. He'd also wondered whether he should throw it in her face.

Daniel's advice now played in his head: *You're Jell-O, dude. If you showed a little backbone, you wouldn't have these problems. Kick her to the curb, and she'll come crawling back. Better yet, get somebody younger who New York hasn't beaten down.*

That's why he'd left her at the Super 8 Friday morning. Returning that ring had pushed him past his limit. He'd feuded with his family over her, eaten spinach for her, even let her arrange his pint glasses into crazy-ass pyramids on the kitchen table for her, but every time he'd surrendered, she'd demanded more. She'd trashed welcome mats, hidden comic books, shut doors as soon as he got home because she said she'd needed time alone. The weirdest part was the stuff she'd moved small fractions of inches when he wasn't looking. A found-art tin-can vase recentered. A desk shifted slightly to the right. The coffee mugs moved behind the pint glasses, instead of up front like the week before. At first he'd thought he was going crazy. Then he'd thought she'd been waging a covert passive-aggressive war, only it was so passive he hadn't even noticed. It was only recently that he'd understood that it was a compulsion for perfection. She was a girl who cared more about appearances than substance. Right then, he should have realized that they were doomed.

Sure, things had started good. They'd been a team. Nick and Nora without the dog. But by the time she'd moved into his apartment, she'd already started treating everything he did with contempt, from shaking hands with strangers too enthusiastically ("Don't be so eager to please!"), to his slumped posture ("Stand tall!"), to the way he was always winded by the time they got to the landing to their third-floor walk-up ("You'd better not keel over!"). Over time that contempt had translated into more closed doors, and more cleaning, and finally, packed bags. Sometimes he'd caught the contempt in her eyes as she'd frowned at him and understood that she was searching for reasons to leave. And how do you fight someone who doesn't *want* to love you anymore?

So, yeah, you have to go after what you want. Yeah, love is all about patience. But maybe it was time he cashed in his chips and started over. He'd settle for lukewarm affection, even smiling but humorless Tonia, his former betrothed, so long as he didn't have to be anybody's doormat ever again.

Just then, the plane began to roll along the runway. Outside, everything was gray, like the rain wasn't clear, but diluted black. Large metal cages in the air. It made no sense to him that these planes didn't come crashing to the ground.

"What are your panties in a bunch about?" Wilson asked.

"Everything," Saraub answered.

"What I don't understand is how you didn't see this coming," Wilson answered.

At first Saraub thought he was talking about Audrey. *I didn't want to see it,* he almost answered, but then he understood that Wilson was talking about *Maginot Lines.*

Most of the calls had come over the weekend, pretty much as soon as he'd accepted Sunshine Studio's deal. The head of public relations at the World Bank, Internal Affairs at Servitus, a member of the House from Oregon, two farmers outside Buffalo, even the spokesman for the EPA. As if they'd been coached, they each said the same thing: they'd decided to withdraw their support for the movie. If he insisted on running their likeness in his film or promotional materials, they'd sue.

At first he'd argued—permission is permission, you can't rescind it. Then he'd pleaded, because no matter what contracts they'd signed, if they wanted, they could tie the movie up in the courts for years. Finally, after call number eighteen, which he'd taken while literally lying between the starched sheets of the Comfort Inn's double bed, he'd given up. By this morning, more than half his interviews had backed out, and out of the ones who'd stayed, only three were worth keeping. Not enough for a movie. Not even enough for a commercial.

"I don't get people," Saraub said, not so much to Wilson, as to the back of the seat ahead of him. "Some of these guys contacted me. They wanted to talk. They thought they were doing the right thing. What could change that?"

Wilson shrugged, and Saraub could tell that a part of him was enjoying this because it proved his cynicism. "Some asshole you don't know from a hole in the wall, but whose boss is one of the main targets of your movie, buys your movie. Two days later half the people in the movie drop out. This is not rocket science. They used all your notes to contact your subjects and showed them some green."

"I can't believe they'd go to the trouble," Saraub said.

"You fight city hall, city hall buries you," Wilson said, then took a slug from the canary yellow Rheingold Beer can he'd filched from the service tray upon boarding the plane. It smelled bad, and Saraub decided that there were greater sins than taking up too much room in a seat; you could be Wilson.

"Three years of my life, all for nothing. I can't believe this is happening," he said. He wasn't just thinking of the movie, but of Audrey, and his white picket fence dreams that he'd been so foolish to dream.

Wilson half snorted, half laughed. The sound was too loud for public, and the woman in the row ahead turned around and glared. "Don't play innocent. You pissed on 'em! Of course they came after you. You want the government to start regulating multinationals, and you're pissing off the coal lobby, the oil lobby, and the big farmers who get subsidized irrigation while you're at it. Servitus has fifty legal eagles on the payroll to deal with guys like you."

"But it's not like any of the footage is a revelation. Everybody knows we're drilling faster than makes sense," Saraub said.

Wilson shook his head. "Hear no evil. See no evil. If nobody has to think about it, it's not happening. This is America, kiddo. Not Calcutta."

Saraub frowned. The baby boomer generation; how quickly they'd turned. "It's not right," he said. "I'm not letting them get away with it, either. I'm running the footage as is. I don't care what they do." Even as he said it, he knew the threat was empty: he was screwed.

Wilson burped again. He'd been out drinking last night, and was still half in the bag. With the five o'clock shadow and oil-stained denim tuxedo he was sporting, he looked a lot like Ted Kaczynski, which explained why, for once, it was the white guy, and not Saraub, who'd been interrogated and searched at the gate before boarding. *If you hate firing people so much, you should just hand him a pink piece of paper the next time he shows up to work drunk,* Audrey had once teased. *Let him figure it out.*

"Hey! Maybe it's got nothing to do with the movie. They just don't like you," Wilson said.

"Thanks," Saraub answered.

"A lot of you not to like." Wilson chuckled in a mean way and didn't bother to hide that he meant it mean.

Saraub sighed, thought about answering, then decided to look out the window instead. Four Air Canada 727s lumbered gracelessly through the storm and down the runway like dinosaur birds.

He could have hired a studio man two years ago, but instead he'd gone with Wilson, who didn't need to be told when to move in for a close-up and intuitively understood the effects of light and shade. On the other hand, there was a reason Wilson had gone from Hollywood movies to television commercials to now, the lowest of the low, documentaries. He was often late and always high.

On Saturday, Wilson had shown up late to the Hart Building on Senate Row, and they'd almost missed the McCaffrey interview. He'd said his flight got delayed, but the truth was, he'd stopped at a few bars along the way.

To save money, he and Wilson shared hotel rooms. Because of that, Saraub had gotten to know Wilson a lot better than he'd have liked. His old-man stink after eating Chinese food was deadly. Worse, he smoked a joint every night to fall asleep. For the most part, Saraub kept his mouth shut and his eye on the prize. So long as the movie progressed, Wilson could order a team of smack-shooting trannie hookers dressed like clowns if he wanted. But last night, while he'd been trying to sleep, Wilson lit up. The sweet smell had itched his throat until it swelled, and he'd had a hard time breathing. With the movie spinning toward oblivion, and Audrey on his mind, he'd snapped. "Open a window while you smoke that, or I swear to God I'll knock your teeth in," he'd yelled into the dark room. Then added, "And thanks for asking me all those times, if I minded. Because I do. I mind." Then he'd rolled over and pretended to sleep.

Old-man legs poking through crusty boxers and yellowed undershirt, skinny Wilson had stumbled in the dark toward the window and tried to open it.

But they'd been on a high floor, so of course, it stayed locked. After looking at the joint for a second or two, he snuffed it, threw on some clothes, left the room, and didn't come back until the morning. Saraub tried to sleep, but couldn't. In the grand scheme of things, he'd overreacted a little. No big deal. Problem was, he hadn't been exaggerating. If Wilson hadn't stubbed that joint, Saraub really might have gotten up and knocked him bloody. That was a little scary.

In the quiet of the empty room, he'd curled his hands into fists and punched the mattress, all the while wondering if Audrey had been right to be frightened of him, which had only made him punch the mattress harder.

"Come on, you're a big guy. You know that," Wilson now said by way of apology.

"Sure," Saraub answered. Another plane in front of them lifted off. Its wings teetered from side to side, and for a moment it looked like it might flip. Instead, it caught its balance and soared. He marveled. How did they manage?

The silence stretched, and Saraub decided to make peace for the sake of tomorrow's final Manhattan shoot. Sure, there probably wasn't much reason to keep going, but he might as well finish what he'd started. "Sorry I snapped at you last night. Where did you go, anyway?" Saraub asked.

"Do you really care?" Wilson snapped back.

"Of course."

"No. I don't think you do," Wilson answered.

Saraub looked at the back of the seat. They'd inched closer to the runway and were now third in line. Lightning streaked across the sky and made everything bright, and then dark again. Rain poured in translucent sheets across the glass. He knew he was supposed to apologize. After that, Wilson's ego would be soothed and the shoot could resume. They'd finish the last interview and call it a day. That was how they'd always worked together. Wilson handed him bullshit, and he ate it all up for the good of the film. But this ring in his pocket was cutting his thigh, and after what he'd been through with Audrey, and now *Maginot Lines*, he was done with giving people what they wanted. "You're right. I don't give a shit," he said.

The air turned to shards of glass, cutting and tense. Wilson's eyes burned holes of rage into the seat ahead of him.

"Fuck you," Wilson said.

Saraub crossed his legs, opened his mouth, closed his mouth. Rain pelted the circular window. Seeking a diversion, he opened his laptop and played the latest D.C. footage. Squinted at the screen and tried to make his vision small, so he didn't have to look at Wilson.

The interview had turned out pretty well, though McCaffrey, the senior senator of West Virginia, sweated a lot, which never looked good on film. Saraub rolled the clip about twenty minutes in. Blue-eyed McCaffrey was wet as a noodle. "The problem," the senator said, "is that regulating these companies starts to look like choosing flowers over bread."

"But bread is a flower," Saraub answered from behind the camera. "A grain. I just saw it in Nebraska. It grows out of the ground. We kill the ground, and it won't grow. We won't be able to eat."

McCaffrey nodded. "That's the other problem—no one is thinking about this in the long term. We're selling our resources to the highest bidders, and in twenty years, we'll look back and slap our foreheads at the idiocy of something like that—look at South Africa and Iraq, for God's sake—but right now, because we see no serious consequences to our actions, or maybe because we've somehow lost our own survival instincts, we keep doing it."

McCaffrey looked directly into the camera when he said this. "We want to compete with the big guns like

China. But they say in another ten years, the annual death toll in China from smog will reach three million. And the thing is, what they breathe, we breathe. The world spins, you know? Why can't anybody ever recognize that the world spins?"

A shiver ran down Saraub's spine, and he shut the laptop. The footage was good. No doubt. Which in its way amplified his heartbreak. His movie was dead. He couldn't do this all over again. He was thirty-five years old, single, a slob. Nothing to show for his hard work except a dirty studio apartment. He sighed. For the first time in his life, the turkeys had him down.

Next to him, Wilson finally spoke. His voice was ragged with fury, and Saraub noticed that his eyes weren't quite focused. The left pupil lazed farther toward his brow than the right. It occurred to him, not for the first time, that booze eventually gives you brain damage. "That McCaffrey guy should climb up on his cross already. There are winners, and there are losers, and he's just mad he's on the wrong side."

Saraub met Wilson's bloodshot eyes. "And what are you? A winner, or a loser?"

Wilson didn't answer for a second or two, because his downhill slide had begun thirty years ago, and his kids and two ex-wives didn't talk to him, and the apartment he rented in Jersey City was full of roaches, and Saraub was the only person this year to give him a job, and by now, it was pity, because his work was shit. "You don't know your ass from your elbow. And these white wetback hicks from West Virginia you think it's your job to protect are a bunch of nobodies," Wilson said. "Worry about your own backyard. Worry about me."

Tears of rage filled Saraub's eyes. "What are you bothering getting up in the morning for, if you really believe that? Don't you see where this is headed? Pretty soon the country'll be bankrupt—we won't be a country. You think the rich'll be happy about the trade they

made when there's nothing left, and their kids are sick
from the factory fumes, because the EPA got disbanded?
Nobody wants this, and everybody knows it's happening, we just don't know how to stop it. That's how
change happens—people like us, forcing it. We have to
try, or else Rome falls. That's the whole point of being
alive. Like this plane, or the Empire State Building—it's
so stupid to build something like that, when chances
are, it'll fall. It's so stupid to try to fly when your feet
work just fine. But we keep doing things like that. We
change our cultures, our lives, even our biology because
change is how we survive. If we give up all that, just
because it's stupid, we're not human anymore. We're
animals.

"It's not about those farmers, or the people in West
Virginia, who keep lobbying for more digging, even
though they're dying of emphysema. Or the power companies that burn less efficiently every year because they
say they can't afford to build new plants, even though
the hurricanes keep getting worse, and we're growing
tropical mold in Mississippi. It's about us."

"You don't know shit," Wilson spit.

The plane picked up speed. Wilson's grin twisted into
a thin line. He crushed the can and burped again.

"You're killing yourself, and I don't like you enough
to watch," Saraub said. The words surprised him, but
he was glad. It was a relief to finally say it.

"So point your pretty little eyes someplace else,"
Wilson whispered. He lifted his crushed beer, then remembered it was empty. So he put it in the seat pocket
in front of him. A nickel tip for the stewardess. Surely
she'd be grateful.

Saraub realized then that he should have fired Wilson
long ago. He should have confronted Audrey, too. But
he'd waited too long, and both situations had gotten out
of hand. The plane rolled faster. Next to him, Wilson
closed his eyes and dozed, or pretended to doze. The

plane nosed up into the sky. Air bubbled beneath the hull, making him momentarily light, and he marveled at the miracle of the Wright brothers, as unlikely as civilization in the presence of barbarians. The engagement ring in his pocket pressed against his thigh. A hard, cold thing. Out the window, the rainy city of Washington got small. They ascended above the black clouds into more black. He couldn't see anything, even though it was morning.

Suddenly, the plane jittered. He gripped the seat rest hard. The nose smashed against a hot-air front, and dropped. Fast. The overhead baggage compartments rattled open. Reading lights along the rows went dark, and emergency lights flickered throughout the cabin, an hysterical orange. Stowed things speared down the aisles and rained on heads; a red duffel bag, small suitcases with wheels, a Twisted Sister poster, some moron's pet parakeet in a tiny cage. It was too frightened to chirp. He reached out to rescue it, but by the time his fingers were in the aisle, it was gone.

The plane kept falling. His skin stretched into a plastic grin like he was on a spinning amusement-park cyclone. One hundred miles an hour? Two hundred? The longer they free-fell, the faster they'd go, and there was no sense jumping without a parachute. The force of acceleration slammed the breath from his lungs. With each passing quarter second—who would have imagined time could pass so excruciatingly—he begged the plane to right itself, but it did not.

The matchbox cars and tiny houses got big again, and the plane dove nose first toward land. His mind spun through images in brief thousandths of seconds that did not register in his conscious state: the time he'd stolen twenty dollars off his dad's dresser and lied about it. The first girl he'd screwed; a hooker named Vanity that his uncle hired as his high-school graduation present. *Maginot Lines.* If he got out of this, he'd make the best movie he could, and if that didn't work, he'd make another movie. Because there's never a good reason to give up what you love when life is this short.

His mind glimpsed still images of all the people in his life. His mother and sisters—who would take care of them? And then, it stopped skipping around, and settled on Audrey Lucas. He realized how lucky he'd been to have found someone to love.

The plane kept falling. Wilson startled awake, and turned to Saraub with an expression of bug-eyed terror. Something warm down below, as Wilson pissed his denim tuxedo. "Wha—" his mouth opened to say as the plane continued to drop.

Wilson's urine heated the seat, the caged bird tried to fly, and Saraub thought about the note he should have left in Lincoln, just in case what had happened between them on that good night had not been a farewell, but another chance. *Come home,* the note should have read. *You're the love of my life.*

27

Islands Collide

Off to work. Hi-Ho!

The hurricane turned day into night. Wind tore through the canyons between buildings and blew Audrey Lucas along the fissure-riddled concrete sidewalks. Leaking rain and packed commuters in merino suits lent an animal scent to the subway. Slowly, people separated from her like they were the sea, and she was Moses. The floor where she stood was red, and she thought the train was a living thing, bleeding and in pain, then realized it was the soles of her own feet, broken by the hula girl. They dried as the car wormed its way downtown, so that by Times Square, she'd stopped bleeding.

At Union Square, the Valium kicked in. The lithium, too. The people around her did not look or come any closer. She felt a little like the wounded chicken, waiting for the rest of the pack to peck her to death.

By the time she got to the office, the jet lag and pills

had hardened her legs like cement. She had to hold the sides of walls as she walked for balance. When she pressed the keypad numbers and opened the door, Bethy jumped out from behind the reception desk and hugged her. "We are SO sad for you!" she said.

The thing in Audrey's stomach squirmed. It gnawed, chewing her soft tissue with sharp teeth. Pretty Bethy Astor with her rosy cheeks, pencil skirt, and two-thousand-dollar black Prada purse. Bird-brained Bethy, whose untested heart was cold as a stone. She went to charity balls for made-up afflictions like Shaking Leg Syndrome, but she'd never taken a subway, nor given a panhandler change. After a company-wide meeting, she'd announced, "Homeless people should just die instead of wasting everybody's taxes." Half her audience had smiled with glee because she'd expressed what they were too sophisticated to say.

A glory tour of Bethy's most asinine declarations: "Black men are lazy. They like white women better because it raises their social status. Also, we're SO much prettier"; "Women shouldn't work past thirty, because after that, their eggs rot, and their kids wind up retarded"; "Men turn gay when their mothers are too needy"; "Jews steal every time you turn your back. They start wars, too. Not in *my* daddy's golf club. Christians only!"

The worst part, Bethy wasn't capable of independent thought, which meant she was parroting somebody else. Her parents, or her private-school teachers, or her buddies eating half portabella sandwiches and finely chopped salads after a couple of sets of tennis at the Westchester Country Club, or the dipshit executives here at Vesuvius, who smiled in your country-bumpkin face, like you and your Indian boyfriend were the lone exceptions to their contempt for everything that was different.

Bethy let go and noticed Audrey's oversized sweat

suit and glasses. "What an interesting new look," she said. "Did you sew that yourself?"

"No, I didn't," Audrey answered. She imagined poking Bethy's eyes out. The juice would run down her face. Not so pretty then, sweetheart. Daddy'll have to buy some Venetian glass, Sandy Duncan style. Then she blinked and tried to chase the image away. Big brown eyes, and Audrey's thumbs, digging in deep. As easy as making a fist. The sound would be a quick, meaty pop. Fluid would splatter while she screamed. The image subsided like drying tears, and she wondered numbly what mean, petty thing had crawled inside her, sowing poison.

"Do you need anything?" Bethy asked.

"How about a raise? Think you can swing that from your trust fund, Bethy? Because I could use a dentist," she said. Bethy squinted in confusion like she had ice-cream brain freeze, and Audrey walked on.

At her desk, she found a bouquet of white lilies. A couple of the smaller buds were still closed, but two had opened to full bloom. Someone had cut the stems on a diagonal to keep them fresh, then placed them in a square, water-filled crystal vase. She'd never been given flowers before, nor owned a piece of crystal. It was heavier than she'd expected. The note attached read: "Sorry, kiddo. Chin up.—Jill." Next to the lilies were two cards. One, a picture of a poodle without caption from the head of human resources. The inside read:

Darling. Let me know if there's anything I can do. Yours always, Collier.

The second note was a Hallmark sympathy card. The outside was carnations, and in black letters the inside read: "Sorry for your loss." Every member of the 59th Street team had signed it.

She sat in her chair with an exhausted *thrump*. Could

feel her pulse moving slowly, like the blood inside her was clotting. Remembered vaguely what she'd done to Jayne's lamp and her clothes. Was frightened by it. Could see that she'd become unhinged. But more than all that, she was angry.

She opened the drawer, took out a .05 width pen. Line by line, over and over she crossed out every signature on the card. Hungover Craig, who spent five hours every night at The Dead Poet on the Upper West Side, drinking his weight in whiskey, then farting noxious tear gas all day at his cube. Sniveling Jim and his excuses, who bragged about the original Lichtenstein *Girl in Bath* hanging in his Park Avenue apartment, like becoming a member of the downwardly mobile, useless class was a badge of honor. Jealous Simon. His designs were more soulless than a Gropius, and if not for his dad, he'd be working for Trump. Louis, Mark, Henry, and David, the incompetent quartet. They talked sports half the morning, went on coffee breaks half the afternoon, then whined about how nobody ever gave them a shot. Sorry, boys, you were right, layoffs are coming early this year.

She scribbled until all that was left was a black card, wet and heavy with ink. Then she pulled down all the things she'd tacked to her cube over the last seven months at Vesuvius. The David Hockney calendar. With her scissors, she clipped it into small pieces that fluttered into the garbage. Next, the *New York Times* article about her award. She folded it on itself before she cut, like making tiny snowflakes. Then the picture of her and Saraub at the Long Beach Boardwalk. After the hot-dog lady snapped the photo, he'd hoisted Audrey over his shoulder and charged toward the ocean as if to throw her in. She lifted her pen, and line by line, crossed out his face. Then her face, too. Then kept going until the gloss was gone, and the black seeped through the paper, an indelible stain.

Her phone rang. Somebody from the 59th Street team, no doubt. Just like Betty had done, they were using her dry. Also like Betty, they wanted more. She imagined grabbing her scissors and snipping the arteries along their necks. Watching the blood gush, the surprise on their entitled faces. She'd get Randolph and Mortimer, too. Slice them up into little pieces, until they were a heaping carnage collecting flies on the office floor. Paint the walls of this entire building red. Then surprise fickle Saraub at his apartment. He'd betrayed her, and now she would separate her love from bone.

The phone kept ringing. She picked it up. Jill's voice. "Audrey. Could you come by my office?"

Jill, with her phony concern, and her bullshit about not making partner because she was a woman. Maybe she just couldn't hack it.

"I need to talk to you."

"Yeah," Audrey said, then hung up and stood.

Fuck Vesuvius. Fuck the rooftop memorial. Fuck the buildings, and cemeteries, and the plaques, and the lilies and cloying baby's breath flowers that piled sky-high, and the mourners who exaggerated their grief because they needed to feel alive. Fuck the widows and their whining and the kids without parents, like the dead hadn't always outnumbered the living. Fuck the holes all over this city, and in her life, too.

She marched, limbs like lead. Her thoughts were all regrets that moved too slowly to register. Valium clotted them like tiny strokes in her brain, so they sparked and died without reaching conclusion: Jayne's hula girl, her clothes, her mother right now, breathing even though she didn't want to, and most of all, 14B. It was doing this to her. It had to be.

Those rational thoughts died as the thing in her stomach suckled and grew. She pictured Jill. Arched brows and stink breath—drink a glass of water, lady! Imagined tearing her limbs away from her trunk, one by one, then setting what remained on fire. She bristled at the grotesquerie of such a notion, then reassured herself with the knowledge that she wasn't alone. Surely The Breviary would understand.

Audrey stopped at Jill's office. She squeezed her hands into fists and pounded the door open. The office was expansive. Ten times the size of Audrey's cube. At first she didn't notice Jill standing at the window. All she saw was the view; Ellis Island lit up against Hurricane Erebus, and little matchbox cars on either side of Manhattan's veinlike highways. She imagined lightning striking the highest point, and setting the whole city on fire. Watching it come crashing down. The dust would be a nuclear winter.

There were tears in her eyes. She felt their coldness on her cheeks. These things she was thinking, she hated them.

"I need to talk to you, Jill," she said. Her voice was a few decibels louder than normal conversation, but Jill didn't turn, or even jolt in surprise. Her nose was pressed up against the glass window while down below, rough waves etched white scars in the water.

She hovered in her boss' doorway, like she'd hovered so many times before, too frightened to speak or call attention to herself, just hoping that after a while, Jill would notice her. She lifted her index fingers beneath Clara's glasses to wipe the tears away, then wondered: *whose sweat suit am I wearing?*

She noticed for the first time that she was holding a pair of scissors. Their sharp twin blades, intended for thick construction paper, were about five inches long. She didn't remember having carried them from her desk, but here they were in her shaking hands, their points exposed as if ready to stab. She dropped them as she stepped inside Jill's office.

"I quit," she said the same moment that the phone

rang and drowned out her words. Jill jumped, but she didn't answer it or even turn away from the window. It kept ringing, shrill and jarring. It pierced Audrey's ears and chest and mind. It woke her up, and the slopping thing writhed.

Tears returned. Maybe they'd never left. Her mother in the hospital with iron wings. Saraub gone. He'd abandoned her. This place she lived, The Breviary: it frightened her. She frightened herself.

She kicked the scissors into the nearest corner and tried not to look at them. Then patted her knees, squeezed her hands into fists, bit her lips, imagined the room in its many possible configurations: desk, chair, bookcase, leather couch, two standing lamps, Wallace Neff photos of old Hollywood glamour houses, fancy as Joan Crawford's palace. In the end, she returned everything to where it now rested and decided how Jill had arranged it was best, and that reassured her. At least someone around here was good at their job.

The phone stopped ringing. Audrey cleared her throat and considered turning tail. Running out of the office, and the building, all the way home to The Breviary.

Jill turned, then jumped. "Audrey," she said. "How long have you been standing there?"

Instead of her usual brown pantsuit, Jill was wearing jeans and a The Who concert T-shirt. The band's logo, the Union Jack, was emblazoned across her chest, and above it in messy red pen, someone had written, *The Kids are Alright*. Beneath the flag, four names were etched in different-colored marker and handwriting, as if added over years: *Clemson, Markus, Xavier, Julian.*

"I just got here," Audrey said. "I need to talk to you."

Jill gripped the side of her desk and slouched so deeply that she folded upon herself. Audrey surfaced from her own grief long enough to feel sorry for her. She looked exhausted. Then again, you reap what you sow: Who the hell has four kids these days, except an egomaniac?

"I need to talk to you, too. I wanted to tell you that I'm sorry about your mother," Jill said. The shirt looked worn, like she'd bought it back in the nineties, when everyone else had been listening to grunge.

Audrey looked out the window. Those scissors. Holy mackerel. What had she been about to do? Kill her boss for sending flowers? "I had to sign the papers to turn off her life support. But I couldn't do it. She's still out there, in Nebraska. Trapped in that bed. My fiancé left me, too. I think I was going to tell him I wanted to get back together, but he left me in a deadbeat motel in Lincoln, Nebraska, before I had the chance."

Jill blinked. Her face was pale. Audrey noticed for the first time that the items on her desk were organized in ninety-degree angles. Not a single pen askew. "He left you in a motel?" she asked.

"Yeah. The night after I had my first orgasm, too. I didn't know they were real, did you?" she blurted this, heard herself, turned red, and lowered her head. But the talking felt good. Less like she was the member of a different species, viewing humans through glass.

Jill wiped her mouth with the back of her hand. Her eyes got wide. Then something unexpected happened. She laughed. The sound was a quick hiccup. "You never talked about that with anyone?"

Audrey shook her head. The scissors in the corner shone like an accusation, and before she had the time to think about it, she picked them up, and shoved them under a pile of drafts on Jill's desk, so she didn't have to look at them anymore. Jill noted this, but didn't comment. "I don't get out much," Audrey said.

"You're an island," Jill answered.

"I don't want to be. I'm trying."

"You don't have to be."

Audrey sniffled. "Sure. I know." If she looked at Jill sidelong, she didn't think the terrible thoughts. The scissors didn't fly up from under the pile and snip.

"Well, like I said, kiddo. Chin up," Jill said. "I didn't know you wore glasses."

Audrey adjusted the black frames on the bridge of her nose. "My mother's. She was an opera singer."

Jill nodded. Then she made a strange sound, like a squeaking animal was trapped in her throat. She looked away fast, but not before Audrey saw her ruined expression. Pruned face, knit brows, tight grin just about to crack. Her pain was so deep that it radiated from her in waves.

"Oh, God," Jill whispered. She held the lower part of her stomach with both hands. Audrey realized that those four names on the T-shirt had to belong to her sons.

"Oh, no," Audrey said.

Jill picked up the cell phone from her desk as if to call someone, then threw it across the room instead. Audrey cringed. It broke into big hunks of black plastic and wires.

"Sorry," Jill said.

Audrey didn't answer. In a way, it reassured her. Maybe, sometimes, everybody goes a little crazy.

"I have to take a leave of absence. A few days, at least." Jill bent down to collect a piece of the phone, then dug her sneaker into it instead. It broke with a single *snap!*

"I bought this for him, in case something happened. I hate cell phones. Just another excuse for those asshole brothers to call me at midnight and tell me about their money problems. Maybe if they stopped hiring their relatives, we'd be in the black."

"I'm so sorry," Audrey said.

Jill nodded, then pinched the bridge of her nose until her eyes cleared. "I've got to talk to you about something."

"What?" Audrey asked, quite certain that Jill knew. The scissors. Her apartment. What she'd done to the condolence cards at her cubicle. There was so little, save this job, that kept her tethered to this world.

"The Pozzolanas sold the company to a corporation based in India. They're announcing layoffs at the end of the week."

Audrey's mouth went dry, and she realized, for the first time in a long while, how much she loved her job. How proud she'd been to finally get here, under the big top.

Jill waved her hand. "Oh, no. You're fine. But we're losing some of the team. I had to switch the Parkside Plaza meeting with the Pozzolanas until next Friday, obviously. But I'm taking a leave of absence, and somebody needs to run it. I was thinking Simon Parker." Jill let this statement hang in the air.

Audrey shrugged. "I gave him a job. How did it turn out?"

"Not good. He's not a creative. But I'm out of options. Unless you plan on coming back this week."

"How far along are we since I left?"

Jill shook her head very slowly, to convey the severity of the problem. "Some ideas. At least you got them stepping up. But I haven't been around, and neither have you. There wasn't enough direction . . . You're good. I should have told you that before now. I see myself in you, though maybe that's not what you want to hear. Want to be a middle manager the rest of your life?"

Audrey took a wary breath. "Not really."

Jill dropped her hands from her temples, turned to Audrey, looked at her for a long while, and grinned very slightly. "Sometimes I want to throw you out a window."

Audrey nodded. "I feel the same way about you."

"Either you do the presentation, or Parker. If the Pozzolanas didn't treat this place like a country club and hire their friends' kids, this wouldn't be an issue. But that's not how they roll. The rest of us do the work for the ones who can't."

Audrey moaned. She thought about all the work she'd done that would be lost if Simon screwed up the presentation, and the client passed. AIAB would hire a whole new firm. Jill would lose her promotion. So, for that matter, would Audrey, who was in line for a serious raise next year. No joke before, when she'd been talking to Bethy; her temporary crown was three years old. She needed a dentist. And maybe staying at work was best. Look how she'd acted all morning. Did she really want to go home, to be left with no one but herself, and The Breviary?

"I think I can do it, but I can't promise."

"Good girl," Jill said. "I knew you'd come through. You always do."

Audrey was moved. It had been a long while since anyone had approved of her. "Thanks."

"Just the truth. Oh, right. The other thing." Jill scribbled something on a yellow Post-it, and handed it to Audrey. "My home number. I'm busy, obviously. But if there's something urgent about the job, or if you trash your place again, give me a call."

Audrey's eyes watered. Was this woman her friend, after all? "Oh, stop," Jill said. "I hate tears."

She tried to return Jill's kindness. "What's his name? The one who's sick?" she asked.

"Was," Jill said. "I just got the call." She tried to smile. Her mouth was a piano string pulled tight.

Audrey stifled a gasp. She knew that if she showed any emotion, it would spread through the air like a sneeze, and start Jill crying. "What *was* his name?"

Jill's eyes filled. She wiped them with the heels of her hands, then leaned on the desk, like it was the only thing holding her up. "Julian. After me . . . People always say you're supposed to face cancer with bravery.

Why would they say something like that? What's the difference?"

Audrey's bad thoughts were gone, and so was her anger. It all seemed so small, in the face of Jill's tragedy. "They don't understand illness. That's why. They want to pretend that they're the lucky ones, who'll never get sick or old. They think it's something you can fight when really, like my mom, it's something you have to accept."

Jill's voice cracked. "Yes. I think you're right."

"Julian," Audrey repeated. "A good name."

"And your mother?" Jill asked.

"Betty Lucas," Audrey answered.

"Betty Lucas. I'll remember that," Jill said.

Audrey took a step in Jill's direction. Jill let go of the desk. They stood close. Audrey was the first to reach out. She squeezed Jill's shoulder, and Jill looked down, so her tears were unseen. "Thank you," she sniffled.

Between different women, it might have turned into a hug, but for them, this was just as good. When they separated, they nodded, as if to wish each other luck.

28

For Whom The Bell Tolls

Back at her cube, Audrey swept up the mess of torn papers she'd left on her desk. The glasses were too heavy for her face and pinched the nub of skin between her eyes, so she took them off and put them in her sweatpants' pocket, then thought better of it and broke them in half. The difference was immediate. Everything appeared brighter, and less like she was viewing the office through a thick glass aquarium.

Her headache returned, but the pain grounded her and diminished the effect of the Valium. She remembered then, that she'd taken lithium, which, in healthy individuals, can induce temporary psychosis. In individuals with family histories of mental illness, it can permanently alter brain chemistry and cause psychosis. She also remembered that she'd been taking it regularly since Saturday. Not so smart.

First thing she did was check messages. About ten were from the 59th Street team, and another five were from the therapists whose appointments she'd missed. The shrink with the Staten Island accent sounded the most annoyed. "It's 6:30, and I'm waitin'!" she'd announced in the first message, and then, ten minutes later. "I'm lookin' at my watch, and it's 6:40!"

"I'm looking at my watch, and it's Monday," Audrey grumbled, then returned the call and left a message: "I had a family tragedy, but I'm still crazy and I still need to see you."

On her desk were the blueprints she'd been working on last Monday. They were marred by about a hundred penciled-in doors. It took her a second to remember that she'd been the one to draw them. They were out of character from her usual doodles in that none were uniform. They weren't even all rectangles, but hobbit-shaped warren holes, squares, even five- and six-sided figures. She began to erase them, then stopped and narrowed her eyes. Something interesting. She tacked the entire four feet of plans along the length of her cube wall and stood back to look.

The placement of the doors followed the imprecise pattern of a swirling conch shell. It gave the design a flow, where before it had been rigid. What if the hedges were curved and lowered in the places she'd drawn doors, so that pedestrians could see clear across to the next hedge? This wasn't a maze at all. People would never feel lost inside it, because on tiptoe, they could always find their way out. The varying heights would make the hedges look like they were growing while people walked. A grin spread across her face. A whimsical, cheerful design. For the first time in her career, she'd created warmth!

She pulled the plan down and began to work. She sketched for hours and got lost in it. The feeling was good and returned a sense of normalcy. When she was done, she looked the job over and smiled broadly to reveal a row of unevenly spaced pearly whites. The plan was good, exactly what the Pozzolana brothers were looking for. Unless they were drunk, they'd approve it. So would AIAB. Her grin got bigger, stretching ear to ear: hot damn!

It was nine at night, and she knew pretty soon she'd have to leave. She thought about Jayne's hula girl, which surely by now she'd seen, and the deflated air mattress, and her clothes. She didn't want to go back to The Breviary. She'd sleep here if she could. But security had gotten tight over the last few months after a couple of laid-off employees broke in and trashed the lobby. After midnight, rent-a-cops patrolled all the cubes, and even the bathrooms.

She decided to delay the inevitable and check her e-mail. Amidst the spam, there wasn't a single note from Saraub. So she composed one:

Dear jerk,

Thanks for leaving me in a motel room. You probably should have kicked in a few bucks for the bill.

She deleted this, and wrote:

Saraub,

I was very surprised by your departure, but trust you know what you're doing. Good luck with your film, and all future endeavors.

That one got deleted.

Next, she wrote: *I'm slowly becoming possessed by my apartment. So . . . can I stay at your place while you're gone? I don't have keys anymore.* She erased that, too. Finally she wrote: *I miss you. A lot.* She pressed SEND fast, before she reconsidered and deleted it.

After that, her curiosity got the better of her, and she searched "Breviary apartment building."

The first link led to an archived *New York High Society* article from 1932: "The Secret History of New York through Its Venerable Grande Dames, IV: Chapter four of a six-part series." She scanned the whole thing, and found the sections devoted to The Breviary:

In 1857, fifteen coal tycoons had an idea. Instead of traveling to faraway summer homes on Long Island and the Adirondacks, they'd build their own, self-contained community in the hills of Harlem. A grand apartment building sequestered far away from the sewaged streets of Washington Square, and close enough to the bucolic Hudson River for daily swims. They'd have no need to send for kith and kin: they would bring the party with them.

They commissioned the popular architect Edgar Schermerhorn to design the building, and he rendered it with his trademark Chaotic Naturalist details, though the building itself was not affiliated with that religion. The Breviary took five years to erect, and its two-degree slant from perpendicular remains a feat of engineering to this day.

In the absence of an Episcopalian place of worship, the fifteen requested that a church be built in The Breviary's lobby, and a rectory constructed out of its basement. The Irish immigrants who laid the stones, resentful of a Protestant God, named their creation "The Dark Church." The name stuck, but its true origin has been forgotten, which is why locals misguidedly claim that the building is haunted.

The Breviary was born in turmoil. The "Great

Panic of 1857" had led to a decade-long economic depression. The dollar's value dropped. Collapsed land speculation, grain prices, and the manipulation of gold's value drove banks into failure. New York shouldered the brunt of the crisis. Riots, most notably between Bayard Street's Bowery Boys and Five Points' Dead Rabbits, plunged the city into chaos. For weeks, the dead were buried along dirt roads in unmarked graves. Violence spread as far north as the Astor Slums of the Upper West Side. Local and state police could not rout the violent tide. Finally, our dear President Lincoln recalled the nearest Civil War regiment from Bull Run to occupy the city and restore order.

Like all storms, the crisis passed, and the city recovered, much like we will recover from our own black Tuesday. When Manhattan yawned, stretched, and awoke from its nightmare, it cast its gaze on the dazzling Breviary.

By far the most regal edifice of its era, if you walk by it, you'll see that it does not face forward but turns slightly to the west, as if posing coyly for passersby. Its limestone is now gray with soot, but its unevenly distributed gargoyles are still sharp as cut glass. Like the city which it inhabits, its strength is a miracle.

Perhaps the most defining aspect of The Breviary is its occupants. Those same fifteen original investors who commissioned the property raised their families on each of its fifteen floors, and it is now their children and grandchildren who reside there. They are members of a genteel and endangered class who still leave calling cards and equip their doormen with top hats. They throw parties each Monday evening, hopping from floor to floor in the small town that is their building. Many of them attended Yale, Harvard, Radcliffe, or Bowdoin before returning home and wedding each other. Each year at their annual New Year's Eve Ball, they raise money for the neighbourhood homeless, and on winter Sundays, they set out a pot of spiced rum, which they serve to the needy.

Reflective of the city in which it resides, The Breviary has not only survived the precarious environment of its birth, but thrived. We are New Yorkers, after all; we will always endure. So if you're in the neighbourhood, you ought to say hello to the residents of the Dark Church of Harlem, and remember that you are one of them!

Reading that, Audrey sighed with relief. So, "dark" meant "Protestant." She could live with that. It made sense that The Breviary's inhabitants were weird. All native New Yorkers are weird. Lock them in the same apartment building for 150 years, and weird easily turns inbred and crazy.

It was late. The pills had worn off and left her exhausted and depressed. She'd gone a little bananas. Not so surprising given the stress and self-medicating, but nothing twelve hours of sleep couldn't cure. She almost closed the link and went home to 14B. But she'd already clicked on the first link, and there were nine left on the page. She didn't like leaving things undone. It was the same as leaving things open. She clicked the second link and her smile drowned.

The article was a personal history piece from the *New Yorker* magazine, written by an author whose name sounded familiar: Agnew Spalding. He'd been involved in some kind of scandal, she thought, but couldn't remember the details. She didn't want to read it, but she knew that if she closed the application on her screen, her imagination would invent something even worse.

The article read:

UP IN THE OLD BREVIARY:
ONE WRITER'S ENDING

I've read these personal histories before. They're pretentious and self-indulgent. My avid readers have come to expect more from me than droll hat tricks, so it was with some reluctance that I agreed to write this article. Let's hope I do a better job than my illustrious predecessors. The bar, at least, warrants no high jump. I'll try not to mention my ethnic peculiarities, cold father, or first sexual experience—disastrous, incestuous, or otherwise.

I was born in Wilton, Connecticut, in 1961, and educated locally, then attended Brown University before moving to my final resting place, Manhattan. Though not a native New Yorker, I've been here long enough to act like one. I can't drive a car; my license elapsed long ago. I can't countenance waiting for anything; even my dry cleaning has to be delivered. I like my lattes with extra foam and 2% milk, but not skim, and I prefer Indian cuisine to Thai and Senegalese. In short, I'm an ass. But there are worse fates for mice and men.

I don't visit Wilton often. Its wide-open spaces exacerbate my agoraphobia. I'm unaccustomed to big blue skies and streets without numbers. Old family friends and neighbors, barely recognizable now, walk with canes and stumped gaits that remind me too much of the passage of time. I'm told that the Wilton I write about bears little resemblance to the genuine item. In my books, kids wear bell bottoms, movie ushers check identification to prevent fifteen-year-olds from entering R-rated movies, mothers stay at home to raise their children, and fathers commute on the 7:08 express to Grand Central Station to earn their families' daily bread. It's not an ideal place to live, but it's predictable, and its values and taboos are clearly defined.

Between my dream Wilton and the real thing are the embellishments of nostalgia. I cannot say which details are true any longer and which are suspect. Perhaps, retroactively, I'm constructing my ideal childhood and tacking it over the one that did not measure up. Together, they are a new fabric. Both visible. And like the boy on the rocking horse who wishes hard enough, both true.

I'd go back to that dream place if I could, just to poke around. But it seems that's impossible. And so, instead, I live on 113th Street in Manhattan. My nine- and eleven-year-old girls share a cramped bedroom, attend Columbia Prep, and quote the *Reader's Digest* versions of Heidegger printed in their English textbooks. I doubt they understand it, but I'm assured by their teachers that comprehension is not the point. They don't understand their favorite pop star's mental breakdown either, do they? But they still discuss it, and her heroin tracks, as if she is one of their friends. I'm often astounded when I hear their dinner-table chatter about one boy's father, who is in jail for tax evasion, the girl who removed her shirt in front of two male schoolmates for a fee of $5, and how they've given up butter, because it's too fattening, even though, ringing wet, neither of them comes close to a buck. They are small adults in children's bodies. Who would have guessed that the democratization of information would also democratize maturity? We're not in Wilton, anymore, Toto.

In my idealized family life, my wife and I

would dress for dinner, discuss lofty intellectual quandaries with our children, and after tucking them into bed, would sit quietly while listening to Wagner and nursing a scotch. The scotch part being essential. Instead, I spend most evenings at the computer while my wife returns phone calls. She wears one of those phones that plugs into her ear, so when she talks, I sometimes forget, and wonder if she's having a schizophrenic break. Who could blame her? She's an event planner and answers at least two hundred e-mails a day.

We don't use our kitchen to cook. We reheat. Last night, after the kids went to sleep, we watched television. The program was not *Masterpiece Theatre,* but a reality celebrity drug rehabilitation show starring washed-up has-beens in all their drug-addled glory, their problems neatly resolved in one-half hour. We learned that the comedian from an 00's sitcom enjoyed his crack from a pipe, while the child star from that same show preferred her self-destruction via sex trade. Was a love connection in the cards between these crazy kids? Would they live happily ever after and drug-free, or, more likely, when the camera faded, and the limelight to which they are addicted ceased to shine, would they crawl back to their former slop heaps, only to make the news once more, this time with the story of their overdoses. Who can resist such titillation!

Bradbury and Debord alike admonished us not to spy on our neighbors, but to learn their names. And yet, we've installed cameras in practically every room of our homes, voluntarily. I cannot help but wonder if Warhol's fifteen minutes, now truncated to fifteen seconds, signals the death knell of the human mind. Where once, it interpreted and recognized patterns, now it regurgitates without comprehension.

The modern world is defined by absence. Religion, family, work, and even our American nationality have lost currency. Instead of finding suitable replacements for the vacuum their loss has created, we deny that they are ailing and cling to their rotting remains, quite aware of the paradox, the hypocrisy, the inevitable corruption. In 1966, *Time* magazine asked, "Is God Dead?" Now the question is reassuringly quaint: it assumes God once existed.

It is the nature of a vacuum to be filled. Our government drops more bombs on more countries every year. Our friends, undependable and temporary, make poor substitutes for our broken families. We are taught that it is our patriotic duty to consume, and so we fill our leisure time with the pursuit of more and better leisure. Our malls have become our churches.

And so I return to the apocalyptic social critics of the 1930s, who've fallen into obscurity over the last few decades, and wonder if their prognostications might have been correct, after all. Perhaps there is a reason for the obesity, and the lawsuits, and the war-waging that erodes our Roman walls. Easy gratification has stunted our development and rendered us eternal adolescents. We find the old and sick distasteful, and so sequester them from our sight. In their absence, we've become so accustomed to having our way that we cannot even perceive our own deaths.

Our wealth has prevented us from having to sacrifice, or even choose. And in the end, what separates us from animals, save choice?

It is with these cheering thoughts that, like Joseph Mitchell before me (though I flatter myself by the comparison), I lie awake some nights and ponder my mortal coil. The bells of St. John the Divine attend my thoughts, chiming the hour, and I examine the unexamined until it frightens me so dearly that I must surrender to my insomnia, and rouse. My perambulations lead me always to the same place. First the church, and then, The Breviary.

For those who've never seen it, The Breviary is a marvel of gargoyles and hand-carved stone. Among the rest of the modern glass condominiums on the block, its sooty façade and westward orientation appear like a twisted, blackened tooth along a gleaming white smile. Even the inside of the place, though its windows are high and massive, is dark.

On more than one occasion, its kind, white-gloved doorman has permitted me entrance to its lobby, and I've sat in one of its red velvet chairs and read a book until dawn. I can't explain why, but its splendor has always made me feel a little closer to the world I wish I inhabited. A fork in the road forty years ago, that would have led to a life, a world, quite different.

It was with a heavy heart that I greeted the news of the Clara DeLea tragedy. I am no innocent to history or human nature. Still, that monstrous act unmoored me. We live in civilized times. We say please and thank you and wipe our faces and asses. Not even our household pets can stand the sight of their own excrement, and yet this woman murdered her own blood. I wanted to know under what circumstances she could do such a thing. I began looking at my wife and daughters differently, at the very notion.

I researched DeLea and found few answers. A history of alcoholism and depression, but I'm in no position to cast stones on either account. She'd never been committed, voluntarily or otherwise. I ran out of things to investigate, so I turned my gaze to the gargoyled creature that had greeted me twice a day, and often in the late evening, for thirteen years.

There are so many remarkable buildings in New York that The Breviary is often overlooked. Few guidebooks mention it, and almost no one but an art history major could identify its design as Chaotic Naturalism. Nonetheless, it is surprising that it has not achieved a cult following, if not for its design, then for its history.

Completed in 1861 in the farmland of what was once Harlem Hills, The Breviary was commissioned by a group of nascent coal prospectors with money to burn. Their incomes increased exponentially during the Civil War, when coal was the only available power source. They provided it to both sides, and though they were charged with treason, the allegations never stuck. By the 1870s, most of them had shown the good sense to start digging for Texas black gold.

The Breviary's architect, Edgar Schermerhorn, led an infamous career. He designed eighteen buildings. All but one were unsound and eventually condemned. Born in Forest Hills, Queens, his training ground was eastern Europe, and when he returned to Boston and New York, he brought the new school of Chaotic Naturalism back with him. After designing his one success, The Breviary, he went on to construct plans for several slaughterhouses in lower Manhattan that would later be proven inhumane. Under his tutelage, the animals were disemboweled. Screaming, they circled the small stables until they bled to death.

Schermerhorn was quoted saying that The Breviary's design did not come from him, but rather, through him. He dreamed it, and when he woke, on his bedside table, were its plans, already drawn. Every effort to reproduce those plans, aside from The Breviary, resulted in disaster.

The building got its name Dark Church, not, as some would believe, because the Irish Catholics, who hauled its mortar resented that its main floor was an Episcopalian Church, but because of what happened after that. In 1886, Edgar Schermerhorn hanged himself from a rafter above the church altar. The noose didn't hold, and he descended thirty feet. The blood from his cracked skull flowed west along the building's two-degree slant. A year later, his wife was quoted in the *New York Tribune* saying that whenever she looked inside The Breviary's stained-glass eyes, the madness of its maker peered back at her. "Like a mollusk trading shells," she'd said, "He fell so in love with his own creation that he climbed inside it."

For those unschooled in backwoods superstition, such acts render a church unsanctified. Though I'm not a religious man, it does bear noting that the church was never blessed after Schermerhorn's death, though it continued to host Chaotic Naturalist masses, a religion its tenants converted to, through the 1970s. It now serves as the lobby in which I now sit and write this article.

Over the years, scandal has plagued the building. In 1916, a doorman who lived in the basement went missing. Two weeks later his body was dug up by a stray dog foraging for food on the grounds that are now St. John the Divine. The original owners of the building did not fare much better. Of the fifteen men and their families occupying its corresponding fifteen floors, only seven survived the Great Depression. The stock market collapse was partly to blame for the suicides, which were a monthly event. The mode most frequently employed was flights out windows, but there were also medicinal overdoses, drownings (DeLea was not the first to engage a tub for her deeds), hangings, slit wrists, and fatal gunshot wounds (two to the head, and one, improbably, to the groin). The vacancies these deaths created allowed those who remained to spread like mold and take over the rest of the building.

On average, 1 in 125 people commit suicide. That number varies by year, but has essentially remained the same over the last century. In New York, the odds are slightly higher: 1:86. In The Breviary, that average is 1:10. Think about that. Since its erection, 2,320 people have lived there. Many moved away. Some stayed. 232 killed themselves. Another 109 were murdered.

There are theories that suicide is genetic. It carries like hemophilia through families. William Carlos' article in *Popular Science* cites two specific genes for self-harm, and his research is currently under consideration at universities across the country. The families who erected The Breviary still own it. Save for the occasional rentals, the same blood lives there now as has always lived there, and it is possible, given their lineage, that they are all distantly related to each other and carry the suicide gene.

My own family, for example, is thick with the blight. In 1968, my grandfather, Thomas Spalding, shot himself with his own revolver like a coward. My mother, who adored him, discovered his gore. In 1973, my sister Carrie, a high-school freshman and gold-medal high jumper, walked in front of a Metro North train on its way to Manhattan. I made oblique reference to it in my third novel, and some critics have postulated that her death is the impetus behind all my fiction. I should correct that here by saying, it's not the act that motivates me, but the mundaneness with which she drank her pulpless orange juice that morning and slung her backpack over one shoulder. In my memory, she turned back after she smiled good-bye, as if she'd changed her mind, and wanted to say more, but had no means by which to express herself. She'd looked to me, the writer, to express it for her.

It is the empty coffin that haunts me, because her remains were washed off the third rail with a fire hose. It is the life she could have led that haunts me, and the possibility, like Clara DeLea, that she knew something I did not. There is a secret there, unfathomable. Possibly divine. I see it every time I pass The Breviary's thick walls, or think of September 1973, when the world was new, and the siren call of train whistles made me think of travel and not tragedy.

When the *New Yorker* requested that I write my personal history, it started me wondering about the trajectory of my life, real and imagined. I have offspring; ten books and two girls. My third wife I are well matched. But still, I wish Carrie had never taken that graceless leap. If she'd lived, I might have stayed in Wilton and lived a different, more contented life. Instead, I try to tell her story, an endeavor doomed from inception that has made me a restless man, unable to make his own peace. If I'm to be honest, none of my dreams turned out like I expected, and my greatest disappointment is myself.

It occurs to me that my sister and the tragic inhabitants of The Breviary had the gift of sight. They saw that fork in the road forty years ago that the rest of us missed, and the paradise lost. They perceived the end of mankind and grew weary of waiting.

I've been walking past The Breviary more and

more lately. I'm drawn to it. Given all that has happened there, I entertain fancies that it is haunted. Maybe it returns what it's been given, and humanity has made for substandard clay. Or maybe we humans blame ourselves too much, when in truth we should look to our stars. Perhaps there are worse things than man can imagine, and they beg our audience through the gaps in our memories, and paths not taken, and old apartment buildings that appear to have grown souls.

I spend my nights now at the building's lobby, and forgo sleep. A restlessness has invaded my gut—a cold, slithering thing that gnaws without cease and calls itself The Breviary. You reading this can visit me, if you'd like. I'm looking for my personal history here. I'm trying to discover the secret. I'm listening to the bells chime, and wondering if they toll for me.

*Agnew Spalding is the Pulitzer Prize-winning author of seven novels, two collections of essays, and a memoir: *THINGS THAT FILL THE VOID: A DRINKING MAN'S STORY* (1984); *MIMIC: SENTINEL* (1987); *CHASING THE DRAGON* (1988); *DARK PLACES* (1991); *DUST OF WONDERLAND* (1994); *THE DARIEN GAP OF CONNECTICUT* (1994); *THE PERRY-WELLINGTON ADVENTURES* (2002); THE DIVINE DEVOE (2002); *A TWISTED LADDER* (2009); *PETRUCHA'S HUNCH* (2012); and *HOW NOT TO BUILD YOUR OWN ATOMIC BOMB* (2012). His death two days after the completion of this article was a profound loss to the literary community. He is survived by his wife Melinda, and daughters Danielle and Dominique.

Audrey read the article, then reread it, then searched "Agnew Spalding" and found his obituary. Suicide. In his apartment, after his daughters left for school, but before the maid came, so that it was she who found his body hanging from a ceiling beam in the kitchen and not his wife. The article noted that his apartment had a view of The Breviary, and his corpse had pointed toward it. Stranger still, he'd shredded the manuscript he was working on, *Generation Vain*, then pulped it into a single upright rectangle with a hole in it. Since he'd deleted all his files, the work was irretrievably lost.

She wanted to stop, but there was no turning back. She clicked the next few links in the queue for Breviary, and found headlines like, "Murder-suicide in Tony Manhattan Apartment"; dated just two years ago, "Woman Hurls to Own Death"; September 4, 2009. Finally, the most recent article, "Bizarre Construction During Final Days." The caption next to the photo read:

> DeLea apartment, July 4: DeLea made a pile of her worldly belongings in this sitting room. All were chopped into small pieces. The weapon has not yet been found. The apartment also suffered from a serious infestation, which authorities believe may have degraded much of the evidence.

Infestation?

The photo showed 14B's den. Above where Audrey's floor was now rotted lay an indistinguishable pile of what looked like trash.

She recalled what she'd done this morning. Her clothes. Poor Jayne's hula girl. The scissors. The card. The ruined photo, her favorite, of her and Saraub. She picked it up now. "No," she whispered at their obliterated black faces. "Please make this not real."

Then, finally, she enlarged the photo. The carpet in the den was red shag, and the walls were red-painted, too. The items in the pile were clearer now. She could make out their size and shape, and in some cases, what they'd once been: Tinker toys, hacked red velvet chairs, book spines, the broken top of a walnut dining-room table. She studied them for a long while, ran the permutations in her mind over and over again, and knew that the pile was not random. Each item was a jigsaw piece. She solved the puzzle of the large object that had buckled 14B's den.

Spalding's pulped manuscript suddenly made sense. She squeezed her hands into fists and tapped one, two, three, four times. Her nighttime construction was making sense, too. Before she died, Clara DeLea had built a door.

At last, she searched one more name. Looked at the image sidelong, afraid that it might peer back at her. Sharp nose and cheekbones. Tailored wool suit, three pieces. In his younger years, he'd been groomed, but by the 1880s, his long, shaggy hair hung down to his shoulders. Edgar Schermerhorn and the bone-fingered man in the three-piece suit from her dreams were one and the same.

The image suddenly came closer, and Schermerhorn got bigger inside the frame. His smile widened. "Your red ants are showing, my dear."

29

Lambs Taste Better Than Pigs

With downtown flooded, the subway got stuck at Christopher Street. There weren't enough cabs, making Hurricane Erebus the great social equalizer. She and her fellow New Yorkers packed like sardines onto the M60 bus. The heavyset Mexican woman to her left wore an extra small T-shirt that read, BUY AMERICAN! She unscrewed a sludgy jar of pickled pigs' feet and tore the flesh with her teeth as she chewed. To her left, a businessman sporting sprayed-on black hair and a shiny Italian suit clung ferociously to the strap hanging from the ceiling. He seemed new to public transportation and wouldn't give anybody else enough room to share the strap.

Everybody was looking everybody else up and down. In her sweat suit and broken shoes, Audrey wanted to hide. She needn't have bothered; unwashed and greasy, nobody looked twice. But then, a skinny black man with working hands shifted his pink Conway plastic bag, and made room for her to sit. "Here," he said, and held his hand over the empty space, so no one else could jump in and steal it. She smiled, grateful.

It was after midnight. As soon as she'd jumped up from her cube (*Your red ants are showing!*), she'd hightailed it into reception, where security had politely evicted her because the office was closing. When she'd gotten out of the building, it had been raining too hard to do much planning save race for the subway. The doors to most homeless shelters closed by 10:00 P.M. She was out of cash until her paycheck cleared on Wednesday. The flight to Omaha and the Super 8 Motel bill had maxed out her credit card, so she couldn't afford another night at the Golden Nugget. Besides, her only currency was her Metrocard: she'd left her wallet at The Breviary.

As she'd stood inside the doorway to her office, rain pouring, she'd made a last-resort call on her cell phone: "Hi. It's me. The girl you loved and left. Thanks a lot. Sorry to do this, but I'm in trouble, and I need your help. Call me back. Like, now." When he returned the call, she planned to beg for the spare keys he kept at Sheila's place, so she could stay at his apartment while he was out of town. Tacky, yes. Unpleasant, without a doubt. But necessary, too.

As for tonight, her options were limited. It was raining too hard to walk the streets. She supposed, like Spalding, that she could pass the time in The Breviary's lobby. Though maybe that was what had gotten him in the end.

She could knock on Jayne's door, and ask, despite hula girl, if she could stay in 14E for the night. Sure, the whole building was probably haunted (or just as easily, she'd lost her wits), but at least she wouldn't be alone. And if that fell through, too, there was always Bellevue. Like mother, like daughter. The nice thing about the men with the butterfly nets: they come to you.

The bus didn't arrive at 110th Street until after 1:00 A.M.

She raced past the Haitian doorman in white gloves and shoulder tassels, who was reading what looked like a Japanese girly bondage magazine: two tweens in braids and short skirts, smooching. Along the ceiling of the raised lobby, which she now knew had been an altar, she spied about ten exposed, brown-stained supporting beams. The middle one was where Edgar Schermerhorn had tied his noose, she imagined. Because it was the focal point of the lobby, and he'd wanted everyone to see his body as they'd exited the lift.

Her mind made a picture: a dapper madman with shaggy gray hair and a three-piece suit; a creaking rope that swung, got rubbed raw, and broke. He was looking down at her now, through the building's eyes. She could feel him.

And how did The Breviary know so much about her? The probe she'd swallowed that lived in her stomach, which had been listening all this time. Spalding Agnew had felt it, too. Maybe it got inside everyone who spent time here. The longer they stayed, the more of their person it devoured, and the more like The Breviary they became.

The elevator took an eternity to ascend. While she waited, she mentally packed: Wolverine, the box full of her mother's things, her wallet, and the soiled trousers, which she would rinse and wear tomorrow. Then she'd knock on Jayne's door. Do some begging, maybe apologize. Or, hang it, blame dead hula girl on freaky Mrs. Parker from 14C.

By the third floor she heard a low-level din. The voices got louder as the cage climbed. They sounded convivial: a party. By the fifth floor, she gleaned snippets of conversations: a woman's laugh, high-pitched and tinkling like a pinged crystal glass; "Baby, you're the greatest!" As she ascended the seventh floor, she saw a pair of feet, then trouser legs and a blazer, and finally, a plain, white mask: Galton. He reached out and grazed her metal cage with his fingers. There were three or four others who'd poured out into the hall. Their necks craned as she ascended. Pretty frocks and black tailcoats. From far away, all their eyes looked black, like the worms inside them had gotten fat. Like they weren't people anymore, but husks.

The talking resumed once she was out of sight. A man with a sandy smoker's voice shouted:

—"There she goes, just like I told you."

—"If it doesn't work this time, I'm building it myself, you Harpy!"

—"Pow! Zoom! I'd like to see you try, whiskey dick!" a woman answered.

Then they were all laughing. The sound got farther away the higher the metal cage climbed. By twelve, it was white noise again.

The doors opened on fourteen. This morning's glaring white bulb hallway had been replaced with soft pink. It gave the impression of a fancy Las Vegas bordello. Someone had poured Love My Carpet in a line all down the red carpet but forgotten to vacuum.

She didn't want to get out. Bellevue, the wet streets, the all-night Dunkin' Donuts, the frickin' subway tunnels with the mole people. Any of those would have been smarter than coming here. But she couldn't turn back now. Grown-ups don't run away from problems; they confront them. Besides, she wouldn't get far without her wallet.

When she debarked, she found Mrs. Parker in her gerbil-elbowed glory standing in front of 14B. At her feet were hula girl's gritty remains. When she noticed Audrey, her eyes bulged. "Eeek!" she shrieked like a surprised mouse, then grabbed the left center of her chest with both hands like her heart had cramped.

Audrey rushed to her side. "Are you okay?"

The woman clutched Audrey's upper arm with bony fingers, then leaned. She smelled like dead skin. "Oh, sweetie," she panted. "You startled me!"

"I'm so sorry."

The woman wore a 1990s, midthigh-length Diane Von Furstenberg v-neck wrap dress. Her knees were wrinkled baby rodents, and her lips were stained the color of blackberries. Dried blood? No, red wine. She blinked her cataract eyes a few times, still recovering, then muttered under her breath, "Sweat suit? Seen that before."

Mortified, Audrey looked down at her loose-fitting pants that smelled, she noticed for the first time, like stale beer, and were stained with what looked like hardened ice cream. "Laundry day," she said.

The woman cocked her head like she didn't know what Audrey was talking about. *Am I losing my mind?* Audrey wondered. "You pointed out this sweat suit, didn't you?"

Loretta squinted, then smiled, like she thought maybe Audrey was high. "Why would I do that? Now, would you be a dear and give me a hand to the elevator? I've got to drop something off on seven. Loretta Parker, by the way. My family goes back to the American Revolution. I was born in The Breviary. So was my father, and his mother, too. Who are you?"

"Audrey Lucas. Pleased to meet you," she said. They didn't shake, and Audrey felt a little like somebody's homeless cleaning lady. She led Loretta by the arm, taking tiny baby steps. The hall light flickered. Everything appeared shadowy and new, like walking through a stranger's house and not knowing which doors lead to where.

"And how are you settling in?" Loretta asked.

"I don't like it here. I'm leaving. Tonight if I can," she said.

The woman made a tsk-tsking sound. "Oh, you haven't

been reading the paper, have you? Not that bunk with that writer, Spalding Agnew?" Loretta's skin was shiny with cold cream, and so thin that it appeared blue.

Audrey nodded. "Agnew. And some other things, too."

Loretta waved her free hand like swatting a fly. "Don't believe half what you hear, and any of what you read. He was a pansy with all that whiny dead-sister bunk. Used to sit here all night and mumble to himself like he paid rent. Bad manners. You give it time, you'll love it here. Besides, The Breve loves you. I can tell."

"Mmm." Audrey took quarter steps alongside the woman's neon pink Cole Haan sneakers. Nice shoes, but not a great match for the outfit. Neither was her necklace—triple-wrapped red plastic beads that looked like they came from a supermarket gumball machine.

"How's your young man? Cuts such a dashing figure with that dark skin."

Another baby step. "Fine, I guess. He's not my young man anymore."

"You don't say?" she asked.

Audrey pressed the down arrow, and they waited. Her clothes itched. They smelled, too . . . whose were they?

"Well, then!" Loretta beamed. "You've got to start coming to movie night. A different apartment every week, always on Sundays. Been doing it as long as I can remember. We watch the classics. They don't make them like they used to. Tonight was my pick: The original Disney *Snow White and the Seven Dwarfs*. What pretty songs! I'd almost forgotten. When you think about it, bluebirds really do sing. You can't help but feel bad for the Queen, though. How was she supposed to eat a pig's heart? A lamb's is much better."

The elevator pinged. Audrey hadn't been listening. She'd been thinking about this woman's bony fingers that squeezed too tight, just like Betty. She'd been imagining lopping them off from the wrist and watching her howl in shock, then feeling bad about that, and blinking her eyes to make the image disappear.

"What about a lamb?" Audrey asked.

The metal door pulled back. "Well, then I'll see you soon." Loretta dropped her slow-gait routine, and leaped, spry as a disco fiend, into the elevator. She smiled at Audrey like she'd gotten away with something as she pulled the metal cage shut. "Buh-bye!"

30

I Hate You!

Audrey turned toward 14B and shook her head, as if cleaning it out: what had just happened? The carpet beneath her wobbled. No sleep last night and pills today. Had the lithium precipitated an hallucination? Had that Agnew article existed at all? She was so tired she was dizzy.

She trod over hula girl, poor hula girl. Even her light-bulb was smashed. The door opened without a key. The light that shone through its crack made two triangles inside the hall, dark and bright, juxtaposed against each other.

She squinted. Hadn't she locked it? She couldn't re-member. But she *always* locked her doors. She lingered over the threshold. A part of her was tempted to sit in the common hall and wait for morning. But Clara's sweatpants—she had to change out of them. And Wol-verine needed water. And her wallet. She took a breath, and plunged in.

Her broken ballet flats *tap-tapped* along the fifty-foot hall. She slipped them off as she walked and noticed for the first time why her feet had been so cold all day. Rainwater had seeped through the hula-girl slashes in her shoes.

In the den, everything was how she'd left it. The clothes a loose carpet. The air mattress deflated. The piano shone prettily, and she immediately thought of Saraub singing an off-key "Heart and Soul": *I fell in love with you madly!* Silly man, he'd sang it like a joke, but he'd meant it for real.

She went to the turret first. Out the window, the M63 opened its doors. Half past one on a stormy Tuesday morning. Passengers spilled out, and umbrellas blossomed like funereal flowers in the swelling rain. She pressed her nose against the stained glass. What if this place wasn't haunted at all, and this specter she was running from was herself?

"It's-after-us-Lamb!" Betty had cried that afternoon in Hinton almost twenty years ago. Her hands had dripped blood on the white diamond kitchen floor. In Audrey's memory, the perfect version of herself, she'd been at school all day. But the truth was, she'd been drinking stolen Canadian Mist behind the restaurant where she washed dishes, then she'd stumbled through town on rubbery legs. When she found Betty with that knife, she'd still been drunk. Not so surprising that Betty hadn't seemed to recognize her at first, given how different she must have looked from that clean-cut little girl she'd once been in Wilmette.

Would the doctors put her in a straitjacket if she checked into Bellevue? She'd be trapped, just like Betty? Would Bethy from the office find out and spread the news like holy-roller gospel: "Audrey Lucas is NUTS!" Her eyes watered at the thought. Bellevue was surrender. She didn't want to live if it meant sharing Betty's fate. Because the damage in that CAT scan hadn't happened overnight. No, it had taken years for the meds to bore those holes into her mother's mind. And the thing is, if you lose your soul that slowly, does it still belong to you?

She decided then. She'd pack her things and leave tonight. She'd take care of herself, like always. If this was all in her head, well, time would tell. But the first step to finding that out was leaving The Breviary.

That was when she noticed that the turret ledge was bare. Where was Wolverine? She surveyed the room. The thing that caught her eye was too disturbing to decipher, so she focused instead on the torn clothes rustling near the heat duct like pigeons' feathers. At the edge of the air mattress, two pairs of shoes lined up like waltz partners, perfectly even. Her soiled pants, which she'd forgotten to soak or even fold, lay on the floor. A three-foot-long rebar with red gristle caught in its wires leaned against the piano. After looking at these things, her gaze returned to its original object: *the door.*

Since she'd left this morning, someone had taken it out of the closet and propped it against the wall behind the piano. It was bigger than when she'd last seen it, before Nebraska. All the loose extra boxes had been taped to its now six-foot-by-eight-foot body, and its handle had been fitted with the hot-water handle from her bathtub. Four rounded spokes like a cross with the letter H in the center.

But the faucet wasn't the most perverse part of all this. Nor the magically appearing rebar with its gristle, nor the door that she'd clearly improved upon during the night, nor even the realization, as she mapped the distances between apartments and elevator in her mind, that Loretta hadn't been startled at all. She'd jumped because Audrey had caught her leaving 14B, where she'd pulled the door from the closet and deposited a rebar. Probably, she'd been the one to put Clara's sweat suit and glasses in the bureau while Audrey had been out of town, too.

But no, that wasn't the worst. The worst was this: at the door's center were two overlapping piles of wet, green mash shaped like oblong wings. They were adhered to the cardboard by tiny, prickling spines. She didn't want to think it. Oh, how she hoped it was not true. But she remembered now, as if from a dream, what Schermerhorn had told her last night as she'd worked: you have to make your door with things you love, or it will never open.

Her sore pricked fingers suddenly made sense. "Oh, Wolverine, I'm so sorry."

She saw now how she'd failed. It was the same old tune that had played her whole life though she only realized it now. The Breviary was haunted. The tenants were in on it, perhaps even possessed by it. From the moment she'd set foot in this building, she'd been in danger. She wasn't crazy and never had been. Just damaged, like everybody else in the world. She'd known these things all along, just like she'd known twenty years ago that she had to leave Betty and start a life of her own. But she'd never trusted herself enough to follow those instincts, and because of that, she'd made a lot of really stupid mistakes.

It was time to leave this place and never look back.

That was when the wall she was leaning against began to hum. The low pitch carried a syncopation that sounded like Schermerhorn's voice: *Audrey,* it whispered.

She did not take stock, or wait for another word, or wonder if she was imagining, or even search for her shoes. She ran for the door. Her third step, she tripped over the air mattress, then crab-walked backward out of the den.

The floors and walls hummed soft and soothing. The tickle diffused through her skin, up her bloodstream, and into her chest and mind, where it woke the wriggling worm. *Shhh, Audrey. Don't leave us,* he chided. *Stop running away for once in your life.* The accent wasn't British like she'd thought, just old-fashioned and sophisticated, like he'd been educated on the Continent in the 1840s.

She moved fast. And then the floors rumbled: *Audrey, darling.* This time it wasn't just Schermerhorn, but Clara, the children (Keith! Olivia! Kurt! Deirdre!), Loretta Parker, Martin Hearst, Evvie Waugh, and Francis Galton. The other tenants, dead and living, too. All different pitches, so dissonant as to be harmonious, but none quite human. It reminded her of the summertime language of locusts.

She scooted faster. Vibrations roared through the floor, met the tips of her fingers and traveled back to her chest. Hot and terrible. The worm chewed. She felt it climb up her gut and expand in her chest, wriggling.

And then, in the den, projector lights flickered. Against the cardboard door, a black-and-white film still shone. The picture showed a split-level ranch house and broken picket fence. A blond man and pretty woman with long, dark hair and dimples. They held a mewing infant in their arms.

Audrey stopped to look. The image shook slightly, but she knew what it contained. Her family before it got broken. *Audrey,* a voice called through the walls and floors and even the air of 14B, only this time, its sound offered comfort. Tears came to her eyes. This time it was Betty.

"Momma?" Audrey asked. The black-and-white image zoomed in on the woman and child. The man disappeared. So did the house, with its broken picket fence. In the picture, tiny red ants crawled across the baby's skin.

Finish the door, Audrey, so we can always be together. The vibrations murmured through the floors, caressing her hands and knees like a warm blanket, while against the door, Betty's image was mute. Only her eyes moved. They followed Audrey like a Cheshire Cat clock.

The worm gnawed on her organs, tiny little bites. "You're not my mother. Betty's gone. She abandoned me," Audrey sniffled.

You forgot your promise, but I didn't. I kept that second-grade picture. You and me, forever. You betrayed me, Lamb. You left me alone in that terrible place. But I forgive you. Finish the door, Betty answered.

The hall light flickered, then went out. Everything got dark, except for the image of Betty holding a baby. The camera zoomed closer. Pretty dimples, vacant smile. Audrey remembered the CAT scan, and the black wings, and that red-ant day in Hinton, when her whole life changed.

"It was your madness chasing us. It was never after me, Momma, because I'm not crazy," Audrey whispered.

It was you, Audrey, the walls echoed with Betty's voice.

She remembered that day twenty years ago. There was more to the story than she'd always allowed herself to believe.

Betty's knife against her throat. Beads of blood. "Shhhh, Momma," drunken young Audrey had whispered, when she'd finally mustered the courage to speak. "Shhhhh. It's your Audrey."

Betty had lowered the knife a little, but not far enough. So Audrey had put her fingers between the blade and her skin, then eased down until she'd knelt over the broken floor. "I'll help, Momma," she'd said. "Look. We'll work together." And so, she'd lifted a clump of dirt. She'd put holes in her own house, just to pacify her maniac mother.

"Look! There's the monster!" Betty had cried twenty years ago, only it hadn't been a monster—but an ant hive, from which an angry swarm had risen. Biting. Biting. They'd flooded the white tiles. Audrey had stamped her feet until the floor was red while Betty had fled. When it was over, the floor was a mess of gore, as if Audrey had done murder.

The cop that showed up hadn't just told her to wear turtlenecks, either. He'd written down the number for a children's shelter. But like always, she'd stayed, and cleaned up the mess, and when Betty returned six weeks later sporting an oozing Playboy Bunny tattooed to her shoulder and a bad case of hep C in the making, she'd cleaned that up, too.

"That's why we always ran, Momma. The ants were always chasing your holes. It had nothing to do with me," Audrey now said as she changed direction, and crawled knee over knee back into the den. Betty's Cheshire eyes went left, then right. Left, then right.

I miss you baby, the walls answered in Betty's voice as the camera zoomed closer. From the bottom of the black and white image tiny insects began to crawl. The baby squealed.

"You were sick, Momma. You were no good to me or anybody else," she said, because she wished she'd said it back then instead of always playing along to keep the peace. Always pretending things were okay, even while her wrists had made a bathtub pink.

The ants covered the baby's swollen face as it raged. The image was still, but the sound carried through the floors and walls. A weeping, furious wail.

We're trapped in here, Lamb. Get us out, Betty said as the image zoomed, and the baby disappeared. *If you build the door, we'll go back to Wilmette, before the red ants came. Just you and me. We'll live there forever, and you can always be my baby. Build the door.*

Sobbing, Audrey covered her ears. The camera zoomed closer. Now it was only Betty, thirty-four years ago. Pretty, with the world at her feet. Against the still frame, an ant darted across the white of her eye, and her skin wriggled.

Audrey touched the image against cardboard. It was soft, like her mother's skin. With her free hand, she lifted the rebar. A steel pole wrapped inside tense, sharp wire. Its opposite end was clogged with fleshy chunks of what looked like rust.

Nobody loves you like we do. Nobody ever will. They'll leave you, everyone one of them. Saraub. Jill. Even Jayne is already gone. But we're here, Lamb of mine.

If she smashed the rebar against the piano, she could use the wood to build a sturdy frame. But they'd known that, hadn't they? Loretta and the inhabitants of The Breviary. That's why they'd left her this bloody present. That's why they'd asked her about Saraub; they'd wanted to make sure she was alone. That's why they'd let her live here for so cheap, and why Edgardo was missing: he'd warned her.

Aren't you tired of fighting? No one else has had to work so hard for so little. You deserve this. Build the door, and you can rest. Momma will take care of you.

Audrey looked at the cardboard construction and realized that it was wrong. Too perfectly flat, too sturdy. It didn't adhere to The Breviary's skews. Just like her dream of Clara's door, it would fall apart as soon as it opened. It needed curves, and functional chaos. It needed an architect instead of an opera singer, or a snotty author of personal histories. She smiled when she understood that 14B had picked her because it meant she was the most special girl.

Audrey hoisted the heavy rebar. The image zoomed closer. Ants scurried. Offscreen, an infant squawked, as if being burned. Betty's face sagged. Her eyes turned black. Something was inside her, wearing her skin like a coat.

Do it now, Audrey. There's not much time. Even buildings have their beginnings and ends.

Audrey blinked. Looked out the window at the driving rain. At her hands, full of tiny cactus wounds. Remembered the dream she'd had the night Betty died, "Better run, Lamb." And those red ants in Hinton, she'd forgotten them, but they'd been real. They'd come out from a nest beneath the floor. Maybe it was even true that they'd followed Betty to every town, because not everyone is lucky enough to be born whole. Maybe some demons are real.

I got tired of fighting, Lamb, the note had read.

She understood then that this thing was not her mother. Nor was it Clara, or the tenants, or even Schermerhorn. This thing that called to her was The Breviary. But there was something The Breviary didn't know because she had not guessed it herself, until now.

She hated Betty Lucas. She wanted her dead. She'd always wanted her dead. Some nights in Yuma, and Hinton, and even Omaha, she'd imagined shoving a pillow over her Betty's mouth while she slept. And every time she'd smoked a joint, or gone for a long walk, or gotten drunk, or cleaned a room twenty times, or even sliced her own skin, it had not been out of self-loathing, but to calm her own red ants, so she didn't lose her temper and shove a knife through Betty's throat.

She lifted the rebar. Her blood ran hot in her veins as she swung. "I!" The rod reverberated in her hands. The wires encasing it twanged against her palms, but her calluses were so thick they didn't cut. She swung again: "Hate!" Swung again: "Ughhh! You!" Her whole body slammed, and then shivered along with the rebar. She swung again: "I hate you!" Again. Again. Again. "I hate you! I hate you! I hate you! I don't want to go back. I don't want it fixed. It's over. It's dead. Why aren't you?"

She chopped Betty Lucas' face. Her black-and-white-film-still eyes bugged in wild surprise. The image bled the color black down the side of the door. As it pooled to 14B's floor, it turned to red. The red turned to tiny, pinching ants that marched down into the rotten hole, and inside the walls of The Breviary. The line thinned as Betty's blood drained dry.

"Hu! Ha!" she cried, as the last of the boxes fell. "Bye-bye!" Wolverine made a clump as he hit the ground. The hot-water faucet rolled lopsidedly from point to point, and her shouts became grunts, and sounds without meaning. And then simply gasping.

All her life, she'd dreamed of raising her voice at Betty. Screaming. Reciting any one of the thousand speeches she'd memorized. Or simply asking, "This life you put me through, have you really convinced yourself that you did it because you love me?" But always, she'd stifled herself. Always, she'd let Betty run the show. Until now.

She kept pounding until the boxes were tiny pieces on the floor that mixed with her clothes and stuck to the reopened and bloody wounds of her feet like homemade Band-Aids. Panting, too tired to strike one more time, she dropped the rebar.

The door lay in a pile.

"Fuck you," she called to her mother, and 14B, and The Breviary, and even God, who ought, once in a while, to take sides.

Audrey, the walls whispered through the vibrations in the floor. It wasn't her mother's voice anymore—it had given that up. It was Schermerhorn, and Clara, and the children. It was the tenants, past and present, too. She could hear their thoughts. All one overpowering thought. The floor rumbled. The walls shook. The vibrations were a furious scream:

BUILD IT, YOU BITCH!

For once, she trusted herself and didn't hesitate. She ran. The walls went red behind her. Water poured out from the open bathroom door as she passed. Her curiosity did not get the better of her. She did not look inside at the tub. Only heard the sounds of struggle. The sickly-sweet voice of the little girl who, in her terror, had accidentally suffocated her baby sister in her arms. "I squeezed too tight, Momma," hard-knock Olivia cried.

And then, the monster, in reply. Her voice strangely kind, like she was doing them all a favor. "Into the tub with you, Ol-lovely, and it will all be over. We'll be together forever."

Audrey turned the handle and escaped 14B.

31

Do Black Sheep Dream?

Out!
    She shut 14B's door behind her, sweat dripping down her brow, arms and back aching from the weight of the rebar. The hall was lit pink as a little girl's bedroom. She stabbed the elevator button, decided it would take too long, and raced for the stairs.

As she ran, she passed 14E, which was dark and ajar. Jayne. Hadn't she mentioned nightmares since Clara's death? And not sleeping? Hadn't she been stuck in this miserable place all week, on a wounded knee?

Audrey swung open the stairwell exit. Jayne was a big girl. She could take care of herself.

The metal fire steps rattled. Her bare feet burned as sores reopened, and she left a trail of blood. Already she knew what she'd do when she got out. Have Tom's Diner call Saraub, and if they refused, call the cops.

Rattle. Rattle. Twelfth floor. She slowed and thought of something. Smashed hula girl still lay in a pile in the hall. Given her ample free time, there had to be a reason that Jayne hadn't knocked, or written a note, or cleaned it up.

Jayne. That nitwit redhead. Audrey cursed her, then sprinted back to the fourteenth floor. She swung open 14E.

"Jayne, are you here?" she called.

No answer, but something in there creaked. It sounded like a rope. While the common hall was lit by a red bulb, once she walked inside 14E, the light left. She looked behind her. Saw the red carpet and 14B's shut door. Then faced Jayne's hall again, where it was so dark that she could not see her hands.

Creeeeaaaak! The sound came from high up, and about twenty feet ahead. What was it?

She reached for a light. Her hands traced cool plaster. Then she remembered that unlike her own apartment, there was no switch, just a string hanging from a bulb about fifteen feet down. She walked farther inside with her hands spread wide. They spanned the width of the crooked hall while she slid her feet across the uneven floor instead of lifting them, to keep from tripping. With each slide, the mouthlike wounds on the pads of her feet gaped, trickling sticky blood between her toes.

Let her be okay. Let us both be okay, she mouthed, though she knew better than to speak, and break the silence. Her heart palpitated faster than when she'd smashed the door, because in this slow-moving dark, she had time to think. The sweat poured from her brow, as if she were still hacking, and she tried not to think about what she'd just come from, because what lay ahead might be worse.

Shhp-shhp was the sound her feet made as they slid. The farther she got, the more distant the common hall appeared. Its light was a pinprick. She wanted very much to run back and meet it. Live in the light, where it was safe. She bit her lower lip to keep from hyperventilating, and reminded herself to breathe. She couldn't leave, because up ahead, she smelled freshly smoked Winston cigarettes: Jayne was here.

Creeeaaaak!

What was that? A part of her guessed, but the rest of her didn't want to know. She moved faster. *Shhp!-shhp!* Then bit her lip, and listened. The sound continued:

Shhp!-shhp!

"Ohhh—" she started, then slapped her hand over her mouth to stifle her own gasp: something was in here with her.

Shhp!-shhp! It came a little closer. The sound was like sandpaper against marble. It came from behind, which meant that it had trapped her inside. She hitched her breath—the beginning wail of a crying jag, then squeezed her mouth and nose together to keep still. Maybe it couldn't see in this dark, either. Maybe if she just stayed quiet . . .

She lifted her feet. Placed them delicately back down as she walked. The thing followed. *Shhp!-shhp!*

So dark in here. Oh, God, and the air, so wet. Where was Jayne?

Shhp!-Shhp!

What *was* that? She let go of her mouth, and her body reacted before her mind could censor it. "Jayne!" she screamed so loud and raggedly that her chest hurt from the expulsion of breath.

Silence answered. And then—*Shhp-shhp! Shhp-shhp! Shhp-shhp!*—it moved faster, and with more urgency. It was coming for her!

She kept going. Bare feet, gently picking their way through scattered objects. Something soft. Another thing, hard, that almost cut. Tears fell like bathwater. She wanted to slide down the side of the wall and give up. Curl into a ball, just like back in the Midwest, and hope her mother didn't see her.

Shhp!-shhp! Shhp!-shhp! It was so close. She could feel its eyes, searching.

She stretched her hands out and felt the walls on either side. Picked up her pace. Behind, like a long-distance dance partner, the monster moved faster, too: *Shhp!-Shhp!*

Suddenly, the left plaster wall was gone. Her hand dangled. She let out a high-pitched breath that made a sound, "Huuhoooh!"

On the left, a small bedroom. It was bright, like a picture from a movie in a dark theatre, even though the hall remained as ink. "Oh," she said. "Oh, no."

All those magazines Jayne had collected. They weren't scattered anymore. They were stacked and taped together into a four-foot-by-two-foot square against the wall. Someone had tried to rend a hole through them for a handle, but the paper was too thick. A tiny door.

She let out a cry. "Jaaa—" she said, then bit down on her lower lip, because the thing was even closer. She could smell it: old, desiccated skin.

Shhp-shhp! Shhp-shhp!

Faster! Another step. Another. As fast as she could, she greased the floor with her blood. Her hand slipped again. Another room. The master bedroom. Bright in there, too. Unmade bed. Wet rubber mattress. All the family photos that had been magnetized to the refrigerator now lay scattered on the floor. In every one of them, Jayne's face had been crossed out with thick, pink pen.

Another step. Another. She raced. Her chest cramped like a heart attack, but still she kept going. .

SHHP!-SHHP! The thing was so close that she could feel the floor vibrating as it raced. In a panic, she gave up her silence: "Jayne!"

Up ahead, something creaked.

"Hold on, Jayne. Please, hold on!"

Panting. Sweat dripping. Her heart slowing now, even though she was more terrified than ever, because her body was spent. *Just a little farther,* she promised herself. Just a few more steps. Because she'd taken—how many? Eleven. The light pull had to be close. She guessed eight more steps.

Seven. Six Five.

Shhp!-shhp! If it extended its arms, it could reach out and grab her. She picked up her pace and tried to put distance between them. *Tear down this place, God.* She pleaded, a silent nonsensical prayer. *Swallow it. Devour it, so that it never was, and never will be.*

Three more steps. She'd pulled ahead of it! But then, shit! Her right foot hooked inside something cold and hard. She spun, but the cold wouldn't let go. She lost her balance. Fell on something hollow and metal. Its rattle echoed throughout the hall. So loud!

Shhp!-shhp!

Metal, everywhere she reached. Her first thought was that she'd landed in a graveyard for the tenants who'd died in The Breve. Over the years their bones, and the metal rods and screws that had held them together had piled here. The thing that was making that sound (*Shhp!-shpp! Shhp!-shhp!*) was a human wraith, guarding its treasure lair.

She grinned with resolve, tight and rictus, then tried to stand, but got caught on more metal (bones!).

Shhp!-shhp! It was close again. Arm's length.

"Help me!" she cried. No one answered. Not even a nosy tenant. Where were they? Where was everyone? "Jayne!" she shouted. No answer. Silence. All alone, just like she'd always been alone.

Shhp!-shhp! She could feel the sonofabitch gaining. Overhead, still that creaking. A terrible sound.

She turned. Her eyes by now had adjusted to the light. She saw. A man, or it had been once. A three-piece suit. It crawled on its hands and knees. Edgar Schermerhorn, only its eyes were black, and its skin hung loose and rotten from its curved, arachnid bones. Its arms were as long as its legs.

With a deep grunt, she hoisted herself up along the wall. Hopped on one leg, but tripped again on the metal ring, and fell again, too. Landed in the same place. Her kneecap came loose. The sound was like an airtight jar twisting open. Explosions of sparks. "Oooowww!" she howled as her body went into cold shock, then scrambled on her hands and good leg, dragging the bum one behind her.

Two more steps. One more step. No more steps. The rope had to be here, in the center of the hall.

Shhp!-shhp!, the thing behind her. She could hear its wheezing breath. Something cold and soft grazed the back of her foot. A finger, perhaps. Or a spider's leg.

"Go away!" she cried as she hoisted herself again, using her good leg and letting the other one dangle. Waves of pain came too fast for throbbing; instead they were an endless red scream. Weeping, she turned her back on it and reached for the switch. She didn't know she was speaking, nor what she was saying as her hands swung blindly through the air: "Huhuh. YoucandoitAudreypleasedoitIknowyoucan huhuh . . ."

Panic. Another cold, soft finger. This time, it grazed her neck. The pull string! Where was it?

Creak! Something warm and wet trickled from above. It dripped along her hairline. A spider's web? She felt the displaced air like a summer fan's soft breeze, and then Schermerhorn was upon her. He pulled her down by the shoulders and onto the floor.

His breath, old and boozy. Too unspeakable to scream. She flailed, tearing away his soft parts as his fingers squeezed her throat. Maybe his clothes. Maybe his skin. And then he was looking at her. Spider eyes.

They stole all the light, so that even his reflection was gone, and she understood now why the hall had been so dark. "No one gets out!" it shouted.

It squeezed tighter. She flailed in the dark with her thumbs cocked, seeking to squash his eyes, and wishing she'd kept that engagement ring, so she would die with something of his still close.

And then, suddenly, the hall lit up. Everything got bright. The man-thing was gone. The hall was empty. In shock, she flailed the air. "Ahhh! Ahhh!" she sputtered, her legs pulled close to her body, kneecap floating. Feet bleeding. Shadowboxing a ghost.

All down the hall were the streaking footprints of her blood, as if she'd walked alone. The tenants watched her from just outside 14E. She noticed this in a flash, then turned her face to The Breviary's heavens. Something dripped. And creaked.

She hoisted herself up. Sparks of pain strong as defibrillator currents pulsed through her skin. Up above, saddle shoes swayed in concentric circles. Their soles were worn to a thin layer of rubber, and wrapped around one knee was a thick Ace bandage. Dyed red hair, faux diamond earrings lining her infected left lobe like decoration. A felt poodle skirt, open and flowing like a flower to reveal pale, bruised legs. Like a dirty old man's joke, white underpants, wet and soiled.

Drip. Drip. Urine pelted Audrey's forehead, because when people die, their bladders release.

She saw now what she'd tripped over. Not bones. A metal ladder, from which Jayne had climbed, then kicked aside. The rope wasn't tied right. Her neck wasn't broken. That was why she was swinging, and the reason the rope had creaked. Too much slack.

She looked lonely as she rocked, so Audrey reached up and touched the sole of Jayne's left shoe. "Silly girl," she said, then burst into tears, as the tenants of The Breviary approached.

32

Baby's Breath

Six days after Audrey Lucas discovered Jayne Young's body hanging from a noose, Jill Sidenschwandt's phone rang. It was two in the morning, and her Madison Avenue bedroom was liquid ebony. Tom reached across the king-sized bed and swatted the antique rotary off the Prince Edward nightstand, then draped his arm over her and squeezed.

Jill burrowed her face into her pillow. "Noooooo," she moaned. It had to be one of the Pozzolana brothers. Not even Tom's China clients had the balls to call this late.

"Are they kidding?" Tom asked, then flicked the Tiffany lamp. Shards of colored glass ignited like a rainbow. "You've got to quit. Start your own business. You paid your dues with those people."

Half the office had shown up at the funeral three days ago. Even Mortimer had put in an appearance. But by now, he and Randolph probably thought her mourning period was over. They wanted her back at her desk.

She flopped onto her back. The ceiling was cracked, which she'd just now noticed. Wishbone-shaped. She winced, and resisted the temptation to make the only wish that mattered.

"They're not kidding; they're just idiots," she said, then remembered that the receiver was off the hook—they might hear her. "Gaaaa," she muttered as she picked it up, then asked, "Hello?"

No one answered on the other line. But she could hear someone's breath. The sound was distant, as if the speaker on the other end was holding the phone at arm's length.

"I can't sleep anyway," Tom said as he sat up beside her. "All these flowers are killing my allergies. I wish they'd just send cards."

Jill squeezed Tom's thigh to silence him. He squeezed back, to be cute. "Hello?" she asked again. More breathing. It sounded further away than before.

"Julian?" she asked, still half-asleep. Next to her, Tom stiffened. It wasn't him; she knew it wasn't Julian. But how could she wonder, and not ask?

When he died, they'd both been at work, and the home-care nurse had been drinking coffee in the kitchen. Her last words to him that morning: a caricature of tough love. Teary-eyed and panicked, he'd asked her whether she believed in an afterlife. It had hit her then, though she should have understood as soon as the doctors gave up on the chemo: her son was going to die.

Shut up and stop worrying, she'd told him. *You've got to be brave and face this fighting, or you'll never get any better.* She'd hated him for just a moment, for having been born, and leading her to this moment of failure as a mother, for not having kept him safe.

"Julian?" she asked again, though she knew it was impossible. Still, it might be the past calling, and this was his death rattle. She could right the wrong, and hear it now and console him, like she should have done then.

Sniffles. "Puh—" The voice said. It sounded feminine, and was followed by panting.

"Who is this?" she asked while Tom switched on the light. Their room was awash with funereal white flowers that smelled worse with each day they ripened. Rancid sugar air.

"Huh, huh, huh," someone—it sounded like a woman— half breathed, half cried over the line.

"Who is this? Tell me who you are!" Jill said.

"Help me," the woman begged. Then the line went dead.

Jill's stomach turned. Something urgent. Something terrible. Her own self, perhaps, calling her from a parallel future, to warn her of what was to come. Only it was too late. Her son was dead. She got up fast and started down the hall to check on the rest of them.

She and Tom had bought the apartment with his trust fund back in the late nineties. Seven thousand square feet in a doorman building in the East Seventies. A long hall connected all the rooms. Up until yesterday, the place had been crammed with relatives. She missed their clutter and hushed voices. The way they cooked and doled out hugs that did not comfort but at least distracted. But Tom's parents had caught a car back to Greenwich, Connecticut, last night, and for the first time since Julian's death, her shrunken family was alone with its grief.

She went to Xavier's room first, and sprung open the door without knocking. One hand clutched a *Hustler*, the other lay hidden beneath the covers. A freshman at New York University, he hadn't been ready to leave the nest and live in a dorm. She'd hoped college would bring friends, or unearth a latent talent, but so far, no dice. His bare chest was hairless and pale. Something about its softness seemed unformed. There was a vacancy behind his eyes. She liked to think he was ditzy, but she suspected it was more than that. His mind traveled to solitary, unfathomable places. No matter how many presents or hugs he got, he was always convinced that the world had done him wrong.

She'd been so busy with Julian that it had only occurred to her at the funeral, when Xavier had sat away from the family and off to himself, that there was more wrong with him than spoiled-kid syndrome. "Why isn't Mercedes coming to clean today?" he asked after the burial, his affect flat as the oil in a level. "I needed somebody to vacuum my room."

Now, in his own world as usual, he pumped under the covers without seeing her. Even in this, his movements were clinical. Though he held the magazine, she did not imagine he was thinking about the black woman with bright pink nipples on the cover, or even of a boy. Nothing so human as that. Just an itch to be scratched. She shut the door and moved on, hating herself as she thought it, but thinking it nonetheless: *Why Julian? Why not Xavier?*

Next, Clemson's room. She found him sleeping soundly. He'd come home from his last year at Harvard for the funeral, and would be leave again in a few days. You'd think he'd have gotten cocky with those smarts and looks, but no. Like Tom, he made a point of putting people at ease. Less like Tom, he always had to win, be it lacrosse, grades, or squiring the best-looking girl to the University Club. If she had any complaints, it was that he was too perfect. People like that, you always wonder what lies beneath. Probably, they wonder, too.

Farther down the hall. She didn't turn on the light, and instead felt her way with her hands through the dark. Last year, when her parents had visited from Dayton during Julian's first round of chemo, her father had asked, "What does the mortgage on this place set

you back a month? Forty grand? You know, there's kids
starving in Africa." Then he'd looked her up and down
like she wasn't his daughter, but a stranger, and said
something she still hadn't forgiven. "There's kids with
cancer. Leukemia. You sell this place for something half
the size and donate the difference to charity, you could
save some lives. Maybe start going to church again and
say a prayer to St. Jude, and you could save *his* life."

"Shut your fat mouth before I shut it for you," Jill's
mother had answered, but by then, Jill was already
in tears. Not a day had gone by since, that she hadn't
remembered those words and wondered if they were
true.

Finally, she checked on Markus. He'd moved into Julian's bedroom after the diagnosis, to keep him company. They'd slept in narrow beds separated by a night
table like an old married couple, and after only a few
weeks, had been finishing each other's sentences. Irish
twins separated by ten months. Markus had been the
most present during Julian's illness, and perhaps the
only one to understand how much that time had mattered. But the end stages had wrecked him. In sympathy with Julian, or maybe in grief, Markus, too, had
lost so much weight that his ribs protruded. He'd even
shaved his head. In a matter of months, both boys had
shrunken inside their skins like mirror-image ghosts.

She opened the door and saw that Markus was not
alone. He'd sneaked his boyfriend Charles through the
service entrance. In sleep, they were pressed together
like spoons in the far bed. She sighed.

She might have found Charles more palatable, were
he not so limp-wristed and fey. So easy to bully, with
simply a frown. The boy was a runaway that Markus
had met in Times Square. His parents had disowned him
at fifteen, and he would have become a street walker
if Markus hadn't helped him get a job waiting tables.
He lived with a bunch of kids in a studio apartment in

the Bronx now, didn't go to school, and dyed his hair platinum blonde. A white cotton sheet concealed their nakedness.

She cleared her throat. Dead brother or no, if she'd done something like this back in Dayton, her mother would have made her pick her own switch, then shipped her to a convent. It occurred to her that she had erred. Nurses, nannies, the house in Amagansett, private schools, then the Ivy League. The boob lift last year that'd had nothing to do with back pain. The constant diets that left the refrigerator bare: four (now three) growing boys, and not a single sandwich fixing. Her job at Vesuvius, which provided her the excuse to neglect her family, when she should instead have quit as soon as she'd gotten pregnant and raised them right.

If she'd been around more often, Xavier might not have gotten lost in the shuffle. Clemson wouldn't be so smug. Markus might have learned affection for the fairer sex. Tom might not have cheated with his secretary, and almost lost his job after that sexual harassment suit that had cost the company millions. The things she'd traded, all for vanity.

The morning Julian died, she'd known it was coming. Had been able to smell the scent of it on his loose skin. She'd opened the window a crack even though it had been frigidly cold, just for some relief from that relentless death stink. She'd understood she ought to stay, but so often these last twenty-two years, her intuitions had proven false. The product of unfounded worries, and guilt for not having been there often enough. Just as easily, the day might be tomorrow, or next week, or fifty years from now. She could not succumb to such fretting when she had work on her desk, and a life to be lived. So she'd left her son with his nurse, and six hours later gotten the call that he was dead. It had taken her more than a day to call family and friends because she hadn't wanted to say the thing out loud.

"Is there an afterlife?" He'd asked, and now she wished she'd swallowed her terror, and told him: *Don't worry, my love. There is a heaven for you on the other side of the stars, and if there is not, I will make one.*

Would leaving him to die alone be her greatest regret? Or would there be more, unfathomable, that would pile over the years so that when she died of old age, she would see two lives, the one she'd lived and the shadow path, full of all the things she should have done. The truth her father had implied: if she'd been a more righteous person, her favorite son would not have died.

In the old sickroom, Markus opened his eyes. Average grades, average looks. No special skills except an ability to put other people at ease, because he so rarely spoke, but always listened. He was the wild card of all her children—stronger than his frail body appeared and kinder than the rest of them, too. His eyes bulged now, and he startled. Next to him, fey Charles grunted.

"I'm sorry," he mouthed.

She waved, to let him know she didn't intend to make a scene. The tips of her fingers flagged up and down in unison. "Ice mother," Julian had once called her, and to her dismay, the others had laughed. Julian was the only one who'd ever teased her, and now she wondered if the rest, even her husband, were afraid.

She leaned in the doorway. Julian's bed was empty and stripped of sheets. On the bureau were piles of clothes that she planned to take to Goodwill. A poster of the Dubai Tower was tacked to the wall, because it scraped the sky, and had reminded Julian of Babel. He'd wanted to build bridges and skyscrapers. Plan the cities of tomorrow. She could smell him in here. Poor Markus, this room was haunted by a ghost.

Markus sat up. His eyes were wet with grief, or maybe shame, as if he believed that for this transgression with Charles, she might love him less. Still sleeping, Charles snuggled against Markus' bare chest, and kissed it.

To her surprise, she wasn't angry. Just grateful to Charles, for transforming this miserable room that would live forever in Markus' memory, into something bittersweet. At least he would not have to be alone on this terrible night.

"I love you," she whispered, because he looked so much like Julian. Because she did love him. Because there was a reason, after all, that she'd left Ohio, and made a new life for herself in New York.

She shut the door. When she got back, Tom was dressed. He'd heaped the white flowers into a black Hefty bag. She nodded her approval, then sat next to him on the bed. "What was that all about?" he asked.

"The person on the phone. She was so sad. I got worried one of the boys was hurt." She weaved her fingers between his and squeezed. These last few days, they hadn't been able to stop touching each other. In their way, returning to the source of their lost son. "I should have been there for him. I wasn't a good enough mother," she said.

He sighed, and she wasn't sure if he agreed or was too tired to answer. "No," he finally said. When she opened her mouth to reply, he interrupted. "No. No. No. No. No."

Now it was her turn to sigh.

His face was clean-shaven, and his hair freshly washed. They were alike in that way: even in tragedy, they firmly believed in the rituals of living. Over the last week, not a single bill had gone unpaid, or report card unchecked, or e-mail unanswered. "When's the last time we were on a date?" he asked.

She shook her head. "It's three in the morning."

"Not for at least a year. Not since he got sick. Let's go to Monteleone's. Have a cold Guinness."

"Is it open?"

Tom tossed a pair of overalls in her direction, along with her twenty-five-year-old Who T-shirt. It was what she'd been wearing when they met, and no matter how much she'd changed since then, he told her he would forever remember her that way: an innocent kid from Ohio who still wrote letters to her grandmother once a month, and loved the Pinball Wizard. The only girl he'd met back then who'd made men wait in the lobby of her building before dates instead of inviting them up. What she hadn't told him was that she'd been working seventy-hour weeks; she hadn't had time for dating. He was the only man who'd stuck around long enough to propose and find out what her apartment in Queens had looked like. Still, it was nice that one of them remembered her youth so fondly.

She pulled the shirt over her head and buckled her overalls. When she stood, she pressed the side of her face into the crook of his arm. Above her, he sneezed. Then said, "I saved the lilies because I know you like them, but let's take out the rest of the flowers when we go."

She and Tom had weathered big fights and big egos, badly trained dogs, sick parents, sick kids, and a year-long separation. She knew then that they would weather this, too. It reassured her that she could believe in that, in him. She'd been wrong last week when she'd told Audrey that nothing lasts because not everything dies. Sometimes love endures.

"Forget Monteleone's. We'll just wind up crying in our beers. Let's walk down Broadway 'til we get hungry."

"Deal," he said.

It did not occur to her until three hours later, as she sat across from her husband eating buttermilk pancakes at Around the Clock on 8th Street and Astor Place, that the voice on the other line had belonged to Audrey Lucas.

33

Bones Break All the Time

A week after Audrey discovered Jayne Young's body, Saraub Ramesh was high on Vicodin, watching the Vikings hose New York. His hospital bed was one of those Craftmatic adjustable jobs, just like he'd seen on TV when he was a kid. The game wasn't nearly as disheartening as it might normally be. Then again, Vicodin.

In the wooden chair next to him, Sheila fiddled. She'd come to visiting hours every day since the accident, and even feigned an interest in football. Tuesday and Wednesday had been season recaps narrated by Mike Ditka. His sisters and their husbands had sat through that. His excuse, as he'd silently watched the boob tube instead of entertaining them at his bedside, had been his drug-induced stupor—it made conversation hard, and ESPN easy. The truth was, he'd never much cared for grand shows of affection, and they'd all kept staring, like the second he turned his head from the screen, they'd pounce, and weepingly declare their love for him.

His cousins, the new Ramesh and Ramesh, had come Thursday and Friday during NCAA rerun games. They'd razzed him about being the only person injured on the entire plane: *You always were a spaz.* Then they'd gotten teary-eyed, which he hadn't expected.

"Why are you always flying all over the place? Why can't you just stay still?" his cousin Frank had asked.

"Because," Saraub answered.

Frank, a man with three kids, a nice house, a cashmere coat, and a smart, efficient wife, had sighed. "And your girl puts up with that. I envy you."

Until that moment, Saraub had always considered himself the black sheep of the family. Over the years, he'd seen less of them because on a very fundamental level, they'd stopped understanding each other. Now, he reconsidered that assumption, and he reconsidered them, too.

That weekend—all twenty-six of them visited. Sisters, brothers-in-law, cousins, nieces, nephews, aunts, and uncles. They brought several four-hundred-dollar bouquets, made a racket, then tromped off for lunch at Ottomanelli's. Their arrival had made him realize what had been missing from his studio apartment in Audrey's absence: noise.

And today, Monday. A week since the accident. Sheila sat next to him, her glazed eyes on the game. Through it all, to his surprise, and perhaps hers, she'd been his constant. She'd cheered teams she didn't care about, yelled at nurses to make sure he got his meds on time, interrogated doctors about their diagnoses, and in general, irritated everyone who worked at New York-Presbyterian into giving him special treatment. It was like an alien had possessed her and forced her into acting like a parent again.

"Here," she now said, and handed him the heel of

some fresh-baked bread while they watched the game. When he dozed sometimes, he woke to find her reading *Vanity Fair* or *Better Homes and Gardens*. Until then, he'd never imagined she was capable of entertaining herself. Always at home, she spent her time dining with friends, preparing meals, or on the phone with her daughters, foisting child-rearing advice and inquiring whether their husbands were spending enough time at home.

He took the bread and chewed. The Vicodin waned in the afternoons, and he was usually a little more coherent. "What's the spice in that? Clove?"

"No spice. It's Pillsbury Italian Loaf. Easy peasy."

He nodded. She put her hand on the bar of the bed, which was as close as she'd gotten, so far, to touching him. Even when he'd first arrived, she'd only leaned over the bed and bent her face close to his. *Open your eyes*: she'd commanded, presumably to make sure he was alive. So he'd opened them.

The landing a week ago had been lucky. If the pilot of the 767 hadn't caught a patch of cold air at thirty-five hundred feet, they might have crashed. Most people wound up unharmed, but like an idiot, Saraub had unbuckled his seat belt to try to catch the flying parakeet. He got thrown, broke three ribs, a cheekbone, and both arms. On the plus side, he'd managed to save the stupid bird.

He'd stayed overnight at the hospital in Bethesda while they waited for Hurricane Erebus to pass. He'd been badly hurt, but none of the injuries were serious. Instead of waiting at the airport, his cameraman Tom Wilson wandered off, then showed up drunk at the hospital the next morning. "Your movie almost got me killed," he'd croaked, then pointed at a mosquito-bite-sized cut on his forehead. "I'ma sue your ass off!"

Saraub had looked at Wilson's red-threaded eyes right

then and said what he should have said a long time ago. "You're fired."

Incoherent and raging, Wilson didn't leave until security escorted him out.

After he was gone, Saraub was not sad, even though they'd worked together side by side for years. He was relieved.

That afternoon, American Airlines flew him first class to JFK, and checked him into New York-Presbyterian Hospital on their insurance company's dime. Probably, he should have been discharged by now, but since he'd signed a waiver agreeing not to sue, they were giving him gold-star treatment. His room was private, he had his own nurse, and his dinner came with a sixteen-ounce bottle of gourmet beer.

His cell phone and laptop were destroyed on impact, so aside from his family and agent, he hadn't talked to anyone in a week. He'd called Audrey every day and left a message from his bedside hospital phone. So far, she hadn't called back. A lot had happened lately. His girlfriend moved out on him, he'd almost died in a plane accident, he'd fired his assistant, and overnight, his promising film debut had morphed into a lemon. These things had given him a new, no-bullshit lease on life. In keeping with that, Audrey's silence didn't hurt his feelings; it pissed him off.

He had one interview left to conduct for *Maginot Lines,* with the former CEO of Servitus. Unfortunately, he'd missed the appointment because he'd been in the hospital, and the guy was now in Europe on an indefinite holiday. Sunshine Studios wasn't returning his agent's calls. Still, as soon as he got out of the hospital, Saraub had decided to finish what he'd started and edit the movie. A recovering idealist, he'd given up high hopes for a wide release, or any release at all, but would instead take one step at a time.

"Lamb?" Sheila asked, then pulled out a Tupperware container from her Metropolitan Museum tote bag. She looked older than he remembered, and smaller, too. She'd stopped dyeing her black hair and let it go white. He admired her more now than he ever had before. She was a strong woman, and on day five of her vigil, while she'd shooed the family out so he could get some rest, it had occurred to him that if he'd acted more like a man from the start, instead of always borrowing money and begging approval because the road he'd chosen was so different from anything the Ramesh family understood, maybe she would have treated him like one. But such is the nature of bones and families alike; they break all the time, and it's how and whether they knit back together that counts.

Sheila opened the Tupperware. "I baked it last night," she said.

He smiled. "They feed me here, Mom. I'll just be full. But maybe you could give it to the nurse, and ask her to serve that, instead of my dinner." On-screen, Biddle caught Manning's pass.

"Oh, I didn't think of that. Good idea," she said, and placed the Tupperware back in her bag. Her hand moved closer to his. "It's not this girl, is it?" she asked.

"What?"

"She didn't put you on a diet, did she? Why doesn't she come? Is her job too important for you?"

Saraub shook his head. He'd called at least ten times this week, and was starting to wonder the same thing. "Leave her out of this."

Sheila sighed. Then sighed again. Saraub looked at her and realized she wasn't sighing, but crying.

"Hey, stop! I'm not dead. It's not even serious. I promise."

"I'm sorry. I'm so sorry!" she'd told him.

"For what? You didn't make the plane crash! I'm fine, Mom. Really."

Her hand clasped the parts of his fingers that poked through the cast. He'd missed his mother; he'd missed the rest of his family, too. "Do you love this woman?" she asked.

He shook his head, like he was disappointed in himself. "Yeah. I do, Mom."

"Well then, I'll try to love her, too." On-screen, the Giants scored a touchdown, which, high on pills, he decided was a sign from God.

"She's had a rough time. She could use somebody being nice to her."

Sheila nodded. "I'll bake her some lamb."

Saraub smiled. Sheila let her hand drop. For the rest of visiting hours, they watched New York steal a victory from Minnesota. When it was over, she reached between his plaster-cast arms and hugged him good-bye.

"I'm glad you're back," he said.

"Me, too, sweetie."

Just two miles away, trapped and bleeding, Audrey Lucas pressed her body against the locked turret window of 14B and screamed into the void.

Part V

Audrey's Door

Not a Case for
the Psychic Friends Network

July 11, 2001

I read Phil Egan's story on the hauntings in The Breviary apartment building with deep concern. He seemed under the misapprehension that ghosts and demons are the same thing: they're not. Ghosts are the lingering stain that humans leave on earth once their mortal coil is abandoned. Demons were never human and don't exist in this dimension. They can only interfere with the lives of men when invoked by séances, or through some other means, offered a portal. The nature of the haunting Mr. Egan described is not specific to any one person, nor does its author seem to want redemption. So you see, it's not a ghost haunting the tenants at West 110th Street. Ghosts can be reasoned with. It's a demon, and the building itself is the portal. I strongly caution against exorcism or the use of psychics under these circumstances, as attention gives these beasts strength. I'd also recommend an immediate evacuation of the building.

Sincerely, Ronald McGuinn,
University of Edinburgh, Parapsychology Ph.D.

Letter to the editor, *Star Magazine*

Fire on the Fifteenth Floor

May 4, 2004

Once again last night, The Breviary reasserted its infamous reputation. This time, a fire broke out on the fifteenth floor after a group of tenants got together and ignited lighter fluid along the hallway carpet. The flames claimed the lives of seven victims, and three more are in critical condition from smoke inhalation.

Mr. Evvie Waugh (78) of 15C, was interviewed at the hospital. When asked why he'd done such a thing to his own apartment, he replied, "I guess we got bored. Nothing happened at the séance, and after all those Manhattans, we were pretty ripped."

Turn to page 6 for details.

From The *Enquirer*

34

The Sound a Trap Makes as It Closes, I:
Backward and Forward, the Same Thing Happens

The night she'd found Jayne's body was a blur. Fast breaths and dizziness. A creaking rope. Her hand extended to the sole of the woman's swaying saddle shoe. She'd held it in her palm, as if to offer it consolation, and imagined a reversal of events: The metal ladder she'd tripped over rising up like a roused beast. Jayne's neck straightening, and the blood flowing from her face so that her skin became pale and freckled again. Her feet gaining purchase on the top step. Her hands swinging backward toward her neck, and loosening the noose. A prayer, perhaps the Lord's, begged backward, too.

She'd inserted herself into the dream. This time, instead of letting Loretta Parker distract her, she got off that elevator and knocked on 14E. Jayne's face peeked out from the rope, eyes bright, just as Audrey's shadow self appeared in the doorway, catching her friend before it was too late.

The dream withered as the tenants approached. Some walked. Some gimped. Some crawled down the hall. They wore suits and fitted dresses, like the occasion of Jayne's death was cause for celebration.

"You did this!" she'd cried as she let go of Jayne's sole and slumped down the side of the wall on her ruined knee. Their man-made faces bent over her. So close their features lost proportion: wide eyes, jutting noses, closed lips, all gargoyle sharp.

"Give it here," a grainy male voice ordered, and something was passed down the line. The man above her had gray, closely trimmed brows, blue eyes, and yellow, jaundiced scleras. He looked handsome and trustworthy as he lifted the needle. "Help me," she mouthed. Then came a prick. Her elbow or her forearm? Her nerves were firing off so many impulses, she couldn't tell. As the cold stuff dripped through her arms, then sloshed its way to her chest, her breath came faster. Her vision blurred and stretched, a movie still pulled taut as skin. She pressed down on her heart as if to calm it as she fainted.

When she woke, a man whose breath smelled like peanut butter was leaning over her. She shuddered and tried to push him away. Then her eyes focused again, and she saw that he was not one of the tenants. Too young by fifty years. His white uniform read: EMERGENCY MEDICAL TECHNICIAN.

Over his shoulder she saw more EMTs dressed in white. Was she in a hospital? A mental institution?

No, there was Jayne. High up, her open skirt like a flower. The EMTs prodded. Jayne's legs swung in tiny semicircles, and then—*clop!* Her loose saddle shoe slipped off her toes and landed between Audrey's knees. Like the poodle skirt, it seemed costume, and Audrey wondered if she'd gotten dressed for her act at The

Laugh Factory three days ago, but lost courage when the hour arrived and never made it to the show.

"How many fingers am I holding up?" Peanut Butter asked. He was shining a penlight in her eyes.

She whispered her answer. "It looks like a thumb."

"Fat hands. Are you okay?"

She nodded, then leaned against the wall and hoisted herself up on what felt like a broken knee. It didn't hurt as much as she expected. Everything felt far away, like she was a spirit tethered to her body by cobwebs.

More people entered the den. A man and woman in plainclothes polyester suits flashed their badges. "Suicide," Peanut Butter told them. "We just got here." Someone shoved the metal ladder aside, while another EMT began to cut Jayne loose from the rope.

The sound was that same *creeeeaaak!* and Audrey remembered, suddenly, the thing that had been in this hall with her. Spidery bones, guarding the trophy of Jayne's body.

Jayne's open, unblinking eyes were fixed upon the long hall. Urine sopped the edges of her doilylike socks. Audrey hopped down the hall as fast as she could, following her own bloody trail, so she wouldn't have to see the girl as she fell.

A few feet down and to her right was the master bedroom. Family photos of redheads littered the floor. Jayne's face in all of them was blotted out. Audrey let her eyes focus on the inky smears, juxtaposed against a sea of voluptuous smiles.

Loretta and Marty Hearst, the guy with Parkinson's, met her halfway down. They scooped their hands under her shoulders and walked with her, little baby steps.

"No," she said, as she tried to break free, but the slanted floor was spinning.

They took her into the common hallway across from the elevator, where the rest of the tenants waited. More then ten, less then twenty. She started counting, but got confused. Except for Francis Galton, their faces swirled. From ten feet away, she could hear the echo of his breath beneath the porcelain mask.

Her heart pumped fast, and she pressed her hand against it, to rub it calm. Her thoughts circled and sank. Rorschach letters and images merged, then separated. Schermerhorn in his suit, only his arms and legs had multiplied, spiderlike, as he perched upon a pile of metal bones—The Breviary was a greedy God. Clara over a tub, slicing length- and width-wise, so that her wound would bear four points. Betty tethered to a hospital bed, dreaming of what she could have been, only she'd been born with black wings too heavy to flap. Jayne, all dressed up, but too scared to go to her act, so she'd stayed home and rubbed out her own face. The tenants at a cocktail party, screaming with delight. And then, in her mind, a terrible door opened, and everything went black.

"Letmeohhh," she whispered. Her voice slurred like her mouth was filled with hardening wet cement. "Ahhllscream."

Their faces up close were worse than she'd remembered. Paper-thin skin pulled so tight it looked as if it might split apart and bleed.

Marty didn't have any eyelashes, and she wondered if it was because the doctor had cut them out when he'd widened the man's eyes. Only his hands showed his age. She remembered, then, that Jayne had known Marty's name that night they'd all crowded outside her door. The sneakered outfit she'd worn on the date with the old man—it had been too casual for dinner at a restaurant, or even a walk in the park, and now she knew why. The date had taken place inside the building.

"Itwasssyou?" she asked lashless Marty as a pair of uniformed cops got off the elevator. "You hurt my best friend?"

Marty blinked his slits. His grip on her arm tightened

until it pinched, and she *knew*. It was him. The man who was so good and kind and full of promise that Jayne had been afraid to say his name. She looked up at him now, and saw that in his vanity, he'd lined under his eyes with brown pencil, and his fake hair was slick with pomade. Jayne. Poor Jayne. She'd trusted too much.

The EMTs were the first to leave 14E. They wheeled Jayne out on a gurney with a white sheet over her body. One of her saddle shoes stuck out. Its sole was broken, and her feet were geisha-tiny. Audrey would have cried, but her chest hurt too much.

After asking some questions of the tenants, the uniformed cops were the first to leave. It happened so fast, and she was shaking so hard, sweating, too, that she didn't think to speak or even try to stop them.

"I can't believe this. Can you believe this?" one of the tenants asked.

"She was always so quiet. I had no idea," Loretta answered.

"—Kept to herself, mostly," Evvie added.

"—Poor girl!" Galton said as he clapped his hands together, unable to contain his jubilation.

The last to leave were the detectives—a man and woman dressed in brown suits a few sizes too tight, like they'd bought them when they got their promotions and hadn't upgraded since.

"Her name was Jayne Young. Her family came from Salt Lake City. Like we told you, Loretta found her and called 911," Marty told them. "That's all I know."

"Terrible," Loretta chimed in. "She left her door open and the light on. I didn't even have to go inside."

"The killer," Audrey said. Marty and Loretta squeezed her arms. The feeling was a sphygmomanometer's sleeve, tightening.

"Killer?" the male detective asked. He had black hair that was gray at the temples, and he looked tired, like he'd been woken from a sound sleep and was still debating whether he gave a shit about the dead girl in the poodle skirt.

"Them. All of them. Got inside her. Mader do it. Sacrifice, so their door would open," Audrey panted.

The man came closer, and Audrey saw he didn't believe. He was looking at her the way people used to look at Betty; with narrowed eyes and poker faces. "How did they do that? Because it looks like she hung herself," he said.

Audrey blinked. She thought she felt a tear roll, but her cheeks were numb. The left side of her chest throbbed, and she wondered if the injection that the kind-looking old man had given her might induce a heart attack.

"Do you know something?" he asked.

"They do," she said.

He looked Audrey up and down, from soiled blue sweat suit to blood-crusted bare feet. "Would you like to come to a hospital?" he asked. Then he turned to the other detective. "Donna? Why don't you call another van for this nice lady?"

She winced. Nice lady—code for crazy. That van wasn't going to a hospital, it was going to Bellevue. She realized then that these detectives were in on it. So were the EMTs. Everybody in the whole world, including Saraub, was in on it. A genuine gaslight, just to drive her mad. They'd done the same to Betty. Jayne wasn't even dead. The tenants had paid her off. All fun and games for the idle rich.

She took a breath. The floor was spinning. The walls were slanted. Nothing in this entire building made sense!

Donna opened her phone. She sounded cheerful, like maybe she got a commission for every lonely woman she helped lock up. "A van—"

Audrey interrupted. "No docore. I'maset . . ." She bit her lip. "She was my friend."

"You sure?" the man asked.

"She's my niece. Too many vodka tonics," Loretta said, then clapped her hands together. "Back to Betty Ford for you!"

The detective waited for Audrey to answer.

"I'ma sore," she said.

He reached into his back pocket and pulled out a business card. Audrey's eyes were so bleary that she couldn't read the number or title, only the name: AIDAN MCGILLICUDDY. "Well, when you're feeling better, if you think of anything you want to tell me, give me a call."

Aidan and Donna got on the elevator. The tenants closed in around her. More than twenty now. At least thirty. Loretta's eyelids blinked over opaque cataracts. The wise, gray-haired man pulled out his needle, and masked Francis straightened her arm. Another shot. Fluid sloshed. The left side of her chest cramped like a charley horse.

The detectives closed the iron elevator gate behind them with a crash. It was then that she realized her mistake. "Waaaait!" she rasped. But by then, it was too late.

35

The Sound a Trap Makes as It Closes, II:
A Little Insulin Never Killed Anybody!

The tenants closed in around her. Cold hands and loose skin. Her feet weren't touching the floor anymore. She felt herself being carried back into 14B. "Soooop," she moaned, as they walked the fifty-foot hall. Their hands were soft, as if they'd never washed a dish or lifted a bag of groceries. But like a game of light as a feather, there were so many of them that they each only needed their fingers to hoist her up over their heads. "No. Peeeease, no."

Into the dark den to find rippling bits of clothes and chopped cardboard and Wolverine, all laced with her blood. Tiny red ants circled the hole in the floor. "I'm-get-you," she said. "Even if I have come back an haunt-you."

"My dear," Loretta answered. "We'd be delighted!"

They laid her on the floor next to the air mattress. Her feet felt cold and stiff, like ice. So did her hands.

She was shivering even though she was sweaty and hot. Loretta and Marty stood over her, while behind, the rest cleared the smashed old door from the room, then piled more moving boxes in its place. To her left, someone returned the grisly rebar to the side of the piano, along with a shiny red toolbox.

"We can't have you calling Romeo!" a man in a blue Armani suit from the early 1960s announced, then shoved her cell phone into his pocket, while an old woman unplugged her laptop and packed it under her arm, and another collected her soiled pants and shoes, so her only clothing was Clara's sweat suit.

Marty held her wrist with shaking fingers while looking at his watch. She was convulsing now, and she didn't dare take a deep breath. Her chest felt like it might split open.

"How much did you give her?" he called into the crowd.

"Nobody ever died from a little insulin. I take it every day," a woman with coarse, dyed-black hair and more gold necklaces than 1980s Mr. T. answered. Marty pumped the plastic mattress with air, then helped Audrey on top of it.

"Oh, stop touching the girls, you dirty old man," Loretta teased.

"Hear, hear, Marty Hearst! Don't play with the girls; you don't know where they've been!" Evvie Waugh shrieked, then slapped Marty on the ass with Edgardo's cane. The sound was sharp, nearly wet, as if it had cut open Marty's thin-skinned ass: *Whhhack!*

Marty grimaced. Tears gathered in the corners of his eyes. Loretta clapped. "Hear! Hear!" And then the rest were clapping, too.

In the commotion, Franics' mask came loose. Audrey gasped. His face was badly scarred. Something had broken the bridge between his nostrils, and it had healed wrong. One side was closed over with skin, and the other had opened up too wide. His left eye was missing, and its socket swelled with infection. It was as if the man had smashed his own face through a window, and then, instead of cleaning it or going to an emergency room, had covered it with gauze and never looked at it again, even while it itched and festered.

"Monsters," Audrey whispered, as the others looked upon his gore, and laughed, clapping all the harder.

"Boo!" Francis shouted, then peered down at Audrey as she convulsed: "BOO!" The tenants kept clapping, only they were jeering, too. Galton leaped across the den, waltzing with an imaginary partner. "BOO!"

In the commotion, Marty leaned too close. She flinched, thinking he might kiss her. Instead, he rubbed his lips against her ear and whispered so fast that she had to replay his words a few times before she understood them. "HoldonOkayHoldon!"

Then he stood and announced to the others, "Someone get her a blanket. She's gone into hypoglycemic shock."

Audrey closed her eyes. Her heart clenched and unclenched. She tried to think of calming memories, to slow down its beating. Her old apartment with Saraub. His hands on the back of her neck. The rooftop design of the Parkside Plaza.

"What-sa matta with her? Why doesn't she have blankets? Is this another homeless?" the woman holding her laptop asked. "The homeless *never* work, they're too stupid."

"—I thought we told Edgardo no dirty girls. Didn't we say that? An architect. A career girl, no attachments. That's what we said," Evvie answered.

Audrey drifted, closing her eyes. Chest clenching, she couldn't catch her breath.

"—And what did he bring us? A psycho or something? Isn't her mother in the loony bin? She gives me the craziest fucking nightmares!"

"—I like them. I haven't been to the Film Forum in thirty years. Nobody here ever dreams anything new."

"—I'm glad Edgardo's gone. I didn't care for his accent. I only like Castilian Spanish. Besides, we should get Irish to clean," the doctor with the kind face announced.

"—It'll work this time. I could tell the second she took the tour. The Breviary likes her." This from Evvie.

"—Shaddup! It likes me better than any of you!" Loretta shrilled.

And then, something heavy on Audrey's chest. It was soft and relieved her shivering. Jayne's pink comforter.

"—Do *you* think it'll work this time, smarty Marty?"

"Yeah, smarty Marty! Yeah! Yeah! Yeah!" Loretta screeched.

Marty cleared his throat. She recognized his voice without having to look because it was ripe with contempt. What was more remarkable, they knew it, and didn't care. From the way they interrupted and shouted, not one of them held another in regard. They'd known each other since they were children. Half of them were probably siblings or at least distant cousins. It occurred to her that after more than eighty years in the same building, without ever having kids or getting jobs, they played the role of children, and The Breviary their parents, in the oldest dysfunctional family in New York.

"She knows what she's doing," Marty said. "The Breviary could get inside the others, but it was like using a pencil to build a house. The tools weren't right. Even when they offered a sacrifice, they couldn't get their doors to open. She will."

"Who will she sacrifice?" Evvie asked.

"Romeo!" Loretta cried. "I knew I liked that darkie!"

"It's all about proper tools," Marty muttered. He sounded like he might be near tears. "None of us were equipped. Not even Jayne. Just this one."

"You're the tool, Marty Hearst," somebody shouted, and they all started hooting again. The sound grew distant as they headed back down the hall.

"—Where's my Mr. Frisky? Mr. Frisky!" Loretta asked.

"—I could kill that stupid cat . . ." This from Evvie.

"Im nadda tool. You cant useme. Not gonna kill my boyfriend I'll kill you!" Audrey mumbled, but by now they were too far away to hear.

"—My apartment is so full of red ants I had to move up to 14A. When are we getting a new super?" Now Galton.

"—I ate your goddamned Frisky, and Toto too," Evvie announced.

Their voices trailed. The last to leave turned out the lights, and everything in 14B went dark.

36

The Sound a Trap Makes as It Closes, III:
Light Through the Keyhole

At first, she chewed her lip to keep from falling asleep. Tasted salt. Tried to frighten herself by imagining Schermerhorn with her in the room. Knew logically that she had to escape but did not feel the urgency. Shaking too hard. Too tired: her chest was a tightened fist.

Insulin. She wasn't diabetic, and two hypodermics of the stuff didn't sound safe. What propelled her was the possibility that she might die. With some of the larger strips of her own torn clothes, she tied her kneecap into place to keep it from floating. She blacked out a few times as she tightened the cloth, but the insulin dulled the pain, and she finished the job.

Hands pulling, legs bent, then straightening, like a frog trying to swim on dry land, she dragged herself out of the den and down the dark hall. The pain in her knee was bad enough that she wished she had the strength to cut it off.

The floors began to hum. *Momma?* a child's voice called. *Is that you?*

"Stop," she whispered as she took another lunge.

In the bathroom, she heard the tub faucet glug. "Please, no," she said as the hall floor, at once carpeted and bare, soaked her (Clara's) sweatpants with bathwater.

Too tired to keep going, she stayed on the ground for a while. Twenty minutes. Kept her hands down over her head so she didn't have to see, and pretended it was quiet. When the shaking relented, and her heart muscles loosened enough for breath to come and go without a fight, she tried again. Crawled five more feet. Then took another break. Counted back from fifty. Wasn't ready. Counted back from one hundred, and started crawling again.

She remembered happier days, even as Clara's children gurgled. She thought about the itchy wool bedspread that Saraub loved, and the crumb-ridden remote control lodged within their futon's deep fold. The time she and her mother had robbed the 7-Eleven of Slurpies and hot dogs, then eaten them in the back of the Chevy. On an empty stomach, Ball Park Cheese Dogs make the best meal in the world. Of her work, and her desk, and the view from the top floor of Vesuvius, and all those pretty things she'd planned to build inside New York's holes.

In her mind, she was already scooting down the emergency-exit stairs on her bottom. Crawling out the lobby, unseen. Calling the cops on these fuckers and incriminating them for Jayne's murder. The hope was a bubble in her stomach, self-contained, unsinkable. That was all she needed, to make it those last five feet.

There was light through the keyhole. Light! Oh, how she loved light! She wanted to live so badly. To feel wet grass with bare feet, and build cities. To marry Saraub, and fill their house in Yonkers with children, and grand-children, and tire swings. She wanted to run from here so fast that she flew.

She counted back from three, then ten, then twenty. With a grunt, pushed her feet against the slanted floor, and stood. Her knee screamed. "Ooooowwwwww," she whispered, as tears rolled, and her nerves came to life—a pinching, throbbing suit of skin. Still, she clasped the gilded wood trim, then the glass knob. Breathing fast but quiet, she twisted the handle. It did not turn. She pulled it. Pushed it. But no. It was locked from the outside.

She looked out the peephole. A black eye with a thin layer of cataract peered back at her. Then the figure stepped away, and she saw that it was Loretta Parker. She waved her index finger back and forth.

"Dirty girl!"

37

The Sound a Trap Makes as It Closes, IV: Katabasis

Days passed. The sun rose, then set, then rose, like a stop-motion camera. When she was thirsty, she slurped water from the sink. When she was hungry, she rationed the leftover Chinese food she'd ordered with Jayne, and when that was gone, just like back in Hinton, she got weaker.

The pile of boxes got smaller. The door got bigger. The humming walls lulled her into a place between sleep and waking life, where around one corner there was a pretty house in Yonkers, and around another there was Schermerhorn, leaning over a tub full of sleeping cherubs while his ghost wife, Clara, screamed.

The thing in her stomach filled the crevices of her body. When she looked in the bathroom mirror, she didn't see her own reflection. Only a black-eyed silhouette that did not quite stand erect. So she broke the mirror, and even broke the chrome toaster, too.

Hours, days, or maybe weeks later, Martin and Loretta returned. Wearing their dusty wool suit and Claudette Colbert silk, they were a mad couple in frayed finery, like ghosts from the *Titanic*.

Marty carried a sandwich and glass of red juice on an antique pewter plate. He bent down and placed it at her bare, crusted feet. She didn't remember how they'd gotten here, whether she'd been sleeping or awake. She didn't know for how long they'd been standing over her, either.

"I don't know why we're bothering. We're not gonna keep her for a pet," Loretta groused, as Marty set down the plate. Her sausage-tight gown was slit down the ass, revealing soiled satin panties full of holes.

Audrey smelled the food. Her mouth watered. She peeled back the bread. Tuna and stale mayonnaise. It had been left out, so its sides were yellowed. Still, she took a bite. It was the best sandwich she'd ever tasted. Her eyes shone with gratitude. Her stomach gurgled, and for few seconds, stopped hurting. She ate slowly, chewing every bite again and again, to make sure it stayed down. The flavors—salt, tuna, sugar, fat—were so crisp that they snapped. And then, something sharp. She bit hard. The temporary crown in the back of her mouth broke in half.

"Ah! Wha—?" she cried, just as Martin coughed, and her tongue traced the outline of the thing that he'd sneaked into her food.

"What? There something in that? Martin did you put something in that?" Loretta whined as he bent forward to inflate the deflated mattress she'd been sleeping in and whispered in her ear quick and pleading with rancid dog breath: "Please!"

"Marty, did you put something in the food?" Loretta

asked. "She thinks she's so pretty but she's not. I could dye my hair brown, too."

Audrey shook her head. Said something that sounded like the old, high-maintenance Audrey, before The Breviary. "I don't like Wonder Bread. It's all corn syrup."

Loretta narrowed her eyes. She bent down, and her dressing gown ripped along its side seam. Flesh bulged. Either she didn't notice, or she didn't care. "Well, la!" she said, pointing her hip to the left, "Di!" the hip went to the right, "Da!" the hip jutted back again.

They left. The sound they made as they clopped down the hall was peculiar. A *clack-clacking,* like their bodies were becoming harder than flesh. They were changing into something spiderlike, just like Schermerhorn.

Audrey finished the sandwich, and felt the most grounded she'd been in days. The most like herself. She waited an hour. Maybe two. She couldn't tell. Was afraid to take Martin's present out of her mouth. She didn't want the apartment to see.

She limped down the hall. Her knee was better—the ligament had reattached, but it still wasn't healed. Same dirty clothes. Hair so greasy it was wet. She spit out half her crown, along with the small brass key. It fit into a knee-height hole at the edge of the door and unsprung the lock. Then she put the key back into the side of her cheek and opened the door.

In the carpet were sandy bits of ceramic and a lampshade. Jayne's ashes? No, Hula Girl's remains. Tears welled. Guilt gnawed. "Jayne," she whispered, then kept limping.

The fire door to the stairs creaked. She squinted, as if to diminish the sound, then began hopping. Cold metal against her feet. She leaped two steps with the left foot, then swung the right leg without bending it. Panting. Panting. The sound of her breath echoed in the metal chamber.

Slap-swing-slap-swing! How many floors? She didn't know. The farther she got, the more she allowed herself to hope.

Slap-swing-slap-swing! The lobby! But then, she looked through the small wire window built into the fire door and saw the tenants. They were out there. Sitting on the antique couches in the former church altar where Schermerhorn's body had once hung. Chatting with each other in old cocktail dresses and faded black suits. Was it Monday again already? Cocktail night for the unemployed? They were drinking Manhattans with cherries. Thirty of them. Maybe more. She was crestfallen, like needles in her stomach, poking holes in a thousand places, until she remembered: there had to be an exit through the basement.

She climbed down one more flight and shoved open the fire door. The basement stank something terrible. Red ants, everywhere. Scampering things, too. Her feet got wet on the peeling, gray-painted cement floors. But at least the lights were on. In her dark apartment, she'd missed light so much. You imagine such terrible things in the dark.

She scooted through the hall, leaning against the wall for balance. There were doors on all sides. A pile of garbage bags lay straight ahead.

She looked for EXIT signs, but didn't see any. Ants scampered each time she stepped. In her mind she dissected them; pulled their chitin inside out, then made them disappear. Made the place smell like roses. Made the air sweet as hash. The visualization worked, and she kept moving.

She pushed open a door on the left. No window to climb through, just a cot and green wool blanket. A dresser with a photo of Edgardo and a portly, brown-haired woman. His wife? And next to that, a photo of a green-eyed brunette standing knee deep in snow. She looked like Audrey, only younger and angrier. Stephanie. So, none of it had been a lie. And where was he, Edgardo? Even if he'd been fired in a hurry, he wasn't the type to leave his things behind.

She tried the next door. Locked. The next. Locked, too. The next, storage. Three rusted bicycles. The old-fashioned, reclining kind from the 1800s. A weathered Genus edition of Trivial Pursuit. A moldy cigar box. A pair of wooden skis. And in the corner, the trappings of the old Episcopalian Church. Crucifixes, chalices, wooden idols of Madonna and Child. Stone carved Archangels Michael and Gabriel. The former banishing Lucifer from heaven, the latter heralding the joyous news of man's redemption. Full of cracks and missing limbs, they were heaped together like junk, and covered in more than a half century of grime.

She shut the door and kept walking to the end of the hall. The stink was overwhelming. She swallowed down her bile and gimped farther. Yes, this place was awful, but at least it wasn't 14B.

She got to the end—the source of the stench: garbage. Grocery bags filled with kitchen offal, black Hefty bags, white toilet-room bags, and random crap piled fifteen feet high. Up above was the opening for the trash chute. A nest of red ants swarmed above the dross. Over the last few days or weeks or months, the tenants must have tossed their garbage as usual, but no one had carried it to the curb. It figured that behind the mess, she could see the red gleam of an EXIT sign.

"Oh," she moaned. "Oh, screw you," she said to God, or herself, or, most likely, the tenants of The Breviary. Then she did a strange jig. Her hands flailed limp wristedly, her head shook back and forth, and she hopped on her good foot. *Rats! Literally!*

When she was done, she sucked up her courage, along with her bile, and lifted the first bag. It made a wet, slapping sound as she separated it from the pack and flung it to the side of the hall. When she lifted the second bag, something squeaked. She would have mistaken the sound for a human scream if she hadn't seen the big-eyed brown rodent. (Rat or mouse? She hoped the latter, but guessed the former, judging by its thick, ribbed tail.)

She scooped five more bags. She was getting there. She smiled at her accomplishment, and imaged the tenants' faces when they discovered that she was gone. Or better yet, when the cops showed up.

But then, something brownish pink peeked out from two plastic West Side Market bags. She took a double take. A triple take. A human hand, and on its fourth finger, a copper ring.

"Oh, no," she cried. She took a breath, turned away, then turned back and pretended that it was not Edgardo at all. It was a mannequin, the kind you use to sew clothes. But even as she lifted another bag, she remembered those tears in his eyes, and the way he'd tried to keep her from moving into 14B, all as penance for Stephanie, who would never know how much her father had loved her.

The smell was coming from him. His body had rotted. Ants chewed. Other things, too. With a few more grunts, she lifted the rest of the bags in her way. The path to the door was almost clear. Only one thing left to move.

"Sorry about this," she said, then closed her eyes, and pretended he was a doll. Shoved him with her bare foot. His skin made a splatting sound, but didn't give. Full of gas and rot. So she bent down and dragged him by the underarms. His neck rolled, and she gagged, then swallowed fast, because she didn't want to lose the only lunch she'd eaten in a week.

His skull was cracked from temple to jaw. The cut was uneven, and the skin around it was torn as if by something barbed. A rebar, she guessed. Her rebar. The tenants. They'd murdered him, then tossed him in the garbage. What a bunch of shits.

She heaved him aside, then lifted one more bag. Then free! She twisted the handle. Didn't believe it. Tried again. Had enough energy, this time, to slam herself against it. Then pulled the key out from her mouth. It didn't fit.

The steel door was locked.

Could she go back and get the rebar, bash the dead bolt? No, the door was metal. The echo would carry through the trash chute and send the tenants charging.

The stench prevented her from wallowing. She started back. Climbed the stairs. Up one flight. Quiet as a mouse.

She considered making a run for it through the lobby, but with her weak knee she wasn't fast enough. Better to wait until they were gone and sneak out. So she waited by the fire door as the hours passed. One? Two? No watch by which to tell. The tenants danced and drank. And drank some more. Spilled their booze on the old altar, laughing gaily, maniacally, like the lone survivors of the Third World War.

She counted them: forty-seven. Wondered if any had left their apartment doors open. Remembered—yes!—some of them might have phones. She climbed the stairs. Up, up, up. Thought the best way to start would be on fourteen. Easier to hide if she heard someone coming. She crept up the stairwell to fourteen and saw that her luck was in. The doors all down the row were open.

She started with 14C—Loretta. She walked down its long hall. *Slip-slide* was the sound her feet made. On her way, she stopped and peered inside the master bedroom. Stacks of china dolls lay on the queen-sized, canopied bed, their cheeks dotted with red circles of blush. Period costume cowgirls, Spanish dancers, Victorians with watching eyes that might goggle closed if you laid them down to sleep. She quick counted seventy-two dolls, which probably meant that they, and not Loretta, slept on a proper bed.

She didn't see a phone, so she kept walking. Into the den. More dolls. This time they hung from fishing-line nooses nailed to the ceiling. Their bodies made a curtain between the den and hall and she had to push them aside to get through.

In the center of the den, she found a half-built door made out of broken white porcelain that had been glued together and covered with blinking dolls' eyes. The door was only three feet tall, and pieces of it had fallen and shattered.

Next to that was a pink princess phone. She picked it up. "Huh!" she sucked in a breath of awful surprise. No dial tone, just ringing, and then a message. "The customer needs to contact accounts payable. Thank you. . . . The customer needs to contact . . . No emergency services in this area . . ."

She hung up.

And then, she hadn't seen. How hadn't she seen? Loretta was sitting at the turret. Drool caked her chin. Her bare feet were bloody, and beneath them were the crushed porcelain faces of more dolls. "Wrong apartment," she said, then resumed crushing, like an Italian peasant stomping grapes. "You live in 14B. Don't forget, stupid."

Slip-slide. Audrey headed back where she'd come. Into the main hall, the kind old doctor who'd shot her full of insulin now lay on the red carpet, nude. His hand covered his privates like a fig leaf over a statue until he waved at her and revealed the hoary mess. She looked away. Was he there at all, or was she mad?

14D. Evvie Waugh. *Slip-slide!* The hallway walls were mounted with dead animal heads. Only, they hadn't been treated with chemicals, and were slowly rotting. The order went like this: moose, bear, badger, panda, bald eagle, gorilla, chimp, and the shrunken African head of a human being. Their skin had all been stuffed, and their eyes replaced with black aggie marbles.

In the middle of the den was a claw-foot tub, in which Evvie, wearing a green velvet dressing robe, reclined with a pile of pillows and a copy of *Decline and Fall*. The tub was Clara's, of course. Propped against its side was Edgardo's cane. So many trophies.

"Wrong apartment. Party isn't until tomorrow night. 14B. You're the host of honor," Evvie pronounced, then returned to his book.

"Thanks," she mumbled, then turned and started out.

14A. *Slip-slide*. Down the hall. All the doors open. Everything empty. Everything dingy. Dried, bloody handprints marred the hallway walls. The low ones belonged to a child, but they got bigger the higher they went. It occurred to her that the prints might all belong to the same person, over a span of fifty years.

Slip-slide. Into the den. The walls were adorned with red smiley faces, and she didn't think it was paint. Not a stick of furniture, except for an old rotary phone. She picked it up. Heard the sound, and at first did not believe it.

A dial tone!

She reached into the pocket of her sweat suit. A piece of paper. Her instincts told her to do this: she no longer remembered why. She dialed the number on the card. An answering machine. She didn't listen to the message, or remember why. Just spoke after the beep. "Hi. They're trying to kill me, and I found this card. My name is Audrey Lucas."

Hung up. Dialed a number from memory, didn't know whose. Machine picked up. Was it late? Early morning? "Hi. They're trying to kill me. My name is Audrey Lucas."

Found a Post-it in her pocket. Dialed the number written there. Behind her in the hall, she heard the *click-clack* of high heels. Ringing, ringing. The phone picked up, but no one answered. "Hello? Hello?" she called. "Please help me. I'm—" then she remembered, "At The Breviary—510 West 110th Street, fourteenth floor. Please!"

But no one answered. Far away, two people talked on the other line. They didn't hear her!

Behind her, the tenants had arrived. Galton, unmasked. His lone eye glared. Loretta. Marty. The naked man. Evvie. The party, too. Still holding cocktails. So drunk they swayed, staggered, and crawled.

She watched, panting. Her breath was as heavy as syrup.

On two, three, and four legs, they advanced. They clogged the hall with their bodies. Arms and legs and torsos, indistinguishable as clumped insects. Their eyes had all gone black. It was The Breviary coming for her. The Breviary never lets anyone out.

She squeezed the receiver. Someone spoke on the other line: *who is this?* The tenants got closer. "Bitch! Bitch! Bitch!" Loretta clapped.

This was happening . . . This was happening?

"Who let her out? Marty, did you let her out?" Loretta asked. Her feet were a puddle of blood. They clacked as she walked, full of doll shrapnel.

Audrey remembered the key in her mouth. They'd take it if they could. But, two inches long and jagged on one end, was it too big to swallow? Then again, if worse came to worst and she died, at least she couldn't build their damn door.

She swallowed. It got stuck. Swallowed again. It tore her throat and lodged inside the wound. She breathed, and air whistled.

They came closer.

And then, on the phone: *Tell me who you are!* It was Jill. She'd called Jill!

She swallowed and lifted the phone to her ear. The key went down, cutting its jagged way along her esophagus. "Hh-hh-help!" she cried.

Loretta pulled the phone from her hand. "I'm Audrey Lucas. I need help!" she shouted, just as Loretta ripped the wire from the jack.

38

The Sound a Trap Makes as It Closes, V:
Build the Door

With hands reaching high over their heads, they played light as a feather. Carried her back to 14B and in their fine, tattered clothes, filled her den.

"Build the door!" Loretta screeched. *Clop-clop!* Her feet were porcelain castanets.

The key cut its cold way down her throat. She coughed blood and wiped it with the back of her hand so they didn't see, then sputtered, "Build it yourself!"

"Bitch! Bitch! Bitch!" Loretta screeched. "I'll scratch your face!"

And then, in the den, Audrey saw what in her sleep state, she'd missed. Her work was almost done. It wasn't shaped like a normal door anymore. Its edges were curved, and it was thicker in the center than at its base. It defied conventional engineering, but she could see that it was strong, and like The Breviary itself, so long as she built a proper frame, would hold. This time, none of the labels were hidden: PALMOLIVE, SERVITUS, PFIZER, HAMMERHEAD, UNITED CHINESE EMIRATES. They'd been cut and taped so that the entire front of the door was riddled with nonsense letters, like English converted into babble.

The hole she'd made for a handle hung only two feet off the ground, as if, when the thing on the other side finally came through, it would not walk but slither. Along the door's perimeter, letters had been cut from the boxes to form a single, repeated phrase:

Abandon Hope. All Ye Who Enter Here.

They laid her on the air mattress. "Finish it yourself," she said.

Martin's voice was low, but no one spoke above it. "We can't. You're the one who can make it sturdy enough to hold. Every time we've tried has been a failure."

"What's on the other side?"

The tenants began to chatter among themselves. Gleeful and twittering. Their time in The Breviary had made them hive-minded. A few, too drunk to stand, were crawling on their hands and knees. Martin blinked his lashless eyes. He'd neglected his eyeliner, possibly because his Parkinson's today was especially severe: he couldn't stop shaking. Then she realized, it wasn't Parkinson's. He was terrified.

"My wife is on the other side!" Galton cried. "She says she's coming back to me."

"The Breviary promised me a pony," the woman with heavy gold chains announced. "Only it's a Pegasus and a unicorn, so I can fly and teleport."

"You're an asshole, Sally." Loretta giggled.

"No, no. It's hell that's behind the door," the good, naked doctor said with a smile, like he was talking about Florida.

"We have no idea what will happen when it opens," Martin said. "But The Breviary wants it, so we want it, too."

"And Schermerhorn, what is he?" she asked.

Marty nodded. "He died a long time ago. The Breviary wears his face."

That was when Loretta pointed at him. "You let her out, didn't you? Fed her that sandwich even though you *know* how much I like tuna fish! Oh, Martin. The simpleton redhead scrambled your brain!"

Martin looked down at his worn-out Hickey Freeman suit, circa 1975, and sighed.

"It was him!" Loretta shouted.

They rallied, and drunkenly shoved him down the hall. A slow-motion shuffle all the way out of 14B. She heard a *click* as they locked her inside, which was soon followed by a low-pitched scream. The sound was cut short, and she knew that Martin, her last ticket out of this madhouse, was dead.

39

Vesuvius

y ou don't have an address in your files?" Jill asked. Collier Steadman's office was a wild assortment of bat-shit nuts. He'd rummaged through street-side trash for his decorative cast- iron plates, which he'd colored over in crayon and used to adorn his file cabinets. Instead of taking photos of his prize-winning terrier poodles, he'd snapped their shadow-images, then blown them up human-sized and hung them along his office walls, so the place looked like a forest of giant poodles.

Collier had been working at Vesuvius since he'd graduated from the Fine Arts Acting Program at Yale, and was now in his fifties. A decade ago, Jill had gone to one of his plays. Ten men who were supposed to represent different aspects of a person's psyche had shouted at one another on a darkened stage. The denouement came when they'd hurled their own excrement in all directions, which, fortunately for the front row, had turned out to be half-cooked brownie batter.

"Fascinating," she'd told him the following Monday. "Really brought me to a place I wasn't expecting to go."

His eyes got watery with crazy intensity, like he'd decided they were kindred spirits. "Most people can't handle that kind of emotional honesty. Darling, it's you and me against the heathens." As he spoke, the poodles had suddenly loomed too large behind him, like he'd been about to get devoured.

Ever since, Collier had always put her requests at the top of his pile. She hadn't worked the day after Thanksgiving in ten years. Schlock Jock or not, that secured for him a special place in her heart.

"Have you tried calling her?" he asked. This evening, Collier looked worse for wear. His skin was waxy, and when he'd leaned over to wave her into his office, he'd dipped the bottom of his pink geometric-patterned tie into his coffee. He was working on a new play set to debut in Bushwick, Brooklyn. A reimagining of *Our Town* with an all-midget cast.

"I've tried her cell, but she's not answering. And the landline I have for her—it's some guy's voice on the machine. Her ex-boyfriend, I think. He hasn't called me back, either. Is it possible she moved?"

Frowning, to let her know what he was doing was against company policy, Collier opened Audrey's file. "It says here that she's on 93rd and York. I've got the same landline number you do."

Jill sighed. After coming home from Around the Clock this morning, she and Tom had made breakfast for the boys. Then they'd all gone to a movie, passing popcorn and large sodas down the long line. They'd even taken Markus' boyfriend Charlie. He'd been grateful as Oliver Twist for the free popcorn, which had prompted her to do something completely un-Jill, and hug him. The slender, nervous boy had hugged her back with all his might, like it was the first time in his life anyone had ever approved of him, which had elicited something even more un-Jill. She'd broken down right in front of the Sutton Theatre. Suddenly, Tom had been holding her, and then Markus, and Clemson, while troubled Xavier had stood a little back. Group hug, they'd all cried, and then, feeling foolish, laughed. A minute or two after that, they'd let go. They went back to the apartment, feeling daunted by such gaudy emotion, but also less bereft.

A few times during the morning and afternoon, she'd called Audrey's cell phone and office phone. Finally, she'd called Bethy in reception and learned that Audrey hadn't been to work in over a week.

That was when she'd told Tom to hold dinner and hailed a taxi. It was after six on Tuesday by the time she got to Vesuvius, and she'd caught Collier just as he'd been putting on his coat. Perhaps even more alarming than Audrey's disappearance, he'd also carried two small denim jackets as gifts for his poodles. Before he'd looked up Audrey's address, he'd made her admire their fine embroidery. "Stunning," she'd told him, and she'd meant it.

Now, Collier flipped through Audrey's file. "No other addresses. Emergency contact is . . . Betty Lucas, at the Nebraska State Psychiatric Hospital."

Jill rubbed her temples. "Psychiatric hospital? That explains a lot."

Collier pressed his head back into his neck like a turtle, and she got the feeling she'd insulted him. "Audrey? She's fabulous. Only one of your team who doesn't fudge her overtime."

Jill nodded. "She's a lovely woman. It still explains some things. Her mother's in a coma, though. I doubt she'll be very helpful."

Collier rapped his pen against Audrey's file. "I don't know what else to do, then."

Jill sighed. "Something's wrong. I'm sure of it. You should have heard her voice. She sounded so frightened. And when I saw her last week, she wasn't herself. You know how she's always alert, paying attention—you never have to tell her anything twice? Well, last Monday, she was a zombie. Don't repeat this to anyone else in the office, please, but I thought she might be stoned."

Collier looked down at the file for a long while, and Jill considered thanking him for his time, washing her hands of this strange business, and heading home, where her life had its own worries. Only, she'd failed Julian not long ago. If she lived another hundred years, she'd never forgive herself for not holding his hand as he took his last breath. If she could help it, she didn't plan on failing anyone else.

Just then, Collier dialed the hospital in Nebraska. "I have an idea," he said, then into the phone when the line connected, "Can I speak with the billing department?"

Jill waited, stunned by Collier's hitherto unimagined deviousness. "Yes. Hello," he said. "I'm Ms. Audrey Lucas' accountant, your patient Betty Lucas' legal guardian. I wanted to make sure you've got her proper address. She'll of course pay what she owes, but she hasn't received any bills." He shrugged at Jill as they both waited. Then picked up a pen. "Yes, 510 West 110th Street. #14B. That's right, just a cell phone. No landline. Exactly correct. Thanks for your time."

What surprised Jill most after he hung up the phone was what he did next. He put his hand over hers, like he was prepared to miss the dress rehearsal for his play, prepared not to feed the dogs for another few hours, all for a woman he knew tangentially, between the hours of nine and seven. Sometimes people surprise you in good ways. "What should we do?" he asked.

She toyed with the idea. It seemed excessive. And yet.

"Call the police, yes?" Collier asked.

She nodded. "Yes."

40

Old Scars Protect Against New Ones

Tuesday afternoon. Eight days trapped in 14B. Nobody had come to find her. Not her office, not her boss, not even Saraub. That kind of neglect leaves a girl feeling less than swell.

Schermerhorn played the piano while Audrey rested. Cocktail-hour entertainment! She'd had a long morning. Her back ached. Arms, too. She'd worked fast since they'd killed Marty. Often, her fingers had moved without her knowledge.

The tune Schermerhorn played was familiar: "Heart and Soul. I beg to be Adored . . . And Tumbled Overboard!" It reminded her of a Harold Arlen song, and now she remembered why his voice seemed so familiar. The accent wasn't British—just rich WASP Connecticut, like his jaw couldn't move more than half an inch in either direction. It was the same man who'd answered the line when she'd called to view the apartment. She'd spoken directly to the building itself.

"Build the door, Audrey!" Schermerhorn cheered. She looked over at her creation. Glued to the cardboard were the shredded trappings of her old life; clothes, the Parkside Plaza plans from the hall, and her air mattress sliced to plastic strips. They fit like flaking skin so that all that remained was the caution:

Abandon Hope, All Ye Who Enter Here.

From the hole in the floor, she'd sawed two sets of two-by-four supporting beams to keep the door from tumbling over. The entire den now sagged, and pretty soon, she expected that it would collapse into 13B.

Ants swarmed the rotten hole and walls. They didn't bite, even though she kept expecting them to. Instead, they circled in and out against the door, like an ocean tide.

"I beg to be adored!" Schermerhorn cried. His skin had sloughed from his bones, and in places, she could see his skeleton. He laughed so hard that tears fell as he sang, like maybe The Breviary itself had gone mad.

Audrey sat on the turret ledge of the empty room. Black-and-white Betty sat next to her. A trick. Not her real mother. But company, just the same. The television blared an old sitcom about single friends living in Manhattan. Betty giggled along with the canned laughter, while the ghosts of The Breviary lined the walls of the den. Each with noose marks, or broken skulls. Bloated faces from drowning underwater. Maybe they hadn't wanted to build doors, either.

"Finish it, my lovely!" Schermerhorn sang.

Audrey looked at the rebar, then the piano. The door needed a solid frame, of course. Something firm, like satinwood. Otherwise, it wouldn't hold for long enough before it collapsed . . . Long enough for what?

She answered her own question: *Silly girl. Long enough for the monsters to climb through!*

At the piano, Schermerhorn cried and laughed. "I fell in love with you, MADLY!" while next to him, the ghosts of The Breviary watched. Some smiling, some seeming themselves, haunted.

What time was it? Afternoon? Morning? Her eyes were heavy, and she knew tonight, when she fell asleep, that The Breviary would consume her, and she'd finish the job.

And what then?

Saraub would come. The last piece of this puzzle. Maybe Loretta would call him and pretend to be a concerned neighbor. Maybe by then, she'd have no control, and she'd call him herself. Either way, once he heard that she needed his help, he'd come running. She would murder him. Skin his flesh from his bones. The door would open then and set something terrible free.

She stood. Thought about tearing down the door, but knew she'd only build it again tonight, and by tomorrow, she'd be too weak to resist.

She tried to push open the turret window, but it was stuck. Betty laughed while somebody on the television broke up with another boyfriend because he looked bad bald. The children howled. They'd been howling for days.

Out the window on 110th Street, groups and couples meandered, and the M60 bus cruised toward the Triborough Bridge. She wrapped the sleeve of Clara's sweatshirt around her hand, then smashed a small, lead-fluted windowpane. "Help me! I'm in 14B!" she shouted, but her voice by now was so hoarse that no one heard.

She pulled one of the shards from the broken pane, a perfectly preserved stained-glass bird, and sat next to black-and-white Betty. She pressed the glass to her wrist. The bird's red eyes watched. "What should I do?" she asked her mother, not mother.

Betty's eyes moved in her direction, but the rest of her

was still. On the television, the friends sang a plucky tune at a local coffee shop: isn't life grand?

"Build the door, baby," Betty said. Her mouth didn't move, only her eyes.

Audrey traced her old scars with the sharp point of the bird's beak. Schermerhorn played louder. She tried to make herself want this. For Saraub's sake, for her own, for the innocents of The Breviary, if there were any.

She closed her eyes, remembered the last time she'd done this. That feeling of freedom, and floating. Watching yourself drift as the water turns pink. It came back to her now, that girl in tan coveralls that she used to be. She was that girl again. Greasy and hungry and useless.

Schermerhorn played louder. The ghosts moaned. The living tenants had gathered in 14A and 14C, and now banged against her walls. The sound reminded her of childhood: bill collectors; angry boyfriends; a manic mother.

The edges of her bird's-eye glass were sharp, but she didn't think the cut would be clean. She pushed hard and broke her callused skin. A tiny scrape. Her scars were already so thick.

"Bitch!" Schermerhorn shouted. He stopped playing and glared. The ghosts wailed. The tenants revolted, pounding so hard that the walls shook.

Her blood beaded. Small droplets thin as dew. "I never stopped bleeding," she whispered.

"I'll take care of you, Audrey," black-and-white Betty crooned without moving her lips. "Trust me. Build the door."

Audrey looked at her hands and wrists. She was sick of scars. Her body had endured so many of them. She was still that girl in coveralls, ugly and invisible. Naïve and too trusting. Easily used. But maybe that wasn't such a bad thing. Maybe that girl was the real Audrey. And all these trappings of her adult life: the cleaning, the nervousness, the hostility, the biting at people she loved most, maybe they were the scars that made the woman shine less bright.

She knew she ought to end this. Thwart The Breviary while she was still in possession of her faculties and had the chance. It would give her pleasure to see the tenants' crestfallen faces and hear The Breviary shriek as she gasped her last breath, and the door went unopened. But neither the old Audrey nor the scarred one was the type to give up. Even in that tub more than twenty years ago, she'd not been frightened or relieved as she'd stood from the pink water and bandaged her wrists with masking tape, but disgusted: how dare she treat herself so cheaply?

She closed her eyes, and in her mind, whispered, "What do I do? Dear God, what do I do?"

Just then, her groin cramped. She doubled over from the pain and remembered that she'd swallowed the key.

41

The Breviary

No thinking creature can tolerate captivity. In the presence of just four white walls, the mind invents. Stagnant air and locked doors skew perception. Eighty-degree angles turn obtuse. Holes form between joists where bricks no longer neatly meet. Smiles become sneers; love skinned leaves the skeleton of lust; and too much sleep unmoors its dreamer. Without the possibility of freedom, the rituals of living are abandoned. Bathing, eating, cleaning, and even language are lost. Things fall apart, and in the vacuum of their absence, madness rears.

The Breviary had always known that it did not belong in this world. And yet, here it remained. Trapped. Alone.

Schermerhorn was the first casualty of The Breviary's rage. He'd never believed in the religion he'd created and had never expected his buildings to stand for more than a few years. The Breviary changed that. Long after he cut its last ribbon and welcomed it to the world, it stayed on his mind. He could not leave the city, nor spend a day without walking by it. He could not go an afternoon without sketching its skewed curves. Eventually, he could not sleep, except in its lobby, where its soft humming soothed him. Finally, he climbed a ladder. The noose didn't hold, and he fell thirty feet to his death. His body was graceful, like a pencil dive, and his blood flowed west.

For a while after murdering its flawed creator, and then wearing his image like skin, The Breviary was content. It played tricks on its tenants, like opening locked doors, and stealing light, and filling tap water with lead. Captains of industry slept in its bedrooms, and at night it whispered poison in their ears, so that it had a hand in the fates of nations and newspapers, Spanish wars, and lovers, young and old.

Outside, New York soared, burned, and, relentless, rose again. Horse-drawn carriages gave way to dynamite blasts through granite, then snakelike subways that screamed underground. Gold-gilded libraries and courthouses with names like Carnegie and Morgan ascended and collapsed. Wilbur Wright flew his glider over Manhattan, the *Lusitania* sank, flappers danced the Charleston, and ten years later men in three-piece suits broke through The Breviary's high-floor windows like witless penguins, trying to fly. Once and future presidents were crowned and killed, fortunes lost, wars fought, spoils divided. Suspension-bridge lights brightened the nighttime Hudson River, while downtown, monoliths and spiteful planes blotted out the sun.

Seven generations came and went while it remained, rooted and unchanged. It learned to hate man for his freedom, and in its boredom it got reckless. It whispered louder and planted itself inside empty stomachs. It drove bodies out windows and heads into ovens. Arsenic into brandies, knives into throats. It haunted its inhabitants with their own dark thoughts, so that with each successive generation, the tenants became more like the building that housed them. They lost compassion for the world outside, and for each other, too.

By the final generation, both building and occupants had gone mad. Like Schermerhorn before them, the tenants, and even the building itself, began to dream. This time, of doors.

They drew pictures, they sketched. They became obsessed. The first tenant used his deceased wife's bones. The door proved a failure, and crashed soon after opening, but in that brief time, through the cracks, he saw a terrible beauty. He loved the black-eyed thing that had peered back at him, because he recognized himself in it. The Breviary recognized what waited on the other side of that door, too, and felt the first pangs of hope it had ever known: beyond that door was home.

Soon all the tenants tried and failed; and then came Clara DeLea, who understood that the price of its opening was blood. She succeeded better than the rest, but in the end, her door was not sound enough to hold and collapsed before anything could climb through. In its fury, The Breviary dragged her back to her clawfoot tub and then shrank inside of her, so that she was forced to see the wickedness she'd done to her children, unmoving as stillborns. In the hopes of safely ushering their souls from the building, she'd slit her wrists crosswise and joined them. In death, her arms were gathered around their bodies in the tub, and her jellied blood layered their skin, as if all five of them had returned to the womb.

And now, Tuesday night, Audrey Lucas shattered the bird-shaped glass meant for her wrists and decided not to go gently into that good night, even while her eyelids got heavy, and the monster inside her grew. Loretta Parker paged through Audrey's cell-phone messages and found Saraub's number at the hospital. She waited, and practiced her speech: "Your friend asked me to call. She's quite ill. A terrible fever. Please, come straightaway!"

Then again, "Your pretty bitch isn't so pretty. We cut off all her hair!" And again, "We slashed her face!" Loretta's cataracts, like the eyes of the rest of the tenants, had gone black.

In 14B, Audrey pinched herself to keep awake, then tore the discarded cardboard boxes into small pieces, and chewed. She would get this key out, one way or another.

The tenants peered into 14B through drilled peepholes in 14A and 14C, or else listened with their ears pressed against the walls. In 3A, Benjamin Borrell put down the cigarette he'd been pressing into his forearm, and smiled. In 8C, Elaine Alexander turned down the volume on her favorite soap, *General Hospital,* and kissed the poster she'd tacked to her wall of Luke and Laura. In 14D, Evvie Waugh lay down on the floor, and beat his arms and legs against the wood until he bled. In 10B, Penelope Falco shaved her head, then her eyebrows, then plucked her lashes, so when the door opened, she'd appear newly born. Her speech finished, Loretta Parker danced in time with Schermerhorn's piano music, her porcelain feet *click-clacking.*

The Breviary watched. Happy for the first time since Martin Hearst threw open its eyes over 150 years ago. Its purpose was finally manifest. It would house the door that destroyed mankind.

42

Doesn't Every Generation Inherit Debt?

Tuesday evening, Saraub waved his mother good-bye, and sat back in the Craftmatic. Flicked the bed remote down and up, down and up. Perused the cable channels. He'd refused today's Vicodin, which suddenly made ESPN's greatest hits a lot less interesting.

He was getting released tomorrow. These seven days of rest had been good for his soul. He'd been working hard for a long time, and it had been nice, for once, to have nothing to do, and not even e-mail to check. He used the plastic prong the nurse had given him to lift the bedside phone. Dialed the first three digits of Audrey's number. Hung up. Enough was enough. She knew where to find him; obviously, she just didn't want to.

His agent had called this morning and told him that Bob Stern at Sunshine had been fired. "What does that mean?" Saraub asked.

"I don't know. How would I know? It means finish the movie and find out."

So that was the plan. He'd finish the movie. And after that movie, he'd make another one. And another one. He'd decided that when he got out of here, he'd leave his studio apartment and move out of Manhattan. He'd find a place in the boroughs where there was space to breathe, with or without Audrey Lucas.

His lunch had come with a free copy of the *New York Post*, and he swiveled his hands inside their plaster to leaf through the pages. The headlines were all bleak. Stocks down. Fraud on Wall Street on the rise. A precarious future predicted for social security and Medicare, now that the baby boomers' health was failing. A line from an economist caught his eye: "This generation has inherited an enormous debt, and I can't believe that it will survive the weight. Indeed, what we may be witnessing is not a recession but the end of an empire."

He thought about that, and he decided that the economist was wrong. Every generation faces its own extinction, and for that generation, it always feels like the end of the world. But somehow, for thousands of years, life has gone on, and even gotten better. Despite the wars and stupid decisions, the racism and despots, people have gotten better, too.

Just then, the phone rang. It took some maneuvering, but he managed to lift the receiver in time. "Hello?"

"Yeees?" a woman's high-pitched voice asked.

"Uh, yes."

"Is this Bobby?"

"Saraub. I think you have the wrong number."

"Oh, no. I mean that other name. That's what I mean. Audrey's gentleman?"

He grabbed the remote, but his fingers couldn't press the mute button, so instead he cricked his neck tighter against his shoulder, so he could hear better. "That's right. Is something wrong?"

"Yes. She's not feeling herself, and she wanted me to call you and ask you to come over. Don't bring anyone. You know how she is—so private."

"What's wrong with her?"

"510 West 110th Street, #14B. Buh-bye!" she shouted, like maybe he was deaf, then hung up.

Saraub held the phone in his hand. *What the hell?* He thought about Nebraska and the way he'd left her while she'd slept. He realized that his anger had clouded his judgment. She was a little nutty, but she wasn't cruel. There could be only one reason she hadn't called or visited upon hearing he'd been in a plane accident: something was very wrong.

He pressed the call button for his nurse and started looking for his pants.

43

The Red Ants Will Carry Away
Even the Last of Your Line

artin Hearst lay broken and unmoving at the top of a garbage heap. Red ants swarmed his skin. It seemed fitting that his family had made its fortune out of digging holes, and he would meet his end inside one, too.

He'd studied the history of this building for years. For instance, Edgar Schermerhorn was his great-great-great-great-great-grandfather's first cousin. If not for that kinship, The Breviary's strange design would never have gotten funding. In 1932, The Breviary was nearly sold by its shareholders after an eruption of suicides, but spared by one dissenting vote: his great-great-grandfather: Martin Hearst III. In Marty's lifetime, the building's foundation had finally begun to buckle, top down. There was a reason no one had lived on the fifteenth floor: since the fire ten years ago, the plaster under the copper roof had caved in.

Martin Hearst the First: The Civil War newspapers

joked that the name was fitting, one letter off from a heart. The stories about him passed down over the generations had become legend. A hardened, self-made man with no patience for the meek, who took what he wanted, and from his neighbors inspired awe. By the time Marty VII was born one hundred years later, the legend was a God.

During the Gilded reign of Martin Hearst II, The Breviary thrived. Crystal chandeliers sparkled, mahogany wood shone, glass gleamed; even the copper roof defied its atmosphere, and for decades stayed the color of freshly minted pennies. The children of The Breviary's elite attended the same summer camps and private schools, shared governesses, and married each other, too. The address became fashionable, and as the building's population swelled, they broke up apartments, smaller and smaller. Twelve bedrooms became six, then four, and finally, two. And if sometimes, the lights flickered, or the doors flew open, such happenings served only to enhance The Breviary's charm.

The third generation started new businesses that brought them to the West Coast or the oil fields of Texas. They intended to return, but never did. The rest inherited family fortunes or found local occupation as bankers, Broadway actors, writers, sculptors, critics, and gossip columnists. They were the first to indulge in the rituals of Chaotic Naturalism: sacrificed animals, séances, dream sharing, scholarship in the occult.

The flapper generation cast aside petty drudgery and perfected the art of the ball. Then one morning over coffee and sodium bicarbonate to soothe the barking dogs that had bitten them the night before, they read about the unfathomable Great Depression. Companies were sold. Family names lost luster. Patriarchs jumped out windows or sold heirloom jewels. They married each other, no longer because the outside world was not good enough but because no one else would understand the humbled majesty of their roots.

Sixth generation. The Harlem address lost its bucolic luster. The tenants talked fondly of the golden years and mourned their lost comforts: summer houses, ski lodges, years abroad in Rome. They saved their pennies, Ziplocked leftovers, hemmed their clothes and passed them down to their children. At night, they imagined the disappointed ghosts of their ancestors whispering abuse in their slumbering ears. They avoided sunlight; it burned their fair skin. They didn't like the jarring sound of street traffic, either. Or the sight of poverty because they knew it was contagious.

Marty remembered the parties back then. His kid-sized double-breasted suit; peeking out from behind his mother's legs to watch dapper men and women trade barbs and cocktails like the last sophisticates hiding from a barbaric world. Monday nights, a rotating group of families had served spirits in their apartments, gatherings that had ended in lamp shades on heads, shared bedmates, words of unforgivable cruelty, and children of unknown paternity. By the arrival of the seventh generation, the place had echoed with emptiness, and the laughter was resentful. The tenants had turned on one another, because there was no one left to blame.

It happened so slowly that at first, none of them noticed. The walls hummed. The stained-glass birds and mosaics sometimes took flight. The hallways constricted like throats. Hinges creaked. Nightmares flew loose from their authors and inhabited the building like cold air.

Finally, the last of The Breviary's line ascended: the seventh generation. The building emptied. By then, more had died within its walls than lived there. The ghosts, echoes of the past, Breviary tricks, even a few genuine trapped souls, walked the halls. Tenants auctioned off the last trappings of their legacies: diamond broaches, Chanel suits, and Tiffany lamps. No longer just a home, The Breviary became their sanctuary. They loved it the way men born to captivity love their masters: reluctantly and with self-loathing. With their last pennies, they paid doctors to score their faces.

For a short time, Marty got out. He sublet a studio in the West Village that he hoped to make permanent. But the rents were raised, and striking out on his own in a new city would have opened too much possibility for failure. He moved back to The Breve, and the elevator doors as they shut had sounded like those of a cage.

Benjamin Borrell in 3A was the first to build a door. Francis Galton came next. After that, 11E. He painted the turret window cadmium red, then tried to walk through it, and fell to his death. 9B followed. Then 8C. Soon, all of them built doors. Even Martin tried his hand at it: he ground all the notes he'd taken researching The Breviary's history into mash and added paste, but without a frame, it hadn't held. In the comfort of their fading privilege, the tenants had lost the knowledge of how to build. It was lost on most of them, save Martin Hearst, that even the blackbirds trapped in glass were sometimes free.

At its height, The Breviary had housed 742 occupants. By the time Audrey Lucas signed her lease, there were fifty-three people living there, and two-thirds of the apartments were vacant. It had been Marty's idea to rent out the fourteenth floor to single women and see what developed. Clara had come closest—for a brief time, at least, something had peered back at them through the cracks. Just as quickly, her door had crumbled. It was then that the red ants arrived. They'd broken out from beneath the floor and swarmed the felled door, gnawing all the evidence that remained. Those ants had infested the building ever since. He'd regretted the drowned children and had wanted to call off the whole thing, but by then Loretta had been calling the shots.

Next was Jayne. A flighty, nervous thing. Bursting

with life. He'd assumed she'd agreed to spend time with him out of pity, or because she needed money. Not that he had any. Two weeks ago she'd taken him on his first walk through Riverside Park. The city had changed so much since he was a boy.

She hadn't been affected like Clara or Audrey. Each morning they'd expected not to see her rise for work, or giggle her hellos as the elevator descended, floor to floor. Waving with glee like a ray of sunshine at each and every tenant. But each morning, there she was. Three months, and all she'd suffered was a few nightmares.

Turned out, it just took longer. After she sprained her leg and Audrey left, they'd locked her inside 14E. She held out for seven days before finally building her door.

He still remembered her shock when he'd come to her room with the others. She'd been on her way to her first solo act at The Laugh Factory, and he'd promised to escort her. Saddle shoes and poodle skirt, she'd fought as they'd filled her apartment. High-kicking the air, she'd bitten Francis, kicked Evvie, even dispatched a right hook to Loretta. And then she'd noticed that Marty was among them. Her shoulders had slumped in submission as she'd asked, "Marty? You, too?"

He visited one more time, at Loretta and Evvie's request. Her hall was dark, and there had been something in there with them, watching. Black-eyed and slithering with rounded, insectile joints, it hadn't seemed as if it belonged in this world. Worse than a ghost. Not human, like a ghost. He'd realized for the first time that this door and perhaps The Breviary itself, were mistakes.

Jayne had shuffled out from the dark. Black eyes. Vacant. But that's what happens when the soul is devoured. In her hands, she'd held the dirty rebar. It was only then that he'd understood; The Breviary needed a sacrifice. Something loved. He'd long wondered why Loretta and the rest had not objected to the time he spent with Jayne. Now he knew: he was that sacrifice.

She'd limped toward him on a wounded leg, dragging the rebar behind her.

"I've been in error," he'd said while Jayne approached: *click-clack-shhp*. Only, it hadn't been Jayne. There was nothing about that husk that he'd loved.

Click-clack-shhp. The sound had been terrible. Snot-nosed and heaving, he'd backed his way down the hall, until he got to the exit. But the door was locked from the outside. Loretta. Evvie. The rest of them, too. His betraying family, whom he'd known the better part of eight decades. They'd locked him in here with this thing.

Click-clack-shhp.

She'd cornered him as he wept. Black-eyed. Bared teeth. Hunched back, like her bones had rounded. She'd pressed her mouth against his ear in that way he'd once found so charming, and pinned him against the door with both arms. He'd closed his eyes, expecting a bite, but instead, she smashed the lock so that it broke. Her delicate hand came back disfigured, the knuckles jagged so that they'd hung loosely inside her skin. "Get out," she'd said.

He'd reached behind him, and turned the knob. Then slipped through as she'd watched. The look on her face had been a snarl of rage, and he'd known it wasn't the monster letting him go, but Jayne.

A few hours later, she was dead.

And so he'd resolved to do his best by Audrey, as he should have done for Jayne. He knew now why the tenants wanted this door, when so clearly, the thing on the other side meant harm. Soon, The Breviary would be condemned. They'd be turned out, every one of them. After seven generations of entitlement, the fall from grace was too great to endure. A door works two ways. The maniacs: they didn't want to unleash anything; they wanted another world in which to hide.

He wasn't dead, though he soon would be. They'd

dragged him down the red-tongued hall. Struck him with their weak fists, then shoved him down the trash chute. He'd heard the crack halfway down. He couldn't move his arms or legs, and was pretty sure, from the cracking sound it had made halfway down the chute, that he'd snapped his spine.

Amidst the ants, open-eyed Edgardo laid next to him. His coveralls were soiled with coffee grounds. It was Loretta who'd heard him warn the girl, Audrey, through the peephole in her wall. Marty had refused to deal the blow. So it had fallen on Evvie Waugh, the only other one of them strong enough to wield the rebar. A hunting man, he'd taken Edgardo's cane for a trophy.

Marty's breath came rasping, and he no longer felt cold, or much of anything at all. The ants converged in a long line across his body, and he thought, for a moment, that he could see the first Martin Hearst, watching him with disappointment now that the last of the line would die with empty hands and a squandered legacy. Dark eyes, a bald crown, and skin sallow from a jaundiced liver. He thought he could see all six dead Hearsts lined up in a row like pallbearers waiting to carry him away with them to the hereafter he deserved. The shadows they cast were not nearly as imposing as he'd imagined, and he felt no shame that he had not lived up to their expectations. Only regret, in what he had not done for himself or Jayne. What a waste, to have lived for wretches such as them.

The ants spread over his chest and got to work, devouring the last of the Hearst line. Before he closed his eyes for good, something else occurred to him, and his smile was bitter. In killing the superintendent, they'd murdered the only person willing to take out their trash.

44

I Weary of the Sun, and Wish the State of the World Were Now Undone

This happened before. Don't you remember the ants, and Hinton?

In her dream, they were Siamese twins again. This version of her mother wasn't black-and-white, but old and wrinkled. Her dress was a hospital gown that fit her like a sail. She pushed Audrey, hard. They came apart so that they were half-women with split hearts and wounded legs, but both were still breathing.

You live in a bad place, Lamb, Betty said.

She was sleeping because the work had been so hard. The piano had made discordant music as she'd chopped, then sawed. Her arms and legs shivered from muscle exhaustion, even in sleep, and she was so hungry she didn't remember her name. She thought maybe it was lamb. The kind people eat.

In her dream, she and her mother were sitting on the

air mattress, watching the door. On the other side, The Breviary's true parents waited. Not Schermerhorn, but the thing that had guided his hand and given him the design for those plans. The spiderlike wraith that had followed her down Jayne's hall. The monster beneath the monster.

She'd tested the door's slant with the level in her toolbox to make sure that it pointed two degrees west. The tenants had provided her with everything she needed.

Just then severed Betty shook her. "You have to get out of here!"

Audrey looked to her left and saw her cleaved heart. No blood flowed, but only two chambers beat in a quiet *lub-dup*. "I don't like moving, you know that. I'm done with motels, Momma."

"Go now, Lamb. Or it'll find a way in. It'll get inside you, like it got inside me." The woman shook harder, and Audrey's breath caught in her throat. Betty was old. A skinny collection of bones and wild, white hair whose jagged bangs had recently been cut. On her far side was an IV tree that dripped fluid into her arm while, in the distance, Audrey heard the steady breathing of a respirator like half of this dream was taking place in a hospital. Was this really Betty, and not a trick? Had she somehow reached out through her coma?

Something wet and warm trickled. Audrey touched her neck and severed chest where tiny drops of blood were beginning to bead. "We're the same. Neither of us were born whole. My heart's all fucked up," she said.

Betty shook her head. "No, Lamb. We're different." Unlike all the other ghosts and hollow echoes that had visited this last week, Audrey *knew* this woman in a way that made her feel less alone.

"I'm afraid," Audrey said. To her left, her cleaved heart bled. The drops coalesced into a red line that thickened. And then the blood began to flow more heavily. Her neck bled, too. "I never stopped bleeding.

From that time you cut me. It's not your fault. We were born wrong, that's all."

Aged Betty reached into her open chest and pulled out what remained of her still-beating heart. "Take this. It belongs to you. I never had one of my own. You shared yours. I'll give it back now," she said as she joined it to its mate inside Audrey's chest. She held it there, firm, for a couple of seconds until the thing stopped bleeding. Her neck stopped bleeding, too. The split healed, and she became whole.

Audrey took the woman in her arms. Betty. She smelled like Baby Soft perfume and Winston cigarettes. Her skin was soft. In the distance, tearing through the dream, was the beeping of a hospital heart monitor.

"Thank you, Momma."

Betty lifted her head. The veins on her neck bulged. Blood gushed as her skin paled. "Get up and get out of here!" she yelled. Then she pushed Audrey so hard she woke up.

The door was humming. The apartment was dark. Audrey woke to realize, with some shock, that she'd just inserted the hot water faucet handle and was trying to pull the door open.

The thing in her stomach turned. She felt it inside of her, growing. Down the hall, water ran from the tub and flooded the floor. "Ohhh," she said. "Oh, no."

She reached fast into her pocket. The key. To get it back, she'd stuffed herself with piano sawdust and cardboard, then flushed it all out of her with a gallon of water. A natural laxative. But when she'd looked out the peephole, Loretta's blue eyes had looked back at her. So she'd waited, and dozed, and finished the door, then dreamed of Betty. The real one, perhaps.

She staggered back now, as the door began to pull from its foundation. Up from the rotten floor, red ants crawled.

What do you have left that you love? It hummed.

Give me its blood and I'll let you see my true face.

The slopping thing in her stomach filled her chest, then her arms and mouth.

Kill him, the walls and floors and door whispered. The sound was deafening. She could hear the tenants through the halls. Their meaningless, frightened thoughts were an hysterical chorus. They banged on the walls. Slowly at first, and then fast. She could hear all fifty-one of them. Reams of spit flew from wrinkled lips. "You're next! You're next! You're next!" they cried.

Kill all that you love, The Breviary commanded.

But she loved nothing. Not even herself. She was dead inside, just an accumulation of scars. The worm filled her body. Her vision got small, then nothing. Her eyes turned black. She saw through The Breviary's eyes. Felt the air through its limestone skin. Felt its fury, that it had been trapped in this awful world, wearing this flawed stone body, for more than 150 years.

First she saw the ants in the basement and the gristle of Martin's and Edgardo's bones. Then floor by floor, every tenant. Every apartment. Every failed door, trash-filled kitchen, and unflushed toilet. She understood why the building loathed them and had played its pranks. She despised them, too. Her gaze ascended. Up, up, up. Ninth floor: the tenants themselves had stolen all the copper fixtures, then sold them at half their value because they hadn't known how to haggle. Tenth floor: Penelope Falco imagined, then wept in fear that she might actually get what The Breviary had promised her on the other side of the door: someone to love. Finally, she saw Saraub Ramesh through The Breviary's cold eyes as he climbed the steps to the fourteenth floor.

She walked down the hall and unlocked it for him, then headed back into the den and located her rebar.

Kill all that you love, The Breviary, the tenants, the ghosts, and even the thing on the other side of the door whispered, just as Saraub Ramesh entered 14B.

45

Let Me In

It took Saraub sixty-five excruciating minutes to check out of the hospital. His cabbie was new to the job, and took Central Park North instead of the 97th Street Transverse. They wound up circling Morningside Park and adding an extra fifteen minutes to the trip. When he finally made his way into The Breviary's lobby, the doorman was gone, and the place was empty. A kiddie porno lay open on the floor.

The more he thought about it, the worse this sounded. She *was* a private person, so why hadn't she called him herself if she'd wanted his help? And where was everyone in this building?

He waited for the elevator for ten minutes, then finally broke open the iron gate, and looked down the shaft. The wire cable had torn, and the car lay crashed in the basement, its roof broken open from the impact of the fall.

He headed for the stairs. After two flights, he was

sweating. It was dusty in here, and he breathed some of it in—a greasy, foul taste that slithered in his stomach. After three flights, he took a break to rest his ribs and leaned against the wall. It vibrated against his fingers.

After a minute or two, he caught his breath and kept walking. Faster. As fast as he could. The building swayed. He could feel it rocking, like the top of the Empire State Building, only he didn't think it had been engineered to bow with the wind: this thing was no longer sound.

At the fourth-floor landing, an old woman peeked out from the fire door. She'd smeared coral lipstick across her forehead and cheeks, but otherwise was wearing nothing at all. Her breasts hung slack around her belly. "She doesn't want you!" The woman giggled. "But they want to wear you!" She pointed and laughed, and he walked faster.

He picked up his pace. It was hard to keep his balance with his arms in casts, so he leaned against the railing. Thought about calling the cops, but didn't know yet what to tell them.

He got to the sixth floor. Sweat dripped from his brow. It was humid in here. Red ants scurried up the steps as if seeking higher ground. He felt something in his stomach. Gnawing. It got bigger inside him, like indigestion.

She said you couldn't make a porn star cum.

Had someone just said something? He slowed. Two steps at a time. Had Audrey been talking about him?

She said she was after your money, only you don't have any. You're just your mother's bitch.

One step at a time.

You never met a Twinkie you didn't love.

He's always wanted a girl like Audrey, who called her own shots. He'd thought she'd seen past his drawbacks. But how can anyone see past 280 pounds?

And these dreams he'd had, of a house. Before Audrey,

he'd used his family's credit card to buy movie tickets.
He'd eaten entire pizzas for dinner, followed by two
pitchers of beer. He'd never paid his bills, or cooked,
or cleaned. These dreams of his, they belonged to
someone else.

He stopped at the tenth-floor landing. The lights
flickered. The banister was hot beneath his fingers. And
why was he doing this? For a woman who'd treated him
like garbage and cleaned their toilet every time he used
it, like she thought his ass germs would put her in a
hospital.

He got to the eleventh floor. Breathing so hard he was
dizzy.

*She's spreading her legs for both the partners at her
office. She was easy, too. All she wanted out of it was
a raise.*

Saraub clenched his jaw. The bitch deserved a right
hook. A tooth knocked out, or maybe her pretty face
slashed, so she'd know how bad it felt to be stared at for
being different.

*She said she'd have respected you, if just once, you'd
punched something besides a wall.*

He got to the twelfth-floor landing. His fury swelled.
He saw, but did not place, the dried and bloody footprints on the steps, as belonging to Audrey. The fourteenth floor. He walked down the red carpet. It was
a mess of white powder and broken ceramic. All the
doors except 14B were open. In 14C, an old woman in a
torn dressing gown pointed at him, and shouted, "He's
here! He's here! I tole you!"

He walked on. A white-haired old man leaned inside
14A's doorway and shot his arm with a hypodermic
needle full of cloudy fluid. When he saw Saraub, he
frowned. "How are we going to get rid of the carcass?
You're too big for the chute."

He turned the handle to 14B. It creaked open. His
panting was fast, and sweat poured. He didn't notice the

running water, or the shadows that raced down the hall and into the den. Didn't notice the Steinway chopped to bits. From its bones and her moving boxes, she'd made a door. The blackbirds in the windows flapped their wings, trapped in glass. Alive. He didn't register this, either. All he heard was that voice in his mind, and the walls, and the air: *Give it to her. She wants it. The only way to keep her in line is the back of your hand. If you don't do it, she'll find a man who can.*

He charged. First walking fast, then running with his broken arms at his sides. Her expression was flat and without emotion. Her eyes were black. She was wearing a sweat suit that fit her like a blanket, and she stank. "You bitch," he said. Then he took a swing with his plaster cast.

She swung, too, but she was faster. He didn't have the time to block the blow. Only heard the sound as his shoulder cracked, and he crashed to the floor.

46

The Tenants

Once Saraub arrived, the tenants lined the four-teenth-floor hallway and began to cheer. Loretta stamped her feet. "It's started!" she cried. Nude Arthur tucked his needle behind his ear. Elaine Alexander slammed her fists against her stomach. Benjamin Borrell tore his hair. Evvie Waugh thought about heaven. "It's time!" they all shouted. "It's time! It's time! It's time!" Francis Galton revealed what he'd done to improve on his artwork: a face without skin.

One by one, every living tenant of The Breviary followed Saraub's path, and crawled, walked, and hobbled down the throat of 14B. Their bodies had become hunched and their eyes black. They clapped and laughed and cried with delight, as Audrey struck his shoulder once more with her rebar.

Seven generations, trapped in this building. No air,

no grass, no sky or sun. They did not care what happened next, so long as it led to an end.

The red ants climbed. Up the steps, through the cracks, vents, and floors. They swarmed 14B, until the floors and walls were red.

47

What You Love Is the Same as What You Hate

A crowd had arrived. The apartment turned red, just like when Clara lived there. The stained-glass blackbirds got loose from the glass and flew circles around the door, in an ever-tightening gyre. The entire building rattled. The floor beneath her cracked, and the ceiling cracked, too. The door throbbed within its frame, and The Breviary trembled with delight.

Saraub lifted his casted arm in defense. His promises and his bullshit, oh, how she hated him. She swung again. Missed as he rolled, double casts flailing, onto his side. The door opened a crack. Her heart swelled: she was such an excellent engineer. But of course, if anyone understood functional chaos, it was the daughter of Betty Lucas.

She drew back the rebar. Saraub's big eyes were cow-like and stupid. Too shocked to react. That's why she was a survivor, and he wasn't. She lifted the pole once more.

"Stop," he groaned. "It's not you. It's the building."

She tightened her fingers and struck again. This time, the bottom of his foot, just to frighten him, because his voice was so familiar. He crawled, using his hips to propel himself backward. Only, the hall was filled with the tenants and ants. Clapping and screaming. His skin was so smooth. Had he shaved for her? Did he know she'd once been a ballerina, or that before Betty went mad, Audrey's best friend's father had owned a Dairy Queen? Did he know that during Betty's final AWOL, she'd gotten beaten to unconsciousness in the back of an Omaha dive bar? Or that Audrey had committed her against her will? On the day she wheeled her into Ward C, she'd told her that the hospital was an airport and that they were going on a vacation to Paris. Did he know the kind of coldhearted bitch she could be, when she had to be?

A tear rolled down the side of her face. "I don't want to kill you. But I have to. It's better this way, trust me."

Behind them, the door opened about a half inch. The space made a vacuum that sucked the light from the room. The ants swarmed. They filled the cracks until the room lightened again.

"Audrey, stop," he pleaded as she followed him down the hall.

The thing inside her squirmed, whispering words of sweetness in her mother's voice. *We girls stick together. No one comes between. Do you know what he did to Jayne? He touched her ass. You saw, didn't you, Lamb? It wasn't your lamp that hurt her feelings so bad. It was the guilt, because she was afraid to tell you. That's why he left you. He raped her, Lamb. It's his fault she's dead.*

"No," she muttered. "Impossible"

Schermerhorn was at her other ear. *He'll be fine, darling. It's better this way. Don't worry your little head. You're one of us, and he doesn't make the cut.*

The door groaned. Along the walls, ancestors of The Breviary watched. And there was baby Deirdre on the floor. Unresponsive, mute. Vacant. She peered up at Audrey with black eyes. "Finish it."

Soon, they were all chanting, even the tenants. "Finish it. Finish it. Finish it."

She could hear their thoughts. They were too far gone to think in words. All was the color red, of madness and murder and frugal love.

She hoisted the rebar.

"Audrey. Think! You'll go to jail. You'll lose everything," Saraub cried as he crawled toward the turret window. Blackbirds struck his exposed skin as they flew, their talons sharp as glass.

"Finish it! Finish it! Finish it!" The tenants trilled. Loretta began to howl. The sound was pained, as if she'd been stabbed.

"Audrey. Put it down," Saraub cried. His arms were plaster wings that reminded her of flight.

She squeezed the rebar. The look he wore was familiar. Even now, his concern outweighed his fear. Stupid man, worried about how his murder might cramp her freedom. So good at caring for other people, so terrible at caring for himself. A red ant climbed along her cheek and bit the bridge of her nose. She realized she'd become the thing she hated most. She'd become Betty's sickness.

The thing inside her lifted her hand against the man she loved. This time she fought it. She noticed her filthy sweat suit and bare feet. Remembered Jayne, and her mother, and herself, all so scarred and raw but fighters, too. Saw Saraub's blood as it coated the plaster of paris. Broken arms—who'd hurt him?

They both knew he could do a lot better than a white-trash hick with OCD. The thing is, maybe he didn't want better. Maybe she made him happy.

"Finish it! Finish it!" the tenants wailed.

She dropped the pole and bent down next to him. "I'm sorry," she said. Around them, ants scurried. There were so many that they looked fluid. They rushed the door, and she remembered, finally, that time in Hinton. Red ants had filled the holes then, too.

"I love you. I'm sorry," Audrey said as she helped him stand. Just then, Loretta hobbled out in front of the door. All around them now, ants squirmed. They filled the ever-widening cracks as the door continued to open.

"I'll do it myself!" Loretta hooted, then picked up the rebar and swung. Only, she didn't go after Audrey or Saraub. She hit the den wall. Plaster chunks broke loose from their wooden beam bones. The others joined her, weak fists punching.

"Fire!" Evvie Waugh cried, and they all cheered. "Fire! Fire! Fire!" A few scurried out of 14B, still chanting.

"What?" Saraub whispered. She squeezed his hand to quiet him. Together, they slid toward the hall, but Loretta spotted them, and blocked their way. "It's my party!" she said. "And you have to stay!"

Panting, Saraub whispered, "I think we can take them."

She doubted this but appreciated his optimism; from the way it slumped backward, she'd broken his shoulder. Supporting him by the waist, they kept going for a step, then two, until the crowd pushed back. Fists flailing, she struggled, punching at random. The sound was like twigs breaking. Saraub threw his body into the crowd. A few, including Evvie Waugh, fell as he jerked his neck back and shouted, "Run!"

The command confused her—did he expect her to leave him? She shook her head and followed him into the crowd. Flailing, kicking, trying to wrest him back. After a short struggle, the tenants had her, too.

The seconds passed. The smell of smoke wafted through the vents. She could feel heat, too, and realized then where the ones who left had gone. To open the door, the tenants were killing the only thing they loved. They were burning down The Breviary. It shrieked its agonized protest, and they shrieked, too. The thing about monsters, they hate themselves most of all.

"Oh, shit," Audrey said.

Saraub stood on tiptoe, to see over the tenants' heads, and called out to her, "We've got to get out of here!" just as Loretta Parker twisted the faucet handle and opened the door.

48

Mother

The door opened. The Breviary screamed in pain and joy. On the other side of the door were the monsters, at last. Spiderlike Edgar Schermerhorn was up front. Behind him were Loretta Parker, Evvie Waugh, Francis Galton, and the rest of the tenants, too. And then, to the left, shadow versions of Audrey Lucas and Saraub Ramesh. Their likeness was unmistakable, only their joints were rounded and their eyes were black. They walked on four legs.

She understood then what was behind the door. Humanity's dark, soulless twins. Cast off by reason and consequence but always searching for ways to return, be it through the subtlety of sickness or the enormity of a door. They were shaped like insects because insects are the only animals that have no souls.

Snarling, they pushed against the boundaries that trapped them inside the door, which would collapse as soon as The Breviary died. From its groans of pain, perhaps even The Breviary regretted what it had done.

"Stupid building. I'm the boss. Me!" Loretta cried. Then she charged the door and somehow raced through its aperture. Her arms were opened wide, as if to give Schermerhorn a hug, but it was her opposite Loretta who caught her, and took the first bite. The rest helped. They pulled her apart. Unsocial creatures, none voluntarily shared.

The building smoldered. Chips of plaster fell, and the door rocked inside its frame. Francis Galton was the next to race through the opening. The same fate greeted him. This time it was Schermerhorn who caught him. The dark, spiderlike Schermerhorn she'd met upon Jayne's death, who'd consumed his human counterpart and had lived here ever since, guiding The Breviary's hand.

"Run!" Evvie Waugh exclaimed, then beat his way backward through the crowd with Edgardo's cane. Some followed him, others followed Loretta.

The shadow creatures pushed against the opening but so far could only lure the tenants inside, and couldn't yet break free.

Audrey could not help but look. Behind the monsters was a red-sunned world with dirt instead of grass and air thick as ashes. Her shadow twin was hunched, with hard features and narrow, ungenerous eyes.

She realized she'd seen this thing before, only back then, she hadn't recognized it. Hinton, 1992.

"We've got to break the door," Saraub said, as the tenants scurried down the hall or else flung themselves inside the door. He lifted the rebar with one of his broken arms. His own shadow self retained his features but stood only as tall as a child. A stunted thing, it sucked its thumb.

"No, it'll collapse before it can open," she told him. "We just have to get out."

He grimaced. "I have to take it down," he said, and

she understood that what he meant was, *every second it stands is an abomination.*

Another tenant screamed as she walked through the door. And another. She didn't hear the sound of smacking lips, or grunts. Even these would have marked a human kind of delight.

The floor beneath them buckled. Saraub advanced too slowly. She took the rebar from him. "Let me."

As she approached the door, she thought about what she'd forgotten in Hinton. Bloody-necked, she'd escaped her mother's knife and bent down over the hole to help dig. One clump of dirt, another. And then, a face. Frantic, she'd clawed more dirt and so had Betty, until they'd unearthed the thing.

Black-eyed Audrey Lucas had peered back at them. Human-sized, a grown woman aged before her time, it had *scritch-scratched* with fingers worn to bones against the floor it was trapped beneath. Though she hadn't recognized it as her twin, in her drunken horror, she'd screamed.

It was Betty who'd stabbed it with her knife. First slitting its throat, then cutting off its head. It was then that the red ants had swelled up from the ground and filled the kitchen while Audrey and her mother had stomped. They'd chewed flesh and blood and bones, until every last bit of the monster was gone.

By the time the ants had finished, she'd forgotten. Maybe it had been too terrible. Maybe it was a secret humans weren't meant to know.

The red ants were not the imaginary symptom of madness, like she'd always believed. They were the gatekeepers that kept the shadow world and the hopeful world separate. Her mother, attuned to both places, had heard Audrey's monster that day and murdered it. And then she'd fled, to escape her own monster.

Audrey swung the rebar. Hard. One hit was all it took because she knew that the top left corner of the frame was the weakest part. The trapped things wailed in fury as the frame crashed down. The cruciform handle tumbled end to end.

She and Saraub backed away. Together, they scrambled down the hall. Behind them, ants swarmed the room. Wood chips, boxes, the air mattress, the ivories, torn old clothes, they chewed and chewed. Gnawing, gnawing, until all remnants of the door were gone.

They stumbled down the hall, where the rest of The Breviary's wild-eyed tenants wandered, aimless. Thick smoke filled the air. By now their bodies were so deformed that they looked identical to their shadow selves. Before she and Saraub started down the stairs, Audrey glanced back once. The entire den was squirming with red.

They gave up trying to limp down the steps, and instead got down on their bottoms and slid. The building creaked and moaned like wheezing breaths. Three more flights—the lobby. At the front doors, they found two police officers in blue uniforms, and behind that, a fire truck. She and Saraub slowed, but kept walking. "Bad fire. Be careful," she said to one of the firemen as they passed.

"Should we go back?" Saraub asked, panting, once they got to the doorman's podium. "See if we can help get some of those people out of the building?" His shoulder was bleeding badly, and he needed to go to a hospital.

She shook her head. "No. They're not worth it."

Just then the chandelier dropped and the old lobby's ceiling caved in. Plaster fell. Cops and firemen headed for the exit. With a loud, ear-rattling moan, The Breviary died, trapping the drunks and monsters and gray-haired children within its corpse.

Holding hands, Audrey Lucas and Saraub Ramesh limped out the door and into the world. They did not look back.

Epilogue

Flight

Dratted Upper West Side Inferno

October 27, 2012

Gothamites' with keen noses know that where there's smoke, there's fire. As by now most readers have heard, the landmark building The Breviary in Manhattan's tony Morningside Heights went up in flames last night. Eighteen residents, with the aid of New York's bravest, escaped the towering inferno. Tragically, another thirty-four locked themselves in their apartments, where help could not arrive, and were consumed by the hellfire. The angels must have been watching, though, because not a single cop or fireman was injured.

Fire Chief Warren Otis gave a brief statement this morning, "Preliminary investigations indicate arson at more than one point of origin, with more than one type of incendiary—basically we found evidence of gasoline in the basement, nail polish remover dumped all over the lobby rugs, and lighter fluid and newspaper stuffed on top of burning stove pilots in many of the apartments." When asked whether the residents had participated in a Jonestown variety mass suicide, he declined comment.

The building was, until recently, privately owned by its blue-blooded occupants, whose median age was eighty-five. Most were related to each other, and all were members of a cult called Chaotic Naturalism. The pseudoreligion predicted a slew of dastardly deeds, such as the death of mankind and a return to the age of beasts. Their masses reputedly took place Monday evenings, in the form of cocktail parties, where they drank the blood of a slaughtered animal. Over the years this ritual apparently proved too onerous, and they converted instead to booze and that rare African delicacy, chocolate-covered ants. Occupants were known for erratic behavior, such as discharging BB guns from their roof, stealing from their cleaning staffs, and making obscene gestures at pedestrians down below.

In keeping with the city's recent love affair with the maudlin, there will be a five-borough moment of silence at noon today to honor the victims, as well as a memorial service at St. John the Divine. Strangers with time on their hands might also want to add their flowers to the six-foot-high clump of baby's breath and hydrangea in front of the building's burnt-out shell.

After the Twenty-sixth Precinct finishes its investigation, the building is slated for demolition. In a new development, it turns out that The Breviary's residents had recently sold their shares in The Breviary to Columbia University Graduate Student Housing in order to cover back taxes. Several months ago, they received letters from the University, as well as the city housing authority, asking them to vacate by summer for reasons of public health, which some reporters believe sparked the mass suicide.

This investigation is ongoing. Turn to page 5 for eyewitness accounts.

From *The New York Post*

We Are All Architects

It wasn't a switch, but a button. A November day in Lincoln, the trees out the window were all barren. She straightened Betty's jagged bangs. Her hands had thinned, and her closed eyes were more sunken. An IV tree fed the tube in her arm.

Audrey knew then why she'd thought her alarm clock read 5:18 that first morning in The Breviary. Because that had been the same time that Betty had entered her coma. It really had been Betty who'd come to her at her darkest hour. She'd broken through Audrey's dreams to warn her and make her whole again. Because love endures all kinds of things. Hurt, betrayal, hatred, bad luck, and even death. "I love you, Momma," she said. "I hope you rest well, now."

The doctor she'd never before met pushed the button, and the respirator slowed, then stopped. The beeping things got quiet. Betty left her flawed, iron-winged body, and Audrey hoped that she was free now, to fly someplace good.

Two days later, she and Saraub boarded a flight from Omaha back to New York. She was wearing his ring again, and though it had only been a few weeks, in this case the human mind proved resilient. They'd both forgotten much of what had happened, except in nightmares.

Saraub's film was almost finished, and he was scheduled to spend the winter editing it. He'd decided to include all the material he'd filmed and face a possible lawsuit once he realized that it was Sunshine that was liable, not him personally. After that, like always, he'd find another mountain to climb.

Audrey's own 59th Street Project had gotten the go-ahead from AIAB, and was under construction. Though she'd been out of the office and Simon had given the presentation, he'd used the new plans he'd found in her cubicle her last night at Vesuvius. Because she'd missed so much work, the Pozzolana brothers had wanted to fire her, but Jill had fought bitterly, not only to keep her aboard but to give her a raise. In the end, the Pozzolanas had buckled though she doubted she'd be staying at Vesuvius for long. She and Jill were talking about starting their own firm and working out of her apartment on the Upper East Side in another year. They'd take David with them.

The flexible hours would come in handy, because that last time she and Saraub had been in Lincoln, they'd conceived more than she'd anticipated. This morning, after her mother's burial, she took a pregnancy test. Only six weeks along, but Saraub had been too excited to contain himself. When Sheila called him about having Audrey over for dinner, he'd blurted the news. To their surprise, she'd ask to talk to Audrey. "Forgive an old woman. Let's start over," she'd blurted into the phone. "Now, what's your favorite dessert?"

And now, here they were, heading down the runway. It occurred to her that all children inherit their parents' debts, and it is up to each generation to determine how, or whether, to repay them. Ahead of them was work and weddings and babies, and dinner tonight with his family for the first time in over a year. Behind them was the hard path that had led them to this good place. And though they were both awed and even frightened by the audacity of the American Airlines 767 as it lifted off into the sky and began to soar, they trusted that it would land safely in New York, where together, they would fill the holes they found there with something better than flowers.